Miss Ruby Midnight
and
Darkboy

DENIS GRAY

MISS RUBY MIDNIGHT AND DARKBOY

iUniverse books may be ordered through booksellers or by contacting:

iUniverse
1663 Liberty Drive
Bloomington, IN 47403
www.iuniverse.com
1-800-Authors (1-800-288-4677)

Because of the dynamic nature of the Internet, any web addresses or links contained in this book may have changed since publication and may no longer be valid. The views expressed in this work are solely those of the author and do not necessarily reflect the views of the publisher, and the publisher hereby disclaims any responsibility for them.

Any people depicted in stock imagery provided by Getty Images are models, and such images are being used for illustrative purposes only. Certain stock imagery © Getty Images.

ISBN: 978-1-6632-0451-6 (sc)
ISBN: 978-1-6632-0459-2 (e)

Library of Congress Control Number: 2020912557

Print information available on the last page.

iUniverse rev. date: 08/20/2020

CHAPTER 1

She was a big, beautiful woman with honey-brown skin—a woman anyone would follow, step by step, down a dusty, dirt country road in their best Sunday dress until they reached church, to acknowledge deep in their hearts that she was the one who would plant herself right there in the middle of the pulpit and sing the church's morning solo with the voice of an angel.

On Sunday mornings, Miss Honey's body whispered divinely while she headed off to Macguire's Baptist Church. Her body had a flood of spirituals in it, songs for singing to the Lord. She was going to make the parishioners sit down with her at the Lord's table and dine with the angels, taking them straight to heaven while sidestepping hell.

"I see you, Ruby!" Miss Honey hollered, as if she were playing hide-and-seek and had just found Ruby peeking behind a blooming bush. "Plain as day!" Miss Honey's big, fancy hat flounced atop her head.

"Oh … Miss … Miss Honey, ma'am."

"Ha!" Miss Honey laughed soulfully, taking a big bite out of the morning air. "Ain't you gonna at least say good morning, Ruby, to Miss Honey?"

"G-good mornin', Miss Honey, ma'am," Ruby said brightly.

Miss Honey stopped in the middle of Golden Road to adjust her fancy-looking straw hat.

"Doesn't wont you to be late f-fo' church, Miss Honey."

Miss Honey continued looking back at Ruby, who, by now, had shortened the distance between them. "Ain't gonna be late for church,

Ruby. Lord knows that. Gotta date with God this morning. No way am I singing for nobody else."

"H-how you know it me, Miss Honey? 'Hind you, ma'am. Think I be quiet. I—"

"Ruby, now, how many mornings does this make, child?"

Ruby started counting her fingers. "Uh, fo'. Fo', Miss … Miss Honey. T-thinks, ma'am."

Miss Honey yelped, hugging Ruby to her ample bosom, the hot sun having layered rings of sweat on her honey-brown skin. She kept laughing. "Ruby, ain't gotta be any smarter than that."

Miss Honey continued to look at Ruby, and Ruby knew why. Ruby stuck out her hand. Miss Honey took it.

Indeed, this was the fourth straight Sunday morning that Miss Honey and Ruby were having the pleasure of walking up Golden Road together. The first Sunday it happened, Miss Honey didn't let on that she heard Ruby's footsteps following her to Macguire's Baptist Church (not a hint or a whisper). But the second and third times, Miss Honey turned, catching Ruby red-handed, even if Ruby had tried everything imaginable to maintain her distance.

Miss Honey and Ruby were laughing like fine rain on Golden Road.

"Miss Honey, ma'am, what you singin' this mornin' in church, ma'am?"

"Oh, I don't know—whatever hits me."

"H-hits you, Miss Honey? Like lightnin' out the sky, ma'am!"

"No, Ruby, didn't say that. Don't want lightning hitting Miss Honey, especially in church—the Lord's house!"

Ruby looked up at her, curious. "So what you mean, Miss Honey? Say … say fo'?"

"Oh, only however God's spirit moves me—hits me—at the time. And the organist can play." Miss Honey laughed.

"Mr. … Mr. Jasper, he play good, don't he, Miss Honey?"

"*Doesn't* he, you mean—don't you, Ruby?"

"Yes … d-doesn' he … he, ma'am?"

"Leave all that bad English for someone else," Miss Honey said, swinging Ruby's hand. "Lord only knows I use my share—but do know better." She looked down into Ruby's startling dark eyes. *Young eyes that search for things, are always searching for things*, Miss Honey thought. "Mr.

Jasper can play up a storm on that organ of his. Mr. Jasper's got the spirit in him, all right. The spirit of song moves—"

"Spirit, Miss Honey? You say it 'gin, Miss Honey." Ruby paused.

"Oh, yes, the spirit. You sing and play the organ with God's spirit in you. It's what can move mountains and people, when it's in you like that, honey."

"It do?"

"Oh, yes. God's spirit's in your bones. Gets right inside them, and it moves. Moves right along with you."

Ruby's dark eyes widened with what seemed to be more interest. She seemed unable to imagine God—or God's spirit—being or moving "right inside" anyone's bones, at least not until Miss Honey said it.

Miss Honey saw how Ruby's eyes widened, seemingly trying to draw more information from her. "God's got bones, Ruby," Miss Honey said, her head arching backward.

"H-he do, Miss Honey? G-God ... do?"

"Bigger than dinosaur bones."

Ruby's little legs kept walking, stride for stride, with Miss Honey's big strides (even though it was more like Ruby was skipping more than walking, kind of like her legs were cheating a bit—but not much).

"Ever see one, Ruby—a dinosaur?" Miss Honey teased.

"Uh-uh, Miss Honey. Leas' not roun' here, doesn'. P-Plattstown, Miss Honey. Ever." Ruby giggled into her hands. "B-but they big, Miss Honey. B-big an' all?"

"Oh, yes. Quite big. But not big as God's bones. Uh-uh. Remember that. A dinosaur's bones aren't as big as God's bones. No way near."

"God, 'cause God got the bigges' bones"—Ruby stopped skipping on Golden Road for an instant, stood in the middle of it, looked up at the sky, and gulped; then gulped a second time, as if she'd gulped in the sky—"in, in the worl', Miss Honey."

Miss Honey looked up at the sky too, once her hand brushed back the front of her big, fancy straw hat. "My, it's hot this morning in Plattstown, ain't it, Ruby?"

Miss Honey and Ruby were parked right in the front of Macguire's Baptist Church on Golden Road. Miss Honey bent over to kiss Ruby's cheek. "See you after church, Ruby."

"Y-yes, ma'am."

"Will be outside, as usual, for you."

"Yes'm, Miss Honey, ma'am." Ruby's eyes twinkled.

Miss Honey was about to turn but didn't. "Singing for the Lord today, Ruby! Good news! A messenger for the Lord!" That was when Miss Honey's head turned, and when it did, the lovely smile on her face—a smile as wide as a barn—quickly faded to sadness. Miss Honey loved Ruby, this little girl who lived in Plattstown.

She walked up the Macguire's Baptist Church steps.

This, she abhorred, this part of her Sunday morning routine, leaving Ruby at the front steps of the church. Ruby couldn't enter the church with her; Ruby was not dressed "proper," not for Plattstown—really, not much for anything in Plattstown.

"Oh, Ruby ..." Miss Honey said under her breath. Sadly, she shook her head. *How many years ago was it when I was that same child in Plattstown, the spitting image of me down to the nothing on her feet—a barefoot child?*

How many years ago was it when she looked like a stray, an orphan child, unkempt, someone who roamed the backwoods, the back roads of Plattstown like a waif—dirty, smelly, nasty-looking, and filthy down to the bone. Her story was no different from Ruby's, except, as a child, her parents had died. Ruby's parents were still alive; they still lived in Plattstown.

"Good morning, Miss Honey!"

"Why, good morning, there, Brother Jasper!"

Miss Honey had made her way down Macguire's Church aisle, and all eyes in the church set on her like a sundial, including Pastor Cornell Mangrove Pettigrew.

Long and as spindly as fine brown rice, Mr. Jasper P. Bean sat on his small wooden organ bench at the church organ, looking over his left shoulder in a curious fashion, with his horn-rimmed glasses on the bridge of his long, tapered nose. "Miss Honey, you know what song you singing this—"

"Singing whatever song you're playing on that fine wooden organ of yours this beautiful Sunday morning, Brother Jasper. Whatever music pours out from your lovely fingertips to me," Miss Honey's rich, syrupy, soprano voice exhorted. "Just don't put me in the key of G!"

"Ha! Got the spirit in you this morning, I see, Miss Honey; it seem like."

"Got it all up in me, Brother Jasper. All the way up in the cracks of my bones this morning."

Miss Honey walked up to where she would sing and where all the church folk sitting in Macguire's pews couldn't wait for her to reach.

The church folk lifted their fans and then began quickly fanning their faces.

"Ruby, honey, this isn't just for the Lord this morning, I'm singing. But for you too, darling."

Ruby was on the side of Macguire's Baptist Church, where Miss Honey had left her.

She looked at the outside of the church, at its dirty white clapboards. She knew what the inside of the church looked like; she had sneaked into it on her own on more than one occasion. She never got caught—never. She was proud of the fact. Ruby's face darkened. She'd never been in Macguire's Baptist Church with people in it, though. She'd never been in it during a church service. Never, not even once. Never.

Maybe it was that she wasn't good enough. God didn't think her good enough.

She liked God. Really liked Him. But maybe God didn't like her. Maybe God didn't like her back. But she—well, He didn't say. He never said she shouldn't go inside Macguire's. She never heard God tell her that.

Maybe it was because she didn't pray. Maybe that was it too—God didn't like that. But she didn't know how. Nobody had taught her. But God still didn't have to like it, that she didn't know how to pray. Maybe everybody should know how to pray. Maybe everybody there is in the world should know how to pray. Some, at least.

It was how she dressed. It was that too. She knew it was. She just knew it. She was smart enough to know it was. Everybody who went to church in Plattstown on a Sunday morning dressed better than her—way, way better. She knew that. God had to know that too, didn't He? He had to—oh well …

Mr. Jasper's organ sprang to life. Ruby practically jumped out her skin, and then she swooned in sheer delight.

When Miss Honey sings, it's like being inside the church anyway, Ruby thought. Wasn't it? Sitting in Macguire's front pew. She could hear Miss Honey as clear as a bell. Couldn't see her, but she could imagine what Miss Honey looked like when she sang her church solo.

Except, sometimes, Ruby wondered if Miss Honey sang with her Sunday hat on or off.

On. On.

Miss Honey sang her church solo with her hat on her head. (Miss Honey had to!)

Ruby fidgeted up until the time Miss Honey sang. And she could always tell when the time came for Miss Honey to sing. The exact time. The spirit (now she knew what it was and meant, Miss Honey having explained it to her this morning) and the church folk would move her. Her body would receive a chill, and she'd be all but frozen, like she couldn't move—not a stitch.

And then the church became the quietest it would be all service, so quiet you could hear a spider walk—not crawl but walk, mind you—across the church floor; it was so quiet.

And that was when Miss Honey would sing.

Ruby hopped up and down like a grasshopper in a thicket outside the church. She was in the shade, on the shady side of the church, even though in the shade the temperature had to be some ninety degrees. But it hadn't stopped from playing as freely as if playing hide-and-seek, not with Miss Honey this time but the wind.

"When, Miss Honey? When you gonna—" And then, suddenly, Ruby's body froze, and she heard that spider walk—not crawl but walk—across Macguire's church floor. "Miss Honey!"

And Miss Honey's powerful voice came pouring out Macguire's Baptist Church like the sun splashing out in a yellow sky.

"Oh … Miss Honey, ma'am …" Ruby jumped back and then jumped forward and pressed her ear against the small church's rugged wood frame. "You, you an' God, Miss Honey. You an' God got bones bigger than a dinesaur," Ruby's small chest swelled. "Big … bigger than any bones in … in the worl', Miss Honey. In, in the worl', ma'am!"

CHAPTER 2

Miss Honey was in a lovely little shop.

She wasn't in Plattstown but a neighboring town. Miss Honey was in this shop for a reason: it was Monday.

Ruby, for the fifth straight Sunday, had walked with her to Macguire's Baptist Church. And, again, Miss Honey had sung for the Lord—but especially for Ruby, especially for that little girl who she kept finding more and more room in her heart for every day. She'd given Miss Honey such joy for living every day.

And after church, at the bottom of Macguire's front steps, Ruby had stood there, as quiet as a field mouse. *This child who has so much love in her*, Miss Honey thought, *who has God's Holy Spirit dancing inside her*. Something, Miss Honey knew, nobody in Plattstown had told Ruby about yet.

Miss Honey felt like singing in this nice shop—*hallelujah!*—but realized it'd be the improper thing to do, and she always did what was proper, no matter the circumstance.

"Afternoon, Miss Honey."

Miss Honey had shopped in this shop before, so she was well known.

"Afternoon, Miss Beatrice."

"How may I help you, Miss Honey, on this fine day?"

"Oh, don't worry any over me, Miss Beatrice. I've got in mind exactly what I want and what I know your shop has in abundance."

Miss Beatrice, whose hair was wrapped in a sturdy, neat, stiff bun, smiled.

"Didn't come all the way over from Plattstown—"

"Now, Miss Honey, Plattstown ain't but a mile an' a quarter out. Northerly, in a northerly direction."

"To socialize, honey." Miss Honey walked straight over to where her immediate interest was. "Came over here to Minesburg to spend my money."

Miss Beatrice more than smiled generously at Miss Honey. "Then I'll leave you to your own particular doings to attend to, Miss Honey."

"Oh, that I know, Miss Beatrice. Am sure of it, honey."

Miss Beatrice's stiff bun seemed to loosen a bit.

Miss Honey was home.

When should I do it—today, Tuesday, Wednesday, maybe? Friday? No … no, uh, Thursday? Maybe Thursday. Give Ruby more preparation. Time. The child needs time. My darling little Ruby.

Miss Honey felt good about herself.

What she had done in Minesburg today made her feel as good as any sermon she had ever heard from a preacher of God's pulpit or any spiritual she'd ever heard sung by a church choir. She'd bought herself a piece of heaven today and was going to spread it around on earth (well, at least around Plattstown).

Suddenly, Miss Honey felt tired. It just came on her like a light breeze that sometimes comes out of nowhere, the air transporting it. She thought about fighting the feeling, not giving in to it, but rethought things. It was late afternoon. Miss Honey walked over to her bed and looked at it, as if the day had indeed been too long.

"Maybe I'd better take to bed. Take an afternoon nap for myself."

Miss Honey began removing her long dress. "I am tired." She felt, resolutely, that she had to concede this to herself. The dress in her hand was pretty. All of Miss Honey's dresses were pretty. There were so many hanging in her closet to choose from that were tasteful and flowery.

"Don't have a model's figure anymore. That was a long time back when Miss Honey laid them dead!"

She pulled a housecoat out of the closet. Putting it on, she walked slowly to her bed. When she got there, she spread her body out on top of it. Comfortable, she shut her eyes and then, seconds later, opened them. "Thursday. It'll be Thursday I'll do it. In the afternoon, I'll make it for Ruby."

Now she could sleep.

"Never been this happy, don't think." But then she thought back to at least one or two very special times in her life. "Uh-uh, no, you don't. The old devil moon's trying to play tricks on me again." Miss Honey wasn't going to let it, though. She knew all about its dirty tricks. "Had some good times. Of course, when you reach my age, all you want to think about are the good times, not the bad. Not the ones that kept you down. Gave you heartache."

Miss Honey thought of Ruby again, of what she'd done for the child in Minesburg that day.

"I was on a mission for God today, Ruby. Do you hear me, honey? In the service of God. The Lord, child."

Those good times—she wasn't going to let them fool her, twist her arm. *Uh-uh, not today or tomorrow or any other day under God's awesome sun.* Miss Honey shook her head, as stubborn as a farm mule. "So leave me alone now! So this old gal can get her sleep!"

CHAPTER 3

There were rows and rows of wooden structures, front and back, on Rumble Way, evoking the image of a crippled man, caved in on one side of his body, sadly leaning on a crutch. Miss Honey stood squarely in front of one of the structures and felt the rain lash them, and the wind shake them, and the mosquitoes buzz in them, and the day's sun heat them into muggy, liquid nights.

It was Thursday, midday.

Before announcing herself to the hovel's inhabitant, Miss Honey made proper adjustments to her big straw hat and steeled her nerves, since she knew she'd need them for today's mission. She never thought she'd have to do something like this—face a day like this—but here she was, and she wasn't going to back down from what she felt was her responsibility to God and herself. Now wasn't the time for second-guessing herself or crumbling. Now was the time to seek God in her heart and to pray with solemn fortitude.

Outside the battered house, propped up on bricks, on Rumble Way in Plattstown, Miss Honey's head bowed.

Miss Honey held her breath after she knocked on the splintered door.

"Miss Honey! Why ... if it ain'ts Miss Honey!" A short, frail-looking young woman with straw-straight hair and an old face stood at the door with shocked eyes.

Millicent Martinson has such a pretty name, Miss Honey thought. "Hello, Millicent."

"Heared you come home. Home to die, Miss Honey."

Could Millicent Martinson know any better? Miss Honey thought. *Could I expect Millicent Martinson to know any better?*

People in Plattstown said Millicent Martinson was a drunk, but right now, she looked sober, even if all the signs of what she was—hair, dress, smell, look—were all in perfect place.

"What you won', Miss Honey? Ma'am? What you won'?" There was a meanness in Millicent Martinson's spare, thin reed of a voice. "What you won' wit' me, ma'am? What you won'?"

"May, may I come in, Millicent?"

"Come in, Miss Honey? Come in?" Millicent Martinson's response was as if she had not given any such thought to Miss Honey entering her shambled house.

"Not, uh, unless …"

"You come in, Miss Honey. Open the doe for you too."

The house's wood-planked floor creaked when Miss Honey stepped on it. Millicent's back had turned to her, and that's when Miss Honey shuddered from her thought of falling through the floor, in a house of rotted wood and an odor matching dead possum in every corner.

There was a ragged chair in the room, but Miss Honey had chosen not to sit in it, although Millicent Martinson hadn't offered. Instantly, Miss Honey felt the house's suffocating, oppressive heat. It was as if her body had been packed solid in mud, and the mud had just come out of a brick oven, smoldering on this hot July day.

Millicent Martinson's fingers fiddled with the front of her tattered dress like a mindless child.

Now settled, and still in control of her emotions, Miss Honey said politely. "Yes, Millicent, you're right, honey. Miss Honey has come home to Plattstown to die." This was fact, pure and simple. "Back home to Plattstown where I started, Millicent. Full circle, honey. Around the map and back, I suppose you could say."

"You a jass singer, ain'ts you, Miss Honey?"

"Uh, I'm—"

"What I heared from roun' here. You a jass singer. Call you a jass singer. Doesn' they, peoples, Miss Honey? Peoples?"

"That I am, Millicent. A *jass singer*, like you, uh, they say."

"You famous, ain'ts you, now? Heared you famous by now, ain'ts you? An' rich, ain'ts you, ma'am? Rich too."

"Famous, maybe"—Miss Honey giggled—"but not rich."

"What—"

"Why, far from it—nowhere near rich."

The remark, further relaxed Miss Honey.

"But what you won' with me? You in the house fo'? Af'noon here?"

That was what Miss Honey was hoping Millicent Martinson would ask. "Ruby, darling. Ruby. Why, I came to talk to you about Ruby, Millicent."

"What she done! Girl done! G-gone an' done now!"

Miss Honey took hold of Millicent's hand. "Nothing, Millicent. Why, nothing at—"

"Nothin!" Millicent did not seem to grasp what Miss Honey had said. "But she always doin' sometin'. Girl always got the devil in 'er. Always. Doin' sometin' bad. Ain't s'pose to." Millicent jerked her hand clean out of Miss Honey's. "S-so if the girl ain't done nothin', why you here? Standin' up in my house this, this way here, ma'am?"

Miss Honey would have jumped straight through the roof if she could have. "I know Ruby, Millicent. Know your daughter."

Millicent, whose eyes appeared tormented—sharing her days with anyone who looked into them—seemed hopelessly bewildered. "My chil'? R-Ruby? You, you know … know …"

"Ruby, Millicent. Yes, honey."

Millicent seemed baffled. "How, how you …"

Inside herself, Miss Honey exploded with excitement. "I'll tell you how. Oh, let me tell you how I know your daughter, Millicent."

Millicent Martinson's face looked like it could not wait to hear how her daughter, Ruby, could ever have anything to do with Miss Honey, a "jass singer" who traveled around the world and back; who was, by all acclaim and opinion in Plattstown, world famous and had come to her house to talk about, of all things, Ruby, her daughter.

Bless the Lord. Bless Him!

It was done! It was done! Accomplished!

Yes, indeedy, this was better than New Orleans, the Mardi Gras and

New York City; better than watching Harry Houdini escape ankle chains and handcuffs; better than Lindbergh's transatlantic flight.

Miss Honey had traveled the world; seen it; was the toast of this town and that town; reveled in fame and the madness of spring; been in love (stormy weather); out of love (blue nights); wore diamonds, minks, furs; rode through Central Park by horse and buggy at midnight; drank bubbly champagne from a silver slipper; knew love—had tasted it on a man's lips when she spread her body open to him like she was a rich man's plate of smoked salmon and caviar.

Miss Honey knew these thrills in her lifetime. But now she was back to knowing the thrill of God, of her Savior—of her blessed Jesus, now back and powerful in her. She'd come home, back to Plattstown, to die (as Millicent Martinson had so bluntly put it). Long ago (twelve years, to be exact), her family had left Plattstown, but she was back—this world-famous jazz singer who had traveled the world and all its many venues. She wanted to come back to Plattstown, back to where she was born and raised, back to her beginnings, to die of her terminal disease.

"I don't know when I began feeling this, Lord; only you do. I put all my trust in your hands. All of it. Every single bit of it."

Was it when her doctor had diagnosed her condition and said she had only four to five months to live? Was it then when this potent pull, this agent of change had swept over her? This old jazz singer, who'd seen the world and been toasted by it, wanted to go back home to Plattstown to die, for some mysterious, cryptic, odd, unrevealed reason, which her constitution stubbornly followed.

Miss Honey was in her room in the boarding house where she was now staying.

"Hallelujah! Hallelujah!" Miss Honey shouted, clapping her hands. "God. Y-You rascal You. Honey, You performed a miracle today f-for me, didn't You, through Jesus!"

She was glad Millicent Martinson had been sober. *God only knows what might have happened between us if she had been drunk*, Miss Honey thought.

Millicent Martinson had listened to what she'd said without once interrupting. She listened to how she and Ruby had come to meet—how

Ruby's and her paths crossed on Golden Road leading to Macguire's Baptist Church on Sunday mornings.

"Millicent listened to me with her eyes open and her mouth shut, all the while. Thank the Lord!"

Miss Honey visualized Millicent: she was an alcoholic. "I've seen them all my life. Smelled them and seen them. Looked into their eyes. Sad. It's always sad."

The husband, Ruby's father, Man Martinson, had run out on his family. Miss Honey knew him and the Martinson family. Man was an alcoholic too. Both parents were alcoholics.

Miss Honey removed her big straw hat and took in a deep but cautious breath.

"Now it's up to me, ain't it, Lord?" Miss Honey asked, looking straight up at the room's ceiling. She grinned. "Me and my bad English—when you know, dear Jesus, that Miss Honey knows better!"

Ruby knew where Harding's Boarding House was located in Plattstown. It wasn't far from Rumble Way, just under two miles east.

Miss Honey. It's all Ruby could think. *Miss Honey. What did Miss Honey want? What could she possibly want?*

Ruby was quite nervous. She thought about how she had looked before. She knew she wasn't pretty. She knew she was a little black girl who was in no way pretty. Black folk in Plattstown never told her she was pretty. White folk never told her she was pretty. The mirror—when she looked in it—didn't tell her either. But most times, she was too scared to look in the mirror to see what she might see.

But she knew what was there; she was ugly. An ugly black girl. A black pickaninny. A black tar baby girl. A black nigger girl.

Ruby rushed along on the road. Miss Honey was expecting her at the boarding house. Her feet were dirty from the dirt and dust of the roads. She'd never been inside Harding's Boarding House. She was excited.

Room D. Miss Honey said room D. Ruby shut her eyes and said it to herself again. *Room D.*

Ruby scooted up the road.

Ruby stood in front of room D; took one enormous swallow.

She tapped softly on the door.

"Miss Honey. It me, ma'am. Ruby, ma'am."

"So it is, Ruby. So it is!"

The door's width (as small as it was) opened as wide as a gulch.

"Af'noon, Miss Honey."

"Good afternoon, Ruby!" Then Miss Honey looked down at Ruby's dirty feet. "Now you know where I stay, honey."

"Oh," Ruby began in her effort to correct Miss Honey, "I knew where you stay all 'long, Miss Honey, ma'am."

Miss Honey kissed Ruby's left cheek and followed her into the front room.

"Uh … uh, nice, Miss Honey."

Ruby took in the place like she'd gulped down one big spoonful of chocolate ice cream followed by another. "Ain't never been in a boardin' house fo', Miss Honey."

Miss Honey made no comment while Ruby acclimated herself to her new setting.

"These, uh, these yo' fershin's in the room, Miss Honey? These? 'Long to you, ma'am?"

She is a smart, curious girl, all right, ain't she? Miss Honey thought. Only Miss Honey had known this all along. Ruby had native intelligence—what she'd had at that age.

"No, Ruby, I left all my furnishings back in New York, honey."

"New … New York?"

"Heard of it, honey?"

"Yes'm."

"From whom, Ruby?"

"My Daddy, Miss Honey. H-him speak of it. Speak of it more'n once, ma'am." Ruby's eyes continued to snoop around the room.

Miss Honey laughed.

Then Ruby's eyes (like a nosy fly) landed, specifically on one of Miss Honey's fancy straw hats. "Miss Honey …"

"Yes, Ruby?"

"Miss Honey, um, um, h-how many hats you got to wear, ma'am? To put on yo' head, ma'am?"

Miss Honey broke out laughing. "Come with me, darling, for you can see for yourself." Miss Honey kissed Ruby's opposite cheek. *What can I do to her hair? What I can do to Ruby's hair?*

Miss Honey wore a colorful scarf wrapped around her head.

Ruby had never seen Miss Honey without something on her head. She didn't know what her hair coloring was, what it looked like. So she looked at her eyebrows, painted a faint brown.

Miss Honey had led Ruby into her bedroom. It's then that Ruby's eyes switched off her and on to all of Miss Honey's lovely hats, arranged throughout the room as primly as red roses planted in a flowerbed.

"Oh … oh, Miss Honey! They … they …" And Ruby's eyes began tracking the hats as if they'd vanish if she didn't.

Now after the discovery and the excitement of seeing Miss Honey's hats, Ruby's curiosity, or worry, or whatever was at play was back because Ruby wanted to know why she was with Miss Honey. Why she'd invited her to the boarding house. The reason for this day.

"Curious, ain't you, child?"

It was written all across Ruby's forehead: an intense curiosity. "Yes'm, Miss Honey, ma'am."

"You know what they say, Ruby: curiosity killed the cat."

Ruby giggled. "But ain'ts no cat, Miss Honey. A-ain'ts, ma'am. Ain'ts."

"Ha. Oh, Ruby, child, God's got His hands on you, honey. Up on your shoulder!"

Ruby took a look at her slight shoulders.

"Ruby, God loves you. God loves you, darling!"

And that's when Ruby felt God or felt something that was strange and wonderful to her, even though she was in Miss Honey's warm embrace.

God do like me! God do like me!

And Miss Honey had her hand. "Close your eyes, Ruby. Tight, now."

And Ruby did.

Miss Honey's hand left Ruby's—and it was as if Ruby was on her own, and Ruby knew Miss Honey was on her own, and both were up to something good—filled with fun.

God do like me! God do like me!

"Oh, Ruby, Ruby. I love this game—don't you?"

"Yes'm. Yes, Miss Honey. I does. T-truly does!"

"How're your toes, the bottom of them doing? How do they feel to you—right now?"

"Tingle, ma'am. My toes tinglin' good, awful good!"

"Yes, yes, Ruby, yes." Miss Honey's voice had scaled down, as if subtly announcing that what was to come had truly come.

Ruby's eyes stayed shut and her fists balled. She was in such a state of anticipation. But then Ruby's body began to cool down, for it could heat back up when the time came. "You ... you gonna sing, Miss Honey, ma'am? What is, ma'am? Like you does in Macguire's Church on Sunday mornin', ma'am? That what you 'bout to do, ma'am—sing?"

Miss Honey planted a kiss on Ruby's forehead. "Open your eyes, child."

The box was big; the wrapping paper white. The red bow, big.

Miss Honey's hand held Ruby's chin.

Ruby looked up into Miss Honey's eyes.

"It's yours, honey. You can take it."

"Mines. Mines, Miss ... Miss Honey? T-take it, m-ma'am? T-take ... I ... I ..."

Tears rolled out of Ruby's eyes, and then found their way onto her cheeks, and then on top of the big gift-wrapped box. "I ... I ain'ts never ..." Ruby's small hand held to the box but didn't yet take if from Miss Honey's hands. "Never ..."

"I'll help you open it."

"No, no, Miss Honey, ma'am. No ... no ..." Ruby said in a dying breath.

Miss Honey laughed. She pulled up a chair. "Then sit on my lap. At least you can do that, can't you?"

Ruby sat on Miss Honey's lap and stared at the box, as if it was never to be opened.

"Ain't you gonna open it, Ruby? You are curious about it?"

"B-but you say cu-*curosty*, Miss Honey, ma'am, curosty it, it kill the cat, ma'am. It, it what you say, Miss Honey."

"Curiosity. So I did. So I did. I'll sing you a lullaby."

"I-I ain'ts no baby, Miss Honey, ma'am."

"I know that."

Miss Honey held onto Ruby as she continued staring at the new store-bought package, staring it down. She decided she was going to wait Ruby out. *Uh-huh,* she said to herself, *I can wait Ruby out. Easy.* All of her years of travel, being a jazz singer, had conditioned her for waiting— waiting for the next town, city, the next stop on the map.

"Where you buy it, Miss Honey, ma'am?"

"What, Ruby?"

"Why, this here, ma'am? This here box wit' the pretty bow in it— that … that got somtin' pretty inside it. W-where you buy it, Miss Honey?"

"Oh … that, that. In Minesburg."

"Never been over to Minesburg, Miss Honey. Ain'ts."

"It's delightful, Ruby. The shops there are simply delightful." Miss Honey sighed.

Miss Honey spied Ruby's eyes as they began to encroach more and more upon the box.

"C-can I shake it, ma'am?"

"What?" Miss Honey said indifferently.

"The box, ma'am. S-some, Miss Honey?"

"Oh that, go right ahead and shake it, uh, some. Nothing inside it's gonna break."

"Um, ain'ts?"

"No."

Ruby shook the box, putting it up to her right ear and then her left.

"See, Ruby? I told you."

Through her dress, Miss Honey could feel Ruby's little rump getting hotter and hotter by the second on top of her knees. *Oh, God loves you, Ruby! God loves you, darling!*

Ruby removed the box from her ear and stared at it for the longest time. "If … if I open it, I … I gonna die, Miss Honey?"

"Oh, Ruby, you ain't a cat, are you?"

"No, ma'am, I ain'ts no cat. Ain'ts gonna never be no cat! Ready say that, Miss Honey … ma'am."

And now Miss Honey couldn't stop have stopped Ruby if she'd tried, for Ruby's tiny fingers scratched at the package like a cat. And it was painfully clear, obvious to Miss Honey, that Ruby knew nothing at all about how to do this thing she was learning—tearing at everything but the red ribbon and big red bow.

"Scratch away, Ruby!"

"Yes'm. M-Miss Honey! I scratchin', scratchin' 'way!"

The box was freed of everything but the red ribbon and bow. Claw marks had been cut into the box the size of a mountain lion's.

Ruby appeared puzzled.

"Let me child. Miss Honey'll take over—take care of the rest of it for you." Miss Honey slipped the ribbon off the side of the box—"The ribbon won't break; see, Ruby?"—and then off the other side—"See?"—and then slipped the red ribbon off the entire box.

"I-I can put it back on, Miss Honey, when, when you through, ma'am?"

"Yes."

"C-can I stan' Miss Honey? Up, up, Miss Honey, on my feets?"

"Why ... stand right up on your two strong feet, child."

"T-to open it."

"Stand, Ruby!" Miss Honey's legs, from Ruby's little rump, felt really warm.

"You ... how ..."

The box looked bigger than Ruby now.

"Lay it on the floor, Ruby. Flat to the floor."

Ruby put the box down on the floor.

"My bredt, Miss Honey. Can taste it." Ruby fell to her knees and opened the box and then leaped to her feet. "Miss Honey! Miss Honey!" Ruby ran from the box, frightened; frightened of its contents; what was in it.

Miss Honey charged out of the chair. "Ruby, what's wrong, child?"

Ruby's eyes were pinned to the floor.

"Oh, honey, honey ..."

Ruby was in tears.

"It's not a mistake. It's for you—what's in the box is for you."

Ruby ran to Miss Honey, hugging her head roughly between Miss Honey's plump hips.

"Ruby, h-haven't you ever seen something pretty? Hasn't anyone ever bought you something pretty before?"

"No, no, Miss Honey. No." Fresh snot ran from Ruby's nostrils.

"Oh, honey."

"Pretty. It, it so pretty, Miss Honey. Ma'am."

Walking back over to the box with trepidation, Ruby's eyes were eager, once again, to look at what was in the box. But then her gangly body turned back to Miss Honey, awkwardly, shyly.

"Take it out the box. Go ahead; it's all right to do."

"Yes'm." Ruby fell silent; her eyes were hungrier than before, more eager to discover what it was that was jolting her. "It ... it ..."

"White. The dress is white. White as a chalk-white sky."

The white dress was in Ruby's hands. Ruby was dancing. "It pretty, Miss Honey! *Pretty!*" Ruby was beside herself, delirious, her feet moving to a tune, turning over and over in her head.

"Ha ... oh, Ruby. Ha. Darling!"

But then, as if lightning had struck the boarding house, Ruby stuffed the dress back inside the box, seemingly frightened by it again.

"Miss Honey, Miss Honey." Ruby was crying. "It, it too pretty fo' me, Miss Honey. It too pretty fo' me." Ruby sobbed.

"Your dress? Y-your white dress?"

Ruby was down on her knees, her thin body bent over at the waist.

"No, uh, darling, God loves. He loves you, child!"

"But I ugly, Miss Honey. I ugly. Daddy, Daddy an', an' Mama say so. But I ugly. Ugly!"

The dress was white linen. Miss Honey had bought in Minesburg in Miss Beatrice's dress shop.

"Why you buy it, Miss Honey? W-what fo', ma'am?"

Miss Honey looked at this black child, in whom she saw so much beauty. "Why, for you, Ruby. You."

"B-but why, why, Miss H-Honey?" Ruby's eyes seemed to be hunting through Miss Honey.

Miss Honey had smacked her hands. "You and me, Ruby, are going to church!"

Smack!

"Church!"

"Sunday morning. We've got a date with Macguire's Baptist Church on Sunday morning!"

Ruby looked stumped. Her head hung crooked.

"Get up, Ruby, and take your white dress out of the box."

And Ruby did. "White, white, Miss Honey!"

"White, white as a chalk-white sky!"

Things had calmed down, and Miss Honey was measuring Ruby from shoulder to shoulder with the white dress.

"Fit, Miss Honey, ma'am?"

"Perfectly!

Ruby smiled.

"You ain't nothing but a little girl, Ruby. All girls are scrawny little things at your age."

Ruby giggled. "You be scrawny like me when you be little, Miss Honey?"

"Just like you, Ruby. No different. Don't let this"—Miss Honey shimmered like an earthquake—"extra load of cargo, extra baggage on my caboose and hips, fool you any, child. There was a time, Ruby—there was a time when Miss Honey was as skinny as a scarecrow too."

Ruby's hand muffled her wild laughter.

Now Miss Honey slipped the ribbon over the box.

Ruby was sitting in the chair, looking down at her dirty feet.

Miss Honey took notice. *Shoes! Shoes! Ruby has no shoes!* "Shoes, Ruby. Shoes. Sunday shoes, honey."

"Yes'm."

Miss Honey rose off her knees. Her arms hugged the box to her ample bosom. "Oh, Ruby, what a fool I am. A foolish old lady!" Miss Honey said, slapping her head.

"Doesn' say that, Miss Honey, ma'am," Ruby said with affection.

"Oh, God bless me. Lord, I-I can't even think past today. To ha … n-never mind Sunday."

Ruby giggled.

"You'll have white shoes with … with—"

"Little white socks, ma'am? Like them other chil'runs does who 'tends them Macguire's Church on Sunday?"

"Will you ever!"

"Can you tell, Miss Honey?"

21

"What, tell what?"

Ruby became extremely bashful. "S-size a my two feets, ma'am?"

Ruby had been at Miss Honey's boarding house for some time now.

"So it's a deal?"

"Yes'm. It a deal, ma'am." Ruby was at the front door when she turned back to Miss Honey. "Miss Honey, ma'am …"

"Uh, yes, Ruby?"

"Is I pretty?"

Miss Honey bent over and kissed Ruby's forehead. "All God's children are pretty, Ruby, darling. Every single one. There are no exceptions. Not one."

Miss Honey was sitting atop her bed. She was exhausted, zapped—she had her shoes off, and when she had her shoes off, that signaled, for her, the end of the day. She supposed it had nothing to do with her illness as much as with the "excitement" that had left her room and should be heading down Plattstown's dusty roads by now and off for home.

But her illness did exhaust her. At particular periods of the day. It was something she'd have to live with for a few more months of her life. The doctor said four or five months, and then her life would end.

Miss Honey opened a big, stuffed cloth bag. Her hand dipped inside the bag and then out. She'd carried mementoes, precious ones, back to Plattstown with her. Artifacts from her travels. Artifacts from the experiences that shaped and formed her.

"My, you were a handsome man, William Malcolm Monroe." Miss Honey was looking at a photo of a good-looking man of light-skinned complexion. "One handsome-looking something you are, Mr. William Malcolm Monroe, now ain't you!"

Miss Honey's hand dipped back inside the cloth bag. The man in the next photo she held was good-looking, his face so dark that it was probably darker than the dark side of the moon. "Beat a path to my door, didn't you, Reynaldo." Miss Honey continued staring at the picture, appreciatively. "Swept me off my feet like a broom!" Miss Honey shook her head, recalling how it had been. "You were *some* man, Reynaldo St. Clair. Some kind of man!"

She put the two pictures back in the bag and returned the bag to the foot of the bed.

Ruby's box was on top of the chair.

"Made a deal, a bargain, didn't we, Ruby? Girl?" She was going to get up but knew better—knew she'd better rest there. The room was by no means cool, but it was pleasant. Miss Honey had one of her colorful scarves covering her head.

Shoes. Shoes. She'd have to buy Ruby shoes. Tomorrow, in Minesburg, at Miss Beatrice's store, she would buy her white shoes.

"Ruby can't wear her white dress without white shoes. How stupid to … No way the child …"

Her hair, Miss Honey thought. *Ruby's hair. The child's hair. Nappy. Snarly as a thick ball of yarn. Ruby's hair!*

"Only the Lord knows."

I ain'ts ugly. I ain'ts ugly. I ain'ts no pick'ninny. I ain'ts no pick'ninny girl. I ain'ts no nigga girl. "But I scrawny like … like Miss Honey say I be."

Ruby skipped along the road as if a song were in her bones as big as dinosaur bones. She felt pretty. It was the first time in her life that she'd felt pretty. *All God's children are pretty, Ruby, darling. All God's children are pretty, Ruby, darling.*

"They is, Miss Honey, ma'am. All God chil'runs is pretty, ma'am."

Sunday, Sunday. I gonna meet God on Sunday.

She'd been in Macguire's Baptist Church—yes, snuck into it—but not on a Sunday was she ever there. Not when God was there. She was sure God was there only on a Sunday; it was when people attended church—on a Sunday—because it was the only time when He was there in church.

"The res' of the week, wonder where He be? What God be doin' up to then?" Ruby looked up at the sky. "Heared you in the sky." Ruby giggled. "Say you the one make the thunder." Ruby looked around her. "But doesn' hear nothin' fo' now." Ruby felt a sweet sensation. "Ain'ts gotta run, does

I?" But Ruby moved from her spot anyway. "Ain'ts gonna strike me dead, is You?" The sky looked calm. "Nope, guess not."

Ruby kept skipping along. "I gonna hear Miss Honey sing in church. Not outside a church Sunday. Gonna be sittin' in a church pew like them other chil'runs."

Ruby began wondering where, just where she was going to sit in Macguire's Baptist Church on Sunday morning, which pew. "The church ain't but so big, no way."

Shoes. Shoes. White shoes with little white socks.

"Mama an' Daddy ain'ts gonna see me. Mama an' Daddy ain'ts." Ruby was going to be dressed up in white, come Sunday morning with Miss Honey. "Miss Honey an' me make a deal. I likes Miss Honey." Ruby looked up at the sky. "You heared me, God?" Ruby asked brashly, challengingly. "Say I likes Miss Honey!" Ruby lowered her eyes. "Miss Honey, when, when she sing, Miss Honey make thunder, God! Sure do then."

CHAPTER 4

The morning woke up at the crack of dawn. It could be heard like organ music. It could be heard as if God had stationed His finest angels in each corner of the sky, like a grandiose chorale, making certain the entire world heard something wondrous pour into their ears today.

It was a high sky.

Already, the crickets had chirped, making their rubbing noises, sounding like an army of sound marching up a tiny hill. Big black bears had yawned. The fields, where the best land in Plattstown was, were the plushest green, as if this was to be the summer of abandoned dreams. Plattstown had a mood woven in it, all right, as if Plattstown could lift heaven and earth up on its shoulders and keep both balanced there, say, forever; that time eternal had some sway. Today was the day to live in Plattstown, even if that person didn't know where it was situated on a map. But it was Sunday morning, and it could be heard in all of its morning glory.

"Ruby, how do you do it?"

"W-what, Miss Honey, ma'am? What I does, ma'am?"

"Keep your feet moving with mine? Step for step, as little as you are."

Ruby was high-stepping this morning. "Doesn' know, Miss Honey. Legs doesn' talk to me, ma'am, while they walkin'. Doesn', ma'am."

And walking they were, Miss Honey and Ruby, off to Macguire's Baptist Church. Ruby was walking in her new bright-white shoes that none of the road's dirt seemed able to catch. Those white shoes shone like silver in the dark. And the white shoes Miss Honey bought Ruby in Minesburg fit Ruby's feet perfectly, just as did the white dress she had bought there.

"Oh, Miss Honey, I can walk in my shoes all day!"

"Child, child. Now, don't let Miss Honey start talking about her feet! Don't take kindly to walking the country roads or Golden Road on Sunday or any other day of the week, for that matter!"

"Yes'm. Yes, ma'am."

The shock was everywhere in Macguire's Baptist Church as Miss Honey walked down the church aisle with Ruby Martinson, holding on to her hand as though she were a living, breathing china doll.

Miss Honey sniffed at the air in a high-hatted fashion, not batting an eyelash regarding that the little girl, Ruby Martinson, was in Macguire's, at her side, in full glory, she knew, of the Lord. The initial "hmm" in Macguire's had turned into a full chorus of "hu-uum."

"Now, Ruby," Miss Honey said, tidying Ruby up for all the parishioners to see, "how about here? How about you sit right here?"

"In the firs' pew, Miss Honey?"

"Yes. Right here in the first pew is good."

"Good mornin', Miss Honey!" Mr. Jasper P. Bean said, looking over his left shoulder, his horn-rimmed glasses gleaming.

"Good morning there, Brother Jasper!"

"Good morning, Ruby!" he said.

"Uh … oh, uh … yes, sir. Good … good mornin', Mr. Jasper, sir."

"I'll take my leave of you now, Ruby. But I'll be right over there," Miss Honey said, pointing her finger to the empty area.

"Yes … yes'm."

Ruby shut her eyes and took a deep breath, only to reopen them. "God. I in God church. How it look on Sunday mornin'?" Ruby whispered.

"Miss Honey, what song you singing this morning for us?"

"'Amazing Grace,' Brother Jasper."

Miss Honey took her seat. She put her pocketbook down on the floor close to her left leg. When her eyes leveled out again, she looked down at Ruby. *The wonders of God*, she thought. *Oh, God's wonders of wonders!* She laughed to herself.

Ruby was being as nosy as a bee with her eyes and mind. But like a habit that was slowly awakening, she was thinking of God. She was thinking of how much she wanted to get to know Him. How much He wanted to know her. She felt as comfortable in Macguire's Baptist Church as her feet had felt in her new white shoes on the road.

Ruby pulled on her short white socks, even if they hadn't needed any pulling up.

Mr. Jasper P. Bean began playing his organ.

It sounds even better on the inside, Ruby thought. She liked the way Mr. Jasper played, letting the notes build up steam and then letting them go like a choo-choo train barreling over train tracks. Ruby had heard that kind of sound before in Plattstown, trains moving on train tracks, going choo-choo.

It was midway into the service, and the collection plates were in the ushers' white-gloved hands. Miss Honey smiled as she watched Ruby's small hand dip into the white pocketbook; it was strapped across her shoulder and hung delicately to her waist.

"You, you welcome, ma'am," Ruby said to the shocked usher, who'd thanked Ruby for her church offering from her white pocketbook.

Ruby took a deep sigh of relief when the collection plate was passed forward to the next parishioner in the pew.

Miss Honey touched the brim of her hat and then looked at Ruby's new white hat sitting atop her head like a pretty snow cone in late July. Oh, the trouble she'd had with Ruby's hair that morning when she got to the boarding house. It was the deal they'd made—that Ruby would come to Miss Honey's room to be dressed in her Sunday wear.

Oh, Lord!

But Ruby's hair was the problem, not the dress, not the shoes or socks or hat or pocketbook but Ruby's hair. It hadn't been washed. Miss Honey didn't want to think when it'd last been washed or combed, brushed, or greased—if Ruby's hair had ever been washed, combed, brushed, or greased. But it was groomed this morning. On this Sunday morning.

Bless the Lord!

The child was so patient, Miss Honey thought. You've got to be patient with life, and, for now, Ruby was. She didn't complain when the chunky comb bit into her hair. Miss Honey knew the comb had hurt Ruby's tender scalp. She sat right there in the chair, as stubborn as the comb was to get to her roots.

God loves you, Ruby! God loves you, darling!

And there Ruby was in the first pew of Macguire's Baptist Church, feeling as pretty as an angel of God.

Now Ruby felt as if she were on the outside of the church, but she was on the inside. She was fidgety. The spirit and the church folk moved her. Her little body had a chill in it. And Ruby knew there was this spider walking—not crawling, but walking—across the floor because Ruby could hear it. Hear it. She couldn't hop up and down (not in her pew) like she did when she was on the outside of the church, but how she wanted to.

Miss Honey stood. And Mr. Jasper P. Bean stretched his long, spindly arms all the way out in front of him, as if he had even more arms to stretch. This was the first time Ruby had seen any of this, standing as a witness to it.

Miss Honey! Miss Honey, ma'am! Ruby didn't know what to call what Miss Honey had inside her throat. She had no words or a vocabulary for it, but she was crying and shaking and felt the bright white dress Miss Honey had bought her in Minesburg touching her skin, touching it, touching it.

Miss Honey do sing wit' her hat on! She do!

Church service was near its conclusion. Only one hymn remained. The church was preparing itself for its final Sunday song.

Up to now, Ruby had not participated in the hymn singing with the church. At best, she'd mumbled whatever the church had sung.

She bent her head, looking down at the floor as the parishioners' spines in the pews were as straight as book spines.

Then Jasper P. Bean began playing the song on his organ. And the parishioners and Pastor Cornell Mangrove Pettigrew sang out the first verse to this well-known hymn. And then they sang the second verse. And then Mr. Jasper P. Bean and his wooden organ got them started on the third verse as the organ began swelling in tension and tempo, and Ruby's head began to lift itself out its lax stoop. Ruby Martinson's eyes stared straight ahead at Miss Honey, whose eyes were shut as she sang. Miss Honey's eyes opened quickly, widely, as her ears heard something straight from—"Ruby, Ruby, God loves you, Ruby! God loves you, darling!"—heaven.

Ruby had sung.

Ruby Martinson had sung in Macguire's Baptist Church in front of everyone.

"Ruby!"

Ruby sat on the throw rug on the floor.

Miss Honey sat in a chair, rocking Ruby from behind. Miss Honey held Ruby tightly beneath her armpits, resting her chin on Ruby's thick, greased, plaited hair.

"Oh … oh, Ruby. The whole church stopped dead. It did, child, when you sang."

Ruby shut her eyes. "Doesn' 'member, Miss Honey. D-doesn', ma'am. Not'in."

"Of course you don't. You were a singer who lost in yourself. Up in yourself."

"Los' … los', Miss Honey?" Ruby's head jerked backward.

"Down in your soul. Your singing was coming out of your soul and into your voice, honey. All your living, Ruby. All of your days and nights—they came together."

Ruby had not understood a thing Miss Honey had just said, but she nodded her head as if she had.

"Oh, you're so young, child. So young. But you know so much already. Your soul is telling you so much." Miss Honey released her. They were in the front room of the two-room boarding quarters. "Excuse me, Ruby."

"Yes'm."

Miss Honey went into her bedroom. She was in there for no more than a few minutes. When she reentered the front room, standing partway in it, she took hold of Ruby's hand.

Languidly, Ruby looked up at her.

"Come, child."

Ruby got up off the rug and onto her feet. She was still attired in her white dress and white shoes. "T-time to take off my clothes, ma'am?"

"No, Ruby. It's time for me to show you something." Miss Honey's skin radiated. The room was a muted gray, appealingly simple. "Here, Ruby!"

Ruby looked at the jazz album making no sense to her.

Miss Honey's name was on the album jacket.

"You famous, Miss Honey. You famous!" Ruby yelped.

"These are records."

"Your pitcher on records, Miss Honey?"

"Well, at least on the album jackets, Ruby." Miss Honey walked over to the old wooden Victrola phonograph machine, which still looked striking. Miss Honey cranked the handle on the Victrola.

Ruby was quite amused.

"Sometimes it's like an old stubborn goat. Ha. It's the only way I can describe it. You got to get it started. But once that happens, it'll work all day."

"Yes'm. Ha."

Cautiously, Miss Honey slid a record out of the album jacket.

"You happy, Miss Honey?"

"Am I!"

Ruby stood near the Victrola.

"Ruby, uh, it's ready."

"Yes'm."

When Ruby first heard the music, she didn't know what to make of it. The instruments her ears heard blending together stimulated her to want to hear more. But then Ruby realized it was Miss Honey's voice. She'd recognize her voice in any kind of music.

Miss Honey hugged Ruby as Ruby's body began twitching. "It's me, Ruby. It's Miss Honey, all right!"

"Miss Honey. W-what you call it? Call it, ma'am!"

"Jazz music."

"Uh … uh, you say jass music, Miss Honey? Jass music, ma'am?"

"Ain't it pretty?"

Ruby was hugging Miss Honey hard.

Miss Honey undressed Ruby as the music blared. Ruby hummed to it, trying her best to understand it; Miss Honey let her.

"Ja-jass music. Ja-jass music, Miss Honey. What you sing be jass music, ma'am."

Miss Honey removed Ruby's dress. Her hat and shoes remained; Ruby looked odd.

"Now, I ain't your servant, Ruby. No way."

"Yes'm. I take my shoes off. An' my socks, ma'am. Do."

"Servant's pay's too low."

Ruby stole a look at the white pocketbook on Miss Honey's bed. "Give all my money to the church, Miss Honey. All the money you give me. I give to Macguire's Church this mornin'. Done wit' it, ma'am."

Miss Honey laid her hands on top of Ruby's shoulders. "I know you did. But why, honey? When I gave you the money this morning, I told you not to put all of it in the church offering plate, only some. You were to save a portion for yourself."

"I know, Miss Honey, ma'am." She paused a moment and then said, "But seem like the church need it more'n I does, ma'am."

"It does, Ruby."

Ruby's candor hadn't surprised Miss Honey.

"Seem like it need few mo' hym'als to sing outta to me, Miss Honey. Fo' Sunday service, ma'am."

Miss Honey looked at Ruby's white hat, and Ruby made Miss Honey wish she hadn't.

"You've got to take it off some time, Ruby."

"I-I know, Miss Honey." Ruby sucked her teeth. "F-feel pretty. Make me feel pretty, Miss Honey."

"You already are pretty. Ruby Martinson's already that—a pretty little girl. Uh, lady."

Reluctantly, Ruby reached for the hat on her head.

"And besides, you're going to wear it next week, your pretty white hat, on Sunday to church."

"I is, Miss Honey?"

"I'm going to wash your white dress and your white socks and clean off your white shoes, and—"

"They dirty, Miss Honey?"

"A little. Only a little. I don't know how you've kept them as clean as you have. Why …"

"God onlies know, Miss Honey. Do," Ruby said, looking down at her shoes.

"Yes, Ruby, God. Only God knows."

"May I help you, Miss Honey, ma'am? May I?"

Miss Honey held Ruby's hands. "And get your pretty hands old and tired like mine?"

Ruby listened to Miss Honey speaking and then to her singing voice—her record was still playing on the Victrola. "You got the prettiess voice in the worl', Miss Honey. The whole worl'."

"Not as pretty as yours. Uh-uh. No, child. Not as pretty as Ruby Martinson's voice."

Ruby had left the boarding house. Miss Honey's body was tired again.

"Ain't never had a day like this. I know I said it just the other day, but ain't!" She closed her eyes and made apologies to no one for her bad English again.

Miss Honey was going to have to help Ruby. In so many ways, she was going to have to service her. She'd come from the same humble beginnings and had wound up dining with kings and queens. Ruby Martinson—no doubt—would do the same.

It would start with her grooming and her language, and then her general feelings toward herself. *They're the basic tools.* This was how she would go about doing the work that had to be done. God had blessed Ruby with something magnificent, something the world, with all its good and its bad, would want. It would demand it of Ruby, like any gold mine that produced great riches.

Miss Honey wasn't going to fight her disease; she wouldn't be that silly. She wanted this time given to her. She wanted to cherish it. She needed this rest for her energy level, for Ruby. Ruby was going to be a great jazz singer one day—somewhere down the road.

She'd heard something great in church that day—a little girl with a magnificent voice. A little girl, already old beyond her years. She had to shout out: *"Ruby, Ruby, God love you, Ruby! God loves you, darling!"*

Macguire's Baptist Church had no way of knowing what had hit it. Ruby wasn't supposed to remember the experience the first time she heard herself sing. When you're deep in yourself, buried deep inside your soul, you never do. Whatever it is just rises up in you and washes over you like a great river, washing you until you're blind. Ruby was there in that greatness, in a context of mystery that leaves no trace or sound.

"I need my strength, Lord. Now I know why you brought me back to Plattstown to die—my mission. What it is. What it looks like."

Miss Honey had not changed out of her Sunday dress. She still had an elegant, graceful look about her. "And didn't you look lovely in your white hat? Didn't you, child? As pretty as a pumpkin, sitting up there in church. The prettiest little girl there, Ruby. Why, prettiest of the lot."

Ruby skipped down the road. Her legs felt springy and light. "I like jass. Like it." Ruby had been saying this over and over since she'd left Miss Honey's room. "Miss Honey gonna teach me how to sing it too."

Ruby stopped skipping and looked at her shadow; then she challenged it. "Say she was." Her shadow did not say anything back to her so Ruby pointed her finger at it reprimandingly. "Do too! Do too! Miss Honey do too!" Ruby put her finger down. "Say I is to learn jass music," Ruby said in a softer voice but then added in a brassy voice, "Jass music!"

The music began circling inside her ear. "Soun', gonna soun' like Miss Honey. Sure is. Gonna soun' like Miss Honey soun'." Ruby laughed. She started skipping up the road again. "Pretty. Jass music pretty. Miss Honey an' ... an' them horns an' things. Make, make jass music soun' downright pretty." Ruby spun. "Miss Honey say I can sing. Never know so 'fore M-Miss Honey say so today. I jus' close my eyes. It what I done, swear—I swear. I jus' close my eyes. It what I done, God, an somtin' come out my mout'. Out my—" Ruby jumped. "Scare me at firs'—then I doesn' know not'in. Stay in the dark like that till Miss Honey, Miss Honey be huggin' an kissin' me an' ... an' Miss Honey got tears swoll in her eyes. When I done."

Ruby scratched at her hair. "Think I be in trouble ..." Ruby laughed. "Onlies know I be in church. Know then I ain'ts done not'in wrong. Jus' meet God. Ain'ts causin' Him no trouble. Scare. Uh-uh, not in church, ain'ts." Ruby had one more road to skip down, Victory Road, and then she'd be home. Victory Road was a long road. "I ... I ... bes' I be walkin' now."

Ruby was in no rush to get home. Walking would take longer than skipping—that she knew. Ruby's smile sat on her face lovelier than twilight. "I ain'ts scared. I-I ain'ts scared!" Ruby had stopped playing with her shadow, this thing that walked with her during the day in Plattstown, wherever she went when the sun was high in the sky. "I ain'ts scared!"

But Ruby *was* scared.

Her mama was in the house.

Her mama was probably drunk.

Her mama would get drunk around this time on Sunday.

She *was* scared.

"I ain'ts. I ain'ts …"

Every nerve and fiber of Ruby wanted to turn around and skip back up the road and back to Miss Honey's boarding house, Harding's Boarding House.

"Them records Miss Honey got. Lissen to them records all day."

Her mama threw things and used words she knew were bad, ugly. Ugly.

"I ugly, ain'ts I? I ugly. Ugly house. Ugly clothes. I … I ugly, ain'ts I? Ugly house. Ugly clothes. Mama drunk. Know Mama drunk on Sunday. Affa church. Affa Miss Honey come from church, Mama drunk."

Ruby looked at the house on Rumble Way, a house struggling to stand up straight.

"Ugly house!" Ruby shouted. She fell down in the dirt. "Fall down! Fall down! Fall down like Mama. Fall down like Mama do! Like … like …" Ruby bit her tears. And then she rose in the road.

"Sing in church today, Mama. What I do. Sing in Macguire's Baptist Church today. In a white dress, Mama. M-Miss Honey buyed me. Goin' back nex' Sunday, ma'am. Miss Honey say. Miss Honey wash my dress, Mama. She say she doesn' wan' me to get ol' hands, ma'am. Ha. Funny, Mama. Miss Honey hands ain'ts ol'. Miss Honey beautiful, Mama. Her hat, her hat wide as the sky, ma'am," Ruby said, heading for her house, heading for home, barefoot.

CHAPTER 5

"Don't be nervous, Ruby. Just hold my hand. Tight as you want. We practiced, right?"

"Uh … r-right, Miss Honey. Uh … we pra'ice, ma'am."

"Now, Ruby, now."

Miss Honey and Ruby stood together. Mr. Jasper P. Bean looked at them and winked. And then Miss Honey started the song, to be joined by Ruby, whose hand, though anchored by Miss Honey's, was still shaking.

But as Miss Honey and Ruby sang together, the tremor began to leave Ruby's hand. Miss Honey's and Ruby's eyes were shut so tight that not even air could squeeze through them. They'd closed their eyes, as Mr. Bean and everyone else in Macguire's had closed theirs. The small church moved as one, en masse, in a sanctified swaying of souls and attitude.

Miss Honey's and Ruby's voices were raising them into greener pastures of God's love.

This time while Ruby was singing, she felt her deepest emotions touch her. She felt a freedom, this place she could play; where the sun shone big and voluminous and golden until the close of day. Miss Honey was there with her, where she played, holding her hand so she wouldn't fly off somewhere inside a wind stream.

Suddenly, from a church pew, Sister Agatha T. Samuels ("Aggie" to her friends) charged to the foot of the pulpit, and her body began shaking as if the Holy Ghost had possessed her. And Sister Samuels began wailing and writhing as Macguire's Baptist Church swayed to and fro, like a mighty ship rocking in a spiritual storm of powerful waves and bold headwinds.

And then Brother Humbert O. Patterson ("Bert" to friends) did the same as Sister Agatha T. Samuels. He charged out of his pew and off to the front of the church, where his body began shaking like a trembling vine.

Miss Honey and Ruby sang and sang while more and more of the church folk ran out from their church pews and to the front of the church, possessed, uncontrollable, shaking with the Holy Spirit as their Counselor and Comforter.

Miss Honey's and Ruby's song, played on the church organ by Mr. Jasper P. Bean, just continued on and on, as if the heavens had been cleaved open and rained down upon them in declaring Jesus stood there with them, naked in the jabbing storm.

Mr. Jasper P. Bean's small head glistened from sweat. And Pastor Pettigrew, with a solid hand, guided the mighty ship with great assuredness and special love.

Miss Honey's hand held Ruby's; both held on, anchored to the task; both singing the struggles of the day and the joys of the night; both involved in God's work from the front of the smallish church, where the long line of humanity had amassed and joined in the service of something even more mighty and magnificent than themselves—this living miracle of souls, alive in the Lord's house, canceled out pain and lifted their faith and trust in God and His steady, labored works for their earthly fulfillment.

Miss Honey undid Ruby's belt and tossed it on the bed. She turned to Ruby and hugged her with all the strength in her. She kissed Ruby. She had kissed Ruby at least a thousand times on her forehead.

"Been every place, Ruby. Sang with great singers, honey, but …" Miss Honey stopped. She just looked at Ruby standing there, as still and innocent as a little bird on a limb. "Thought my heart was going to burst, child."

Ruby took Miss Honey's hand again. Ruby kissed it.

"Oh, honey."

Ruby walked Miss Honey over to the Victrola. "Miss Honey, can I hear you sing, ma'am? Hear you sing through the machine, Miss Honey?"

"W-what again?"

"Y-yes'm."

Miss Honey giggled. "Church wasn't enough? Didn't fill your bill?"

"Jass, Miss Honey, ma'am. Jass music."

"Y-you like jazz that much?"

"Yes'm."

"You *are* a jazz singer—you know that, don't you?"

"Yes'm."

"I know I told you that before. And you don't know, don't quite understand any of it."

"No, ma'am."

"But you are, Ruby. You've got a natural feel, a natural rhythm. What jazz singers have. Have to have." Miss Honey put a record on after she'd cranked the Victrola, much to Ruby's delight.

"I-I does, Miss Honey?"

"Yes. Don't have to teach you nothing about that. You were born with that. God gave you a voice and rhythm, and with it will come a style, a style all your own."

Ruby understood none of this; her face mirrored this limitation. "J-jass, Miss Honey?"

Miss Honey's fingers picked at Ruby's dress and then smoothed it out evenly, flat. "There're still things I have to teach you, though." Miss Honey's record played in the background.

"You does, Miss Honey?"

"Oh yes, child."

"I gotta wait, Miss Honey, ma'am?"

On the following Sunday, well after church service, not a soul was in Macguire's but Miss Honey and Ruby. Miss Honey sat on the organ bench while Ruby stood.

"Ha ..." Miss Honey looked around the church. "Glad we didn't sing to empty pews this morning."

"They be full, Miss Honey."

"Full."

"Full."

"People stood outside the church door this morning, Ruby, waiting to get in. Standing room only. Couldn't have squeezed another soul into Macguire's with a shoe horn!"

They glanced at each other, for they knew why the church had been filled.

"Now, Ruby, let's you and me get down to the business at hand." Miss Honey had carried a good-sized handbag to Macguire's this morning. She pulled the music out of the bag and set it on top of Mr. Jasper's organ. Then she spread out the sheet music.

"Jass music, Miss Honey?"

"Uh, no, not in church. You don't play jazz music in the Lord's house. No way do you, child."

"I, I …" Ruby's head was shaking. "I doesn' under—"

"Jazz music ain't bad, Ruby."

"Sin, sin—"

"No, honey, it's not sinful. It, well, it just doesn't belong in God's house. It's how most people feel, especially colored folk—the religious kind."

"Oh."

"But you'll understand in time. Don't you worry." Miss Honey pointed to the sheet music. "Church music, Ruby."

"Church music, Miss Honey."

Miss Honey struck a note on the organ. She could play both organ and piano well. "I'm going to teach you how to read music today."

"R-read music, ma'am?" Ruby's eyes bugged out. "R-read, y-you can *read* music?"

"That you can. As plain as a book." Miss Honey grinned. Her feet were on the organ's wooden pedals.

"Uh, ain'ts good at readin'. Book readin'. Writin' neither, ma'am," Ruby said, her head half-bowing.

"I'm going to teach you all three!"

"You, you is?"

"Yes, I am, Ruby. But first, we're going to start with music."

"Readin' music, Miss Honey," Ruby said, delighted.

"Reading music."

Miss Honey and Ruby were at it for a while. As Miss Honey had correctly assumed, Ruby was a quick learner—very.

"*A*, Miss Honey. That note a *A* ma'am. A on the scale." And then Ruby hummed the note.

"Excellent, Ruby!"

"*B* nex', Miss Honey, ma'am. Hmm."

"Right on pitch!" Miss Honey skipped up the scale.

"D, ma'am."

"Hum it, Ruby."

"Hmm. E, Miss Honey!"

"And?" Miss Honey's eyebrow arched.

"Hmm."

"Ha!"

"I-I readin' music, Miss Honey?"

"No, Ruby. But you will. In due time."

Miss Honey chose to stop. She put the sheet music away. She'd put it up on the organ stand as an enticement for Ruby (like chocolates), if for no other reason.

"We gotta, gotta stop, Miss Honey, ma'am?"

"Yes, for now."

"I can go on, ma'am. I-I ain'ts tired. Jus' gettin' started, seem like."

"I know that, but I am, honey," Miss Honey said, faking.

"You, you is, ma'am?"

"Aren't you hungry, Ruby? Know I am." Miss Honey feigned hunger.

"Uh." Ruby, it seemed, had to think that one through a bit more; let it tumble in her head some.

"I've never cooked for you, Ruby. And I'm a good cook, darling. A darn good cook!"

"B-bet you do be, Miss Honey."

Miss Honey got up from the organ bench. "So you're saying," Miss Honey said daintily, "a big, full-figured woman such as myself better be a good cook. Is that it?"

Ruby saw the play, the fun, in Miss Honey's smile. "Yes'm."

Miss Honey grabbed Ruby. "What am I to do with you!"

"Hee-hee."

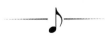

Back in Harding's Boarding House, Miss Honey and Ruby had eaten eggs, potatoes, ham, and grits. Ruby had two big helpings of food; Miss Honey, one.

Miss Honey was washing the dishes. She was in a red polka-dot apron. Ruby was in Miss Honey's bedroom, listening to her records. By now, Ruby knew how to operate the old Victrola, Miss Honey having showed her and entrusting Ruby with it. The phonograph was all Ruby's, and Ruby was having a ball, going through Miss Honey's large stack of records.

Miss Honey was drying a glass when she heard Ruby's miraculous voice, singing along with the record—not note for note but adding her own originality to it with tremendous ease.

Miss Honey stopped wiping. She listened. This was a dream come true: teaching someone; certainly, a child as eager and bright as Ruby Martinson. It wasn't Ruby's fault she couldn't read or write; Miss Honey's own experience in Plattstown matched Ruby's. It was Plattstown's white men's hatred of "their" blacks that imposed educational limitations. It was the white man's hatred of blacks that produced black sharecroppers, itinerants, drifters, drunks, jail bait; lucky to be alive—to survive this worthless, valueless state of being. The black man's social status attained through the South's oppressive, strong-armed will.

After leaving Plattstown for the North at age seventeen, Miss Honey began her formal schooling at age twenty-one. She learned how to read and write and speak good, "proper" English and lost her Southern accent. In her gut, she relentlessly asserted her overriding desire to do that, to improve, to look better in the world's eyes.

But it was really for herself that she'd done it. And now she could see that same spark in Ruby. The same spark in Ruby's eyes. Ruby, whether she knew it or not, had this burning desire in her too. And it was Miss Honey's job as Ruby's teacher, mentor, and someone who recognized it to develop it, to bring it out of her.

"Ruby catches on to things fast, so fast," Miss Honey said to herself. "Her mind isn't going to let her rest. Not for one hour in a day."

And what happened back in Macguire's, the church today, with her testing Ruby's ear on the piano to see if she had good pitch (excellent), she had to get back to the boarding house to feed Ruby. She had to. Give her at least one cooked meal today. If it was the last thing she'd do today, that was it.

Unconsciously, Miss Honey drifted into the front room's archway, looking into the bedroom.

Ruby's eyes were shut tight so she didn't see Miss Honey standing tall in the doorframe.

"Child, if you ain't something!" Miss Honey whispered.

When Ruby went to put a new record on the turntable, she saw Miss Honey standing in the bedroom with the towel and glass. "Miss Honey."

"Now don't let Miss Honey get in your way," Miss Honey said, turning to go back into the kitchen.

"Miss, Honey, which o' these records yo' fav'rite, ma'am?"

"Hmm ... let me see. Why I—"

"Ain't play through all them yet, so doesn' know which to say be mines, ma'am."

"But you will, won't you?"

"Yes'm. Gotta learn the words."

"But once you learn them."

"Gotta feel them. I-I know, Miss Honey."

Miss Honey was shocked. "Why, Ruby!"

"I-I say somtin' wrong? S-somtin' bad?"

"No, child, you said everything right."

Ruby returned to the chair. "Like this one, ma'am."

Miss Honey lay on the bed, forgetting all about drying the dishes. "Me too, Ruby."

"How get yo' voice to come through that machine way it do, ma'am? How, Miss Honey?" Ruby frowned.

"Don't know, Ruby. But much smarter people than me do."

"Hmm. An' what 'bout them instaments an' or, or—"

"Orchestra, Ruby. Oh, those engineers; they find a way." Miss Honey chuckled, her hands smoothing out her housecoat.

"Who they, Miss Honey?"

"Engineers—oh, you'll find out one day."

"I is, Miss Honey?'

"They're going to have a love affair with you, Ruby Martinson."

"I-I ain'ts got me a boyfriend, Miss Honey."

"Oh, Ruby …"

Miss Honey was singing about lost love on her record that she and Ruby listened to.

Ruby shut her eyes. She didn't like boys, at least not the ones in Plattstown—them! *What a disgusting thought*, Ruby thought.

Two months later

It was late September in Plattstown, and what was good about Plattstown in the summer was good about it in the fall: its air's seductiveness. It was the mixing of Plattstown's flowers, their fragrances, tender and kind and arresting and pleasing, and seduced any stranger, enticingly, by one quick wink of the eye.

Fragrances and experiences are what Miss Honey and Ruby were breathing in, routinely—as if queens of privilege and the divine. Miss Honey was teaching Ruby things at a breakneck speed. And Ruby was learning them, absorbing these things as if her very life depended on it. Not obsessively—no, not at all—but with magic's grace.

Ruby had memorized Miss Honey's songs, setting every one to memory, like she'd grown three brains inside her head where she stored things like a mother squirrel.

Even Miss Honey was stunned by Ruby's feats.

But there was something about these two—a fluidity, a rightness to them that made everything between them work with ease, very naturally. Miss Honey had Ruby on a string, a long one, playing a game of passion, as both were passionate in this endeavor, in this easy-as-pie collaboration.

Jazz.

Miss Honey was teaching Ruby jazz—the rudiments of it; its structure and form. Ruby read music like she could read it with her eyes closed, blind to the musical page, as if she were making her own musical notations on the music's page. Ruby read notes with the accuracy of a metronome beating time. She dived into the musical waters and came out of it with the biggest fish, making the biggest catch of the day.

And Ruby was reading. She was reading books Miss Honey had

brought from New York City to Plattstown. And Ruby was writing. Miss Honey was teaching her how to write.

Ruby seemed to instinctively sense, to know, what it was all about, what Miss Honey was doing for her. Miss Honey had spoken of singing for kings and queens and heads of state. She told Ruby of another world, a world Ruby's world was wrapped in, a world Ruby knew nothing about.

"It's like stepping out of here and going to nearby Minesburg, where the pretty shops are. Someplace, honey, you know nothing about. Nothing. Nothing at all."

That was how Miss Honey tried explaining it to Ruby—that plain, that simple, that uncomplicated. Ruby had to know there was someplace better than Plattstown, someplace better than where she was. She had to know there was a world that she could live in that could give her things she never dreamed—a world that was waiting for her gift, to carry on something others had given their lives to. Now it was her turn for the same.

Miss Honey's health—well, it was declining. Her doctor had predicted it would. Month by month, he said it would. Miss Honey wasn't seeking a miracle. She was only content that God was back in her life and using her as He was. She was content that she'd come back to Him and that He was there, that He had reaccepted her into His kingdom—at least that was her perception.

Each day, she felt closer to her God. Each day, she felt Him calling her home, preparing her "dying bed" (which the words to the old Negro spiritual "Fix Me, Jesus" plainly expressed).

At night, when Miss Honey was in bed, she knew that one day she would wake, not on earth but in heaven. Dying did not frighten her. She knew that one day her body would be too tired and sick for anything to frighten her; that her last days on earth—when they ended—had been peaceful and good, complete with service and reward.

CHAPTER 6

It was late Saturday evening. Miss Honey had washed (a pre-Sunday ritual by now) Ruby's white dress and socks and had cleaned off her shoes much earlier in the day. As for now, she was admiring them. Tuesday, she thought, she'd go back into Minesburg to Miss Beatrice's shop and buy Ruby her new Sunday attire. She hadn't told Ruby—it'd be a surprise.

Miss Honey touched the material of the white dress. She hadn't decided on the color of the new dress for Ruby. *Maybe yellow—yes, yellow,* she thought. Ruby would look pretty in yellow. Still, she would leave her mind open and see what Miss Beatrice had in stock, but it had to catch her eye immediately; it's how she shopped.

Tomorrow would mark the ninth straight Sunday that she and Ruby would march up Golden Road to sing in Macguire's Baptist Church. Miss Honey looked down at Ruby's white shoes. *Ruby stands so tall in them on Sunday mornings,* she thought. *So tall!*

Miss Honey looked at the time; it was ten twenty-five.

"Five more minutes, and I'm in bed. Ha. Fast asleep. Dead to the world."

It was later—much later—when Miss Honey awoke to a rapid pounding on her front door.

"What in God's name!"

The fists pounding the door continued unabated, beating it in what seemed to be a rage.

Miss Honey rushed to her feet and snatched the robe off the back of the bedroom door. She didn't bother to turn on the bedroom light but quickly hustled from the bedroom into the front room.

"Who …" she asked herself as she unlocked the door.

The woman stood there, as drunk as any drunk.

"Millicent!"

The slip of light from the hallway light shone across her face.

"Get, get outta my way!" Millicent Martinson said, her body banging into Miss Honey's front room wall. "You, you get outta my goddamn way, woman!"

Both stood in the dark.

Miss Honey couldn't see Millicent Martinson's eyes; she could only imagine them: red, angry, blistering, gleaming. "Let me turn on—"

"Doesn' need me no light to tell you what I gotta, you black heifer!"

Miss Honey turned the room's light on.

Wildly, Millicent Martinson flailed her bony arms and then fell to the floor. She got on her hands and knees and struggled to lift herself. Wildly, her arms flailed in front of her, and her body crashed into a wall. Her eyes whirled in her head, unsettled and unmanaged. She came off the wall, staggering toward Miss Honey.

Miss Honey stood her ground. "What's this about, Millicent? Tell me, between you and—"

"Stealin', stealin', stealin'." It was all Millicent said; her tongue was drunk too.

"Stealing?" Miss Honey said in shock.

"Stealin', stealin', stealin'." Millicent grabbed Miss Honey's robe, seemingly out of anger but to hold on to something too, to maintain her weakened balance. "My, my little girl. My Ruby!"

"Ruby!"

"You black heifer!"

"Ruby!" Miss Honey repeated in disbelief.

"My little girl! My daughter!" Millicent's fists pounded Miss Honey's chest, beating it with the same rage as they'd beat the door.

Miss Honey grabbed Millicent's bony wrists.

"Let go! Let go a-me! Let go a-me, goddammit!"

Miss Honey held Millicent's wrists tighter, not drawing a word from her own mouth.

They looked at each other—Miss Honey's eyes steady; Millicent's eyes fluttering.

"Teachin' 'er things. What … teachin' things she oughta not know!"

"Reading, writing—"

"Teach the girl things she oughta not know!"

"Millicent, honey—"

"Get yo' goddamn hands off me, black bitch. You black, yellow bitchuva whore!"

Miss Honey let go of Millicent's wrists.

Millicent stumbled, then staggered. "C-come back to Platt-Plattstown to die, doesn' you, M-Miss Honey? D-doesn' you!" Millicent taunted, her eyes not fluttering.

"Why, that's common knowledge, Millicent, why I'm back home."

"Ain't it, though. Ain't it, though. Leaves here. Too, too good fo' here, huh, Miss Honey?"

Miss Honey did not reply.

"Huh! Huh!"

Silence.

"Go off, go off"—Millicent laughed wickedly—"from here." Her head jerked backward. "Famous, ain't you, Miss Honey? Travel the worl', Miss Honey, doesn' you? Ha. An-answer me, woman. Answer me!"

"Yes, I traveled the world, like you said, Millicent. I traveled—"

"Learn you to speak good English too, d-doesn' you?" Millicent stepped toward Miss Honey again.

Miss Honey nodded.

"Famous. Famous. Jass singer, an' you come t-to Plattstown like you ain'ts no ways better than res' a us back in Plattstown. Y-yo' poor ol' nigger-ass. H-hear me, woman? Goin' to all them fancy-up places an' come back to die, likes the nigger you be. R-right here in Plattstown. L-like res' a us.

"Ha ha."

Millicent swung her fist at Miss Honey but missed, falling to the floor. When she got back on her feet, her body was weaving. The skin on her knees was torn; her dry, straw-straight hair, wild; her look, frightening.

"Dressin' 'er all pretty-up. White dress an' all. Shoes. Hat. She ugly! A black pick'ninny! Black tar baby! A nigger chil'!"

"But Ruby, Milli—"

"Ain'ts gonna be no church morrow! Ain'ts gonna be!"

Miss Honey's body buckled.

"Ain'ts goin' off to—"

"No, no, you—"

"Ain'ts gonna be no church for that chil'!"

"No, no, you can't do that, Millicent! You can't take that away from Ruby!"

"Who gonna stop me? Y-you, Miss Honey? You?" Millicent wagged her finger madly in front of Miss Honey. "You! You! Bitchuva black yellow whore!"

"You can't do this!"

"Ha!"

"You can't do this to R-Ruby, Millicent. Take this from her. This is Ruby's only chance. The only chance she has. Her only hope!"

Millicent Martinson hitched at her loose, dirty dress, as if she were hitching at pants riding her hips. "Hell, I ain'ts. I Ruby mama. The chil' mama. Hell, I-I ain'ts. She mines. R-Ruby 'long to me. Black ass brung her into this worl'. Nine mont's. Nine mont's. Bleed 'er out my cunt. Bleed 'er out my cunt hair. I the chil' mama."

Miss Honey staggered like a drunk. "God. God gave her an instrument. Ruby, a gift, a voice to sing with. A—"

"So's the girl can wine up like, like you, Miss Honey? 'Dentical? Like you. Ha!"

"God, God gave Ruby—"

"Singin' in church, is you? God? Singin' the devil song?" Millicent's eyes squinted and then became meaner and wider. They targeted Miss Honey. "Heared what they say, goddammit, woman! 'Bout my chil'. 'Bout Ruby. Roun' here. All right. What you an' 'er does ev'ry Sunday mornin' when you go off to church? Got folk heeber-geeberin'. Got 'em heeber-geeberin' in church. Seein' the devil. Shakin' wit' it. Goin' mad wit' it. The devil in 'er. You put the devil in my chil', in my onlies chil'!" Millicent shrieked. Her body was shaking.

"Stop it! Stop it, Millicent!" Miss Honey grabbed her by her shoulders. "Stop mocking God!"

She spat into Miss Honey's face. Her spit sat large on Miss Honey's face. "Ha!" She spat into Miss Honey's face again.

Miss Honey stood there, taking it, as Millicent's spit rolled down her face. She released Millicent's shoulders. "I'm tired, Millicent. Tired, honey."

Millicent circled her.

Weakly, Miss Honey walked over to the front room's couch and sat.

"Dyin', ain't you?" Millicent said cruelly. "Heh, heh. Dy-dyin', ain't you, Miss Honey? Slow, slow, ain't you, Miss Honey? Dyin' slow, ain't you? L-like poison? God, heh, heh, God. The devil in you now. Doin' the work he know. Know to do to you, Miss Honey. Workin' on you. Workin' on you good."

Miss Honey closed her eyes. "Go, Millicent Martinson. Go. You've done what you came here for. Go now." Miss Honey opened her eyes. "I won't bother your daughter. I won't bother Ruby ever again."

"Steal-stealin' 'er 'way from me, woman. Tryin' to steal my onlies daughter 'way from 'er mama."

"Ruby ain't singin' no mo."

Miss Honey fell back into the couch. Her strength returning.

"Heh. Heh."

Millicent looked so ugly to Miss Honey—so disgustingly ugly.

"Better not 'ear that pick'ninny girl sing not'in out 'er mout' in my house. Ain't lettin' the devil enter t-through in my goddamn house!"

"She'll run from home one day. Same as me."

"Black ass ain't goin' nowere. Nowere. Stay r-right were she be. Die 'ere like me—'er mama!"

Miss Honey's back reared forward from the couch. "Not Ruby! Ruby's going to leave you, Millicent. One day. One day," Miss Honey taunted.

Millicent covered her ears. "Shut up! Shut up, you whore. Black whore!"

"Ruby's going to sing. Sing, Millicent, sing to the world!"

"Shut up! Shut—"

"Ruby's a jazz singer!"

Millicent swung at the air with her fists and again fell to the floor.

Suddenly, Miss Honey had the compassion to help her to her feet—a

Christian urge—but she rejected this notion. She watched Millicent Martinson, who seemed more drunk than before, try as hard as she could to put herself back up on her feet.

She was on her knees and then toppled over on to her side, as if she were a baby, just learning to crawl. She paused, and her tongue slid out of her mouth and licked her finger, and then she let the slimy saliva on her finger try to heal the red tear on her knee. Her eyes became blank when she again tried to get up on to her feet. Flat on her backside, she rolled over on her right side. Her hands darted out, helping to prop her and straighten her body. She stretched her legs out and began coming up as one, as a unit that was complete and whole. She kept doing this until, finally, she stood.

Millicent Martinson began to weave, as did her eyes, everything about her, as if she were going to fall again but did not. She looked to the front door, seemingly thinking it was someone. A door she'd talked to before, when she first entered the boarding house, when it was all she could talk to, the shut door in front of her.

"Ru-Ruby ain'ts gonna leave me. Ruby loves me. My, my daughter loves me." Millicent Martinson staggered toward the door. Her hand pressed on the doorknob. She seemed to be marshalling her strength.

The door opened—and then slammed shut.

Millicent Martinson had gone as she'd come.

Miss Honey was back in bed. Her head was heavy. Her head was drunk with fear. Ruby was all she could think, was all she could say: *Ruby*.

Miss Honey still could smell the liquor that had been on Millicent Martinson's breath, soaked in it, drunk with it, lingering in her nostrils. What would she do to Ruby tonight? What had she done to Ruby already, before she showed up at her door, drunk? She'd walked through her front door.

Millicent wanted to take the world from Ruby. She never wanted Ruby to know the other world Millicent had heard of but never had seen. She only wanted Ruby to know her world, Plattstown, which had made her a drunk.

Miss Honey tensely held onto herself.

Sunday. Sunday without Ruby. "W-without that child." Miss Honey closed her eyes to pray but couldn't.

This wasn't going to shake her faith.

No. No. She'd seen worse things in her life; this wasn't the worse she'd seen. There had to be struggle; there had to be the impossible dream made possible. Ruby had a beauty in her, incandescent, even militant. It had to shine. No matter if Ruby did not know or notice or even understand it; it was shining in her. It was there, burning like a flame, inexhaustibly. It would penetrate any darkness in her life. She would be able to depend on it. It would breathe, making the determination and will she already had inside her manifest.

But how far would Millicent Martinson take this thing? Would she forget about it in the morning, when she was sober, when the alcohol emptied out of her blood? How far would she take this thing with Ruby? Had it been her or her liquor talking?

At some point in her life, Ruby Martinson would run away from home, from Millicent and Man Martinson. Now that she had discovered, through the glory of God, what she was, who she was, Ruby would run from home.

"You are a jazz singer, Ruby, like me," Miss Honey said to the darkness.

CHAPTER 7

On Sunday morning, Miss Honey walked out of Harding's Boarding House. The sun was out, vivid. Her heart wasn't in it, but she had to serve the Lord. It was Sunday, and she had to praise the Lord. It was Sunday, and she had to give all her praises to the Lord in song.

Miss Honey was on Golden Road, off to Macguire's Baptist Church. Her heart wasn't in it, but she'd sing for the Lord this morning—give Him all the praise.

And then Miss Honey stopped on Golden Road to look behind her.

Miss Honey had sung that morning, in Macguire's Baptist Church, as she'd never sung before. It felt as if she were singing for two people. Her singing that morning had brought her great joy. For those few minutes of song, God had freed her soul of its troubles. But troubles there were, festering in her, unmitigated.

"Ruby." Miss Honey had to say it as she began her walk home, entering upon the road. "Ruby."

She wasn't going to hang her head. She wasn't going to do that. She was going to look at the sun and let it bathe her eyes. She was going to hum—yes, hum the Lord's songs, the Lord's spirituals.

"Afternoon, Miss Honey!" Augustus H. Mack waved.

"Afternoon, Brother Mack!" Miss Honey waved back.

"Miss church this mornin', Miss Honey. But heared you from the road. Sound so lovely."

"Why, thank you. Thank you, Brother Mack."

Mr. Mack waved. Miss Honey waved back.

"No trouble—not at all, Miss Honey."

Miss Honey walked erectly, energetically, and then her body began to collapse, to fold in. It was the strangest thing, Miss Honey thought, that her mind was trying to defeat her spirit. But she was tired of fighting her mind; was exhausted by the effort. This thing was bigger than she was, much larger.

She looked up Golden Road, knowing the walk, the distance it took to get back to Harding's Boarding House. Her big straw hat shielded her eyes satisfactorily from the sun. She felt big, not small. But she had shrunk. She could complain about her feet, the high heels being harsh to her feet at this time, at this precise moment, but it didn't interest her to complain—something so small, frivolous. How could she?

At this part of the road that Miss Honey was passing over, both sides of the road were clumped with thick bushes for possibly two hundred yards; then stopped.

Miss Honey was about one hundred fifty yards in when she heard, "Psst. Psst. Miss Honey. Miss Honey!"

Miss Honey thought she'd been struck by lightning. "Ruby!"

"I here, Miss Honey! I here wit' you, Miss Honey, ma'am!" Ruby slipped out of the thick clump of a bush, parting it.

Miss Honey grabbed her. "Honey!" She held Ruby's face, looking into it anxiously. "Ruby."

"Mama doesn' hit me none, Miss Honey. Throw things. Throw things. Mama throw things, ma'am. But doesn' hit me none, ma'am."

Small victory, Miss Honey thought. *Small, small victory, Ruby.*

"But, but your mother, Ruby—Millicent. Where—"

"Mama drunk. Drunk 'bout now, ma'am."

Miss Honey shuddered.

"It how I run out the house, ma'am. Like I does."

"Ruby ... Ruby." Miss Honey cried, hugging Ruby to her.

"Doesn' cry, Miss Honey, ma'am. Doesn', doesn'."

"You've been through so much, Ruby, in your young life, child." Miss Honey wiped her eyes, wishing to please Ruby, this little girl.

They began walking down Golden Road. Ruby had her arm around

Miss Honey's waist, and Miss Honey had her arm around Ruby's shoulders. Miss Honey looked down at Ruby's hair; it was back to looking "that way" again.

"How much time do you have, Ruby?" She knew that Ruby knew—it felt like a game she and her mother played.

"Plenty, Miss Honey. Mama fall down. Ain't gettin' up fo' long time yet, ma'am. Yet. Yet. Could poke 'er wit' a stick, ma'am, an' Mama doesn' wake. Feel not'in.'"

But it's not a game, Miss Honey thought. What Ruby and her mother, Millicent, did wasn't that.

"Do it one time, poke Mama wit' a stick, ma'am."

Does she ever cry? Miss Honey thought. *Does Ruby know how to cry anymore*?

"Hee-hee."

Ruby looked up at Miss Honey. "You look pretty, Miss Honey. Pretty this mornin', ma'am."

"Why, thank you, Ruby."

Was Ruby going to talk about them going to church together, singing together? Did Ruby miss it?

"Always look pretty," Ruby said. "Always. 'Specially on Sunday, ma'am."

"Thank you."

She's especially talkative today, Miss Honey thought.

"Hee-hee."

"What, Ruby?"

"Got me a hat to wear, Miss Honey."

Miss Honey could barely swallow her saliva.

"White, Miss Honey. White hat. What gonna 'appen to my white hat?"

Miss Honey was crushed.

"An' my white dress, ma'am? What gonna 'appen to my white dress?"

"Why, why, R—"

"Mama say I can't sing no mo'. In church. In Macguire's Baptist. It, it what Mama say."

No longer could Miss Honey speak.

"Doesn', Mama doesn' hear me sing no way. Doesn' know how I sing no way. I sing in the fiel's. Out in the fiel's."

"God," Miss Honey began to say, "will make a—"

"My shoes, ma'am, Miss Honey. What 'bout my shoes an', an' white socks, ma'am? What gonna 'appen to my dress?"

What could she promise Ruby? What did she know? "We have to trust God, Ruby. In God. God loves you. God loves you." It was all she could offer. *Was that enough?* Miss Honey thought.

Ruby quieted. She held Miss Honey's hand. "God like me, don't He, Miss Honey?"

"God loves you, darling." Miss Honey swung Ruby's hand. They were at the boarding house. "You mustn't come in, Ruby," Miss Honey said nervously.

"No, no, Miss Honey. Yes'm."

"We might forget the time. You know how we girls get."

"Yes, yes'm."

"You'll go straight back home, won't you?"

"Straigh'. Straigh' as a arrow, Miss Honey."

Miss Honey laughed.

So did Ruby.

"Nobody can take your voice from you, Ruby."

"Nobody, Miss Honey?"

"You and those eyes. Your magnificent eyes."

Ruby blushed.

"I love you child."

Ruby smiled. "I-I still a jass singer, Miss Honey, ma'am?"

"Ha. One in a million!"

"That many?"

"Oh …" Miss Honey decided not to explain it, for when Ruby got older, she was sure she'd hear the expression "one in a million" said to her a million and one times, anyway. "Straight home now. You go now. Straight as an arrow, promise?"

"Yes'm. Promise."

She looked down at Ruby from porch-level.

Ruby was off the porch and on the dirt road, looking up at Miss Honey.

Miss Honey could see that Ruby felt lost. "How many Sundays straight did we go to church, Ruby? To sing, honey?"

Ruby checked her fingers. "Eight, Miss Honey. T-times, ma'am." She balled her fist. "I … I miss it, Miss Honey." Ruby stood in the sun. "This mornin'."

"Me too, Ruby."

Miss Honey turned and walked into the boarding house, and Ruby turned and walked toward home.

Several days later

"Come in, Ruby."

The tap on the door had been barely audible. Ruby came through the door. Miss Honey was on the couch, generously spread.

"Miss Honey, you restin', ma'am?"

It was all Miss Honey had been doing of late, for she was declining at a faster rate than first realized. "Yes, Ruby."

What was happening between Miss Honey and Ruby now was not like before. Millicent Martinson had crushed the purity out of what they'd had like a kingsnake. The relationship Miss Honey and Ruby had now was guarded, squeezed in between Millicent's drunken episodes.

"May I pull up the shades, Miss Honey—fo' you, ma'am?"

It was a question asked many times before.

"Yes, Ruby. Let in the light, child."

And up the shade rolled.

Miss Honey lifted her head. "You may turn on the light too."

The light popped on.

Miss Honey's face was pale, was without make-up.

"Miss Honey …"

"Don't I look pretty, Ruby?"

There was a reluctance on Ruby's part. "Yes, yes'm."

Miss Honey's head was in a wrap. "I'm still a pretty old lady," Miss Honey boasted playfully.

"Pretty, Miss Honey. P-pretty, ma'am." She went over to Miss Honey.

Miss Honey did feel pretty now, not something she'd concocted. "Where's your hand?"

"Here, here, Miss Honey." Ruby giggled. "Here, ma'am."

"Mmm." Miss Honey took Ruby's hand and smoothed her hand over it, as if it were a smooth pebble. "Your hands aren't rough, child."

"Soft, Miss Honey?"

"They're going to stay that way: soft. My baby's hands are going to stay—"

"Ain'ts no baby, Miss Honey. Ain'ts no baby, ma'am." Ruby pouted.

"Of course you aren't. I mean it affectionately. I meant it ..." Miss Honey made room for Ruby on the couch as she pulled her to her. Ruby sat. "Rest on me. On Miss Honey."

Ruby's head rested on Miss Honey's breasts.

"Oh, why, doesn't that feel good, Ruby?"

Ruby shut her eyes and her nose breathed in Miss Honey as if she were sweet, mixed milk. They didn't say anything for the longest time.

Finally, Ruby said, "Miss Honey ..."

"Yes?"

Ruby paused a moment and then said, "Your heart, ma'am. Your heart beatin' fas'. Fas', fas' as raindrops does, Miss Honey." Ruby's ears pressed harder into Miss Honey's breasts.

"It is?"

"Yes'm."

"Ha."

"Hee-hee."

"Like a marching band, Ruby?" Miss Honey yelped.

"Uh, yes'm."

"Yes, yes, like a marching band, Ruby. Like New Orleans," Miss Honey yelped again.

"New, New 'leans?"

"Orleans, Ruby."

"Oh, Or-Orleans."

"Yes."

"Jass music in Orleans?"

"Yes, plenty of it."

"Miss Honey, yo' heart re-really beatin' now. Fas'. Fas' like, like a storm, ma'am!" Ruby pressed her ears harder to Miss Honey's heart.

"It was a long time ago. Knew a lot of people in New Orleans."

"Jass peoples?"

"Indeed, jazz people. Didn't know how good I had it then. How sweet life was then. Was a wild thing, though."

"You was, ma'am?"

Miss Honey caressed Ruby's thick plaited hair as if stroking a wild cat. "Yes, me, Ruby. Miss Honey."

"Hee-hee."

"Wasn't always a lady like now. Uh-uh. I could raise me some—oops!"

Ruby giggled some more, since she was well aware of what Miss Honey almost had said.

"Yes, Ruby," Miss Honey continued to reminisce, "those were good times. Darn good." She took in a deep breath, and then let it all out.

Ruby took in a deep breath, and then let it go.

"Copying me?"

"Yes'm." Ruby giggled.

"Ruby."

"Yes, Miss Honey?"

"When you become a jazz singer, child, you're going to travel, darling. Travel like nobody's business. Sing before kings and queens."

"Like you, Miss Honey? Like you tell me you done, ma'am?"

"Yes. You've memorized all the songs off my records, haven't you? Every single one."

"Yes, yes," Ruby eagerly replied. "Yes'm."

"Oh, Ruby, you're a smart child!" Miss Honey gushed. "But when you travel the world, you've got to act like a lady. Carry yourself like a lady. Speak like a lady. D-do you understand what Miss Honey's telling you?"

"Y-Yes'm." Ruby stiffened. "Yes, Miss Honey."

Miss Honey's eyes became more desperately serious, it seemed. "English."

"En-English."

"Your English will improve." The next few words charged out of her mouth. "It will have to!" Miss Honey relaxed. "Like you have an excellent ear for music, you must have an excellent ear for English."

"If I gonna sing fo' kings and queens, Miss Honey!"

"Exactly!"

"Ha."

"Oh, Ruby, I love you to death—to death!"

"What that mean, Miss Honey: love me to det, ma'am?" Ruby said, her mouth gaping open.

"Oh."

"Somtin' else I get to know 'bout when I older than now, ma'am? Aint's fo' now, ma'am?"

"Yes, honey."

"Good."

♪

More time passed between them.

Miss Honey had not wished to think about Millicent Martinson. She was drunk, hungover—it was why Ruby was there with her, why Ruby was able to come to Harding's Boarding House to see her. Miss Honey had not wished to think about Millicent Martinson but here she was, on the couch, thinking of her while she held Millicent's child.

Oh, if only things could be different. But life wasn't made up that way. It was made up of backgrounds and experiences that shaped things, that gave things order, prescription, no matter how good or bad they turned out.

Ruby was meant to be in this situation, just as she was meant to be in hers. This child resting on her breasts today was meant to be where she was in Plattstown. All of this background, history, the experiences she was having were there to shape her, make her who she would one day become.

She could be as wild as Millicent Martinson. *I have a past*, Miss Honey thought. She was a woman of God now, but she could have been as ugly-acting as Millicent had been when she came to her door and entered her room that night.

She was a tough gal who could fight like an alley cat and was as strong as a bull (more than one man told her). *Yes*, Miss Honey thought, *I was all those things at one time. Not a bad woman but a wild one.*

Men, sex—she had sowed her oats. There was a time when she would have knocked Millicent Martinson clean on her backside. Hit her so hard she'd forget today, tomorrow, and most of next week! *Ha! Oh yes, there was a time, a time all right.*

But she'd had to be that woman for her to become the woman she was now: someone who appreciated the sunrises and the sunsets. Someone who could look at life and say she'd lived it, every square inch of it, and understood its possibilities. Someone who had no regrets—not one in her heart.

And now it was Ruby's turn in this enduring, ongoing cycle of life, on this treadmill. This little girl would have to make her way through the thickets and thorns, sort out things and learn from them. This little girl who lay her head on Miss Honey's breasts, with her eyes and thoughts shut off to the world at present, who didn't know what was before her—a future that would take her off to wonderful, exotic places, as sure as day passes into night.

Miss Honey looked down at this bright child; then a thought leaped out at her, something for her to give serious consideration to. When finally she decided on it, she shut her eyes serenely, peacefully. She couldn't believe what she'd thought or how cleverly it'd been conceived, yet she recognized its sentimentality.

"When Ruby wakes," she whispered, "I'll do it."

Miss Honey had been keeping watch over Ruby for so long that they were beginning to breathe as one, Miss Honey catching on to Ruby's rhythmic pattern.

When Ruby stirred, Miss Honey became fretful. "Ruby …"

"I fall sleep, Miss Honey." Ruby rubbed her eyes. "You fall sleep too, Miss Honey? Like me, ma'am?"

"A little—just a little, darling," Miss Honey winked.

"Ain'ts tired, Miss Honey?"

"Now, can't an old gal like me keep some secrets of her own, Ruby— for herself?"

"Secret—"

"Under her wig. Have a little privacy?"

Ruby hiccupped. "Oops." Ruby had hiccupped as if air had gone down the wrong windpipe. "Sorry, ma'am."

"About us, Ruby. Thinking about us," Miss Honey confessed. "Excuse me."

"Yes'm."

Ruby seemed a bit disconnected by losing her comfortable pillow but got up to make way for Miss Honey.

"Be right back."

"Yes'm."

Ruby sat back on the couch, twiddling her thumbs, waiting.

"See, I'm back."

Indeed, Miss Honey had returned to the front room. In her hand was a beat-up old suitcase that looked as if it knew the world and, by the same token, the world knew it many times over.

Ruby stood.

"Sit, child. There's no reason to stand."

Ruby sat back down on the couch. Miss Honey sat beside her. "You see this?"

Ruby was all eyes. She couldn't help but see the big suitcase on the floor; what Miss Honey had put there.

"Me and this suitcase—well … we've got many a memory and story to tell." Miss Honey laughed.

Ruby's feet jigged atop the floor.

"Excited, excited to know what's in the suitcase, aren't you?"

Uncontrollably, Ruby's eyelids batted. "Yes'm!"

"Want to open it?"

"Why I … me, Miss Honey? Me!" Ruby's feet stopped jigging on the floor, and her body rolled forward and over the suitcase. "This way, Miss Honey?"

"Exactly. Untie the two leather straps."

"Like this, Miss Honey?"

"Uh-huh."

"An' the zipper? The zipper—"

"Unzip it."

"Like this, Miss Honey?"

"Tell me you ain't been doing this all your life!"

"Know you teasin', teasin' me, Miss—"

"Now open it. It'll open out for you."

"Open it, ma'am?"

"It won't bite. Nothing's going to jump out. Maybe old ghosts—"

Ruby jumped back.

"But nothing more."

Ruby was petrified.

Miss Honey leaned forward and opened the suitcase. "See."

And what was in the suitcase, Ruby saw as plain as day. "Miss Honey, ma'am, a record, ma'am. It … it onlies a r-record, ma'am."

"A record."

Ruby stared at the record. "One a yo' records, Miss Honey."

"Yep."

"Why, what it doin' in yo' suitcase, ma'am? Why it not wit' the res' a dem records in the room?"

Miss Honey picked up the record and pressed it to her bosom. She sighed heavily. "Ruby, if only I knew."

Ruby looked into the empty suitcase and shook her head again, as if looking for explanation.

Miss Honey shut her eyes. They were moist. But for now, her eyes were looking at Ruby, drinking her in, as if the sun had spilled milk. And what she had thought about while Ruby slept, could be realized.

She withdrew the record from her bosom.

Ruby, for some reason, felt magical.

"Ruby …"

Ruby's eyes grew wider.

"Take this." Miss Honey handed the record with the cover to Ruby, whose little fingers trembled. "You carry this with you, Ruby, in your suitcase wherever your travels take you."

Ruby's hands no longer trembled as she took the album in her hands and sighed as heavily as Miss Honey had. "May … may I play it, Miss Honey, on the Vi'trola, ma'am? In the room, now? Now?"

Miss Honey's eyes sparkled. "No, not today, Ruby."

"But—"

Miss Honey's hand covered Ruby's mouth. "Don't you worry, you'll know when, just when to play the record."

To Ruby's ears, it was magically said. And Ruby closed her eyes, as if magic were in her; as if Miss Honey had put her under a magical spell.

Miss Honey shut the suitcase. She brought the suitcase up to knee-level, then stood. "Excuse me, Ruby. I'll be right back."

"Yes'm."

Ruby pressed the record flat against her chest. She was attempting to hear it; her ears were attempting to hear what was recorded on the record. The sound, the music.

Miss Honey came back in the room. She observed Ruby attempting to do the impossible by offering up sounds and notes in her head. *She could never be right about those sounds*, Miss Honey thought. *Not them, never.*

Ruby was embarrassed. "Oh ... Miss Honey, ma'am."

As soon as Miss Honey sat next to Ruby, Ruby stood.

"I ... I ..."

"You've got to go. Of course you do."

Ruby hugged Miss Honey's record to her, then put it down, and then hugged Miss Honey as tightly as was possible.

"Oh, Ruby—you hug like a bear. A big, old bear!"

Ruby smiled.

Miss Honey wanted Ruby to hug her again but didn't intimate it to her. But Ruby came back into her again, lovingly.

"You tired, Miss Honey."

"I am. Miss Honey is."

Miss Honey's record was back in Ruby's hands.

"You look so pretty, Miss Honey."

"That picture of me on that record cover was taken a long time ago. Mind you." Miss Honey smiled.

"Mean now, Miss Honey, ma'am."

Miss Honey suddenly looked frightened, for she felt sick, very sick.

Ruby picked up the record again.

"It's yours forever." Miss Honey coughed. "Forever, Ruby."

Ruby backed away from Miss Honey, taking short, awkward steps from her. Miss Honey said nothing but coughed into her hand. Ruby had reached the room's door.

When Ruby's and Miss Honey's eyes met at the door, Ruby ran back to Miss Honey, and Miss Honey's hands held each side of Ruby's head and she kissed her forehead, powerfully.

"Now, go, child. Go now, Ruby."

"Yes'm."

And so Ruby turned a second time, turning herself back to Miss Honey, taking short, awkward, backward steps, her hands holding on to the record potently; her eyes looking at Miss Honey, potently.

"Good day, Ruby."

"G … good day, Miss Honey, ma'am."

The door opened and then closed. Ruby turned and looked at the door, then down at the record, and then wound down the short hall.

Miss Honey lay down. She was too tired to go into the bedroom. *Besides*, she thought, *the couch feels comfortable*. She'd been lying on it for most of the afternoon. "Ruby," Miss Honey said, "Ruby, honey, you've got my life in your hands." A motherly emotion overcame her. "You're carrying my whole life in your precious hands, darling."

Where can I hide it? Ruby thought with some enterprise. *Where can I hide Miss Honey's record?* She sped up and then slowed down in her walk. She sped up; she slowed down; this odd pattern; this hesitation of will; this overwhelming uncertainty.

"Mama … Mama …" She knew her mother must not find it. "N-not ever. Ever." Ruby knew that. But where could she hide it, something as fragile, as delicate as a record? It must not get broken, not Miss Honey's record. She had to keep it forever, for a lifetime—that much she understood about Miss Honey's record, which she was holding on to.

Ruby thought hard. She had to come up with something. She really had to use her brain for this. Miss Honey said she was smart, didn't she— didn't she, Miss Honey? Ruby calmed; she'd come up with a solution. "Mama, Mama ain't gonna fine Miss Honey record. Uh-uh …" Ruby shook her head mightily.

Ruby was home. The house was still.

Ruby scooted off to her room and then out. She knew she could make noise in the house and it wouldn't matter, but she had not. The room was adjacent to hers.

Her mother lay on the rough floor, drunk—passed out. When she lay like that, Ruby often thought she was dead—or maybe she wished it.

Ruby did not have Miss Honey's record. She had not brought it into the house.

Now Ruby was in the kitchen; the front door opened into the kitchen. Ruby knew what she was looking for. She knew they had a sack. *Yes, a sack*, she thought.

Soon Ruby had the cloth sack in her hand. She jumped up and down with glee but without her voice teasing out a sound.

Silent—Ruby was silent with joy. And after doing this, this simple child's act, Ruby ran out of the house knowing, exactly what she'd do.

She was at the back of the ramshackle house on Rumble Way, this feeble house that sat on battered brick. Ruby stooped, and under the house she scooted, with the ease of a gopher in dirt. Ruby was in dirt, the worst kind of dirt—dry, parched, caked. She was on her hands and knees in the dirt. But all that mattered to Ruby was the record, Miss Honey's record; she had to protect it, keep it safe, and carry it with her forever—for a lifetime.

The record was in the sack. It was protected. Ruby had put the record in the cloth sack. Her mother wouldn't miss the sack. Her mother would never know it was gone; it'd vanished from the house. Her mother would never miss it.

Ruby put the cloth sack down on top of the dirt. Her eyes looked down at the dirt, accepting her challenge. "Mama ain't gonna fine you. Mama ain't."

Ruby began scratching. Her fingers began scratching away at the dirt like a cat, feverishly. The pebbles in the ground felt Ruby's little fingers scratching at them. This little girl was in this blazing, possessed panic, doing something Miss Honey had entrusted her to do.

"Uh! Uh! Uh!"

Digging.

Clawing.

"Uh! Uh! Uh!"

Digging, clawing her way through dirt, making the hole deeper and deeper, wider and wider, so the record inside the cloth sack could remain buried in the dirt—not be seen or heard by anyone above ground.

"The hole. The hole big 'nough. It big 'nough!"

Ruby was joyful. She looked at the record. "You doesn' stay down there all the time. I come for you ev'ry day. Take you out to the fiel's w-where we sing an' play."

With pain, Ruby picked up the sack and put it down into the hole. She hesitated, then began patching the exceptional-sized hole up with dirt.

"Gonna be hot, I know. But gonna be cool nights too—when the winter come. An' oh, rain—the rain too."

Ruby patted the dirt down with her hands. She looked at her hands; they were dirty, obviously. But for Ruby, it was worth it. *What I did for Miss Honey's record*, Ruby thought, *was worth it.*

Miss Honey had been coughing badly. She had to get up from the couch. Her head felt light, her eyes unfocused.

What time is it? she thought. *How long ago did Ruby leave?* Right now, she had no idea.

Miss Honey strained to get to her bed. And when she did, Miss Honey felt rocky. Suddenly, she thought of New Orleans, the riverboats, the waterways. *Funny*, she thought, *how the past has been obsessing my mind more and more each day, bringing the past back to me, into sharper focus.*

Miss Honey coughed, and when she did, she felt a terrible strain in her throat. She looked at the hand she'd coughed into and felt the spit in it. In the darkened room, she couldn't see the color of the spit but had a good idea of its color.

She coughed again, twice.

Now, in her bedroom, Miss Honey turned on the light. Blood. She saw she'd spit up blood. It had stuck to the palm of her hand. Anxiously, Miss Honey rubbed her hand against her dress, wiping the blood in it.

What time is it? How long has Ruby been gone from the boarding house? Nine forty. It was 9:40.

Miss Honey hadn't eaten; she wasn't hungry. She was at her bed, and then she just fell on it, letting her body go. She lifted her leg, straddling the bed, onto the floor, then onto the bed. Miss Honey's head was swimming in turbulent waters—that's how it felt. Then her head began banging. Banging, banging, furiously.

She coughed; it was a hard cough. It was produced in an extreme way.

She'd spit out a piece of saliva bigger than before, redder, meaner-looking than before, into her hand—blood. Miss Honey trembled. Her entire body trembled. It felt as if it had fallen under an enormous pressure to seize itself, to make Miss Honey certain of what it was doing. Whatever methodology was now in place had now taken over.

"God ..." Miss Honey thought of Ruby and her voice in Macguire's Baptist Church, exploding out from those around her like a giant eruption of earth. "Ruby, honey ..."

Ruby's white dress hung where Miss Honey could well see it. "Angel. Angel—pretty as an angel, you were, Ruby."

And then the dress, Ruby's white dress, looked ghostly, of a different sort.

Miss Honey no longer coughed. "I ain't afraid of you. I'm not afraid of you. You can come for Miss Honey if you want." She continued staring at Ruby's white dress on the hanger that had now been transformed back to something grand, something special, and something wonderful—the way she first had seen the dress in Miss Beatrice's dress shop in Minesburg.

"Ruby. Ruby'd look pretty in it, wouldn't she? Wouldn't she? My little Ruby will look pretty in it."

Miss Honey tried getting up but couldn't.

"Ruby, come over here, Ruby, honey. Come over here, darling. Come, come to Miss Honey in your pretty white dress, child."

Ruby, in her pretty white dress, began coming toward Miss Honey in this vision of her.

"Oh, Ruby." Miss Honey felt peaceful; at peace. "Ruby, let me kiss you, honey. Miss Honey kiss you, darling."

But instead, Miss Honey felt Ruby's lips press onto her forehead.

"Ruby." She paused a moment and then said, "And your hand, Ruby. Where's your hand, child?"

And Ruby's hand was there for Miss Honey, as always.

"Yes, yes, it—here it is, Ruby. Here it is. R-right here." Miss Honey shut her eyes. "Oh, the world is beautiful, Ruby. It's beautiful. Sang before kings and queens. Oh, sang on riverboats and in speakeasies and ... and cabarets. Ha. Sang to the world. World. Hear me, child? Hear ... of course you do. God loves you, Ruby. God loves you, child." Miss Honey opened her eyes. "Now, run home, Ruby. Go ahead. You get on home. I gave you the record from out of the suitcase, honey. Time for you to run home now. You said you'd carry it. Of course you did. Miss Honey hasn't forgotten. Carry it, Ruby. Wherever your travels may take you, child, in the world."

Miss Honey's head had been cleared of its trouble. She felt like she was floating in water—her body on top of the water, not in it but on top of it, floating. "Oh, God. God." Miss Honey took one last look at Ruby's white dress and saw Ruby in it, like it was a Sunday morning, and she and Ruby were heading down Golden Road and off to Macguire's to sing while Jasper P. Bean played.

Miss Honey saw this as plain as day.

♪

Ruby looked around her room, as if hearing termites chewing in the battered house's wood. Maybe termites were chewing in the house's wood. Ruby giggled. *Bet they are*, she thought.

Ruby was in bed—her flaked-off-paint thing. Sinful. The mattress smelled of urine from the years when Ruby had wet the bed. It was a nasty smell, a smell Ruby smelled through her eyes first and then her nose. Ruby lay in this bed, hearing termites, as if they had songs in their teeth, singing through the house.

It's the record, though, isn't it? Ruby thought.

Her bed was above the record she'd buried in the dirt, only this afternoon. She'd buried the record in that spot for a reason; it was the record, Miss Honey's singing to her, not termites in the wood.

Ruby was in panties, nothing more. Her little body was sticky with sweat. August's air had tricked September.

She heard her mother. Her breathing was like the roar of a train rolling down train tracks. She had awakened before the night had arrived and hadn't said much; she didn't have to—just made sure Ruby understood that.

Ruby flipped onto her side. She was happy. She'd done something today that would be a part of her life forever and ever.

"I hear you singin', record. Hear you comin' through the wood. Use to come out Miss Honey suitcase but not no mo'. Come up through the wood now."

Ruby hopped off the bed and pressed her ear to the scarred floor. "Yep, comin' up through the wood, all right."

Ruby's imagination was alive, was yawning as wide as a big black bear before a winter's nap. Ruby began humming to herself. "I ain'ts gotta worry 'bout Mama, uh-uh. Ain'ts gotta worry 'bout nobody. Sing like I won. Sing like I won. Lissen to the songs like I won."

Ruby was sitting on the floor now, having crossed her legs in front of her, as if sitting around a bright fire. "Gonna stay up all night if I can. Ain'ts fallin' sleep. San'man ain'ts comin' fo' me tonight."

Ruby leaped to her feet. She looked out the window and saw a star in the sky. It had a smile in it. *How high is it?* Ruby thought. *How high in the sky is it? How high your arms gotta reach for it? Wonder, I wonder if Miss Honey see it. Wonder if Miss Honey lookin' at it like me.*

Ruby frowned. She remembered back to the boarding house. *Miss Honey looked tired*, she thought. But even still, Miss Honey had looked pretty.

"Miss Honey can't look not'in but pretty. You lookin' at the same star I is, Miss Honey, ma'am, in the sky? Sure be pretty, ma'am. Tonight, Miss Honey."

Ruby turned, then tiptoed to her door, and then to her mother's door. "Ain'ts gonna ever catch me, Mama. Ain't," Ruby whispered defiantly. "Hear me, Mama? Say ain'ts gonna ever catch me an' Miss Honey, Mama."

Ruby tiptoed back inside her room. She peeked at the star in the sky again. "Miss Honey lookin' at it. Miss Honey, know you is, ma'am." Ruby lay back on the urine-stained mattress. "Music comin' up through the wood, Miss Honey. Music. Jass music. Up through the wood, ma'am."

Ruby's eyes were wide open. She couldn't have blinked them if Miss Honey had bought all the white dresses in Minesburg for her to wear to Macguire's Baptist Church. "Stay 'wake all night. N-night long. Stay 'wake all night lissenin' to Miss Honey music. Say it fo', doesn' matter. Say it 'gin, doesn' matter. Say it when I wonts—doesn' matter."

Ruby smiled like the star in the sky. "Do, do it, Miss Honey? Ma'am?"

CHAPTER 8

Ruby hadn't visited Miss Honey since Wednesday. Today was Monday. She was going to visit Miss Honey today. To visit Miss Honey on Sunday wasn't a good day for her; it had too many memories in it—all good.

Yesterday, Ruby had Miss Honey's record all day long. She took it out into the fields with her and played it and played it and listened to it and listened to it until she was dizzy-headed. She'd never had so much fun by herself. She and Miss Honey's record had so much fun together. She just held on to the record, keeping it near her chest, smothering it with joy.

It was afternoon, a few minutes past twelve. Miss Honey was up; Ruby was aware of that much about Miss Honey's habits. She'd been up for a few hours, Ruby thought. She decided not to get to Harding's Boarding House too early—there was no rush.

Ruby skipped along the dusty road, then ran into the open field, putting a stiff wind in the high blades of grass. She was moving fast. There was another road—Thunder Road—that she had to cross before she got to Miss Honey's boarding house.

Ruby headed for the bushes. She liked doing this, going into the bushes and then jumping out of them, as if she'd just sprung out of nowhere, invisible then visible. But first, Ruby always peeked both ways up the road, as if giving warning to the unsuspected, even if no one passed when she jumped out of the bushes on any occasion.

Ruby then peeked to her right and then her left. But when she peeked to her left, from out the bushes, she saw townsfolk down the road, a bunch of them.

It startled her.

The people were at a good distance, so, for the moment, Ruby couldn't tell what was going on. But she could feel her heart racing. And these folks up the road were moving slowly, as if in no rush to get to where they were going; as if they were moving from sheer repetition.

Ruby hid herself away in the bush, better than before. A leaf here, a leaf there, but she could see, though not as far up the road as she'd have liked. When these people got closer, she would be able to see everything there was.

But Ruby listened. She listened to all the feet in the dirt, covering distance, covering it ever so slowly, as if the dirt would put layers of dust on top of their shoes, making them practically invisible.

She was patient, even if she was holding her breath, keeping it still, keeping her from moving. Her eyes had not twittered; she was in this golden silence, hiding in a bush, making no noise, cloaked, invisible. Ruby listened; but for the shoes on the road, it was all silent, as silent as her—but there was a march in those townsfolk, a practiced march in them, a procession—slow, solemn, spiritless, not confused by duty or obligation; the ongoing trial to end.

Ruby looked and saw a wooden casket raised on six men's shoulders—three men on either side of the casket.

Ruby's skin split open, and she felt something deep in her rock her so hard that she could barely breathe.

And she saw the woman, the last woman in the procession, carrying it—one of Miss Honey's fancy straw hats.

Ruby cried out, *"Miss Honey!"*

But the funeral procession kept moving forward up the dirt road, as if it had not heard her, heading for Macguire's Baptist Church.

"Ma'am, ma'am …" Ruby had fallen; she'd collapsed. Ruby's body was in the tall grass blades. She tried standing but was like a fledgling, her legs too weak and new for her to stand. Ruby's body sped into hysteria. Her fingernails did the same thing as they'd done to bury Miss Honey's record, scratching, clawing, and tearing apart the patch of dirt. "Ma'am, ma'am."

She knew how to cry. She'd not forgotten how to cry.

Ruby was crying.

Ruby had no idea of how she'd gotten there. She had no way of knowing. But Ruby was there, at Miss Honey's boarding house.

She didn't know how she knew that Miss Honey's door would be unlocked—but it was. Ruby stepped into the front room. She shivered in fear. She was afraid but, at the same time, unafraid. She was afraid of getting caught, but at the same time, she was unafraid because she was in Miss Honey's room. Miss Honey was there. Miss Honey would protect her. Miss Honey would watch over her.

How had she known that?

Shadows cloaked the room, dark shadows, even if it was still afternoon.

"Miss Honey, I here. I here, Miss Honey, ma'am."

Ruby knew Miss Honey had come home to Plattstown to die. Ruby knew that. It wasn't something she and Miss Honey ever had discussed, but she knew Miss Honey had come home to Plattstown to die.

"Ev'body know it, Miss Honey. Ev—" Ruby looked beyond the living room, beyond that room. Her eyes looked off to the bedroom as she took one step, one tiny step in the direction of the bedroom. She was walking yet did not know how, but her determination was such a force.

"I here, Miss Honey."

Ruby was in Miss Honey's bedroom. This room wasn't as dark as the living room—a dark gray but no more. Ruby looked at everything there was in the room. "Yo' hats, hats, Miss Honey, ma'am. Yo', yo' hats."

Ruby sobbed, seeing them on parade. Some hats were in boxes, but most were left out for display. Ruby touched one of the hats, one with a fine feather in its silk band. When she touched the feather, it tickled her fingertips, only Ruby didn't giggle—not on this occasion. Ruby just let it happen, not reacting one way or the other.

The suitcase—Ruby's eyes saw Miss Honey's old beat-up suitcase.

"Miss Honey, the suitcase empty, Miss Honey. Not'in but air, ma'am."

And then Ruby panicked. She was taking too much time. She was supposed to be in there and out of the room. She wasn't supposed to be taking this long.

Ruby looked. "I here fo' it, Miss Honey. I here fo' it, ma'am."

She was in tears but fought through them—her tears, her grief. She saw the dress, the white dress hanging. She knew Miss Honey would want her to have it.

"How I gonna carry it?" Ruby said. "Miss Honey, ma'am, how I carry it, Miss Honey? I carry it home, ma'am?" Ruby looked at the suitcase. "No, Miss Honey. No, ma'am!" Ruby screamed, knowing she couldn't take the suitcase.

But then she saw the box. Miss Honey hadn't thrown away the dress box.

"The box, Miss Honey!" Ruby was elated. She held the dress by the neck of the hanger. "Fol' it. Fol' it. How you fol' it, Miss Honey?"

Ruby didn't want to do the dress any harm. She didn't want to put a wrinkle in it. Ruby's head wouldn't think for her. She'd never folded a dress in a box. Whatever she wore never came out of a box. "Help me, Miss Honey. Hel-help me, Miss Honey," Ruby pleaded.

She had to get out of Harding's Boarding House. She had to get out of that room; she didn't want to get caught. They'd think she was stealing, that she was a bad girl. They'd forget all about Sunday mornings and how she and Miss Honey went off together in that white dress to sing at Macguire's—forget all about that. They'd think she was stealing, that Ruby Martinson was stealing.

Ruby stuffed the white dress in the dress box. "Done, done, Miss Honey!" She began backing out of the room, stumbled, and then stopped, remembering. "Oh, Miss Honey, Miss Honey, ma'am." Ruby sobbed. She could feel Miss Honey's lovely lips warm her forehead, kissing her there; her cheeks warmed too.

Then she ran for the front room door with the large box in her small hands. Ruby followed the roads but didn't take them. She was hiding herself away. Then she thought of Miss Honey while lugging the dress box. She realized where Miss Honey was going to be buried: behind Macguire's Baptist Church. There was a cemetery behind the church. Miss Honey would be buried there.

Ruby was happy. She would visit Miss Honey there. She would look for her gravestone. It would be easy to find, and then she and Miss Honey would sing—sing together there in the cemetery.

Ruby kept traveling along, shrinking away from her own shadow. Not even her shadow must sense her whereabouts, she thought. But now, more than ever, Ruby wanted to sing like a jazz singer. Sing like what Miss Honey said she was. "I see you, Miss Honey, ma'am. I see you."

And Ruby ran like the wind. She ran for home. Rumble Way.

She had to get there before her mother came out of her drunk. I ain'ts gonna get caught. Nobody gonna catch me, Miss Honey. Nobody gonna know. White dress mines, Miss Honey. 'Long to me, ma'am. Does, Miss Honey!"

Ruby's voice sailed through the wind—outracing it, outspeeding it—gazelle-like.

Ruby burst into the house and then into her room. For a second, Ruby heard nothing but her breath, and then she listened for her mother's. She looked at the box and then put it down on the floor, standing it upright. Ruby was apprehensive, almost to the point of fear.

"Why ain'ts you breathing, Mama? Why ain'ts you doin' that? Why ain'ts yo' bredt loud?"

Ruby looked into her mother's room and saw nothing—at least not her mother. Ruby trembled. Where was she? Where was Mama? She'd left her drunk, on the floor, passed out!

Ruby ran between rooms, in and out of rooms, like a chicken with its head cut off—so primitive, Ruby looked.

But then Ruby pitched herself against the house's grimy wall and slumped. And as Ruby's body slid down the wall, she shut her eyes, confused, perplexed, strangely defeated.

"Miss Honey dead. Mama gone. Miss Honey dead. Mama gone. Miss Honey dead. Mama gone." Ruby repeated it over and over, tears welling in her eyes, rhythmically, increasing, and ballooning; her tiny chest heaved in and out, mercilessly. "Miss Honey dead. Mama gone. Miss Honey dead. Mama gone."

Ruby couldn't control her body or stop it from falling off to the side like a wooden soldier. "Miss Honey dead. Mama gone. Miss Honey dead. Mama gone."

Then she stopped what she was saying when her ear, pressed to the wooden floor, began hearing, listening to the music coming up and out of the record from below, down in the ground where Ruby had buried Miss Honey's record. The sound was coming up through the floor's wood.

"La di, la di, da di da. La di, la di, did da, did da!"

"Girl! Pick'ninny girl! Black tar baby girl! Nigga girl!"

"Mama!" Ruby screamed, turning her head.

"Miss Honey dead! Yo' Miss Honey dead!"

"Mama, Mama!"

"You run off, pick'ninny girl! Black tar baby girl! Run off!" Millicent Martinson's shadow hovered over Ruby. "At 'er fun'ral, girl! Miss Honey fun'ral!"

Ruby scrambled across the filthy floor. "No, ma'am. No, Mama!"

"The devil take 'er. Now you singin' the devil song, girl! How I catch you!"

"No, no, Mama! No!"

"You singin' Miss Honey song. Catch you. What I tell you? Tell you, pick'ninny girl!"

"Weren't, weren't!"

"Heared you!"

Why wasn't she drunk on the floor? What had happened?

"You go off to 'er, doesn' you, girl! Doesn' you!"

"Miss Honey dead, Mama. Miss Honey dead!"

"How you know, girl? How? Tar baby girl. How you know if you doesn' go off to 'er!"

"Know, Mama. Know!" Ruby blurted.

"You see them walkin' wit' er. Carryin' 'er 'long Golden Road in, ha ha, in a casket box. You on Golden Road. Out the house. 'Bout. 'Hind my back."

"No, Mama, no!"

"Pick'ninny girl! Pick'ninny girl!"

Silence.

And then Millicent Martinson laughed. "What this? What this, girl? What this you got?"

Ruby scrambled. "Not'in, Mama. Not'in." Ruby grabbed the box, clutching it to her chest.

"Bring it here, girl. Nigger girl. Bring it here."

Ruby halted, then shoved the box at her mother. Her arms stretched all the way out in front of her.

Millicent Martinson snatched the box from Ruby's hand. Her eyes looked around the box as if it were hers. "Who been to Minesburg I know, girl? Who you know in Minesburg? Fancy boxes in Minesburg, pick'ninny girl. Fancy clothes." Millicent Martinson was taking her time; she seemed in no rush to end this, what was being done. "Gotta mine to go over to Minesburg, girl. See if you steal somtin' out them shops."

"No. No, Mama, I doesn' steal not'in doesn', doesn' 'long to me, Mama!"

Millicent sneered.

Ruby's eyes were searching just now, trying to look straight through her mother.

But Millicent Martinson wasn't having any of this. Her eyes turned sharply from Ruby's. Anger was in her wide, deep bloodshot eyes, seemingly reddening them more. She stood there, as if poison knitted together her veins, her frailness, this wisp of a woman, who still had liquor in her that'd not been tamed.

Millicent lifted the box above her shoulders while looking down at Ruby, and she flung the box against the wall. The box hit the wall and then its contents jumped out: the white dress.

"The devil dress! The devil dress!" Millicent screamed.

"Miss Honey! Miss Honey!" Ruby screamed.

"The devil dress! The devil dress!"

Ruby scrambled on her hands and knees toward the white dress on the filthy floor, but Millicent's body blocked her. "You stay were you be, black tar baby girl!" Millicent's neck snapped around to the dress. "Heared Miss Honey buy you a Sunday dress to sing in, heared it, pick'ninny girl."

Ruby was silent, scared. Ruby scrambled like an animal, back to where she'd been, to where it seemed safe.

"Pretty, ain't it, Ruby? Pretty, ain't it?"

Ruby was nonresponsive.

"Pretty white dress, girl. Pretty." Millicent's hips swayed.

Ruby cowered.

"You an' Miss Honey."

"Yes, yes'm."

"You an' the devil!" Millicent's foot kicked the box.

"No. No. No, Mama—ain't true. Ain't true, Mama!"

"You an' the devil! You an' the devil! You an' the devil, heeber-geeberin', heeber-geeberin'!"

Ruby scrambled toward the dress again, not wanting any harm to come to it.

"Get back! Get back, girl—fo' I …"

Ruby scrambled back.

"Ain'ts gonna harm it, girl. Ain'ts gonna do not'in bad to it, girl. Not'in bad to it."

Ruby's eyes seemed to sink into her soul.

"So pretty, Ruby. Pretty it be. Pretty white dress on the flo', girl." Millicent picked up the dress, dangling it from her hand. "Doesn' 'long on the flo', Ruby. Not Miss Honey dress she buy in Minesburg. Over in Minesburg." Millicent looked down at Ruby. "See yor mama ain't so bad. As that. See yor mama been to church, Ruby. Pray, pray wit' a preacher man. Was baptize in church. Marry in church. Sin in church!" Millicent laughed a piercing laugh. She turned.

Ruby leaped to her feet.

Millicent ran off into the kitchen with the white dress. "Miss Honey dead. Ain't ever gonna go to church no mo'. Devil woman. Devil woman!" Millicent looked around the kitchen; Ruby froze.

"Scissors! Scissors!"

But Ruby knew there were no scissors in the Martinson household.

"Cut it! Cut it up!" Millicent screamed. "Cut it to sheds, girl!"

Ruby's head banged in pain.

Millicent, wild-eyed, was beyond speech; her movements were jerky, beyond comprehension.

Ruby charged at her.

Millicent raised her hand, threateningly. "Gonna smack yor black ass, black tar baby girl!" Millicent ran for the front door and then out into the yard.

Ruby ran after her. "Miss Honey! Miss Honey!" Ruby screamed.

"She ain'ts never gonna sing no mo', Miss Honey. She mines. Mines. Pick'ninny girl mines! Gonna stay right here wit' 'er mama. Girl ain'ts gonna run off; ain'ts gonna run off to sing, to sing fo' nobody. Gonna die, die in Plattstown like 'er mama gonna. Like, like 'er mama an' my mama, an' my mama an' you, you does, Miss Honey. You, Miss Honey. You die, Miss Honey. You die in Plattstown, Miss Honey. Like alla us die!"

Millicent Martinson's hands began to tear Ruby's white dress, and then, with her bare teeth, she bit into the dress, ripping it apart, into shreds, with sharp teeth, into white linen strips in the front yard of the ramshackle house. The dress covered more and more of the ground, as if a cloud of snow had fallen out of the sky in big white chunks in Plattstown in the summertime.

CHAPTER 9

Eight years later

In three days, Ruby would turn fifteen. The coming of birthdays never excited Ruby. She was not excited to know that her birthday would be in three days. For her, it would be just another day in Plattstown.

How had the past eight years of Ruby's life been? Hard, very hard. No longer had she felt like a wild, lost, inadequate child, rooted to nothing. She prayed to God every night. What Miss Honey had taught her in that brief period of her life, it seemed, no one had taken from her.

Ruby spoke to Miss Honey every night after praying. It was the last person she spoke to before bedding down. And when she went out into the fields, she sang up a storm. She sang all of Miss Honey's songs at least two times—sometimes more.

She hadn't lost her dream. Not the young child or the teenager. Ruby was going to become a jazz singer, like Miss Honey said, come hell or high water. Ruby Martinson had decided that the moment that Miss Honey had told her what she was.

Ruby could smell him like stink.

She was carrying a bucket of water; she'd gone to Miss Florence's place down on Rumble Way to get the water. Miss Florence had a water pump and was nice enough to share it with the Martinsons.

Ruby wasn't far from the house. She could smell her daddy like stink.

He was back. Man Martinson, her daddy, was back. He'd come back every now and then, stay a few days, and then be gone. He got as drunk as her mama. He drank like her and was a drunk like her.

Why doesn' they die?
Why doesn' they die?
Why doesn' they die?
Why doesn' they go way?

Sex—yes, Ruby knew about sex, a girl of fourteen, going on fifteen in three days. Her mama, at one time, said what she and her daddy had was love. But already, Ruby recognized the difference. What she and Miss Honey had was love; what her mama and daddy had was sex.

She was afraid to go into the house, even at this early time of day. Ruby opened the waist-high rusted gate and was on her property. Ruby retrieved the bucket of water she'd put down on the ground.

"I-I ain't goin' in. I ain't! Daddy home. My daddy home!"

Ruby ran to the back of the house and went under the house; she squirreled to where her body could still fit without producing discomfit. Ruby dug up the record, Miss Honey's record, holding it tightly to her young, budding breasts like she had when she'd first held it, when Miss Honey first had given it to her.

"Miss Honey. Daddy back, Miss Honey. He come back home, ma'am." Ruby put the record back in its hole and covered it with the same dirt. "I doesn' know what to do, Miss Honey. Tell me, ma'am. Tell me."

It took a few more minutes before Ruby calmed and was in much better control of herself. "Three days, Miss Honey. Doesn' matter, ma'am. Doesn'. Ain't gonna be fo'teen no mo', ma'am. Gonna be older than fo'teen. It gonna 'appen, Miss Honey."

Ruby darted out from under the house. She stared out into the distance, daydreaming.

"Girl! Girl!"

Ruby turned.

"Why doesn' you bring the water in the house, girl? Like you s'pose to. Tell you to!"

She was barefoot and looked nasty.

"What slowin' you!"

Then he came out of the house—Man Martinson. He was tall, dark, handsome, and strong—and as mean as a rattlesnake. "Black tar baby ain'ts doin' 'er chores 'round here no mo', Millie!"

"Ain'ts 'bout that," Millicent Martinson said, turning to Man Martinson. "Man."

"Then what?" Man Martinson said, glaring at Ruby. "Oughta put the back a my han' to the girl. Do like my daddy do me: beat the girl black!"

"Tell you, ain'ts gonna be that, Man!"

"Beat on you, woman!"

"Yeah, me, Man, but not the pick'ninny—I die firs', Man."

"Get that bucket a water in 'ere. Tell you. Get in 'ere wit' that bucket a water, girl. I thirsty!" Man Martinson stomped back into the house.

Ruby grabbed the water bucket's handle.

Millicent raised her hand, as if to strike Ruby. "What you doin', girl? Daddy home!"

"Yes, Mama. I know. I, I know, Mama."

"Get up them stairs an' into the house. Yo' Daddy home. Back. He come back home, girl."

It was nighttime.

They'd had sex; Ruby had heard them. She always heard them. They might as well be in her room, sleeping next to her in her bed—it's how well she heard them when they had sex.

They drank and then had sex, making noises like they were dying.

Ruby had been trying to sleep for—she didn't know how long it'd been, but it'd been for a long time; that much she knew. She'd prayed and spoken to Miss Honey but was awake.

She heard footsteps in the dark.

"Oughta beat you, girl! Black tar baby! Beat you black! Fo' what you does this mornin' to me!"

Ruby's eyes saw the big dark figure from the bed. "Daddy! Daddy!"

Millicent exploded out of the dark and jumped on Man's back. He tried to shake her off but couldn't, the angry energy in her making her strong.

"No! No, Man! Ain'ts beatin' my chil'. Ain'ts beatin' Ruby. Already tell you that!"

Man Martinson grabbed Millicent's arms, pried them apart, and then threw this light sack of weight on his back and into Ruby. "Ha, ha, ha!"

Millicent sprang back on her feet, even while drunk. She was naked; Man was in his drawers.

"You gonna die tonight, woman!" Man boasted.

"Ain'ts 'fraid a dyin'. You know that. Tol' you that, Man. Was born to die, Man. Ain'ts 'fraid a hell!"

"Ha." Pause. "Ain'ts gonna kill you, woman. Uh-uh. Let the liquor do that. The good times do that. Ha."

"Ha. Uh-huh. Uh-huh." Millicent laughed. "Liquor, good times, Man."

"Ho-hokey pokey. Sex, woman!" Man said, swiveling his hips. He grabbed Millicent, picking her up in his arms.

And Ruby was no longer there in the room—invisible, no longer someone to fight over.

"Ha!" Millicent laughed.

"Kiss me, woman!"

"Liquor on yor bredt, Man. Got liquor on yor bredt!"

"Goddammit, woman! Kiss my ches', then. Kiss my dick, then. Kiss my toes, then!"

"In bed, Man. In bed, Man. I kiss alla them, Man. In bed!"

And Man carried Millicent out of Ruby's room and back to their room, where they could do those things. Ruby could hear them through the wall, as if they were still there in her room, dying.

CHAPTER 10

Today was Ruby's birthday.

Today, Man had thrown his shoe at Ruby's head. It was deep into the night. Ruby had decided, on her fifteenth birthday, to run away from home. She had packed. The few clothes she had were packed in a cardboard suitcase she'd found, serendipitously, on the road a few days back.

She'd snuck around the house. This was the best time for her to go: both Millicent and Man Martinson had drunken themselves into a stupor. Ruby had the cardboard suitcase and the record—Miss Honey's record.

No tears glistened in Ruby's eyes when she reached the house's front door. She saw the outline of her mother's naked body on top her father's naked body from where she stood.

"Bye, Mama. Bye, ma'am."

Ruby opened the front door of the house. She stepped out of the house.

Ruby was on a dirt road in the dark. Her stomach belched out hollow sounds, but her ears were accustomed to it. Was she afraid? No. The way Ruby walked in the dark on the road proved this.

"Ain'ts gonna miss me. None a them gonna miss me. Pick'ninny girl! Black, black tar baby girl! Nigga girl! Ain'ts gonna miss me. Ain'ts wort' penny a gum. Ain'ts wort' it, I know. Ain'ts wort' not'in."

The night air was crisp, invigorating to the senses. Ruby was hungry but about as alert as a cricket at sunrise. "Ain'ts 'fraid on the road. Ain'ts 'fraid out here. 'Fraid back there. In there. B-but not out on the road."

The suitcase wasn't heavy. Ruby paused. "Comin', Miss Honey. Comin'. Be there soon, ma'am. 'Nough, ma'am."

The moon was tall in the sky, in full splendor. It draped over Miss

Honey's headstone, seemingly smiling saintly sweet down on it. Ruby smiled back at the moon. She knelt. "I know you know I 'ere, Miss Honey. Know you know I runnin' way from home tonight, ma'am." Ruby shut her eyes. "I feel you, Miss Honey. Do. I-I feel the weight a yo' bones on me, ma'am." Ruby was silent for about three minutes. She stood. "I on my way, Miss Honey. On my way now, ma'am. Ain'ts comin' back. Uh-uh. Not never. S-so it be the las' I gonna see you 'ere, ma'am. In, in Macguire's Baptist Church cemetery, ma'am."

Ruby had yet to take any further steps in the direction of Golden Road. "Got yo' record, Miss Honey, in the suitcase, ma'am. Today I be fifteen, Miss Honey. Fifteen. How ol' you be when you run 'way from home, Miss Honey? Plattstown, ma'am? Ain'ts 'fraid, Miss Honey. 'Fraid a not'in. Travel 'lone. The roads. Gonna be a jass singer, ma'am. Runnin' 'way to be a jass singer, Miss Honey. Like, gonna be like you, a jass singer, ma'am. Gonna wear fancy hats an' white dresses. Gonna do that, ma'am. Yes'm. Promise, Miss Honey. Promise." Ruby crossed her heart. "Suitcase ain't heavy. Uh-uh. Carry it to the moon an' back, Miss Honey." Ruby smiled. "Ain'ts much in it." She giggled. "Gonna go, Miss Honey."

Ruby nodded her head up and down. "Gonna go now. I, I promise Miss Honey, ma'am. Late already." She snatched the cardboard suitcase. "Ain'ts comin' back, ma'am. Ain'ts," Ruby said assertively as she marched away from Miss Honey's headstone in the back of Macguire's Baptist Church. "Mama die 'ere. Daddy too. They die 'ere, Miss Honey. Bot' does."

The moon was off Ruby's back but was still draped over Miss Honey's headstone, creating lively light.

Ruby's voice came out of the end of the darkness in the cemetery, where dead bodies beat to morning and night silence. "I ain'ts dyin' nowere near Plattstown, ma'am, when I die. Uh-uh, Miss Honey. Uh-uh. Nowere near."

CHAPTER 11

Darkboy and Tennessee were showering in a public bathhouse: FOR COLOREDS ONLY.

The bathhouse was a collection of rusty pipes, crumbling walls, cracked floors, and squeaky doors. And if the showers' hot and cold water flow balanced out equally when mixed, it was a sacred miracle—hallelujah! Obviously, with its being an establishment for the black community, there were no city codes to enforce.

"Hey, Darkboy, pass the soap, would you?"

Darkboy passed the bar of soap to Tennessee.

"What's left of it." Tennessee grimaced.

"Yes, uh, right, that's about the size of it, Tennessee." Darkboy laughed.

Darkboy and Tennessee were musicians—Tennessee, a guitar-picker of blues; Darkboy, a drummer of jazz.

Two dark shadows spotted the cracked tile walls.

"Your last night in these here parts, right?" Tennessee said.

"Right, last night."

"Sure you wanna go?" Tennessee asked cautiously.

"Positive."

"Chicago, she's calling that bad, huh?"

"Man, Tennessee, a thousand times worse than you can imagine." A bright smile crackled Darkboy's face.

Tennessee passed the bar of thinning soap back to Darkboy. "You know they play mostly blues up there, Darkboy. Don't bother any with nothing else—practically. For me and my twelve-stringer. Me and Baby Love. Not you."

Darkboy applied the fuzzy white washcloth to his stretched neck.

"Jazz plays second fiddle. Takes a backseat to the blues in Chi-cago, naturally. Ha, ha."

"There're jazz clubs," Darkboy said with utmost confidence.

"And you're guaranteed to find you one. No doubt, as far as I'm concerned." Tennessee whistled. "Cold as a motherfucker up there, so I hear." Tennessee did a shimmy shake in emphasizing his point.

"Ha ha. No matter how much blues they play, huh, Tennessee?" Darkboy winked.

"Cold as a motherfucker in Chi-cago!" Tennessee said with extra grit.

They toweled body parts lazily. The quiet in the bathhouse at this time of night seemed to have thoroughly relaxed them.

"Mmm … nothing like a shower to cool off from a hard day's work," Tennessee said.

Darkboy wiped his closely cropped hair.

"Man, Darkboy," Tennessee said strongly, "how in the hell you wind up with the name Darkboy? What in the name of God was your parents thinking?"

"Thinking, ha ha, Tennessee?" Darkboy said laying his dark hand on Tennessee's likewise dark shoulder. "Well, I guess my mama and daddy thought the white man would call me 'dark boy' behind my back so decided they'd let him call me Darkboy to my face. Yeah, I suppose it *was* that—what both thought—at the time."

"Why, I like them, uh, your folk already. A whole bunch of liking! Louisiana boy, you say, right? Born and bred? New Orleans? No wonder you so hopped up on jazz. Cozy with it and all. Jazz ain't nothin' but down there in them scuffling neck of the woods. For sure. Playing out the bayou."

Darkboy's smile lit up the bathhouse.

Now they were out of the bathhouse and away from the building's dim front light, facing a dark road that divided in four directions.

"Boy, if we don't look like two country gentlemens of the highest rank!" Tennessee said.

Darkboy nodded. "We do, don't we?"

"You a good-looking boy, Darkboy. Look like you always got a pretty feather stuck in your cap."

"Uh, thanks." Darkboy smiled modestly.

"Got money in your pocket, ain't you—for Chi-cago?"

Darkboy blushed. "Hmm. Uh, yes, probably enough for a week."

"Typical. Typical jazzman, man," Tennessee said, as if a bluesman was different. "Well … okay." Tennessee put down Baby Love's guitar case to shake Darkboy's hand in the dark. "Good luck to you. Godspeed. That's from me and Baby Love. Going out to y'all, now."

"Thanks. I'll need it."

"No, sir," Tennessee said, shaking his head as if a wasp had stung it. "Beg to differ; you a drumming fool. One drumming fool, man. Got all the talent in the world and then some!" When Tennessee got some thirty yards away, he turned and waved at Darkboy, who, of course, waved back. "Just keep it light, Darkboy. Clean and light. Shit …"

Jimmy "Darkboy" Slade had been a drumming fool since he'd first heard the drums, the marching drums, in New Orleans, playing through the streets like galloping horses, like proud sound, like drums out of Africa. But when he first heard Chick Webb, he thought he heard perfection— how remarkable a set of drums are.

Chick Webb. Chick Webb.

"Well, the time has come," Darkboy said, "and I don't owe anybody any money down here. Not a red cent, man."

Of course, Jimmy Darkboy Slade was joking, simply using a trite expression in order to pass the time, for Jimmy Darkboy Slade was as honest as the day is long. He never borrowed money from anyone, not even if he spotted a stray penny on the ground. Jimmy Darkboy Slade was raised honest, as honest as a day is long.

"Ha."

Darkboy had a lot of travel in him. He'd been traveling since he was sixteen. He'd been to this town and the next, but he still looked like a boy who was maturing into a man, day by day, but hadn't quite gotten there.

Physically, Darkboy wasn't as tall as he'd like but was tall enough by most folks' standards. His build was slight, like a jaybird's, and he had teeth as white as chalk, and he had a natural smile—one that stayed with any stranger he met.

Darkboy came from a loving family in Louisiana—mother and father, two brothers, Dexter and Ellis Jr. His parents recognized his talent right off, much to his father's delight and his mother's chagrin. When Darkboy left home at age sixteen to become a jazz musician, Darkboy's mother, Louisa, had not wanted him to go, but Darkboy's father, Ellis Sr., knew Darkboy had to go.

Darkboy whistled the same tune Tennessee had been whistling in the bathhouse. If he was nervous about setting off to Chicago, he didn't show it. Darkboy had a philosophy about life that, at his tender age, he couldn't fully express, but he knew it to be there, fully formed, at his beck and call.

If I have to be a blues drummer in Chicago for a while, then I'll be a blues drummer in Chicago for a while, Darkboy thought. *Been everything else, it seems, why not a blues drummer in Chicago?*

Darkboy was carrying his drum kit that was in zipped cases, and a suitcase as big as Alaska. Darkboy was on a long, dark, rugged dirt road. He thought about his mama and daddy. "You'll get a letter from your son soon, Mama, Daddy, as soon as I step foot in Chicago."

Jimmy Darkboy Slade always had written to his mama and daddy back in New Orleans since he'd left there a few years back. The local mailman there, Glendale Lee Roundtree, routinely beat a path to the Slades' door, with a letter from their son, Jimmy Darkboy Slade, in hand.

Darkboy could see Mr. Glendale Lee, his sprightly step, his tattered letter bag, his electric smile. *It'd certainly brighten the dark road I'm on,* Darkboy thought. Get him faster to Chicago than what it seemed. "Even for a young boy like me." Darkboy smiled. "Who knows how to walk a country road, uh, in the dark?"

CHAPTER 12

There was a veil of smoke, so much smoke that Darkboy couldn't have seen Mona Lisa's smile in it if he'd tried.

The Bluelight Café. Chicago. Chi-town. Blues. Jazz. Party town. Party until the liquor in the Chicago bars ran dry–sat on empty.

Darkboy was there in Chicago. He'd been in Chicago for six days, going on a week. He was playing in a blues band, was a blues drummer–a Chicago blues drummer, seeking a jazz band. The jazz band over at the Bluelight Café, a blues player had informed him, was looking for a jazz drummer.

After a few weeks in Chicago, this is what happened for Darkboy and his drums:

"So, you're Jimmy Darkboy Slade?" the tall middle-aged man said, striking a match, making a bright blue flame. "Long Ray's the name. Play bass fiddle, and do most of the composing for the band."

"Glad to meet you, Long Ray."

The match went out. Long Ray inhaled. The smoke had to navigate through a long, tubular system (it was presumed) before Long Ray Davidson exhaled, which it did. "Smoke?"

"No."

"Drink?"

"Yes."

"Good," Long Ray said. "Now about that drumming job."

"Right."

"See you brought your equipment with you."

"All the way from—"

"I know, I know—no need to tell me." Long Ray Davidson laughed. "I know the travel route. By way of—"

"New Orleans."

"The city of jazz! Cradle of jazz!"

"Uh, you might say," Darkboy said proudly.

"I do say," Long Ray said as proudly. "Okay, listen, the band plays in … in another ten minutes, okay?"

Darkboy's pretty white teeth sparkled.

"Got you a helluva smile, Darkboy. Women must love the hell out of it!"

"Uh, uh-huh."

"Could charm the drawers off a snake, I imagine. I mean, if you tried, wanted to, uh—that is?"

"Uh, uh-huh."

"You're my kind of cat, Darkboy. My kind of cat, man!"

They were standing by the bar. Long Ray looked at it through the Bluelight Café's smoke screen. "Now, let's get down to business, Darkboy, shall we?" Long Ray arched forward. "Listen, we all drink. Hell, you know the deal, so I ain't telling you nothing new." Anxiously, Long Ray drew on his cigarette. "The last drummer I hired was a drunk. Plain and simple. Drank too much gin. Was drunk before the Chicago bars opened. Before the band's first downbeat. Thought more about drinking than he did drumming. He crawled out the Bluelight Café every night of the week on his hands and knees. How he handled the job. Fit with the band."

Darkboy shook his head.

"Tried helping the young man, me and the rest of the cats. Called on our experience, what we know—we're like that. But he acted like we were handing him down some hand-me-down clothes. Second-rate advice. The young man rejected our help. Just flat out rejected it. Was a decent drummer too. But gin was the young man's downfall. Uh, obstacle. Gotta know when to get off the gin wagon before the wheels begin falling off. Uh, coming off. Hits a ditch or crashes into a wall."

Darkboy felt he had to say something. "Yes, yes, I drink liquor, but my drumming comes first, always, Long Ray. Always has. I can't sleep a wink at night if … if my drumming's not right. If I had a bad night on the bandstand."

"Believe in practicing, Darkboy?" Long Ray asked devoutly, divinely, more like a preacher man than a jazzman.

"Wherever I can."

"No matter what time? The hour?"

"Whoever looks at a clock when it's time to practice? When it comes time to practice music."

Long Ray thumped his chest, then again for good measure. "Hey, not me! No way! Never hear anyone accuse Long Ray Davidson of that—that's for sure. Man, I follow the golden rule too. A jazz man's golden rule too when it comes to practicing." Long Ray's arm snaked around Darkboy's shoulders. "Hey, let me introduce you to the fellas in the band."

"Great."

"But first, what you drink?" Long Ray asked, again looking over at the long bar through the thick haze of smoke.

"Bourbon will do."

"For now?"

"For now," Darkboy agreed, smiling.

Darkboy had been formally introduced to the jazz quintet: Long Ray Davidson, bass; Johnny "Cool Hands" Dockery, piano; Pinky Irving, reeds (tenor sax, alto sax, and flute); and Louis "Loose Lips" Lawrence, trumpet.

Darkboy's drums were set up on the Bluelight's bandstand. Darkboy's foot worked the bass drum's foot pedal for a few seconds, kind of giving it an opportunity to bask in its own glory.

Long Ray stepped up on the bandstand with an air of diplomacy and good will. He looked into the overhead colored lights. His skin coloring was eye-catching, and his moustache trimmed as neatly as a golf course's slick greens.

"Hey, we're back, and where I come from—Waco, Texas—it's reason enough for everybody's applause."

So the medium-sized gathering in the smoke-infested den, the Bluelight Café, applauded.

"When last we gathered here, the band didn't have a drummer. Was drummer-less." Long Ray squirmed. "But no more. Because either through luck or charity—take your pick—we took care of that sorry-ass situation."

Darkboy managed an embarrassed smile to crease his lips, as if he'd just got caught jaywalking on a Chicago street by a Chicago cop and was ticketed.

"So, go on, Long Ray," one of the Bluelight's patrons said.

"Yeah, that."

"Yeah, that!"

"His name's Darkboy. Jimmy Darkboy Slade. Stand up, Darkboy, and take a bow in the Bluelight. Let the folk gathered here get to know you."

Darkboy stood up to a smattering of applause.

Long Ray placed his hand to his right ear, then leaned his head in Darkboy's direction. "So, where did you say you're from again, Darkboy?"

"Louisiana. New Orleans, to be exact, Long Ray."

"That's what I thought you said. Louisiana. New Orleans, to be exact. City of the drum—if I'm not mistaken. Play it at funerals, don't they? The routine?"

"Yes, we do."

Long Ray caused his backbone to dip and sway, and then, slowly, he strutted across the bandstand as if his legs were testing air. "Sorta march like this down there in New Orleans, don't they, Darkboy?"

Darkboy grinned. "Sort of, Long Ray. Sort of."

The folks in the Bluelight Café were enjoying the short, extemporaneous shenanigans between Long Ray and Darkboy, along with the band.

Darkboy sat down on the stool behind his drums.

"Tired of talking, huh, Darkboy?"

Darkboy crossed his drumsticks in front of his chest, as if it were some kind of trademark he'd invented and worked out for himself.

"Me too. Say it's time to wake folk up in Chicago, if they ain't already woke. Let them know the Super Chief ain't the only train blowing its way through Union Station tonight!"

Darkboy sidled up to his drums to wait for Long Ray Davidson's decisive downbeat, Chicago-style.

"Uhhh—"
Blam!

"Let me shake your hand, Darkboy, and welcome you to the band, man! Man, damn—ooo-wee, does the band have itself a drummer, man. Ooo-wee, Darkboy!" Long Ray shouted.

The band stood in line to shake Darkboy's hand. It looked like a receiving line for a dignitary, a statesman, someone of the highest, finest breeding.

Pinky Irving's tenor sax dangled in front of him. He had yet to unhook it from its strap. "Darkboy, man, I ain't never gonna complain to the owner about lack of heat in the winter in this joint—not after tonight's blowout session!"

Darkboy shook Pinky's hand, which had three rings on five of his fingers. Pinky was fleet-fingered on his sax, so the three rings on his five fingers, apparently, weren't a hindrance.

"Could cook up a month's worth of bacon and eggs on them drums. Make a meal. A real Southern banquet," Pinky said.

"They were popping, Pinky. Popping, weren't they? Thought them snake skins were popping popcorn," Loose Lips said.

"And Loose Lips digs him some popcorn, Darkboy."

Darkboy was taking all of this in with unassuming pleasure.

"But Darkboy can play like a moon setting on a lake now, too," Cool Hands Dockery, the piano player, said. "Like a Mozart sonata."

"Yeah," the band chorused.

"Got the touch of a heart surgeon at work," Pinky said.

Now everyone was pretty much on their own. Only Long Ray was keeping an eye out for Darkboy, being he was the band's bandleader.

"So where you staying in Chicago anyways, Darkboy?"

Darkboy zipped his cymbal case. "Uh, the Mercy Hotel, Long Ray."

"Hey, why don't you stay with me?"

The way in which Long Ray said it, it was as if Darkboy were saying it to himself, *Why don't I?* "I—"

"Got room for you and your drums."

"You—"

"Plenty. All the room in the world."

Darkboy's face still registered a look of total disbelief.

"Ha—it's like I hit you square between the eyes with a snowball, ain't it?"

Long pause. "W-what's that—a snowball?" Darkboy frowned.

"Oh, that's right—you're new to Chicago. These parts. You've still got Louisiana in your blood. But don't worry, Darkboy; you'll find out soon enough. Boy, will you ever. Waco, Texas, had never heard of a snowball either—but it has now!"

Darkboy laughed lightly at what seemed the ominous prospect of his first encounter with a Chicago snowball.

"Well, is you is, or is you ain't gonna be my baby?"

Darkboy's pretty smile shot to the surface, seemingly cracking through the confusion. "Mmm, since you put it that way, Long Ray—I guess I is!"

"Mercy Hotel, looks like you just lost yourself a house guest!"

Darkboy and Long Ray were out on Chicago streets. It was raining. "Better than snow, Darkboy," Long Ray remarked.

Since Darkboy still didn't know anything about snow, he really couldn't offer anyone any expert opinion to say which was better: rain or snow. Both were without umbrellas. The rain fell on bare heads.

The apartment building's hallway wasn't well lit. Every third step over the hallway's floorboards produced a potent creak. It was as if each squeak had a squawk with the landlord (a history of them). But it hadn't mattered to Darkboy. He was too overwhelmed by this good fortune that had come, seemingly, from out of the blue.

"Don't expect too much. Anything too fancy now. Just reasonable. It's not the Taj Mahal." Long Ray opened the apartment door and snapped on the lights.

"Hey, nice. Nice!"

"You sure, Darkboy?"

"Sure, Long Ray."

What Darkboy saw of Long Ray's apartment, he liked indeed.

It was a five-room apartment with high ceilings and three wide windows with great views. The bare but clean-looking walls were painted a chocolate brown with cream-colored trim. This area of the apartment was kept neat, certainly reflecting Long Ray's personal attention to detail. If there was dust on the floors, Darkboy didn't see it.

"Let me show you to *your* room," Long Ray said.

He snapped on the light in that room.

"F-fine," Darkboy said. "This'll fit me fine."

"Got another room; it's a little smaller—who knows?"

Darkboy understood what Long Ray was suggesting—getting at. "The more the merrier."

"Yeah, we're all living on a shoestring, Darkboy. True for everyone who calls himself a musician in this world."

Darkboy paused to reflect. "Sometimes, though, Long Ray, it feels more like a rope tightening around my neck."

"Does, doesn't it, though, Darkboy. But then again, we ain't being hung by the neck by none of those Mississippi crackers, now, are we?"

"No, it just feels like it sometimes. Sometimes it really does, man."

To a jazzman, it was late night; for anyone else, an early morning. It's just that the sun hadn't come up through the window on Darkboy's and Long Ray's first day together. Darkboy was dressed, so was Long Ray.

"Darkboy, practice. Practice," Long Ray said reverently.

"Long Ray … you know you just said it like someone down on their knees, praying."

"Did I?"

"Pretty much." Darkboy leaned against one of the front room's bare brown walls.

"Been practicing on this bass since"—Long Ray held his bass—"boy, it has been long, hasn't it? When you stop to think about it. Add up the years."

"Any other instruments along the way for you?" Darkboy asked.

"Uh-uh, just the bass. What about you?"

"Clarinet. It was when Daddy played Sidney Bechet on the phonograph. Recall it to this day."

"Damn, damn—know you quit the clarinet! Got hot in the kitchen, huh? Was smoking up a storm in there?"

"That night. That very same night!"

"Uh, then?"

"Then the piano."

"And so?"

"My daddy played Art Tatum on the phonograph."

"Ooo-wee, your daddy sure was cold. Cold as ice. Downright abusive, man! Know you switched instrum—"

"To the drums."

"Then?" Long Ray lit a cigarette.

"Yeah, thought I was Africa, Long Ray. A continent. New Orleans. A funeral march. Chick Webb!"

"Chick Webb—that drumming fool! He's your hero? The man on the drums for you?"

"He's my hero all right. The man in the shining armor," Darkboy said with reverence.

"So what about 'Papa' Jo Jones?"

"Him too." Darkboy's eyes sang drum solos. "But ... but mostly Chick Webb." Darkboy looked at Long Ray and anticipated another question to roll off his tongue. "And don't ask me why, because I ... I really couldn't tell you. Not to this day, man."

"So, your daddy likes jazz?" Long Ray said, flicking the ash off the cigarette and on to the floor.

"Daddy—does he!"

"You love him a lot, don't you?"

"To death, Long Ray."

"Where'd you practice, uh, at home?"

"Down in the basement. Mostly there."

"What about your neighbors?" Long Ray chuckled.

"Complained to Mama."

"She didn't like jazz."

"But not to Daddy."

"Knew better."

"Daddy said the neighbors said I sounded like Chick Webb. He'd tell me, 'Uh, Darkboy, neighbors say you learning them drums. Sound, sound like Chick Webb'!"

"Did you?"

Darkboy's back popped off the wall. "Who knows?"

Long Ray knew better than to jostle what appeared to be the sentimentality of the moment for Darkboy.

"What about your daddy and your mama, Long Ray?"

"Daddy? My daddy? Mean as poison, Darkboy. Wouldn't feed him to a swine. Not to a Texas pig. It'd kill the pig. Kill the motherfucker dead. Dead on the spot." Long Ray ground his cigarette into the floor. "If it wasn't for this bass fiddle, Darkboy—if it wasn't for this bass ... I, I swear, I ..." Long Ray clutched his tall instrument. "It saved my life. What, literally. Did it ever. Unless I might be dead in Texas. Truly. Dead and buried there a long fucking time ago."

Long Ray lit a fresh cigarette. His hand shook. He took a number of short, successive puffs from it.

Darkboy buttoned the right cuff of his shirt. "Who, who plays the bass like no other for you, Long Ray? Who's your hero? Your knight in shining armor?" Darkboy hoped the question would free up the tension in the room.

"For me, none other than"—Darkboy could hear a drum roll—"Jimmy Blanton himself. Who else?"

"A Tennessee boy. Chattanooga."

"He had country dirt in his shoes but made those big city cats sit up and take notice."

"Duke, you mean?"

"Dirt in his shoes but big city dreams in his pockets."

"I guess like all of us."

"What a band, huh, Darkboy? The best band in the land, before or since."

Long Ray and Darkboy looked at each other, practically giddy, like big-eyed kids—never mind Long Ray's advanced years.

"Practice!" Then Long Ray looked out the apartment window. "Gee, man, the sun's up?"

Darkboy looked out the same window. "Not unless you painted the sky black, man."

"Not me, Darkboy. Would've painted it darker."

"Dark as me, Long Ray?"

"No, darker, Darkboy."

Darkboy was enjoying this repartee. "What if I asked you to call me Jimmy and not 'Darkboy,' Long Ray?"

"I'd still call you Darkboy anyway, Darkboy," Long Ray shot back. "Your folks, they really did love you." Pause. "And about you being a Louisiana boy and me a Texas boy—I kind of let that slip back at the club. Had band business on my mind then. But—"

"I know."

"We, I mean, we are next-door neighbors on the map. Surprised you never knocked on my back door before. You never—"

"Are we going to practice or what?" Darkboy asked.

"Not without your practice pads, which I know you've got."

"Right. Right. Be right back." Darkboy scampered off to his new room in Chicago.

"Darkboy, don't know how many times I've listened to Jimmy Blanton on record. Might be too afraid to count," Long Ray shouted to Darkboy between rooms.

"Bet not as many times as I've listened to Chick Webb."

And Darkboy thought of his daddy, and Long Ray, coincidently, thought of his.

The next morning

Darkboy patted the bed. It was as lumpy as a plate of boiled potatoes. *What did I expect*, Darkboy thought, *a bed of roses?* The apartment sounded quiet—lonely.

Last night Long Ray said he'd be out the apartment before Darkboy woke. "Got me a day job. Elevator operator. Need just two hours sleep. You know the situation."

Boy, oh boy, did he know the situation—*did* he.

Darkboy made the bed. *This will be my last day of luxury,* he thought. He had to get over to the Mercy Hotel and pack his suitcase, then check out.

Before turning in last night, Long Ray let him know, his *day job* was at the Mayflower Hotel in downtown Chicago, and that the hotel needed dishwashers. He said they always needed dishwashers at the Mayflower. Darkboy knew how to wash dishes. He'd be off Chicago's unemployment rolls by no later than tomorrow morning—guaranteed.

The bed was made. Darkboy patted it again for good measure. "Me and you are going to have to get along, looks like," Darkboy said, as if he were bonding with the lumpy mattress. "After the first shock, it wasn't that bad. Really … really, it wasn't," he said in a kinder, gentler voice.

Darkboy walked into the front room. He was dressed. Before leaving, he looked to make sure all the apartment lights were off—out of habit. At home, hailing from a family of five, it was something he was in the habit of doing before leaving the house. "People can't afford to throw money away," Darkboy's father would remind him. "Every penny's got a place. And every light's got a switch."

All the apartment's lights were off. Darkboy was about to lockup. Long Ray had given him a spare key.

Darkboy opened the door but didn't walk out the apartment. For some odd reason, even to him, he walked over to the smallish room, the one for now unoccupied but with what looked to be a sturdy bed with a lumpy mattress.

Long Ray's a generous man, Darkboy thought. *A give-his-shirt-off-his-back type of fellow.* Darkboy moved toward the apartment's front door. "I wonder who'll be coming to Chicago next. Who'll need a nice place to stay? I wonder."

CHAPTER 13

The boxy radio blared the blues. The heat in the kitchen had to be hovering near 120 degrees—easily. Between the blues and the heat, even the devil might hop on the first midnight train for Georgia.

It was Darkboy's first day as an official dishwasher ("suds buster") in Chicago's Mayflower Hotel. It was why Darkboy was down in the "dungeon." He had a legitimate, bona fide excuse for being there; it's where his day gig was, down in that potboiler of a room.

Darkboy was sweating like a stick of dynamite about to blow or, at the very least, someone who was standing near a stick of dynamite about to blow. But the crusty, salt-and-pepper–bearded old gentleman, who he worked next to and who went by the name of Hambone Hamilton, was hardly breaking a sweat while washing those dirty, caked hotel dishes. So Darkboy had to assume Hambone Hamilton had seen a whole lot of worse days than even the blues on the blaring radio was speaking of to all who were within listening distance.

Darkboy blew on a few beads of sweat trying to reach his forehead, where all that gunk dripped from. What was Darkboy thinking while he washed another dirty dish? More about tonight than anything else. More about tonight and the music and the band and what it was going to play at the Bluelight Café than anything else. There was a tingle of happiness in Darkboy, a sweet satisfaction of being at the right place at the right time in his life.

Often, Darkboy thought about the great mysteries of life. Often, he thought of his travels—where they had taken him. Leaving home at age sixteen hadn't been easy but was the first step in making the journey. Even at sixteen, he knew no one could teach him about the life he wished to live but life. He knew he had to get out there in the world and live it; live the life of a jazz drummer if he wanted to be a jazz drummer. There were no shortcuts—just back roads. There were no back doors to get to the front door. Something at the beginning of the journey had manifested this fact.

Maybe it was Chick Webb.

Maybe it was in the drum kit, his drumming. Maybe Chick Webb explained what a jazz drummer's life was like in his drumming—its elegant, magnetic sound.

Darkboy smiled broadly. He liked the thought. It made a world of sense to him. Darkboy wiped his forehead clean with his hand (not blowing on it with his breath this time) between dishes.

"Man …" Hambone Hamilton said.

"It, it's hot down here," Darkboy said.

"Weren't 'bout to say that," Hambone Hamilton intoned matter-of-factly. "'Bout to say, man, that man can sure sing them blues." Hambone Hamilton's skin was as dry as a fresh piece of hambone.

Darkboy's ears paid more attention to the blues music spinning out the radio. "Oh … yeah, he sure can."

Hambone's eyes targeted Darkboy suspiciously. "Now, what you say you play, boy?"

"Uh … uh …" Darkboy stammered nervously, as if he were about to break his first dish on the job (God forbid!). "D-drums, sir."

Hambone Hamilton nodded, undoubtedly unimpressed.

"A … a jazz drummer," Darkboy said.

Not a word came out of Hambone Hamilton's mouth, as his sweatless hand reached for the radio knob on the shelf just above his head. He turned the radio's volume higher. "Jazz," he said, looking over to Darkboy with worn eyes, "makes a man sweat. Blues, on the other hand," Hambone's deeper-than-an-ocean voice echoed out, "make a man feel what it was he sweat."

Darkboy shut his mouth. What the hell could he say?

What?

What, man?

Time for Darkboy, down in the Mayflower kitchen, was moving about as slowly as a snail hitchhiking a ride on one leg on a five-lane highway heading South. Even if Darkboy's body was under far better temperature control than before, his mind still thought back to those hot, muggy, late-summer Louisiana afternoons, when even the fish and frogs in the bayou refused to jump. The heat of the day made them so repulsively lazy that they'd fan themselves in the crook of the shade with little relief.

"Darkboy!" It sounded like a cannon shot heard around the world, but it was only Long Ray. It appeared as if he had the wind at his back. "Just thought I'd come down here to the dungeon to make sure they're treating you right."

Long Ray was about to acknowledge Hambone Hamilton, but Hambone acknowledged him first.

"Where's Ike sleepin'?"

"And a good afternoon to you too, Hambone."

Hambone grinned.

It was the first time all day Darkboy had actually seen him smile. *Now,* Darkboy thought, *Hambone Hamilton should do that more often.*

"Keeping busy, Darkboy?"

"I'm building a small fortress. Care to join me?" Darkboy teased.

Long Ray chose to disregard him. "Hot as hell down here. They never turn the temperature down. Hell, need to."

"What? Too tough down here for you, Long Ray? Skin ain't tough 'nough," Hambone snarled. "We field niggers down here."

Darkboy froze.

"Ah, get off that 'field nigger,' 'house nigger' crap, Hambone, when you know good and well you never picked a day's worth of cotton for Mr. Chuck in your life, man!"

But Long Ray and Darkboy knew Hambone had probably picked a whole lot of cotton for Mr. Chuck in his lifetime. He'd missed slavery but knew all about sharecropping.

"Won't be too tired from your day job, Darkboy, to play tonight, uh, will you? Cramp your style?" Long Ray asked.

"No."

"A drummer and a bass player," Hambone muttered disparagingly

"What? You've got something against that?" Long Ray laughed. "I know, I know, you want me to play 'real' music, don't you, Hambone? What your argument always is. Am I right?"

Hambone wiped his hand in a towel and rubbed his salt-and-pepper beard.

"Listen, Hambone, we play the blues every night at the Bluelight too. Put it on the menu." Long Ray sighed. "We haven't forgotten." Long Ray shook his head.

"Didn't—ain't said you do, Long Ray. Ain't gotta put words in my mouth," Hambone retorted.

Suddenly, Darkboy liked this dear old man.

"Better get back, Darkboy," Long Ray said.

"Uh-huh, Long Ray, 'fore Ike wake!" Hambone said.

"So I gotta cut my visit short."

Darkboy's arms wrapped around half a stack of dirty dishes, sliding them down into the sudsy dishwater.

"But before I exit for my fan-cooled elevator with a stool, let me say—earnestly, from one lover-ly jazz musician to another lover-ly jazz musician—Darkboy, you look funkier than a skunk walking down Michigan Avenue on a short leash!"

"Let me and Darkboy be!" Hambone said in defense of Darkboy.

"And as for you, Hambone," Long Ray said, dashing for the exits as if a wind had hit his back, "you haven't sweat a day in your life!"

"Not since God make sweat!"

Hambone smiled at Darkboy, and Darkboy could feel the time down in the Mayflower's hot-as-hell kitchen move a lot quicker around the clock.

CHAPTER 14

Three months later

A drink was in Darkboy's hand.

"Hey, Darkboy!"

"Hey, Pinky!"

Pinky Irving wore pink suspenders. He was a "Dapper Dan," a lady's man—someone who always kept cash in his right pocket and a dame's telephone number in his left. He looked around the Bluelight Café with a certain air of expectancy. "Hey, where's Long Ray?"

"Oh, he's coming."

"Look, don't worry, Darkboy. When I don't see you with Long Ray— shit, I make the same inquiry."

"Long Ray's beginning to feel like my shadow, Pinky."

"Long one."

"Uh-huh, six foot plus of—"

"Must be a great feeling, 'cause Long Ray's a great cat. The finest in the litter. Hey, Bartender Bob, you can hit me up with a tall highball, if you will, my good man."

Bartender Bob, ginger-colored, light on his feet, and always quick with an off-color quip, handed Pinky his drink.

Pinky gulped it down. "Man, oh man, I did have a thirst. I needed that one." Pinky pointed his finger at the glass. "Another hit'll do me fine, Bartender Bob. Can measure it out the same, my good man."

"Pinky, if you want the bottle I'll gift wrap it for you."

"Ha." Pinky was more deliberate in drinking the highball this time, with, it seemed, more patience. "Hear Long Ray's calling a little confab before rehearsal."

"Oh, right, Pinky," Darkboy said casually.

"Know what about?"

"Yes, I do. Long Ray, uh, wants to get us on the road. Uh, the band, that is—out on the road."

"Oh, no, that bullshit again," Pink said disgustedly.

"Again?" Darkboy said quizzically.

"Yeah, it's what I said: again!"

"Why ... I ... I ..."

Pinky slammed the whiskey glass down on top of the bar. He looked inside the whisky glass, drew a breath, and appeared to take his time before speaking.

"Pinky, look, uh, I'm at a loss here. Help me out, would you, man? P-please."

"With pleasure." Long pause. "Look, nobody wants nobody out of the Bluelight Café in Chicago, man." Pinky sighed. "You don't put that kind of off-the-track crap on your résumé–you get me? Is that simple enough?" Pinky mimicked a club owner reading a musician's résumé. "Chicago? Bluelight Café?" Pinky pinched his nose, as if it were in a Chicago dump. "Got a bad odor to it, Darkboy. That's what. Long Ray, he's just spinning his wheels–treading water. Lucky just to be keeping himself above water."

Darkboy was stunned. "But we're all great musicians," Darkboy countered, but suddenly, he was oddly unsure of himself.

Pinky slowed down on his take on things. He had a heart and soul. He didn't want to take Darkboy's away—not this early in the game. "Uh ... you're ... a young jazz cat, Darkboy. I'm an older jazz cat. You ain't been at this kind of business long. I have. Get me?" Pinky deliberated more. "After a while, well—it ain't about talent, you see. Who's gifted or not. A ... uh, a lot of times—and you can trust me on this—it's about luck. Luck—luck, and timing. Luck and timing—and even then, who's to say? Say you're lucky. Get me?"

Pinky, with his drink, walked away from the bar, leaving Darkboy sitting there on the wooden bar stool in a state of personal reflection.

Darkboy pretended he wasn't bothered by what Pinky had said, but he was. Pinky Irving had told him something of value, something both wise and lofty—and he knew it. If he was to get an education, then he must want one. It was as clear as that. He mustn't look for things that were not there, no matter how lofty his goals or dreams. No matter the rainbow. No matter what world he put them in his dreams, they had no life without his life.

Darkboy turned to Bartender Bob for a refill, but Bartender Bob had vanished. Darkboy looked at his empty whiskey glass on the bar and nudged it aside with his forefinger.

What's a jazz musician's life anyway? But who was he to stand in the way of a person's—in the way of what Long Ray was going to propose to the band? Who am I to … to do that? Darkboy felt humbled by the thought.

Long Ray operated an elevator; Darkboy washed dishes. They were great musicians; this was their lives. He had no reason to bitch or moan or try to turn the moon blue if it was purple. He was in this thing with Long Ray, solid. He was in this thing, chasing butterflies without a net. He was in this thing, morning to night, dawn to dusk; in it to stay. Not run away from it—hightail himself from it.

Pinky reappeared, putting his glass back down on the bar.

Darkboy looked to his right and then to his left.

"Where's Bartender Bob?" Pinky asked.

Darkboy looked to his right and then to his left.

"Lost too, huh?" Pinky said.

Darkboy shrugged his shoulders. "Guess so."

"Damn, Darkboy, can't depend on you for nothing!"

Darkboy tapped his foot on the floor with style. "What about—"

"Yeah," Pinky interrupted, snapping his fingers.

"The beat," Darkboy finished.

"Steady."

"Freddie," Darkboy said.

"Man, wouldn't trade any of this shit in for nothing in the world, Darkboy, nothing—not even horse feathers!" Pinky's voice zinged. "What time'd you say Long Ray's meeting for tonight was?"

"Uh, I didn't."

"Hey, don't start playing with me, man. Messing with an old cat like me. Better not play with your elders, young boy," Pinky said, his cheeks looking about as pink as pink paint. "And, uh, listen, Darkboy, what I said before—"

"I thought it through," Darkboy said, cutting Pinky short. "Pinky."

There was this mellow, cello-sweet silence between them.

"Good. Good. Glad you did. Can always find ghosts in the dark if you look hard enough. Take a liking to … Shit. Yeah. Shit."

Long Ray's meeting had concluded, and the band and its five able-bodied musicians were about to play to an average-sized audience who were sitting at round tables in the Bluelight Café.

Long Ray's meeting had covered two special items of importance: one, Long Ray asked Loose Lips Lawrence if he would act as the booking agent for the band, to which Loose Lips agreed. And two, Long Ray and the band members finally came up with a new band name, other than the Bluelight All-Stars—a moniker they'd been stuck with for over seven months.

Their new name, beginning tonight, starting at this very instant, without any further ado and to be announced by Long Ray from the Bluelight bandstand tonight, was,

The Windy Wind Five (that's no *jive*).

Darkboy held his high-hat in his hand. He was about to clamp it to the stand when he heard a voice from the bottom of the ocean's cellar climbing confidently to the top:

"Ladies and gentlemen, it is my proud, distinguished honor to announce tonight that the four gentlemen and I, who form this musical aggregation standing before your lovely eyes tonight …"

So what if Long Ray is being a mite longwinded, Darkboy thought.

"With pride and pleasure, would like to announce …"

And repetitive.

"Before you and all the world …"

And overreaching.

"That from this night and what will be forever more …"

And downright melodramatic …

"Will no longer be assembled as the 'Bluelight All-Stars,' something quite ordinary, passé, man. "Long Ray's eyes dashed over his shoulders and back to where Darkboy sat in the darkened backdrop—this had been planned long before they took to the bandstand, that Darkboy would execute one of his world-famous New Orleans drum rolls.

Darkboy, though, hustled up one drumstick, fumbled it, caught it again in his paw, and then beat the drum one time.

The Bluelight crowd and the formerly named Bluelight All-Stars were in a state of tears.

"Uh … uh … Darkboy," Long Ray said, temporarily distracted; thrown off his game.

"S-sorry, L-Long Ray." But now Darkboy displayed his world-famous New Orleans drum roll with his almighty drumsticks.

Rat-atat-atat-atat.

"Say, Long Ray, sure you ain't forgot the new name of the band by now?"

"Why, not at all, Joe," Long Ray replied to Joe Flowers, a Bluelight regular.

Rat-atat-atat-atat.

"The Windy Wind Five!"

"Don't hear you too good, *Long Ray!*" Joe Flowers shouted.

"Didn't?"

"No!"

"Said, the *Windy Wind Five!*"

"Sa-a-ay now," Joe said sweetly.

Rat-atat-atat-atat.

The first jazz set was, as most jazz cats would say, in the bag. The second set was about to commence.

"How's it feel, Darkboy, playing under our new name and billing, the Windy Wind Five?" Long Ray asked.

Darkboy still had to get used to the new moniker, even if he and Long Ray had thought up the name only two days ago while walking home from the Mayflower.

"Come on, come on," Long Ray encouraged him.

"Still have to rub it in my bones some more, I guess. The name still sounds kind of funny. Odd to me."

"I know, but before long, it'll feel like an old suit that's been hanging in your closet forever. Been rained on a few times. Shrunk two sizes."

"It's a hit, though, Long Ray. Everybody thinks it's hep."

"Who's patting whose back, Darkboy?"

Darkboy extended his arm. "Sorry, but my arms can't reach that far to my back."

Long Ray extended one of his more-than-long, rubbery arms backward. "Don't worry; my arms can, without a problem."

Then Pinky made his way into the picture. "Cheese!"

"Man, if you don't get out of here!" Long Ray said.

"Thought you and Darkboy was posing for a family photo, for a family album, since you cats was smiling like cat whiskers," Pinky said, strapping his sax across his chest. "You know what, Long Ray?"

"No, what, Pinky?"

"Was thinking …"

"Which is dangerous, not only for humans but animals of any species, man," Long Ray said, winking at Darkboy. "So out with it. Come on."

"So, yeah, how about some blues in this set? Something that sweats you good and hard. That makes your soul wanna holler like a hog!"

Long Ray looked at Darkboy, and Darkboy looked at Loose Lips, and it carried down the line to Cool Hands and then returned to the original point of origin—hot-eyed.

"Do I look like the last fool standing in Chicago or what?" Long Ray said. "Ain't gonna be a witness to my own death. Murder!" Long Ray laughed. "You cats got my vote. The green light. The blues it is—and as many times as you want to play it. It's all right by me for the next set."

Long Ray knew not to mess with the blues, argue with it, or with the Windy Wind Five, for that matter, from the Bluelight's cramped back room.

By now in the Bluelight, the Windy Wind Five had turned the blues inside out and outside in. They'd drift into a blues tune, play a standard or an original tune, and then drift right back into a blues; tag on a blues line, a blues melody, that would make anybody who was listening sweat in their shoes, old or new.

The audience tonight at the Bluelight Café was, seemingly, at the mercy of the band. It was as elastic as a rubber band ready to snap at any minute when such provocation appeared. Right now, all heads in the Bluelight hung low, as low as the blue smoke, not yet scaling skyward or to other places, just settled in for the time being in a subtle, gritty groove.

Long Ray opened his eyes, for some reason, and when he did, he saw her through the filmy smoke. He saw this person, this girl, this lovely, lonely figure sitting in the front row of chairs, as if the smoke had manufactured her, made her, as surely as the blues, what the soul knew and tried its best to explain.

Long Ray's eyes normally already would have been shut again, only they were not. For Long Ray was fascinated by this figure. He was fascinated by this girl who was dressed in black—as far as he could tell. Long Ray couldn't keep his eyes off her.

Long Ray wondered, pondered.

Darkboy's eyes were shut.

Darkboy was sweating as freely as he would in the Mayflower Hotel kitchen, down there with Hambone Hamilton—nothing had changed. His touch on his drums was deft, polished to perfection. Darkboy's thoughts had little range; they'd gotten only as far as Hambone Hamilton.

Hambone Hamilton would love this moment; he'd eat it up, Darkboy thought. For Hambone could pick cotton to it, or lay a piece of tough railway track to it, or lift a riverboat's bale of hay to it. Hambone would enjoy these moments—the blues, in all of its surprise and infinite wisdom.

Darkboy's eyes had not opened; his soul felt good, satisfied, right now. And then his eyes did open, and he saw her too, as Long Ray had—this girl, this lovely, lonely figure sitting in the front chair in the Bluelight. Sitting in her chair as if the blues had conjured her up so that black magic could somehow coexist in the world in order to bedevil it.

She was pretty, gorgeous, with the shining skin of a black angel. She didn't have to be this pretty, but she was. Suddenly, Darkboy knew she was someone he'd never ever forget.

Darkboy felt the heat of her speak through him as his drums spoke the blues; felt the searing stirrings in his soul.

Pinky Irving was soloing, and his horn—tenor sax—sounded as if his guts had twisted far into the saxophone's solid metal, each note growling as blue as the last, as if a mule were on Pinky's back, as if one was sharing with the other their great earthly burden.

But then the band put the final touches on the blues tune, letting loose its last rugged, contested breath.

Long Ray placed his bass fiddle against the stage's back wall and then stepped forward into the spotlight, where all the club's smoke seemed to have stopped en masse.

The spotlight appeared to shrink with Long Ray standing in it. "The blues. The blues …" Long Ray shook his head as if he had yet to shake the blues from himself. "Who's black and doesn't know it? The blues."

"*A*-men to that!" someone in the Bluelight crowd said.

"It wakes you every night," Long Ray said, "that is, if it'll let you sleep at all."

"Hey, not me, Long Ray. I get my sleep!" said Joe Flowers. "Ain't nobody messing with me and my nine hours. Beat them bad-ass blues black and blue if they mess with me. Uh-uh, them blues better stay away from my doorstep at midnight; in fact, all night!"

"Uh … of course, Joe," Long Ray said deferentially. "We didn't mean you, but … but everybody else who's in here. Everyone else who's sitting here and has some sweat in them." Long Ray's body took up more of the Bluelight's spotlight. "The blues is our story, our history," he said to the all-black Bluelight gathering. "We live it every day."

"Ev-er-ry day!" Joe Flowers said.

"Glad we agree on something tonight, Joe. Two of us," Long Ray said. Joe Flowers laughed.

Darkboy couldn't keep his eyes off her; neither could Long Ray.

"What about you, little girl? What about you? What's your blues?"

And the girl, the young lady, sat in her chair as if she hoped a cricket would sound to break the silence trapping her in it like a zipped glove.

Where? Who? How? These were questions Long Ray couldn't seem to answer: where this young lady had come from, or who she was, or how old she was.

"So young, so young, and and you're here at the Bluelight Café, uh, listening to jazz."

The patrons in the Bluelight Café were drinking her in, looking her over. Their eyes brushed over her slowly.

Darkboy's heart went out to her. He wished Long Ray hadn't started this thing he was doing; that the girl could've just sat there at her table and be left alone and not put upon; not feel the hot spotlight of attention.

"You—"

"I love jazz."

The voice out this young girl, Darkboy thought—someone Darkboy wished to protect—seemed too frail and vulnerable, and had spoken in a tone beyond imagination.

"You ... you do?" Long Ray stuttered.

"Yes, sir, does sir, does ... I ..." Her voice sounded like honey pouring out of a bottle.

"You know what, young lady? I bet—just bet—you do."

Darkboy leaned over his drum set, for he felt better about this now, what was developing between Long Ray and the young lady, who had all but captured his heart and tossed a thick net around it.

"How old, I mean, how do you know about—"

"I'm a jazz singer," she interrupted.

Long Ray's long legs buckled.

Darkboy's body drew back from his drums.

"A ... a ..." Long Ray stammered.

"You heard what the girl said, Long Ray," Joe Flowers said. "She said she's a jazz singer, man!"

"Yeah ... yeah, Joe. I heard her," Long Ray said impatiently, waving Joe off. "You mean to say you sing jazz?"

"Yes, sir."

Long Ray's head shook as if the blues wasn't quite finished with him yet—not by a long shot. "Why ... that's great, uh ... uh ..." He seemed to be searching for her name.

"Ruby, sir. Ruby Midnight."

The name seemed to inject a new pulse into the room. "Did ... did you say Ruby? Ruby Midnight, little girl?"

"Yes sir, sir. Ruby Midnight."

Time seemed to freeze in the Bluelight.

Then …

"Ain't you at least gonna invite the young lady up to the bandstand, Long Ray? Joe said. "Show her off? Where're your manners, man? The girl, Miss Midnight, says she's a jazz singer."

It appeared Long Ray couldn't think straight, that he could hardly keep his head straight on his shoulders. He was too busy considering whether fate had dealt him this hand.

What if she can't sing? What if this young lady, this little girl, can't sing? Her dress is black. But her name–Midnight. Ruby Midnight. And she is in the Bluelight Café, the blues, fate–whatever religion is, it's tricky–downright clever yeah, tricky.

Ruby Midnight stood up at the table, as if Long Ray's invitation had already been extended to her, a foregone conclusion.

Long Ray felt greatly relieved. "Yes, c-come up to the bandstand, little girl." His hand reached out for her with great care.

Ruby took it.

Ruby was up on the Bluelight Café's bandstand.

Darkboy felt her.

Ruby turned. Now everyone in the Bluelight could see her—most of Long Ray and some of Ruby Midnight in the spotlight.

"What do you want to sing?" Long Ray whispered, loud enough for the band to hear. "You go ahead and name the tune, uh, song you want to sing for us, uh, now little girl, and we can play it," Long Ray said, looking respectfully at the band "Even if you decide, uh, someway, to make up your own song key."

But the Bluelight's mood seemed to suggest that this "little girl," Long Ray was referring to wouldn't have to make up her own "song key." Miss Ruby Midnight knew the song key probably as well as midnight knew what time of night to show.

"Yes, sir." Then Ruby Midnight's face turned to the Bluelight's microphone, and she opened her mouth, and her voice traveled into it for all in the Bluelight Café to hear.

Darkboy's hands trembled in a flash.

Long Ray urgently pulled his bass off the wall.

Ruby Midnight stood at the Bluelight's microphone, waiting for the band to join her in song, to make music with her in the soft stage lights and the gray, lazy, swirling smoke.

But it was the shock of her voice that Long Ray and Cool Hands and Pinky and Loose Lips and Darkboy had to recover from first. It was the beauty of her tone, how she made the air turn from gray to pink and then an iridescent rainbow.

The Bluelight's audience shut its eyes and could feel the journey in her, the peaks and valleys, where each section of the journey resonated in her heart.

And the Windy Wind Five shut its eyes, playing, feeling the joy in her, where the journey had brought her, the one-nighters, saloons, jazz joints along the way. This person who told them she was a jazz singer—someone like Ma Rainey or Bessie Smith—as if wishing to burn a new star in the sky that was all her own, had set a diamond in the constellation's crown and wore it like a golden tiara.

Her face was pretty, as they'd hoped it to be, and Midnight—Ruby Midnight—the name.

She was through with the first song, and it was as if she really hadn't sung, that there were so many more songs in her to sing before she was through for the night.

The smoke in the Bluelight Café stopped.

Ruby Midnight was singing "The Man I Love."

How many more songs had Ruby sung in the Bluelight? How many songs had the audience in the Bluelight demanded Ruby to sing?

The audience was standing on its feet, applauding her, this someone in a black dress.

"Ooo-wee, Ruby! Ruby, bow, Ruby. Hell, bow!" Long Ray hollered.

Long Ray was the first one to grab Ruby and kiss her cheek.

Then, just when the applause seemed to die down, it built back up again, bigger, louder, monstrous—lovely.

"Ruby! Ruby, bow, darling, bow!"

Ruby had bowed as Long Ray had said, as Darkboy watched her from behind, knowing what she must look like from the front, having memorized cheek and bone and smile together.

Long Ray applauded frenetically. "Keep applauding, folks, 'cause I don't know if Dinah Washington ever passed this way, through the

Bluelight. Even if Dinah never sang here at the Bluelight, all of us—we'll all know that Ruby Midnight did."

"Darn … if, if that ain't the God's honest truth!" Joe Flowers said.

The applause swelled. Ruby bowed and smiled, coordinating one with the other, feeling Miss Honey's breath of life breathe over her, splashing ocean warm.

Finally, the Bluelight had emptied.

"Con-congratulations, Ruby. Congratulations!" Loose Lips Lawrence was busy shaking Ruby's hand with all his might. "My, my name's Loose Lips Lawrence. Can call me L. L. for short, uh, if, if you'd like. Okay by you."

"Just call him Loose Lips, Ruby. Don't let them loose lips off the hook that easily," Pinky said. "None of the band does."

Ruby smiled.

Pinky took Ruby's hand, kissing it. Ruby blushed. "Pinky Irving, my dear." Then Pinky's body reassumed its former proper posture. "I just kissed a legend. A living legend! I've heard them all come and go. Ruby Midnight, sister, my dear child—I just got my religion back!" Pinky squeezed her hand. "You made me feel things tonight, young lady, I ain't felt in years. Moons. Things I … I just haven't felt, yeah, in … in years."

Ruby turned to Darkboy. Darkboy felt tongue-tied. Ruby didn't seem to mind, for she was thinking of Darkboy, how he looked, how he'd played the drums for her and made the music feel just right on the Bluelight bandstand.

"Dark … Darkboy …" he stuttered, coming from the back shadows to introduce himself. "Jimmy Darkboy Slade."

"Drummer, par excellence!" Long Ray said.

"I … I know," Ruby said.

And Darkboy realized it was the first time Ruby had spoken to anyone since introductions began.

"Thank you," she said.

"For what?"

"Fo' playing like you do."

Darkboy's heart played tag with itself. "You ... you made it easy, easy for me, Miss Midnight. Q-quite easy for me."

Darkboy looked around the bandstand. Long Ray, Loose Lips, and Pinky had joined Cool Hands at the bar. Bartender Bob was pouring drinks for the band. Darkboy glanced over to the table, just to his right. "We can sit ... if, if you'd like, Miss Midnight."

Ruby nodded.

Darkboy and Ruby had just gotten to the table when Long Ray came over and joined them.

"Ruby," Long Ray said, sliding the chair from under the table. "I looked up, and there you were." Long Ray squared his tall body off to Ruby's. "Like you came from out of the midnight. It was the damndest thing."

Ruby's mystery seemed to linger in the air.

Darkboy's discovery of her was identical to Long Ray's, so he understood, firsthand, Long Ray's confusion. On the Bluelight's bandstand, he had closed his eyes, then opened them, and what he saw was Ruby Midnight— and what he imagined was the end of a dream.

"Ruby, are you old enough to drink," Long Ray said.

The person had beady little eyes and a mousey physique and had darted, like a bullet, across the Bluelight floor in his cheesy suit and slick black hair, straight to Ruby's table. "Ruby, Ruby Midnight—now that's a name we ain't gonna have to change, now, are we, Ruby?"

Ruby's response was poor. Her confidence was gone.

"Zack Macketts. Zack Macketts is the name, Ruby, the owner of the Bluelight Café."

"Hel ... hel—"

"Nice to meet you, Ruby. Grand to make your ac-quaintance!" Zack Macketts stood at the back of Ruby's chair. "So if you'll come with me to my office, Ruby, we can talk some."

"Yes, yes, sir." Ruby, in her black dress, got up from the chair that Macketts was helping her with.

"My office is over there, Ruby," Macketts said, his hand at Ruby's back, strongly urging her forward, steering her toward the smoothly painted door. His head turned. "By the way, boys, nice job you done for me tonight." Macketts turned back to Ruby. "Ruby, Ruby Midnight—why I … I like it, Ruby. No. No. Ain't gonna have to change it a bit. Nothing, the name, Ruby. Nothing!"

And before the Windy Wind Five knew it, Zack Macketts and Ruby Midnight had vanished into Macketts's office.

"Sonuvabitch! Fucking sleaze ball!" Pinky slapped the top of the bar. "God made all things beautiful and pure so the devil comes along—"

"And take them away, Pinky," Long Ray said, disgusted.

"Steal them away, you mean. Take gold out of the earth. Plunder it, man," Cool Hands said. "Plunder it."

Ruby was facing Macketts's desk, but Zack Macketts was standing behind her, over her, painting pictures in the sky of sunrises and sunsets. "Ruby … Ruby, I can see it now …"

Ruby's body began to twist and turn in the seat, but Macketts's tiny hands quickly grabbed Ruby by her shoulders, recentering her. His hands flew back into action, back to painting wonderful pictures. "Ruby, how would you like to headline with the boys?"

Ruby said nothing; she just sat there in her poor dress, with nothing but black in it.

"Yes, yes, Ruby. I hear you saying yes, Ruby. Sure as I'm standing here. Yes. Yes." Macckett's eyes lit up. "And the money, Ruby." Macketts darted from behind Ruby to the front of her. "Don't worry about the money."

Ruby could see his beady little eyes clearly, the glint and glow in them, looking through her, beyond her—skimming mountaintops.

"It's how we all do business around here, the musicians and me, Ruby, my dear!" Macketts said.

Darkboy drank his scotch in silence. He wanted to protect Ruby. Already, he wanted to protect Ruby Midnight, build a castle around her in the sky. Keep her away from the world—the wolves devouring the world day by day, limb by limb. Long Ray and the rest of the band were talking, but he didn't hear them, not really. Usually, they'd be out of the club and on their way home. But not tonight. Ruby Midnight was in Zack Macketts's office, behind his door.

How long had she been in there? How long would she be in there? Not long—that was for sure. But she was in there, and once someone went in there, the same person never came out—not as the same person who entered.

The door opened.

Ruby came out of the office alone.

Darkboy saw her trying to smile her pretty smile, but it'd been besmirched, sullied, cheapened—set upon.

"Ruby, are … are you all right?" Long Ray said.

They took her by the arm to the table—the table where first Long Ray and then Darkboy had spotted her through the club's thick gray haze.

Ruby was shaking badly. "Drink, drink. I … I …"

"Here, here, Ruby," Pinky said, handing Ruby a glass of gin.

Ruby took the glass, drank it straight down, and wiped her mouth with the back of her hand. "May … may I …"

Pinky was back with a second glass of gin. Ruby drank it down the same as she'd drunk the first glass.

Saddened, Darkboy watched this.

When Ruby was through with the drink, she handed the glass back to Pinky, who stood near her. "Thank, thank you, Mr. Pinky, sir." Ruby smiled, and there was still some sweetness in her cheeks.

Darkboy was in love with Ruby Midnight as sure as God made little green apples.

"Where are you staying in Chicago? Y-you got a place to stay?" Loose Lips asked.

A pain struck Darkboy's heart. *Can't you see the cardboard suitcase hugging Ruby's leg, Loose Lips? Can't you see how Ruby's trying her best to hide it, man?* Darkboy thought, upset with Loose Lips at this really stupid question.

But Long Ray was quick to seize the moment, size up the situation, and get things back on track. "Ruby—hey, Ruby can stay with us, right, Darkboy?"

"Yes, right, Long Ray. Right."

"We've got a room for Ruby back at the apartment."

It was a humid night in Chicago as Long Ray, Ruby, and Darkboy stepped out of the Bluelight. Ruby walked between the two men. Long Ray wheeled his bass along the sidewalk with one hand and carried Ruby's suitcase with the other. Darkboy didn't seem to mind; he was lugging his drum kit.

While walking, Ruby suddenly looked back over her shoulder, back at the Bluelight Café in darkness. Long Ray pretended not to see this; Darkboy did the same.

All they talked about on the way to Long Ray's place was music—music, music, and more music—until it was shooting out their ears, as thick as wax.

Ruby laughed, and when she did, Darkboy felt as if sparkling rain was saturating him.

Long Ray was naming jazz musicians like crazy, as if he'd held a roll call. He knew this musician and that musician, who wrote which tunes, when and where, and which bands played them. Long Ray's brain was encyclopedic, full of facts and figures and dates he'd share with anyone who chose to listen.

As they drew nearer to the apartment, Darkboy's heart beat faster. He hoped, wished, and prayed that Ruby would like the apartment, even if he knew she came from very little, like all of them.

Long Ray stood back from the apartment door—in fact, he stared at it—and then cleared his throat. "Well … here we are, Ruby. Destination accomplished."

"Yes … yes, Long Ray."

"Now don't go crazy." Long Ray laughed.

"Try, try not to, Long Ray," Ruby said.

Ruby looked at Darkboy. Darkboy smiled.

Long Ray walked up to the door. "Okay, here goes!" Long Ray unlocked the door, swinging it open.

And Ruby liked the apartment—did she ever!

Darkboy's worries were quelled.

Long Ray put Ruby's suitcase down as Ruby looked around the place. That was when Darkboy vowed to himself that Ruby Midnight would have a new dress color to wear. (Oh, yes. *oh, yes!*) Ruby Midnight would be as special as Lena Horne; one day Ruby Midnight would be as special as her name.

"And *this* is your room, Ruby."

"M-mines, Long Ray?"

"Yes, Ruby, honey." Long Ray walked over to the bed. "The, uh … the mattress, well … it's a little lumpy," he grudgingly confessed. "But, uh, once you sleep on it for a while, settle in, you'll be able to smooth it out, I'm sure, just like … just like cream butter!"

Ruby giggled. Then she looked shyly at Darkboy, who was standing just outside the door. "What you think, Darkboy?"

"Uh … uh, about what, Miss … Miss Midnight?" Unexpectedly, there was a magnificent pretense in Darkboy, as if Ruby were a God-sent angel he was trying his darndest to impress. "Oh, those lumps?" Darkboy stepped into the room, authoritatively.

Long Ray muffled his laughter. He knew full well what Darkboy was up to with Ruby.

Darkboy walked directly over to the bed and firmly patted the mattress. "Oh, uh, these lumps?"

"Yeah, those, Darkboy, those."

"Why, uh, uh, Long Ray is … is quite right, Miss Midnight. Uh, once you sleep on them—the lumps, that is—uh, from night to night, that is, uh, yes, everything …" Darkboy's hand glided over the lumpy mattress. "Everything—the lumps and all, I mean—yes—they, uh, will smooth themselves out like cream butter, like, like Long Ray said, uh, uh, Miss Midnight."

It was 3:59 on the nose. Ruby lay on her lumpy mattress. "Miss Honey."

"God loves you, Ruby! God loves you, darlin'!"

Miss Honey was the first thing that came to Ruby's mind. The road had been long and hard, but now she was in Chicago. She'd wandered around. Wandered? She knew just how to wander in a town now; for her, it'd become an art—from town to town, city to city, back road to back road.

119

Had she thought about her parents, now that she'd been away from them for so long? Rarely. Did she think Millicent and Man Martinson had thought of her since she'd run from Plattstown? No.

"Darkboy," she whispered. Ruby didn't feel the lumps in the mattress; she only thought of how smoothly Darkboy's hand had glided across it and how smoothly Jimmy Darkboy Slade had played his drums behind her. It was all she'd heard when she sang—Darkboy's drums. *Darkboy is beautiful, like a girl*, Ruby thought. *Delicate eyes, delicate black skin. Darkboy is beautiful, like a girl.*

Since her departure from Rumble Way on the night she hid in Plattstown's darkness, stealing away in it from the ramshackle house, from Macguire's Baptist Church's weeded cemetery, she'd met men and had been in their company because of what and who she was, a jazz singer. But none had been so beautiful to look at as Darkboy. The drums were in him, in his skin. He was the jungle one minute—wild, exotic—and a summer night the next—sultry and warm.

Ruby rubbed her arms and thighs. She'd never had a pulse in her like this: hot, strong, sudden. What had happened to her? What had Jimmy Darkboy Slade done to her in one night of drumming in the Bluelight Café?

Ruby felt the first lump in the mattress. She laughed, while thinking back. How many worse beds had she slept on? How many bad floors? Somewhere off the side of the road? A barn? A railway car? Somewhere where the scare in her bones numbed her to sleep. Somewhere where she had to steal breakfast to make do for supper. Somewhere. Somewhere. Everywhere.

After two years of travel, Ruby felt as if she'd been no place good and every place bad.

And this night, she'd been led into a room by a short, pudgy white man who was trying to sell her the world. Mr. Macketts. Zack Macketts. He was going to pay her. He was the owner of the Bluelight Café–Mr. Zack Macketts. "Headline with the boys, Ruby," he'd said.

She'd felt Zack Macketts's hands in the air, up there, doing strange, weird things. Why look? Why? She already knew what his hands were signifying to her. She had to pay her dues; it's what jazz musicians said— how they talked. She'd heard it from town to town, from place to place.

He let her walk out the door on her own. He had nothing more to say to her—to do with her. Mr. Zack Macketts. She'd said yes. It was all he wanted her to say. It was all he wanted from her.

"Gonna sing in the Bluelight Café wit', wit' Long Ray an' Darkboy. It feel right. G-good."

Ruby thought through all the Windy Wind Five's names. And she liked the Bluelight Café's name. "The Bluelight Café. Oh, Miss Honey, ma'am."

The cardboard suitcase was open. Its articles had to be unpacked.

CHAPTER 15

Darkboy pulled up his socks. His eyes looked like two potholes in winter, only it was summer. *I must be quiet as a mouse*, Darkboy thought. *Quiet as a mouse nibbling on cheese.* "Who … who says I'm, I'm not being the fool?"

But Darkboy had to be quiet. Ruby was in the apartment. It was as if the Queen of Sheba had taken up residence. "Long Ray, I can hear you being quiet this morning too." Darkboy laced his shoes. He'd pressed his pants. He was going to look sharp, stay sharp—wear pressed pants every day. "Stand in front of the mirror all day if I have to."

Shhh, shhh, Darkboy reminded himself. *Ruby, Ruby's sleeping.* He didn't hear her behind the door. She had to be sleeping like a baby. *She should*, Darkboy thought. Last night was her night. She woke up the world. Now it was time for her to sleep—return to normal.

"Have to buy a mirror, though," he told himself. "A floor mirror. I-I mean it. I have to look at myself from top to bottom before I go to work, uh, from now on, man."

Long Ray stepped out the tiny bathroom, slipper-soft.

Darkboy and Long Ray gave one another the "hi" sign. Long Ray pointed to Ruby's door; then used his hand as if it were a pillow. *"Solid,"* Long Ray mouthed. *"Ruby's sleeping solid, Darkboy."*

They passed each other like proverbial ships passing in the night. Long Ray placed his ear to Ruby's door. *"Glad Ruby doesn't snore,"* Long Ray mouthed again.

Darkboy grinned and then thought, *I wouldn't mind it if Ruby Midnight snored; it'd probably sound like an evening breeze caressing the trees.*

Darkboy felt like washing a ton of dishes at the Mayflower with

Hambone that morning. He and Hambone were going to wash three thousand dishes between them, whether Hambone wanted to or not. *Who knows?* Darkboy thought. *It could be more—far exceed that modest number.*

Ruby was up and about in the apartment. When her eyes finally caught up with their ability to see again, Ruby saw the note on the kitchen table. It was from Long Ray.

> Ruby you from down the way so Darkboy and me know you know how to scratch you up a decent meal. Im leaving you this music to read through. Its something you might want to sing tonight at the Bluelight Cafe. The songs I been working on just needed to find the right singer to sing them thats all.

Ruby had informed Long Ray that she read music–she wasn't bragging at the time, mind you, just furnishing Long Ray with her résumé.

Ruby read through Long Ray's music and loved it. *This is great music Long Ray has composed*, Ruby thought. The music, the lyrics—they were woven perfectly together, in Ruby's humble opinion. And Ruby could read words much better now. She'd made it her business to improve her reading.

She picked up a new piece of sheet music and then paused. "I got to get me a job like Long Ray an' Darkboy."

Long Ray and Darkboy had mentioned their day jobs at the Mayflower Hotel to her. She wanted to do her share. "Got to get me a job. Mayflower Hotel sound like they hiring." Ruby giggled. "Sound like it to me. Ironing, domestics."

The apartment door opened at 5:06 p.m.

Darkboy saw Ruby was wearing the same black dress she'd worn last night. He knew it was the only dress Ruby owned. He knew, when the time came, Ruby Midnight was going to have a new dress to wear. He knew Ruby was going to have high-back shoes and was going to look like Lena Horne, or a chorus line, or the Cotton Club, or like Harlem at night, when folks said Harlem was all "dressed up."

"Hi, Long Ray … Darkboy."

"Hi, Ruby, darling," Both replied.

Darkboy ducked into his room.

"Ruby, did you see my note this morning, honey?"

"Yes, Long Ray."

"So … uh, what do you think?"

"They great, Long Ray. Great!"

Long Ray wiped his brow with tremendous vigor. "Ooo-wee! Looks like they passed their first acid test. Ooo-wee!"

"Who you speaking? Me, Long Ray?"

Long Ray hugged her. "Yes, young lady, you."

"I look them all through," Ruby said proudly.

"Every single one of them, Ruby? You hear that, Darkboy?" Long Ray was as excited as lightning in a bottle. "Ruby read through all the tunes, all of them!"

Darkboy came back into the room. "Miss … Miss Midnight did?"

"And Ruby liked them!"

"She really … really like them, Long Ray?"

"Yes, really, really liked them, Darkboy." Long Ray unloosed Ruby and headed straight for his bass.

"Want for me to sing them tonight, Long Ray?"

Long Ray half turned. "C-could you, Ruby?"

"That what you say in your note."

"Oh. Ha ha. I know. Ha. I-I did, didn't I?"

Darkboy wanted to say, *"Who are you trying to fool, Long Ray? Ruby's got your number, man."* But instead, he said, "We're going to turn some heads our way tonight, Long Ray. Looks like, wouldn't you say?"

"Yeah, Darkboy. Aren't we, though," Long Ray replied with much anticipation.

That night at the Bluelight, Ruby knocked the audience dead, singing Long Ray's songs.

Ruby brought the house down. And so the Windy Wind Five's love for Ruby rose even more since she'd made Long Ray so happy. Long Ray had cried in front of everybody—Joe Flowers, the gang of folks.

Ruby had sung so pretty that Pinky said she could flip a penny up to the moon, and it would come back down a dollar. "Too bad," he'd continued, "Ruby doesn't have a barrelful of pennies to flip because the Windy Wind Five would be rich by now!"

"Broke a string on my bass tonight, Darkboy!"

"What? I didn't notice. Your bass sounded the same to me."

"Man, you better stop with that jive. You know good and well you heard my bass string snap as loud as Pinky's pink suspenders."

Ruby came out of the Bluelight's ladies' room. Long Ray and Darkboy stood. Ruby was taken aback by the attention.

"For the queen," Long Ray said. "The Queen of Song." Long Ray took her hand. "Thanks again, Ruby."

Ruby looked over to Darkboy and then back to Long Ray. "They so easy to sing, Long Ray. They was wrote for a singer."

"But not just any singer. I was saving them for someone special like you," Long Ray said with great charm.

"Good night, Ruby," Loose Lips said as he passed by the table.

"Night, good night, Loose Lips," she said.

"Hell, what?" Long Ray said. "We don't rate, Loose Lips, me and Darkboy, all of a sudden?"

Long Ray and Darkboy were drinking scotch; Ruby, gin.

"Looks like it's about time to scoot, don't it, folks?" Long Ray asked as he drank what remained in his glass. Ditto for Darkboy and Ruby. "Helluva night, is all I can say. One helluva night!"

Long Ray could still hear his songs echoing in his head—the songs that Ruby had sung so splendidly.

Soon, Long Ray was rolling his bass away from the Bluelight Café.

Darkboy was saddled with his drum kit. And Ruby was walking as free as a bird.

Long Ray took account of Ruby. "Ain't you glad you ain't a bass player or drummer, Ruby?"

"Sure is, Long Ray," Ruby said, taking account of Long Ray's hint.

"You just have to carry yourself around town, and that's it. Your voice." Long Ray laughed.

"But your fingers don't get colds in them—not like singer's throats do," Darkboy countered.

"Correct, Darkboy," Long Ray agreed. "Never thought of that. Get many colds, Ruby?"

"No, Long Ray," Ruby said.

"Good blood?" Long Ray asked.

"That's what it is?" Darkboy asked.

"Must be, Darkboy. Must be," Long Ray said.

"Since you said it, huh, Long Ray?" Darkboy said.

The three laughed.

"Good night, one and all," Long Ray said emphatically, after placing the bass down on its side.

Ruby stood in the middle of the floor in shock since it was still early— at least for Long Ray.

"Going to my room and get some *real* sleep tonight. A few hours' worth." And into his room, Long Ray ducked.

"Does, does you know what happen, Darkboy?" Ruby finally asked.

Darkboy remained immobile, then said. "No, I, I don't Miss—"

"Why does you call me *Miss Midnight* an' not *Ruby*, like the others does, Darkboy?"

I do, don't I? Darkboy thought frantically. "May-maybe I'm afraid to call you anything else, Miss, uh, uh, Ruby." Darkboy sighed. "I-I'm sorry, Ruby."

"Y-you ain't gotta be, Darkboy."

"Well, I guess," Darkboy said, looking at his room door, "since Long Ray—"

"My name ain'ts Midnight, no way, Darkboy. Wasn' born wit'," Ruby said, fumbling with a button on her dress.

"It isn't?"

"Uh-uh." Ruby twirled as if she were a little girl in a mix of honey.

To Darkboy, it was sexy—really sexy.

"I give myself that name."

"Like my mama and daddy gave me the name Darkboy."

"My real name be Martinson," Ruby said forcibly, only to Darkboy, it was the first time he'd heard Ruby sound angry. "Ruby Martinson."

"Martinson to Midnight?"

Ruby stood directly in front of Darkboy; her body shadowed most of him. "I be singing in a place—"

"One of those places," Darkboy said. It was just the way Ruby said it, like it was a place Darkboy knew well too.

"Yes, Darkboy, one a them places. An' …"

"Yes, Ruby? Yes?"

"An' this man, this man stand an' say, while I be singing, 'Girl,' he say, 'sound like you come out the midnight.' Same way as Long Ray say, say, Darkboy. Same as Long Ray do."

"And you knew then?"

"Know then. I, yes, I does."

"Midnight. Miss Midnight, instead of Miss Ruby Martinson. Miss Ruby Midnight was born."

"Midnight—it prettier than Martinson. Way."

Darkboy could have said, *You're beautiful with any name, Ruby*, but he didn't.

"Was thinking at the time, Darkboy, a changing it."

"It's going to look good in lights, Ruby—great."

"Think so?"

"Just great."

"It don't gotta be."

Darkboy shook his head. "Uh … it doesn't have to be what?"

"In lights."

"You do know what I mean, don't you?" Darkboy wished he hadn't asked the question, as if Ruby was stupid or something.

"Star, Darkboy."

"Yes."

"You talkin' 'bout me a … a star. Don't gotta be, you know." Ruby was behaving like a young, awkward person again, someone who'd left Plattstown, pouting.

"But you will, Ruby, whether you want it or not. Your voice, your singing—it's not going to let you be anything else. Your talent."

Seconds later, Ruby yawned.

"I guess you're tired, Ruby, after tonight."

"A, a little."

"I guess it's catching—Long Ray first, then you." Darkboy yawned. "And now me."

"Good night, Darkboy."

"Good night, Ruby."

Long Ray heard the two bedroom doors—Ruby's and Darkboy's—close simultaneously. His stunt had worked. They had to find time alone in order to produce desirable results. "Both of them were in the front room a long time," Long Ray said to himself. He looked at the shaft of moonlight slicing through the window and then rolled onto his other side. "I just hope Darkboy stopped calling Ruby 'Miss Midnight.' He's changed his tune. Miss Midnight—even if Ruby's royalty, man."

Next morning

Ruby walked into the kitchen.

"What are you doing up this early, Ruby?" Long Ray asked. Before Ruby could answer, he said, "You're not supposed to be up with us. Right, Darkboy?"

"Uh, right, Long Ray," Darkboy agreed.

"Listen, Ruby, Darkboy and I have to get up early. But there's nothing for you to do but sleep in the morning, like a queen. Right, Darkboy?"

"Uh, right, Long Ray."

"So turn yourself around, and head back to your bed," Long Ray said.

Instead, Ruby stepped up to Long Ray as if she were the next in line at a Harlem rent party. "Gonna get me a day job this morning, Long Ray, at the Mayflower Hotel, where you an' Darkboy works. They hiring on over there. Know that for sure."

"Day job, Ruby? Mayflower Hotel? You?" Long Ray asked.

"Yes, yes, Long Ray."

"Hiring, are they?"

"Yes, Long Ray," Ruby said with a peachy but determined smile. "I dressed okay for a interview? Long Ray? Darkboy? Ain'ts I?"

"Yes, fine, uh, Ruby. Great," Darkboy said.

"Yeah, great, Ruby, like Darkboy said," Long Ray told her. "Except you're not going with us to the Mayflower this morning. No way. Or any morning for that matter."

"Why, Long Ray?" she asked.

"Why, because you're a star, Ruby. A born star. Me and Darkboy, we'll take care of things around here. Right, Darkboy?"

"Right, Long Ray!"

"See, Ruby?"

"B-but ..."

"Things are going to be different for you than anywhere else you've been till now," Long Ray said. "Lord, God, Jesus—there's not going to be any clawing and, and scratching in Chicago for you. Not in this town. Maybe some place else, honey, but not here in Chicago with us."

Darkboy's eyes were intense, like Long Ray's.

"But I work all my life at somtin', Long Ray," Ruby argued. "D-don't stop doing that."

"We know that, Ruby. Hell, don't we? But you're a jazz singer now. Why, those folk, man, at the Bluelight the past two nights, told you that, honey. You're in our hands now," Long Ray said. "The Windy Wind Five's."

Ruby was deeply touched.

"So back to bed you go, Ruby!" Long Ray said.

But Ruby wasn't through. "I make breakfast for you an' Darkboy in the morning, then."

"That's out the question. Darkboy and I have managed up to now. Been doing just fine in the breakfast department, right, Darkboy? Now," Long Ray said sternly, "you're going to make Darkboy and me late for work if you don't drop the subject, immediately—if not sooner."

And with that settled, Long Ray deliberately sped like a bullet out of the kitchen.

Ruby stood over by the stove, flummoxed. "What I s'pose to do all day, Darkboy, while you an' Long Ray gone? I ain'ts never have time on my hands 'fore."

"Relax, Ruby, I-I guess you should just relax before your life gets too hectic."

"Hec, hec …"

"Busy, Ruby. Busy."

"You smart wit' them words, Darkboy."

"Ruby, you will be too, one day."

"Wanna be, Darkboy. Do." Ruby's body slumped. "Wanna be so bad. Be smart wit' them words one day."

Darkboy felt her frustration. "You know, I better take off. Long Ray's probably two blocks up the street by now. You know, with his long legs and all."

"Least, Darkboy."

"Well, see you, uh, this afternoon."

"Gonna study Long Ray songs all day. Do better than what I does them last night."

Darkboy made his way out of the apartment to catch up with Long Ray and his long legs, but he said to himself as he headed down the hallway and then the stairs, "How could you, Ruby? How in the world could you possibly sound any better than what you did last night at the Bluelight? Would you care to explain that one for me, please?"

CHAPTER 16

The Windy Wind Five had been knocking them dead in Chicago.

Ruby Midnight had been knocking them dead in Chicago.

Ruby was going on her tenth week at the Bluelight Café. She ruled Chicago's Southside like she was Al Capone, with a voice instead of a tommy gun. And Chicago's musicians and singers had been flocking in droves to listen and learn from Ruby Midnight and the Windy Wind Five–both so much at the top of their games.

Music critics wrote about Ruby in those Chicago newspapers, like Walter Winchell gossiped. It seemed all of Chicago's music critics had been coming to the Bluelight to hear a star being born right in their midst. And all of them seemed hell-bent on thinking (quite naturally) that they had the skinny on her, Miss Ruby Midnight, this unparalleled jazz diva. This rising star, this sensation, was gaining broader and broader attention and appeal by the minute.

> Miss Ruby Midnight sings like no other jazz singer alive.
>
> Miss Midnight can sing a man and woman's lifetime in one single, tormented note.
>
> A gem of a Negro girl, who soon will own the jazz world. Gosh ... what a *dame*!
>
> Miss Ruby Midnight is the hottest thing to hit Chicago since the great Chicago Fire of 1869.

Miss Ruby Midnight has made this music critic a true believer that there's a she-devil in Chicago and that she sings the blues nightly at the Bluelight Café!

And was Ruby ever singing the blues. So Hambone Hamilton dropped by the Bluelight to see for himself just what all the rage in Chicago was about. And Hambone told Darkboy the next morning, while washing a few stacks of dirty dishes in the Mayflower dungeon, that last night he'd sweat through at least five handkerchiefs!

In fact, Hambone told Darkboy that this girl, Miss Ruby Midnight, reminded him a great deal of an old jazz singer who'd had quite a successful career, who went by the name of Honey Gillette. Darkboy was acquainted with Honey Gillette's recordings.

"Ask Ruby if she's heard of her," Hambone said, "and then get back to me."

But Darkboy forgot to ask Ruby, and Hambone's memory proved to be about as faulty and trustworthy as Darkboy's. Miss Honey's name, therefore, never came under discussion between Ruby and Darkboy.

It was just Darkboy and Pinky at the club's long bar. Bartender Bob poured their liquor in the glasses.

"Who said, 'Loose lips sink ships'?" Pinky asked. "Who said that? It's what I told the cat, Darkboy. I don't get up in nobody's business but my own. Shit. So the cat, he was selling his Fuller brushes at the wrong damned door for sure!" Pinky snapped his suspenders and then edged up to Darkboy's shoulder, as if he was testing his breath. "Darkboy, you been seeing what I been seeing? Lately? What's been flying around here in the club?"

Darkboy checked out the joint and then answered, with mild mystery striding through his voice. "Around here? No, I haven't, Pinky. What?"

"Ain't noticed, Darkboy? What? You haven't got a clue?"

"No, I said I—"

"A bug? Not even?" Pinky asked.

"Really, I don't. I'm as blind as—"

"A freaking bat!"

"Okay, okay—blind as a freaking bat!"

"You see them cats lining up, don't you?"

"Them cats? What cats lining up? Where? Down at the race track? At … at, uh, Little Al's Betting Parlor? Where, just where, Pinky?"

Pinky shook his head in total disgust. "No, Darkboy. No. Here, right here, on this fucking plot of green earth in the Bluelight." Pinky half smiled. "They're lining up in front of Ruby's door, Darkboy. Ruby's freaking door, man!"

Pinky had sounded the alarm. Darkboy's face turned green. No, Darkboy wasn't as blind as a bat, not at all. He'd seen those stage-door Johnnies (as they were called) as well as everyone else. He'd seen them. Damn-tooting!

"I don't mean to hit you with bad news, Darkboy, but—"

"No … no," Darkboy said, trying to shrug off the whole thing as nonchalantly as if it were a fly buzzing his shoulder, "I thought you were talking about something else. You, yes, you caught me off guard, com-completely, I guess."

Pinky leaned away from Darkboy's face.

The next few seconds dragged on for Darkboy.

"Lookit, I know you got you a sweet tooth for Ruby." Already, Pinky's words were sailing at Darkboy as if they were on a collision course. "Gosh, man, who doesn't know that? But lookit, listen, shit—you better hurry and put your order in, put your postage stamp on the girl. Do that, especially since them Sugar Daddies I'm referring to are beginning to form a long—I mean a *long*—line at Ruby's door with them boxes of roses and sweet dark chocolate candies, man. Dig what I'm saying? Hepping you to?" Pinky patted Darkboy's back. "So I'm just tugging your pant leg on it. Tugging it hard, man. *Real* hard for you."

And so Darkboy knew the band—every single one of them—knew how he felt about Ruby Midnight. How in the world could he hide it? They heard it in his drums too. No longer did they hear Chick Webb in his drumsticks when it was Ruby Midnight.

Ruby Midnight.

Pinky's hand fell away from Darkboy's back. "So did I hit you too low below the belt with this, Darkboy? Because if I did, man, I'm sorry."

"No. No, Pinky."

Pinky drew Darkboy to him in a fatherly fashion. "Been there, you see. Down that sunlit road. It ain't easy to navigate. Gets …well, it ain't at all easy. But it's worth it in the end. Man," Pinky said, shaking his head. "Every night you can't sleep, it's worth it. Don't let nobody tell you different. Love's worth everything you got in you."

"You think I'm in love, Pinky?"

Mischievously, Pinky's hand felt Darkboy's forehead for its temperature. "Shit, ha ha, you got all the known symptoms of a lovesick cat. Damn, man!"

Darkboy laughed. "Never felt this way before," he said, removing Pinky's hand. Darkboy had to admit his head had felt like it was running a high temperature.

Pinky's face turned serious again. "Uh, you've laid with girls?"

"Yes."

"A lot?"

"Enough."

"Umm … right, right. You enjoy it? Sex?"

"Pinky, come on, man." Darkboy shrugged his shoulders in macho fashion. "Of course I enjoy it."

"But not as much you're going to with Ruby, the first time you lay down with her. Uh-uh. None of it's gonna be sweeter, as sweet as it's gonna be with that young lady. Shit, no. Ha ha."

To say Darkboy was surprised by Pinky's comment would be like saying he would be surprised to see a green elephant in a champagne glass (not unless he was drunk, wrecked totally).

"Yeah, Darkboy, speaking from experience—and don't worry; I've had plenty—there ain't nothing like the 'real thing,' baby—and I ain't pulling your freaking leg neither, Josephine!"

Darkboy began walking over this new ground that'd just opened to him as if land mines were hidden at every turn.

"Why don't—haven't you hit on Ruby? It's what the whole band's been asking. Long Ray, included."

Darkboy's eyes squinted. "Daren't, Pinky. That wouldn't be right. Proper decorum."

"Decorum! Proper—the hell with proper decorum. We're talking about love, man. Love. *L-o-v-e!*"

"Thanks, thanks for everybody else's concern," Darkboy said sarcastically, "but I can handle things."

"Up to now, you ain't. Look, man, them Sugar Daddies are lining up at—"

"Pinky, dump it, dump it, would you? I don't care how much you mean well for Ruby and me. I got principles, standards."

"Principles, standards—you gotta toss them out the window when it comes to love. You gotta."

"Ruby lives in the same apartment with Long Ray and me. It, well, it wouldn't be right, Pinky. All wrong, in fact."

"Right, wrong … okay, okay, damn, man. Have it your way. Shit. Stick to your—what? Your damned principles, as you call them, man." Pinky slid his left hand down in his pant pocket, then yanked it out. "Hell, what a young boy like you know about principles anyway?" Pinky chuckled. "Okay, okay, Darkboy, I'll get off your toes." Pinky's voice mellowed out. "I just don't want you to lose her. You understand what I'm saying, where the hell I'm coming from and getting at? Not a young lady like Ruby. You understand what I'm imparting to you, Darkboy? Advice I'm handing down to you, as an older man?"

"Don't worry, Pinky. I'm not going to let it happen. I'm not going to lose her."

Pinky picked up his drink and walked halfway across the club's floor. He turned around to Darkboy. "You know how many stars there are in the sky, Darkboy? Shit, ever count them?" Pinky's eyes shot upward.

"No," Darkboy replied, thinking Pinky's question ludicrous. Really, really ridiculous. Without merit.

"Neither have I. Neither have I … not once," Pinky said, lowering his eyes. "But I know I can tell you when the sky's missing one."

Darkboy was in the Bluelight's bathroom, pretending he was using it, but he really was there to range through thorny thoughts. It was what he did, currently, trying to get the helicopter in the air to land down somewhere safe.

"Sweet tooth? Sugar Daddies?" Darkboy spoke to himself in the bathroom mirror. "Stage-door Johnnies?" Darkboy scoffed. "I ain't jealous." He seemed to boast to the mirror. "I've always had a sweet tooth for the ladies. Always." Darkboy bopped his head with defiance. "I'm just shy with Ruby; that's all. I know she means something more, far more to me than running through a sweet rush of words."

But the Sugar Daddies were real, and the stage-door Johnnies were too. All of it was real, happening in real time. Happening before his very eyes. But nightly, he and Ruby said things to each other through the music, didn't they?

Darkboy swung around excitably. "My drumsticks, and bass drum, and snare drum, and cymbals, and top hat, and tom-toms, and sock, and trap drums have been telling her from the time I first saw her." Darkboy fidgeted. "But how am I going to work out this tricky situation?" Darkboy stepped away from the mirror. "How does Ruby feel—really feel—about me?"

Darkboy began washing his hands in the sink, even though there'd been no need. And then his system was jarred for a second time. "Make … make love to Ruby? To Ruby Midnight?"

The thought alone petrified him.

Hurriedly, Darkboy wiped his hands with whatever was available. Now he wished he'd spit those words out of his mouth before using them and out of his mind before thinking them. He hadn't even held her hand or looked into her eyes.

Make love? To Ruby Midnight?

He'd not made love to a woman he loved. He'd not done that. Pinky made it sound so special. Would it be like that—as special as Pinky made it sound—to make love to a woman he loved?

Chick Webb played his drums that way; it was something he loved, his drums. But this was a woman he was talking about, not a drum set.

"I'm a young Louisiana farm boy. I guess I'm young and wet behind the ears when it comes to love. When it comes to the real thing." Darkboy wrung his hands as if he were wringing water out of the sea. "But if I ever make love to Ruby, this … this Louisiana farm boy, watch out. Yeah, man, watch out."

Darkboy did an imaginary drum roll with his rubbery wrists. "Sparks are going to fly!" And now he'd considered the thought of making love to Ruby and had spoken the words, but, actually, for now, all Darkboy wanted to do was hold Ruby's hand and look as far down into her eyes as possible.

Yes, Darkboy thought that would be awfully special for him for now.

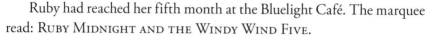

Ruby had reached her fifth month at the Bluelight Café. The marquee read: Ruby Midnight and the Windy Wind Five.

Ruby didn't cotton to the top billing, not at all, but it didn't bother the band, not at all. It'd known worse, far worse. Long Ray, when he first saw what Zack Macketts had done, summed it up for the band as best he could: "It doesn't matter who's on top, Ruby, as long as the music gets played, honey." This was Long Ray's take on the situation.

Through her musical association with the band, Ruby was singing better and better. And another thing: Long Ray's apartment now had three of Ruby's show wigs in it and six new store-bought evening dresses. Ruby's cardboard suitcase, the one she'd been carrying with her since she'd run from Plattstown, was to be put out in the apartment's back alley tomorrow night. Ruby just hoped, in her heart of hearts, that some lucky hobo might come around, for he could maybe cut a good pair of shoes from it.

Ruby and Darkboy talked a lot, just between themselves. Long Ray had gotten into the habit of walking in front of them, rolling his bass, when they left the club.

Ruby and Darkboy seemed to be two entities, lingering behind Long Ray. Long Ray's shadow never encroached on theirs; it didn't come close.

Long Ray held a bottle of champagne in his hand and poured it into six champagne glasses before the band's rehearsal. "I feel like a father who's just given birth to twins!"

"You change diapers, Long Ray?" Pinky asked.

"Never mind, Pinky!" Long Ray said, turning his attention to Ruby. "Ruby, stand!"

Ruby stood.

"Ruby, sit. I know how you are, honey, when it comes to these things." Long Ray laughed uproariously.

Ruby sat.

"Okay, all you cats can stand and bow or whatever you care to do in front of Ruby. Because we owe all of this to her. Our dear Ruby."

The band stood and bowed to Ruby, who laughed extravagantly.

"As for me, Long Ray," Pinky said, "I'd like to make a toast—"

"Later, Pinky. First things first."

"But—"

"Ruby," Long Ray began, "this is your day as much as ours. Now don't say nothing, anything, honey, because you are the one who made all of this possible. It's called 'star power.' Remember those words because you've got it—loads of it." Long Ray put his foot up on a chair. "They didn't want to hear our name unless they heard yours first. Am I right, Loose Lips?"

"You bet," Loose Lips agreed. "Yes indeedy. You're dead right on that!"

"You put the Windy Wind Five on the road, and we're grateful to you, honey, for that. You walked into our lives at the right time, like a black angel sent from … to us from God. And you put us back on the road. Back out into the world again. We missed it. I think I can speak for all of us. No matter how bad we used to complain about the travel when we played for other outfits, combos, we missed it. Missed the hell out of it. It hasn't been easy, Ruby."

Ruby felt terrific.

"So we're toasting you today. You're a very special young lady. Besides being the greatest jazz vocalist God ever created, you're a decent human being. So, fellas, here's to Ruby!"

"Here's to Ruby!" they all chorused.

They waited for Ruby to drink her champagne, and then they drank theirs.

"Now, Pinky," Long Ray said, "what was it you wanted to say?"

"Say … hell, Long Ray. Why, we're out of damned champagne! What the hell's there left to toast!"

Darkboy was on his way in from the Mayflower. They'd agreed to hold his dishwashing job open for however long he was on the road with the band.

Darkboy was carrying a cake in a bag. Hambone had baked it; it looked lopsided. *Ruby is great, isn't she?* Darkboy thought. The band owed her everything. Star power—Ruby had it in spades! Everyone, all the Chicago clubs, were trying to get her into their clubs to sing, but Ruby wouldn't sing with any other band but the Windy Wind Five—that was how all of this good fortune had evolved for the band. Ruby told any inquiry made to her that she wasn't going anywhere without the Windy Wind Five as her backup band.

Long Ray told her to forget about the band, them, their ambitions, and think only of her career, but Ruby stood her ground, wouldn't budge, moved nary an inch. Finally, Long Ray threw in the towel. He knew he was up against someone who was as stubborn as an Arkansas mule, so he mildly surrendered.

This was going to be a great experience for all of them. They got along like family. And even Darkboy had to think there weren't many bands in the land as good as theirs. They really made great music.

Sweet music.

Ruby was as nervous as nervous can get. From the Bluelight Café to …? She messed with her show wig, teasing it. She got up and opened the bedroom closet. *Dresses*, she thought. *Dresses. Who would've believed?*

It was happening too fast, and it had begun to frighten her. The pressure, at times, was unbelievable. It was a good thing she had the band and Darkboy for support. She'd be lost without them, badly. She had no idea how to do this, to be a star without them. How had Miss Honey done it? Who had guided her? Who took Miss Honey by the hand and led her? *Miss Honey.*

Ruby looked at the wig and then laughed out loud. Miss Honey and her wigs. How she wore them wigs, whenever she performed.

A headliner.

She was a headliner. She was going to a new town, leading a band. But she was a singer, a jazz vocalist. She couldn't lead a flea to pee. It's how she felt, no matter how disgusting it sounded. It's how she felt; she couldn't lead a flea to pee.

She began crying. "I … I ain't not'in. I ain't not'in. You hear me? I ain't not'in!"

Darkboy entered the apartment alone—Long Ray had stopped off at the cleaners—and looked around. Usually, when he and Long Ray got home, Ruby was there in the front room, poring over music. Today, she wasn't. Darkboy was disappointed. Ruby's bedroom door was closed.

He was about to go into the kitchen when he heard sobbing. *It's Ruby.* He gently tapped on her door and called, "Ru-Ruby?"

"T-that you, Darkboy?"

"Yes."

There was a moment of silence before she said, "I'm all … all right."

She knows I heard her, Darkboy thought. "Ruby, are you sure?"

"Yes. Am."

"Okay." Darkboy decided not to take it a step further.

"You … you can come in, Darkboy, if … if you like. I'm decent an' … an' all."

Ruby's door opened, and Darkboy walked into her bedroom. Ruby was on her lumpy bed.

"Things at the hotel go all right for you, Darkboy?"

Darkboy felt foolish, standing there with the cake, even if it was in a brown bag. He was surprised Ruby hadn't asked him about its contents.

Ruby did look at the bag, but then her eyes turned into the wall. "Been cryin'. Ain't shamed to say so."

Darkboy was looking for relief, so he put the cake on the floor. "We don't have to go, Ruby. The band. We can forget about it. We—"

"Will they like me, Darkboy? They, they gonna like me?"

"Everybody does. When you sing. Everybody."

"At the Bluelight …"

"I'm nervous," Darkboy said.

"'Bout your drummin'? That?"

"Yes."

"You don't show so. Why don't you show so?"

"Ha. I don't know. Maybe I'm too scared to," Darkboy said shakily.

"Scared—that be funny, Darkboy. Too scared to be scared."

Darkboy laughed. "I know. But maybe it's how to explain it. For myself, it is, at least."

Ruby looked away from him. "I ain'ts a star, Darkboy. I ain'ts what they make me out to be. S-saying I is. I … I can barely talk good."

"But you're getting better, Ruby. I mean, much better."

Ruby's eyes continued to stare into the wall.

"Ruby, you are what you are."

"I … I doesn' un-understand, Darkboy."

"Heck, Ruby, I don't know what I'm saying. I'm trying to sound smart, in-intelligent, wise and all, but—"

"When you get old, Darkboy? When that happen for you?"

"Darn't Ruby. I don't know. I don't know the answer to any of this— what we're going through and why we're going through it, not on my life."

"Darkboy, y-you doesn'?"

"What? You thought I did?"

"Ha ha. Uh-huh, a little."

"What, this much?" Darkboy asked, pinching his fingers apart so that a pinch of salt could sift through.

"Uh-huh, least that much."

Darkboy increased the margin. "I've got to give myself a little more credit than that."

"How you talk so good, Darkboy?"

"Read and listen, like you. You're doing now."

"Fast. Do it come fast, your learning, the way you speak?"

"Ruby, you know what?" Darkboy said, as if looking for a needle in a haystack. "I don't even remember. I can't, just can't recall right now."

"It what I wants for me so bad. To talk good. To talk smart—po-polite." Most of Ruby's tears had cleared her face. "Feel better. Does."

Darkboy loved her. Oh, how he loved Ruby Midnight! This singer of songs, so young—yet so much a woman, so certain of her inherent sexuality.

"Darkboy, what you got there on the floor?"

"Cake!" Darkboy reached for the bag. "Hambone baked it for me. It's a going-away present from Hambone to us."

"Gonna cut me a slice? Of your cake—for me?"

Her voice is this sexy thing, Darkboy thought. She was putting this thing in him, sweeter; had to be sweeter than Hambone's chocolate cake in the bag.

"What kind, Darkboy?"

"Chocolate. Dark chocolate."

"Mmm …"

Already, Darkboy could taste the dark-chocolate cake. He wanted to take Ruby's hand and lead her off to the kitchen to cut her a slice of cake, but he thought better. *Decorum, Darkboy, decorum,* he reminded himself. "Ruby, you want yours now, before dinner?"

Long Ray barged through the front door, full steam ahead, carrying his cleaning. "Man, Mr. Clarence's Cleaners cleaned my suit like new. Got rid of all them grease spots. Hallelujah!" He looked at Ruby, then at Darkboy, with his cake, his forward-lean pointing toward the kitchen.

"Hambone's cake is gonna have to wait," Long Ray said. "I'm cooking tonight!" Long Ray had just sabotaged Hambone's chocolate cake. "Just listen for the downbeat, kids. When I call you for dinner!"

CHAPTER 17

The sun was high in the sky.

"Now, look here, folks, this ain't no luxury liner heading for France. Just a small bus with us on it!"

"Sam Waters put gas in it!"

"Pinky, something like that *would* come from you."

"Don't want it running out of gas halfway down the road, especially not a dark, deserted country road, Long Ray. Who knows what's out there, moving on them at midnight?" Pinky sat in his seat, flooding the world in pink. "The Windy Wind Five's got enough on its mind without having to worry about a bus running outta gas halfway down the road. Damn, and us pushing it."

The bus was an old, short, snub-nosed yellow school bus. Sam Waters rented them out for all occasions. The Windy Wind Five had rented one for its two-city tour: Kansas City and Saint Louis, Missouri (or bust!) and then back home to Chicago (or bust!). The instruments (drums, bass, and trumpet and sax cases) were nestled on the bus's rear seat, safe and sound.

"If you sleep on the bus," Long Ray said from the middle aisle, "please don't snore—at least not unless it's in case of an emergency. We'd like this two-city tour we are embarking on to be as—"

"Where do we pee, Long Ray?" Pinky interrupted.

"Hey, Pinky, Pinky, R-Ruby. Ruby," Cool Hands cautioned Pinky. "You've got to show better respect than what you already have for Ruby, man."

Pinky's head turned to Ruby. "Oh, sorry, Ruby—but, uh, Long Ray, where do we urinate, man?"

143

"Off the road," Long Ray said, embarrassed. "Off the road, okay?"

Ruby giggled.

"In the bushes," Loose Lips added.

"Figured. Once we get down the way, okay. That redneck cracker ain't gonna let us do nothing but pee in his damned bushes. Help them grow."

Ruby was sitting next to Cool Hands. Cool Hands seemed proud of this fact—that Long Ray had designated him as Ruby's seat mate on the long trip, as if he were her official chaperone, even if none of the band, of course, would dare lay a hand on her.

Cool Hands smiled at Ruby, and Ruby smiled back.

"Okay, here goes …" Long Ray said.

Long Ray was the driver. He sat behind the steering wheel. It wasn't that he'd given up his night job as bandleader; Long Ray was wearing a variety of hats on this trip to Kansas City, Missouri. "'Show me state'— Kansas City—here we come!"

"Ain't saying Kansas City," Pinky grumbled, "until we get outta Chicago first. Not in Sam Waters's big bucket of bolts."

Later into the trip

It was dark outside. Something, whatever it was, had been whistling in the dark on this deserted patch of road for the past mile and a half. At least, that's what Long Ray had heard. Sure, someone on the bus was snoring like a log, one of the Windy Wind Five, but it wasn't that. Uh-uh.

Pinky sat at the window seat, with Loose Lips next to him. Loose Lips had to stand for Pinky to step into the aisle.

"Not again," Loose lips groaned. "What'd you have for breakfast this morning, Pinky, a gallon of orange juice? Man, your kidneys must be shot. What? You can't hold your pee in anymore?"

"Just stop the bus, Long Ray. Brake it!"

"For the nineteenth time!" Loose Lips grumbled.

"Yeah, Loose Lips, for the nineteenth freaking time!"

"Pinky," Long Ray said, smiling in the dark, "I've been, uh, hearing something for the past mile or so, following us down the road. Whistling in the trees."

"Woo!" Loose Lips said.

"Woo—hell. Whatever it is, it ain't got a chance in hell. I'll drown the sucker!"

"And be sure you wash your hands, man, when you're finished," Loose Lips said.

Pinky grumbled and was off on the side of the road, doing his roadside business in the bushes.

Long Ray had something in mind.

Pinky boarded the bus, zipping his pants. "Ah, relief. Killed a batch of worms. Shot them suckers dead."

Long Ray was standing in the middle of the bus aisle. "Lookit, everyone, since we're here and have covered a lot of ground in one day, we might as well just spend the night."

"Here?" Pinky said.

"Here," Long Ray said.

"Gee, Long Ray, ain't you got a lot of class."

"Let the man do this job, Pinky," Cool Hands said.

"Cool Hands is right," Loose Lips said. "Long Ray calls the shots, not—"

"I mean, it is safe, isn't it, Pinky? Am I mistaken, or was it you who just said you just killed a batch of worms out there?" Long Ray's grin gleamed. "So, uh, what do you say, Darkboy? Ruby?"

"Uh, it's between you and Pinky, uh, Long Ray," Darkboy said.

"H-how I feel too, Long Ray. Same as Darkboy do," Ruby said.

"At least the toilet's located right outside the door. Right? In case Pinky has to go again. I don't think we can top that for convenience," Long Ray said.

Long Ray parked the bus on the shoulder of a dark road that looked about as deserted as the garden of Eden. A yellow bus couldn't hide in the dark—even if Sam Waters's bus was more dingy than yellow.

"Darkboy, am I exhausted," Long Ray said in a light voice.

Darkboy snuggled his head in his pillow. "Haven't touched my drums all day."

"Ditto me and my bass."

"Feels funny. Odd, though," Darkboy said.

"Sure does. You know, we're gonna play up a storm once we hit Kansas City. Take the bumps and grinds of the road—this trip—out on our axes."

"I'm going to play pretty, Long Ray."

"Now, you know I'm not going to put a hurt on my bass. Not that! I think this is going to be the start of something big, though," Long Ray whispered into Darkboy's ear.

"T-think so? Y-you mean with Ruby, uh, don't you?"

"Yes. Uh, right. We're as talented as hell, Darkboy, but it's all about timing in this music business."

"And luck, uh, right?"

"Been at this a long time. This music, man; have I ever. Don't, don't want to say Ruby's our meal ticket to fame, better days, 'cause that's not what I mean. But I-I've been waiting a long time, Darkboy. Given up a lot of stuff in my life—wife, family, even friends. Not that I'm complaining, just keeping the scoreboard from cheating me out of my hits and runs. At bats. But Ruby's the big time. We know that. With that voice. She ain't about back roads and beat-up buses rented from Sam Waters off his car lot. Us sleeping out on the shoulder of a road out in no-man's-land in the middle of the night. That … that no one could find if they tried. Put it on a map. Circle the damned thing in red ink." Long Ray chuckled and lay his head comfortably back on his pillow. "She's about other places, Darkboy. Faraway places I used to dream of. Where the day never became night, and the night never became day—and the stars, well, they never knew the difference. You know, Darkboy, where Satchmo played."

Darkboy chuckled.

"And, and Ruby's singing my songs, Darkboy. *My* songs, man. Hell. The songs I wrote. Imagine that good fortune."

"It is a dream come true."

"Could stretch it to heaven, like saltwater taffy."

"I wonder how Ruby's taking to the trip so far," Darkboy mused.

"What? You mean you haven't talked to her?"

"Uh, no, not really. Not with Cool Hands guarding her, so far, like Fort Knox."

"Yeah it seems that way," Long Ray said, cracking up. "Cool Hands is taking his job seriously."

"Too seriously, if you ask me."

"Don't worry, Darkboy. There's going to be time for you and Ruby on this two-city tour, man."

"There … there. What do you mean by that?"

"Out of the twelve days on tour, we've got two days off between the two gigs. So we can lay over one day in Kansas City, and then swing into Saint Louis the following day."

Darkboy got Long Ray's drift.

"So don't worry," Long Ray said. "I'll find something else to occupy Cool Hands's time. Take the cat completely off the case. That's what a good bandleader on the road's all about."

"Right, Long Ray," Darkboy said, convinced.

Long Ray turned to Darkboy; Darkboy heard him in the dark. "You two deserve time together. You know, I know what's going on. It's no secret to my ears."

"Well, to be honest, Long Ray, Pinky and I did discuss the matter a … a few days ago in the Bluelight—you and the band picking up on, on Ruby and me. Not that I mind or really care."

"She's what you're dreaming about now, what's sticking to your dreams."

"Every night and every day, Long Ray."

"Kansas City ain't far off—at least according to my map," Long Ray teased. "Uh, by the way, Darkboy, want to help me with the driving tomorrow? I need a helping hand. You *do* know how to drive, don't you?"

"Tractors. You know I'm a farm boy, like you. Had plenty of practice driving tractors back home."

Long Ray didn't respond, for he'd shut his eyes, and now his breathing was near a snore.

Darkboy shut his eyes. *How's Ruby doing?* he wondered.

And he thought it again—then, nonstop.

Ruby was wide awake, even if her eyes were closed as if she'd gone off to dreamland. But she hadn't. Ruby was rooted in the now of things; all she could think about was Darkboy. She missed him today. It wasn't like when he went off to the Mayflower Hotel in the morning and came back in the evening. Today, Darkboy was on the bus with her, but she had little access to him. He was out of reach of her, in a way. She'd hoped for more on this trip to Kansas City.

Whose fault was it? Hers, his, nobody's? She thought Long Ray would maybe let Darkboy sit next to her on the bus. Why hadn't he? What was wrong? Why Cool Hands?

Cool Hands breathed lightly at her side, no heavier than air, but it traveled through Ruby's ear as if she could hear oceans rise and fall. She'd heard about oceans, read about them. One day she wanted to cross an ocean, a body of water, with Darkboy.

It sounded so romantic, something suddenly so real and set in her mind. Who understood her more than Darkboy? Who understood her silly thoughts more than him? She was learning from books, from spoken words, gaining more confidence to become what the world wanted of her.

But who understood her more than Darkboy?

She stopped listening to Cool Hands's breathing. Her eyes opened. "Darkboy."

Ruby hoped tomorrow would be much different than today for her and Darkboy. She wasn't quite ready to fall asleep. She didn't have to dream about anything when her dream was right in front of her, right down the aisle, off to the right, right next to Long Ray, who was asleep and could be heard loud and clear.

Smoke? Smoke? Who was the one who said the Bluelight Café contained all the universe's smoke? Now, the Hey-Hey Club, *it* had smoke. Billows and billows of the gray, thick stuff. It was as if it had rolled out of a roaring canyon. And so, that would be a great question to posit: Why do jazz clubs have to have so much damn smoke in them, as if by mandate or by some preposterous jazz requisite?

And whose smoke curled and intertwined effortlessly with all the other smoke, meshing as one, sedately, in the historic black club? None other than Long Ray, who was dashing the cigarette into an ashtray at the gorgeously carved, curved oak bar of great repute.

Long Ray made an about-face. He wasn't far from where Ruby was in the back of the club, applying her makeup for tonight's long-awaited performance.

Ruby looked into a vanity mirror, applying eyeliner. Her hand was steady, but her stomach felt like a nest of vipers. *It's fast approaching*, Ruby thought. Soon she would be on the Hey-Hey stage. She was thinking of the words, the music, this and that, the Hey-Hey crowd. She wanted to be liked. She wanted the Hey-Hey Club to like her. How much did it know about the Chicago critics and what they wrote about her? "She-devil singing nightly at the Bluelight Café." "Girl singing sensation."

But all if it meant nothing? Immediately, she had realized this. Tonight was all that mattered—what the Hey-Hey's customers felt. What they thought of her and her singing.

"Long Ray," Ruby said suddenly, surprised. She dropped the eyeliner pencil. It fell to the floor.

Long Ray bent over to pick up the eyeliner pencil. "Here, honey. You're nervous as all get-out."

"Yes, Long Ray, I is." Ruby turned back to the mirror, looking blankly into it.

"Ruby, you'll do fine, just fine tonight on stage in front of this Kansas City crowd. There's no difference between the Bluelight and the Hey-Hey Club. It's just the Hey-Hey Club, honey, has more smoke." Long Ray laughed.

"It do, Long Ray?"

"Man, Ruby, does it. We won't be able to find ourselves unless we feel for each other on the bandstand. And I got out those grease spots in my suit at Mr. Lawrence's cleaners—what?—for this?"

Ruby laughed more; she had no other choice, it seemed. Then she got back to putting the eyeliner on her eyelids. One eyelid was done.

Darkboy entered the room.

"Long Ray, the smoke—"

"Yeah, I know, Darkboy."

Long Ray looked in the vanity mirror at Ruby's reflection. "So, uh, you know what songs we're starting off with, the order, don't you? Of course you do, Ruby," Long Ray said, catching himself. "Nerves, nothing but nerves. My skin's ravaged with them too, honey."

The other three members of the Windy Wind Five suddenly showed up in Ruby's dressing room.

"The smoke out there," Pinky complained. "You seen—"

"Yeah, Pinky. Uh, Darkboy and I were just talking about it." Long Ray threw his hands up in the air as if absolving himself of blame. "Can't blame me. You don't see me smoking."

"But you were out there, Long Ray," Cool Hands said. "That's evidence enough. I'd—"

"Let's pray," Pinky interjected, cutting off Cool Hands.

They held hands.

"God," Pinky began, "I been playing these jazz gigs a long, long time. Man. But for some reason, tonight, my stomach's in a god-awful fit. Got a million of them nasty butterflies in it. It just ain't me, though; we all got them—the whole band. I can feel it. Really can." Pinky seemed to swallow deeper into his throat. "Just give the band the strength to do well tonight. To do its best. And Ruby, our dear, dear Ruby—let Ruby sing as pretty as the star she was born under. And powerful enough so her voice can penetrate all that damned smoke out in the club that Long Ray and the rest of them conked-headed cats blew out and left in the Hey-Hey Club for us to battle. If, uh, You're getting my drift up there. *A*-men!"

They opened their eyes, and everybody, on cue, stepped back but Darkboy. And before Darkboy realized it, he was the only one still in the dressing room with Ruby.

"Ru-Ruby, we're alone."

"I know, Darkboy," Ruby said, looking into the mirror, seeing Darkboy and only Darkboy.

Darkboy laughed. "Those sneaks."

"I'm glad, glad."

"Me too."

But then Darkboy looked down at his shoes; his feet began to shuffle.

"Uh, cat got your tongue? What it got?" Ruby had put her eyeliner pencil down on top of the vanity table.

"Seems so, doesn't it?"

Ruby wore a blue gown, something that made her dark skin look extra pretty.

Lovely, Darkboy thought. "Pinky's prayer …"

"Were beautiful, Darkboy. Pinky pray beautiful when he pray."

"Since he meant every word."

"I feels it, Darkboy."

"Every word. You were born under a star, like Pinky said. He was right, you know."

"You too. You ain'ts no different from me, what I can tell."

Darkboy shuffled his feet again. "But you were born under a special star."

Ruby stood. She was wearing high-back blue shoes. "I'm scared, Darkboy. Scared!" She grabbed him and held him. It was the first she'd ever held him.

Darkboy smelled Ruby's perfume. It smelled like no other woman's perfume. He held her without saying a word, but he knew his body felt solid, like oak, like something with old mountains in it.

"I'm ... I'm scared," Ruby said.

The emcee dashed onto the bandstand as if bees were attacking him from behind. He was as short as a two-cent ice cream cone and about as smooth as a Lester "Prez" Young saxophone solo. "I'm back! We've heard the band; now it's time to hear the wo-man of the band. The baddest female singer in the land. Sam, Jake, whatever's your take!"

Darkboy's sweat dripped from his hands and onto his drumsticks like a leaky pipe.

"Really," the emcee said, pinching the tip of his red fedora with pizzazz, "she's the lady of the land who has brought her band to the Hey-Hey Club so she can knock us all dead—if that's at all possible, or impossible, to do!"

Darkboy had a knot in his stomach as wide as the Hoover Dam. *This is unfair*, he thought. *So unfair*. Ruby was only a girl—not a "woman." The Hey-Hey Club was packed to the gills, though, for this "girl."

"So without any further ado, the Hey-Hey Club is most proud to present, direct from Chicago's Bluelight Café, Miss-s-s Ru-u-u-by Mid-d-d-ni-i-ight and the Windy Wind Five!"

Darkboy performed his famous New Orleans drumroll.

And Ruby stepped out onto the Hey-Hey stage and looked like a woman, not a girl. There was applause galore, but there was equal chatter, and glasses clinking, and the toss of dice hitting the crap tables (one more time) from the far recesses of the club, and the ruckus, and good, free spirit. The audience's applause had ebbed.

Ruby adjusted the mike to her height. She stood perfectly erect. There wasn't a drop of perspiration on her. Her skin was as dry as the Mohave Desert.

Many of the patrons had shifted their eyes away from the bandstand and off to other things and places.

Ruby turned to Long Ray, and then, as per usual, to the entire band. Long Ray was to execute the downbeat.

Long Ray leaned into his bass and said, "Uh-one, uh-one, and uh-one, two, three."

And so Ruby sang into the microphone.

The Hey-Hey Club was being sanctified by Miss Ruby Midnight and the Holy Ghost by one note, and now two, and now three … and now a cascade of them. The band arched gracefully over moons with her, clinging to the madness of Ruby's vocal genius and the beauty of their beloved in her blue dress, blue shoes, singing, blowing notes out of her mouth as freely as a swinging gate, a hurricane, desperately grabbing on to tempo with Ruby. Ruby all but stomped through blues tunes, respectfully, on the Hey-Hey Club's bandstand in Kansas City, Missouri, where only the deepest joy sprang alive in her.

Now Ruby hummed through the song's chorus in a long, soothing breath with a spellbinding effect, as natural as growing grass after a light, steady sprinkle of sparkling rain.

The band was back on the bus.

"Should be a limo!" Pinky said. "The way we tore up the Hey-Hey Club. Run Ruby for president of these here United States, pardner!"

The band was on its way back to Miss Katie's farm on the outskirts of town. It's where they stayed on the tour. Miss Katie had a huge spread of land. It's where many jazz musicians laid over, paying a small fee, when they came to Kansas City to play. Miss Katie loved jazz, but she was confined to a wheelchair. She did little venturing of her own into town.

Darkboy sat next to Ruby on the bus. Indeed, Long Ray had found something for Cool Hands to do: drive the bus! Cool Hands had wondered when Long Ray would ask him. He looked quite cool while driving the bus.

Ruby was out of her wig and gown and high-back heels. She and Darkboy were sitting in the dark, listening to the bus tires dig into the road.

Ruby and Darkboy were exhausted from the performance. The Windy Wind Five was exhausted. There were over twenty standing ovations and seven encores, all sung by Ruby. Ruby's voice felt—at best—threadbare.

"Darkboy." Ruby's head lay against the side of the window.

"May-maybe you shouldn't talk, Ruby. Uh, save your voice for now," Darkboy said worrisomely. "Tomorrow night, we're going to do this all over again. Don't know how many encores they'll ask you to sing."

"It turn out great, don't it?"

"Yes, even though I was dead tired, I still could've played my drums all night, I suppose."

"Still got snakes in my stomach up to the third song I sing. They still there for me. Least up to then." Ruby sighed. "Then I feel better. Feel free, like the songs coming to me easy."

"You won them over right off. Within an instant on the stage."

"It what it feel like to you, Darkboy?"

"Right away," Darkboy said, nodding his head. "They loved you from the start. The first note to the last."

"They do? Love me, love me, Darkboy?"

"You must've felt it, Ruby. Every inch of it tonight."

Ruby didn't respond.

"I … I know I did."

"From your drum set," Ruby jested.

Darkboy laughed. "From my drum set."

"You play great tonight. Chick Webb, he be proud."

Darkboy had told Ruby all about Chick Webb, from beginning to end.

"Guess what, Ruby? My mama and daddy would be proud too." He turned to look at Ruby. Was she ever going to mention anything about her parents? Ever? He wanted her to. Oh, how he wanted Ruby to, but he wouldn't coerce her, force her into anything.

"You know, Ruby, there are times—I mean, sometimes you remind me of an old jazz singer I've listened to on record. She sang in New Orleans, they say, on Beale Street and on riverboats running the Mississippi River."

So many jazz singers have done that, Ruby thought. *So many.*

And then, for some odd reason, Darkboy didn't elaborate.

Ruby twisted in her seat. "Who, Darkboy? Who that be—jazz singer on record you speaking?"

"Oh, Miss Honey Gillette."

Ruby was jolted.

"Hambone mentioned her the night he came to the Bluelight to hear you sing. I meant to mention her to you before but forgot. I believe she died some time back. A few years ago, I believe."

Ruby could barely breathe. Whatever had been private for her now seemed to have become public. Miss Honey had been world famous. She was known by so many jazz musicians, but still …

Of course, in the bus's dark shadows, Darkboy was unable to see Ruby's face. He could not see her upset.

"By the way, Ruby, who were your singing idols? The singers you liked?"

Silence.

"I mean, I loved Chick Webb and Papa Jo Jones and Gene Krupa, and a dozen other drummers, as you know. But what about you? Who were singers you've liked that made you want to become a jazz singer?" His head turned to her. "Was … was it—"

Ruby interrupted him by pointing to her throat.

"Sorry. I'm sorry, Ruby."

"It all right, Darkboy. But may-maybe I oughta rest my voice some. D-do like you say to do 'fore. Don't know how many encores the band get tomorrow night."

"Don't worry; it'll be a lot. Wait and see."

"Hope so. Do."

"The Hey-Hey Club in Kansas City already loves you like the Bluelight Café in Chicago. You've already won them over."

"God loves you, Ruby. God loves you, darling!"

The arrangement in Miss Katie's barn went something like this: Loose Lips and Cool Hands, bunkmates; Long Ray and Darkboy and Pinky, bunkmates. Ruby, of course, had her own private quarters.

The old barn was partitioned off by Miss Katie, wood panels making it seem like rooms but without doors. She must have been striving for privacy and came close but fell somewhat short, architecturally speaking. Miss Katie's house was thirty yards out from the barn, and the two outhouses were about fifteen yards from Miss Katie's house.

The Windy Wind Five was honored to be guests in her barn. Miss Katie was an icon, a living institution in Kansas City, God's sweet jazz messenger.

Kansas City weather had yet to turn cold, but Miss Katie said it was hard on everyone in the winter in the barn. She also told them there was an army of blankets to go around. Woolen blankets, thick, "spine warm."

Ruby was in her living quarters on her cot. She couldn't sleep; tonight wouldn't let her.

The Hey-Hey Club spun in her head. The screams and yells—near pandemonium; all the applause. She did take Kansas City by storm, as Long Ray had predicted. *The band played great*, Ruby thought. *They played with so much love in their hearts.*

If Ruby'd had her druthers, she would walk out Miss Katie's barn, look up at the sky, and find a star—any star, as long as it looked down at her. She was so lucky. She'd breathe in the night air and let its scent settle in her. She'd just keep breathing and breathing, nonstop.

That was the kind of mood she was in, as delicate as the night wind, winding its way through Kansas City. And Darkboy—he'd been magic on his drums tonight. She felt every pulse, every beat, and she followed him to wherever his drums led her.

They'd sat side by side on the bus, and she felt her heart do something stupid when it happened. It was as if they were on a date, girl and boy. A real grown-up date.

Darkboy loved Chick Webb, but when he mentioned Miss Honey …

"Miss Honey, ma'am."

Ruby wanted to say Miss Honey's name strongly but could only whisper it. Darkboy had said it; she'd said nothing but felt everything. She was still holding on to Miss Honey's past. The beauty of it. She couldn't share it, not even with Darkboy; that hurt.

Miss Honey's record was in the suitcase, there in Kansas City, with her. Wherever she traveled, Miss Honey's record traveled too.

Ruby trembled. Darkboy had used Miss Honey's name.

Darkboy.

Darkboy loved Miss Honey's singing. When would she tell Darkboy about her and Miss Honey? He had to be told about Miss Honey. He had Chick Webb, and she had Miss Honey. Darkboy never had met Chick Webb, though; he only knew him through records. But she knew Miss Honey. She knew what Miss Honey looked like and how she walked and talked; how she smelled and felt. Her touch.

Ruby could look at a star now. Any star, sitting in the Kansas City sky over Miss Katie's farm, would do now. She'd take in the Kansas City air and think of the Hey-Hey Club tomorrow night. And Darkboy playing his drums behind her. And then riding back to Miss Katie's farm on the band's bus, side by side, girl and boy, as if they were on a date in the heartland of Kansas City, Missouri—so beautiful, beautiful, beautiful.

What was happening nightly in the Hey-Hey Club was the wildest scene the wild, wild west had ever cooked up. There was Wyatt Earp, Doc Holliday, Billy the Kid, and scores of other western heroes, legends, villains, hombres, and scoundrels, but none with the reputation of killing their victims sweetly by poisoning them from a harmless-looking wine glass—not the way Ruby Midnight was doing it at the Hey-Hey Club.

Her singing, combined with Long Ray's songs, had been killing the Hey-Hey patrons sweetly, nightly. It was a wonder Kansas City had not posted MOST WANTED signs for the capture of Miss Ruby Midnight throughout the heart and breadth of the Missouri territories, warning folk of this infamous woman of song, this ferocious man-killer who was still on the loose, she and her notorious jazz band, the Windy Wind Five, who were out of the Chicago, Illinois, badlands.

And with this amazing success, the band and Ruby were having a total ball.

CHAPTER 18

The day was as bright as Nebraska corn, but it was a Kansas City sun. A yellow car was parked in front of Miss Katie's barn. Long Ray stood in front of the barn, beaming like no way would he find the off switch in his back to stop it.

"Pinky, you can bring the kids out of the barn."

Pinky snapped his pink suspenders, snapped his heels, and gave Long Ray a snappy salute. Ruby and Darkboy had been in the barn, stashed away in there like stowaways. Loose Lips and Cool Hands had been keeping a watchful eye on the pair, as duty demanded.

The barn door opened. Darkboy shaded his eyes, as if the Kansas City sun had blinded him or the yellow car had. Ruby was in casual attire, but there was a slight rustle in her demeanor, once she spotted the car.

Long Ray kicked the car's right front tire. "Looks good, doesn't it, Darkboy?" Long Ray walked over to the other side of the car and kicked the car's left front tire. "Runs damned good. Road-tested it. Uh-huh. She's all yours, Darkboy. Yours and Ruby's, to ride around in for the day. No band rehearsal this afternoon for you kids. The afternoon's yours and Ruby's to spend together as you please."

Ruby and Darkboy were shocked.

"Rented it—the car, that is." Long Ray dug down into his pockets and out came a receipt and the car's keys. "You and Ruby might need these," Long Ray said, dangling the keys. "That baby's a lot easier to drive than Sam Waters's bus. Man!"

All eyes turned to Sam Waters's rented bus, basking in the Kansas City sun. The bus looked as if it might melt like butter in the sun.

"So are you kids going to get in, or do you want us to do that for you too?" Long Ray asked. "'Cause we will, you know."

"No, no, that's o-okay, L-Long Ray," Darkboy said. "N-no need to."

Long Ray handed Darkboy the car keys. Pinky escorted Ruby over to the pretty yellow hell-on-wheels. The car was a two-door roadster, a convertible with the top down, sporty-looking. Something that could zoom down a Kansas City road like a spaceship circling the galaxy.

"Drive safely, Darkboy. Avoid any ditches, man. Inconveniences. Don't forget; you've got precious cargo aboard," Pinky said.

"Yeah, Darkboy!" the angry mob yelled.

"Don't get lost, Darkboy. But if, for some reason, you do, there's a road map in the glove compartment, as insurance."

"Great, Long Ray!"

Ruby and Darkboy covered some ground in the roadster.

Darkboy really knows how to drive this car, Ruby thought.

Darkboy felt Ruby's eyes pressing on him. It felt the same as when he played his drums, was doing a solo spin. As always, he felt like showing off for Ruby, but he knew he was playing music, and you don't show off with music; you feel music. But now, driving a car, he could show off, unless he ran the car into a ditch, which he would be sure not to do!

The car wound around another bend.

"Darkboy, you sure know how to drive this car."

"Can you drive?"

"Uh-uh."

"Ever want to learn?" Darkboy shifted gears.

"Yes. Yes," Ruby said slowly, then began building on it. "Uh … yes, yes, Darkboy. Yes."

The car braked. "I could teach you how now, you know."

"Teach me to drive? T-this car?" Ruby said, amazed.

"It's what I said."

"Me!"

"Now. Right now. It'll be easy."

And as if there were springs in his legs, Darkboy sprang out the car and seemed ready for action. "Want to? I won't teach you unless you want me to."

Ruby hesitated only for a moment. "Yes, Darkboy!"

Darkboy ran halfway around the car. "Then I'm at your service, Miss Midnight. Complete service!"

"You isn't gonna go back to calling me Miss Midnight again," Ruby said with a pout. "Is you?"

"Just for now, Miss Midnight, while I'm in your service. Giving you driving lessons."

Ruby's pout hadn't changed. Darkboy helped her out of the car.

"We ain't gonna get in trouble, is we?" she asked.

Darkboy winked. "Not unless you speed. Or hit a cow. Or a pig crossing the road."

Ruby laughed. "Oh, Darkboy, you nothing but a big tease. Ain't complaining, though."

"No, it didn't sound like a complaint."

It was a riot, Darkboy teaching Ruby how to drive a car. They laughed and giggled so much that it made them both sick. If they laughed again, it might split them in two.

A driver, Ruby wasn't. Oh, she was determined, all right—a great sign—but stop and go was her biggest achievement to date. Darkboy felt as if someone were punching him in his back and then knocking him in his chest so he could be punched in his back to complete the wretched cycle. He sadly concluded that Ruby needed a lot more driving lessons.

"Come on," he said with a laugh. "Ruby, I thought we agreed, two miles back, that there'd be no more laughing until we got back to Miss Katie's farm."

"Ha. I know," Ruby said, her fingers wiping tears from her eyes, "but you ... you ..."

"I know; I almost turned red when—"

"I almost hit me that cow—"

"Crossing, ha, the road. You should've seen—"

"I do, Darkboy. The cow owner turn red too, just like you does."

"Right, right, you did. Instead of keeping your eyes on ... at least you were going only five miles an hour."

"Was, Darkboy?"

"Three to five, tops?"

"Oh."

They were practically back to the farm. They still had to perform at the club tonight, but they'd had quite an afternoon outing. It definitely had relaxed them.

"Gonna really sing tonight, Darkboy. Ain't bragging on myself or nothing."

Darkboy took a goodly dose of Kansas City air in his lungs. "Ah … nothing like good old country air, Ruby."

Ruby took a deep breath of air in her lungs.

"Copycat."

"Ain't."

"You are."

Ruby pouted.

"And you can pout all you want, Miss Ruby Midnight, and it's not going to help your case. Not with me."

Ruby crossed her arms in front of her and kept the pout on her mouth. "Darkboy, you mean."

"Taught you how to drive today, didn't I?"

Ruby broke out laughing. "You ain't tellin' i-is you? Long Ray and—"

"Uh-uh, no, not the way you shift car gears."

"Gonna do better next time. Next time you take me out driving."

Will there be a next time? Darkboy thought. "Right, right, Ruby. Next time."

Long Ray had slipped out the barn with his pack of cigarettes.

"Hey, Long Ray," Darkboy greeted him.

"Had to take a drag," Long Ray said, looking down at his cigarette. "Figured the band had enough smoke for one night. Hope the club in Saint Louis isn't as smoky as the Hey-Hey." He took notice of Darkboy—especially his eyes. "Your eyes, they're actually shining in the dark. Man, like gems!"

"They … they are?"

"Yeah. Hell, yeah! Ask me if I've ever seen anything like it." Long Ray grinned. "Ask me." He planted himself in front of Darkboy; at least, that was how it felt to Darkboy. "Let me take a closer look at you. Examine you. What are you up to, man? What is Jimmy Darkboy Slade up to, anyway?"

How can I hide it, Darkboy thought, *the feeling I have inside when it reflects on the outside so much? It's penetrating right through me.*

"I know you sat next to Ruby on the bus again tonight. On the way back," Long Ray joked, "which seems to be habit these days."

Darkboy grabbed Long Ray's arm. Long Ray almost dropped his cigarette. Darkboy's grip was that urgent.

"Hell, what do you do to get a grip like that, Darkboy? It ain't from drumming. Must be from alligator wrestling in the bayou, or good old gumbo soup!"

Darkboy's eyes shone even more, and his grip on Long Ray's arm strengthened. "I have a surprise!"

"Which is?"

"I love Ruby."

"Darkboy," Long Ray said, "we know that. Been written across your forehead in invisible ink for everybody, all us cats, to read. So tell me something new, huh?"

"I ... I really love Ruby, Long Ray. And I've, I've really thought about this."

"If this is about you and Ruby—"

"It is."

"Then maybe I can help you but not like this. With you being a bundle of nerves, man. A nervous wreck." Long Ray took a drag on his cigarette and then tossed it to the ground. "Talk to me, Darkboy. Tell me about love, man."

"I've thought about it, really."

"You can't think about it, Darkboy. You *feel* it, like the music in—"

"No, Long Ray, about what I have to do."

"So that's the surprise?" Long Ray pulled the pack of cigarettes and matches from his pocket. He lit a cigarette and puffed on it until it glowed orange in the dark. "Then talk to me, Darkboy," he said softly, "about your surprise. About love, man."

The yellow car was still Darkboy's to drive. Long Ray had made it so, had rented the car out for a lifetime, so it seemed to Darkboy.

The car was parked a distance away from them. Darkboy and Ruby were on a street in Kansas City where Scott Joplin had walked—or someone famous. It was a busy street. There was traffic and lights that seemed they could light night into a new day. There was a current of romance in the air that buzzed magnificently.

"Darkboy, what you thinking?" Ruby asked.

Darkboy had been silent for some time. It was probably the longest he'd been this quiet around Ruby since they'd met. "Who knows?" Darkboy replied cheerily.

"You thinking an' you don't know what you thinking?"

"Boy, y-you sure know how to make me sound stupid or foolish, Ruby."

"Don't mean to."

"I know you didn't."

"When I gonna talk better than now, Darkboy? I do!"

"Ruby, d-don't worry. You will. Will soon."

"Think 'bout nothing sometimes too."

"Y-you, you do? So I'm not the only one—not alone, then?"

"Uh-uh."

"So what do you think about when you think about nothing?"

"Nothing!"

"Ha. We should be a comedy team."

"Not just jazz?"

"Make people happy."

"Like that, Darkboy; make people happy."

"Something you do through your singing, Ruby."

"And you, your drummin', Darkboy."

Darkboy smiled. He knew Ruby; one compliment deserved another. But what he did on his drums couldn't compare, not even in small measure, to what Ruby did with her voice. It wasn't a compliment to be taken with a grain of salt, for Ruby meant what she said, only she still didn't feel comfortable being the center of attention, not under any circumstance.

"Ruby, want to head back to the car?"

"Uh-huh. We walk a good ways, seem like."

Right now, at this particular moment, Darkboy's stomach was grinding as if it were grinding bricks. He was seeking an intimacy with Ruby, something dedicated to a lifetime of sharing.

"I like walking; what 'bout you, Darkboy? Plattstown, I run through the fields. They all pretty an' nice. Walk some"—Ruby giggled—"but mostly run. Miss that part a the South."

"Me too."

Darkboy and Ruby kept walking and drawing nearer and nearer to where Darkboy had parked the yellow roadster. All of this, what he had set out to do, was supposed to have been done before he and Ruby reached the car. It was to have been done under a Kansas City lamppost, one shining rays of love from its filament.

"Darkboy, y-you know how many cities we gonna be to, uh, 'fore we through? Miles we gonna have to travel, one day?"

"Ha, what the future looks like, you mean? Bet you Pinky could tell us. All about a musician's life."

"Pinky an' Cool Hands both, for sure."

"Have suitcase, I guess, will travel. The world is a jazz musician's home. Haven."

"I want it to be, Darkboy. For me."

"You do?" Darkboy asked, surprised.

"Yes. I ain't never have no real home. None to speak of."

What Ruby said struck Darkboy deeply. What had she just said about herself, intimated to him?

"When I on the bandstand an' sing, does ... I, I doesn't know ..."

"Say it, Ruby?"

"Feel so free, Darkboy. Like I running through the fields in Plattstown inside. All the time, time. Doing that."

They were but a block away from the car. Darkboy looked straight ahead and then over to Ruby, whose smile still resonated. Both were about to pass by the lamppost on the broad street near the intersection.

Darkboy grabbed Ruby's hand. It startled her, and it took another five steps for them to get over to the lamppost, right under its pretty shine, and for Darkboy to drop to his right knee and look up in the full polish and beauty of Ruby's eyes, her dark face, at the woman he'd loved since the moment she suddenly appeared in the Bluelight, since he'd seen her through its veil of slow-rising smoke.

"Ruby Midnight, will you marry me? Will you become Mrs. Jimmy Darkboy Slade?"

CHAPTER 19

The next day, August 19

It was a gorgeous day in Kansas City, Missouri. The Windy Wind Five, plus Ruby, were in Kansas City's city hall. Ruby and Darkboy stood in front of the justice of the peace. Long Ray had given Ruby away and also doubled as Darkboy's best man.

"I-I do!"

"I now pronounce you, man and wife," said the justice of peace. "You may kiss your wife, Mr. Slade."

Their two eyes met, and they knew this would be the first time they'd kiss, something the Windy Wind Five had suspected.

Ruby placed her arms around Darkboy's shoulders and slowly drew him to her.

They kissed.

The band roundly applauded Ruby and Darkboy.

Long Ray had found a decent hotel for the newlyweds. Something not as fancy as the white man's hotel but what a black man in Kansas City could provide for himself.

Long Ray had parked Sam Waters's bus in front of the hotel. Long Ray, Ruby, and Darkboy stood at the hotel's tacky front desk.

"Catch up with you kids in Saint Louis. You know you've got until

Friday at four. The rehearsal's for four o'clock Friday." Long Ray hugged Darkboy and then Ruby. "I love you two kids."

The bus horn sounded. *Honk.*

"Must be Pinky," Long Ray said. "Oh, well."

Honk.

"Yeah, it's him. Loves the key of B-flat, doesn't he? Oh well."

"See you in Saint Louie, Louie," Darkboy said.

"So, in two days."

"Bye, Long Ray." Ruby said.

"Bye, Ruby. Uh, Mrs. Slade."

Honk.

"Cat never changes key."

Long Ray left.

Darkboy and Ruby looked at each other, as if they were lost stars.

Darkboy looked down at the suitcases. Ruby reached for hers.

"No, you don't have to, Ruby. I'll carry it in."

Darkboy felt his nerves cracking open. *This is different*, he thought. This was far different than their riding in a yellow roadster with the top rolled down on a Kansas City road on a fun day.

"W-what room is it a-again, Ruby?"

"Room six."

One day, we were friends; the next, husband and wife, Darkboy thought. *So fast. So damned fast.*

"Uh … you, you go first, Ruby. Uh … Mrs. …" He couldn't say it, finish it. It was far too new to him, too sudden to think about: he was someone's husband. He was having second thoughts.

Ruby's forehead wrinkled in puzzlement. "Room six, Darkboy. You hardly can see it, but …"

"If … if you say so, Ruby," Darkboy said anxiously.

"It what it say. Room six." Ruby had the room key. "Open it, Darkboy?"

"Yes, yes, Ruby. Of, of course. Please."

Ruby stuck the key in the lock and opened the door.

Both stood outside the door, Darkboy with the suitcases in his hands and Ruby with the room key in hers. Both gazed into the dark room.

Seconds passed, but both still stood there at the door, as stiff as brooms.

Darkboy, red-faced, put the suitcases down. Even Ruby understood what a bridegroom was supposed to do, traditionally, for his bride.

"Ruby, s-sorry."

Within seconds, Darkboy had swept Ruby off her feet and into his arms, holding her, carrying her into the hotel room, where a bed sat in the middle of the room, obvious but oh-so-small.

Ruby's arms were tight around Darkboy's neck, hugging him to her. "Thank you, Darkboy."

Darkboy put Ruby on the bed and turned to retrieve the suitcases from the hall. He carried them into the room and put them on the floor. He began to breathe heavily in the dark room. "The lights. I forgot to turn on the lights."

Ruby giggled.

Darkboy opened the room door so light could enter the room. "There—there's the light switch, Ruby."

Playfully, Ruby shook her legs atop the bed. "Know you was to find it, Darkboy. If you look for it good 'nough."

Now that they could see each other again, they laughed at each other.

"Ruby, are you sure we're … we're Mr. and Mrs. Jimmy Darkboy Slade? We just got married?"

"Sure!" Ruby laughed. "You wearing you a black tuxedo, ain't you? Yes, think I know what being married feel like from what it don't."

"After"—Darkboy glanced at his watch—"what? Three hours and a few minutes thrown in of matrimony."

"Like you say, Darkboy, a being Mrs. Jimmy Darkboy Slade."

"Happy. Are you happy, Ruby?" he asked, walking toward the bed.

Ruby swooned. "Yes, yes, Darkboy."

"S-so am I."

"Be angry, mad if you say you ain't." Ruby got off the bed.

Darkboy's eyes snaked around her. The midnight-blue dress she wore to city hall—he wanted to think of Ruby as a she-devil in a blue dress, only for now, he was still too nervous. "Are you hungry?" he asked. "I-I saw a store about a half mile away. Down the road. I could go down there and could have them fix us something."

Ruby had seen the tiny store too, but her appetite was not for food—and Darkboy had sensed as much. He felt Ruby's voice sing in him, his playing his drums, them making the music. Him following her, her following him; always in perfect sync. The mystery of what they were was as clear as a waterfall, overpoweringly quiet.

"Kiss me, Darkboy. Not like you do at City Hall. Uh-uh, n-not like that." Her hands touched him, and Darkboy's entire body hardened. Ruby's arms encircled Darkboy's trim waist, and Darkboy's lips could taste the sweetness in Ruby's lips without his touching hers. They kissed differently than at City Hall, and their hands searched each other in hidden rooms, in dark closets, in secret passages of the mind and heart. Darkboy held tightly to Ruby's body as he walked her over to the room's light switch (eyes open) and flipped it off with his fingertip (eyes shut), while his mouth continued to make love to Ruby's neck, ears, her tender, hot pieces of skin; their bodies united.

Ruby's dress was off her, her slip shining in Darkboy's eyes. He slipped one thin strap off Ruby's shoulder, then the other. Darkboy smelled Ruby's breath, pleasantly scented and strong.

Ruby's hands rode evenly over Darkboy's supple back, from his shoulder blades down to the small of his muscled back. This drummer boy. This African boy. This drummer man, virile as the drumbeats of Africa.

Darkboy was ready to taste Ruby, this black woman whose breasts rose up to him like the rich hills of Africa. "Ruby, I-I loved you from the first night I saw you."

"Darkboy … Darkboy … I-I a virgin."

And so Darkboy's body became a gentle ship, as gentle and loving as Darkboy could have dreamed of ever making it move in the warm Louisiana waters back home that he'd swum in when he was young—innocent and naked.

The room's lights were off. Ruby and Darkboy lay in the narrow bed, resting.

Earlier, Ruby had told Darkboy all about herself. How she had moved from place A to B and X, Y, Z, with no man ever touching her. With no man ever asking her to pay him rent with her body. She never had to run from a man, not from anybody, Ruby said, or fight a man for what was hers but he thought was his, when he figured that a knife and a black heart owned the night.

Yes, Ruby had told Darkboy she was a virgin throughout her travels. At eighteen years of age, Ruby was a virgin until tonight, until Darkboy made love to her, made her a woman.

We were jazz together, Darkboy thought. They made love together like music, jazz, Yardbird, Hawk, Prez. Like him drumming and her singing. Him coaxing her, his drums urging her, until Ruby Midnight screamed her song, euphoria, an ecstasy out of her throat.

I'm the one, Darkboy had thought. *The only one. Man. Ruby was a virgin, and now she isn't. She's Mrs. Jimmy Darkboy Slade.*

Darkboy felt like a klutz, for his foot had slightly nudged Ruby's leg inadvertently.

"Sorry, Ruby. I-I think my foot must've fallen asleep."

Ruby's eyes had been closed. Her head rose off of Darkboy's chest. "It all right. I weren't sleep no way. Was resting."

"Tired, aren't you?"

"Uh-huh," Ruby said, childlike.

Inwardly, Darkboy laughed. How could Ruby go from a sultry woman one second to an innocent girl the next?

"Sex, it always make you tired af'erward, Darkboy?"

Darkboy had told Ruby of his sexual exploits with other women, that he was not a virgin. Ruby never expected him to be a virgin. Not a boy Darkboy's age.

"Seem, though, my body ain't never gonna be same again, Darkboy. Like it always gonna be tired this way."

Darkboy kissed Ruby's eyelids as his head tilted downward. "Don't worry; you'll gain your strength back. Suddenly, it'll return to you without warning." Darkboy smiled.

"Sex, it beautiful, ain't it, Darkboy?"

"With the right person, it is, Ruby."

"It … it ain't otherwise?"

Pinky came to mind before Darkboy answered. He remembered what he had said about sex in the Bluelight. "Not … not always." And Ruby had proven Pinky's point to Darkboy.

"But as Mrs. Jimmy Darkboy Slade, it do, Darkboy?"

Darkboy nodded, but something leaped into his mind. "Ruby, your name!"

"What, what 'bout my name?"

"Oh, oh, I mean your stage name."

"S-stage name?"

"Ruby Midnight."

"Yes, uh-huh. Mrs. Ruby Midnight Slade," Ruby said proudly.

"That's what I mean—you mustn't change your stage name. It's too beautiful."

"But I-I want to change—"

"But you mustn't. No, no, you mustn't change it. It's a name people are … are just now getting to know. Used to hearing."

"But I marry you, Darkboy. To you," Ruby said strongly. "I your wife. I gotta take on your name. It the Christian thing to do. A-ain't it?"

"Yes, no, I mean it. It doesn't have to be, Ruby. It's on our marriage certificate. See, see, it's there. It's official. But you're Ruby Midnight. Not Mrs. Jimmy Darkboy Slade. To the world, that's who you are."

Ruby understood but then didn't. She'd become something new only to go back to something old, what had been. "I know it on a mar'age 'tificate. The piece a paper, Darkboy. But doesn't you want to see it in lights? 'Ruby Midnight Slade' in lights?"

Darkboy drew Ruby back to him. "My name's good enough in lights. There's no need for you to."

"No?"

"No."

Ruby lay her head back down on Darkboy's chest and felt her strength return to her body—she hadn't noticed until now—just as Darkboy had said it would.

Darkboy felt it too.

Darkboy had left the room. Ruby was on the bed, with only a top sheet covering her. The bottom sheet was red from Ruby's blood. She'd bled badly. But Darkboy had been gentle. She didn't want to cry but had. It hurt. Darkboy's penis, it hurt her.

But she was determined to withstand the pain, knowing this much about sex, what it took for a woman the first time, having sex.

169

Darkboy was trying to secure a new sheet for the bed. He was out at the hotel's front desk. Ruby hoped she hadn't embarrassed him—or them, for that matter.

She was in a slip. She would stay in a slip. She felt comfortable around Darkboy in a slip. All the months of her and Darkboy and Long Ray living in the apartment together, the modesty they maintained between them, and now this openness. She felt comfortable around Darkboy either in a slip or naked.

Darkboy had been patient with her, gentle with her from the start, with someone who knew nothing about sex, a virgin, who'd sung about it in a song on a bandstand but knew nothing about it, how it really was, really felt for a man to be inside a woman, for a man to make love to a woman. Darkboy told her it was the best way, the way they'd had sex, with them in love. Already, she liked it.

And then, fast, in a flash, while her head lay on Darkboy's warm chest, awake, she'd thought of her mama and daddy, the sounds she'd heard, that she remembered them making, released from their room next to hers—clawing, scratching apart the bloodied air like scissor-nailed rats; Man Martinson's and Millicent Martinson's drunken screams.

But Darkboy made her scream in that way, drunkenly. She was like her mama and daddy, Man and Millicent Martinson, then. Darkboy's body on top of hers, strong and potent. And beneath him, she'd felt the same potency in her body, the same willingness to please and be pleased, an animal lust, her breath, her eyes—that shocked her, something real and sudden and frightening exploding inside the spaces of her head.

Sex, what is it? What is it that could do those things, these things? Ruby thought.

Darkboy's penis had felt so good inside her, once she'd cried, once the pain left her. And when it was over, she felt her blood, but Darkboy knew it was there all along on the sheet, stained there.

She'd wanted to see it for herself, so Darkboy turned the light on for her, and she saw it, her blood, how she'd bled. The blood signified to her that she was no longer a virgin but a woman, Darkboy's wife.

Ruby wanted to fling herself up to the sky. "I ... I Mrs. Jimmy Darkboy

Slade. Got me a husband, Miss Honey. Ma'am. Ma'am. A beautiful man. Got me a husband, Miss Honey. A ... a beautiful man, ma'am."

"And I a jazz singer too," Ruby said, touching her breasts through her silver slip, remembering how Darkboy had made love to them. Miss Honey had made her a jazz singer, and Darkboy—Jimmy Darkboy Slade—had made her a woman.

Darkboy was back from the front desk.

"Got it, Ruby. A new bedsheet."

Ruby sprang off the bed, running to Darkboy as if dashing out in a sun shower.

"Oh, Ruby, I wasn't gone that long, was I?"

"Seem like it. Do, for me."

Darkboy blushed.

"Let me, Darkboy."

Darkboy handed Ruby the sheet. "I can help, Ruby."

Ruby was at the bed. "Ain'ts gonna let my husband do not'ing on our wedding night. On our honeymoon."

"Noth-nothing?"

"Not'ing, Darkboy."

"But you're the star in the family."

"Uh-uh. Not at home. At home, I Mrs. Jimmy Darkboy Slade. Who I is, Darkboy."

"And on stage?"

"Miss Ruby Midnight." Ruby tucked the bedsheet beneath the mattress.

"Man, Ruby, I'm glad we finally got that straightened out." Darkboy laughed.

Ruby laughed. "You the boss, Darkboy."

Darkboy grabbed her from behind, his slacks warm. "What boss?" He kissed her neck. "When you know you can twist me around your little finger at any time you want."

"I ... I can?" Ruby relaxed back in Darkboy's arms.

"Yes, you can, Mrs. Slade."

"But I still got to fix the bed, right?"

"Well ... since you started ... no sense in stopping you now."

I going to love being married to Darkboy forever and ever and ever, Ruby thought.

They'd eaten. They'd had sex.

Ruby was on the bed, looking at sheet music. Darkboy was in a chair, drumming on practice pads.

"Ruby, I forgot—completely forgot!"

Shocked, Ruby's head swung around to Darkboy. "What you forget?"

"Mama, Daddy! I haven't told my parents I—you and I got married."

Ruby relaxed. "Oh, I ..."

"Thought it was serious, huh? Well, let me tell you—it is in my family. They'll crown me if I don't tell them."

"So how they gonna know to crown you, Darkboy, if they doesn't know we married? How that?"

"Oh, they have ways, Ruby. Believe me, my parents have ways of finding out things."

"They ain't ghosts, is they? Your parents?"

"Ha. S-sometimes I think they are. I just know one thing: I'd better write them and fast."

Darkboy headed for his suitcase. "Uh, besides, all they have to do, on the map, is hop over Arkansas, and they're here. It's Louisiana, then Arkansas, then Missouri."

"Oh."

How much education does Ruby have? Darkboy thought. *No matter her travels. Those places were that—just places to her, long stretches of land, roads, forgettable by name, if not by memory.* "I've got writing paper." He opened the suitcase on the floor. "Here, here it is," Darkboy said, showing it to Ruby. "Now for the pen. Got it. Here it is." Darkboy raised the pen. "Now I can breathe again."

"Good. Don't wont to see you blue in the face."

"Ha."

"How, how you think they gonna take to it, Darkboy? Y-you takin' on a wife? Me?"

"Daddy, fine. Mama, well …" Darkboy's lips twisted. "I … I don't know, Ruby. Mama can be difficult." He came over to the bed and sat next to Ruby.

She put her head down on his shoulder. "Never tell my mama an' my daddy." Her voice was unrecognizable to Darkboy. "Hate them, Darkboy. Hate Mama an' Daddy!" Ruby trembled. "I-I doesn't think a them. I-I ain't mean or not'ing. Mean or, or not'ing!"

Ruby struggled with her emotions.

"Doesn't know if Mama, Daddy dead, dead or 'live, since I been gone, Darkboy. I leave home. R-run from home. "I doesn' think a Mama an' Daddy. I … you lucky, Darkboy. Lucky."

"Yes. I-I am."

"Write your mama an' daddy. Got reason to. G-good 'nough reason to."

Darkboy felt he was a part of this now, this drama, what seemed the psychological war within Ruby. He'd been holding her as if he could control her emotions, for them not to twist and turn and bend and mangle.

"What did they do to you, Ruby? P-please tell me."

"My mama, she drink," Ruby said, softening her voice. "My daddy too. They get drunk. Doesn' know the difference 'tween night an' day. Drink all day. Drink all night. Drink … drink all day, all, all night."

"R-Ruby." Darkboy's tone was fretful. "Did, did they hurt you?" Roughly, he turned her to him. "Hurt you, baby?"

"Mama doesn' let Daddy beat me, on when … when Daddy try."

"T-that's something, Ruby."

"But she don't love me, Darkboy. Uh-uh, not that."

"But she—"

"Fight for me t-that one time. Mama mean as sin to me. Mean as Daddy be."

"But only when she was—"

"Mama always drunk. What it seem. Doesn' know Mama to be sober, hardly."

What am I doing? Darkboy thought. *I can't make rain fall from the sky, wet the ground. I can't make the ground turn over new fruit, yield it bountifully in winter. And I can't make Ruby love her mother when she hates her.*

"Hate Mama!"

"Ruby, don't!"

But Ruby broke away from Darkboy. She was brooding.

Darkboy looked down at the pen and paper. Ruby looked at them too. She rushed back to him, holding him.

"I sorry, Darkboy!"

Darkboy slipped his arms around her waist. "Your life was so much different than mine."

Ruby sobbed. "Want you to know. You my husband, my best friend."

Darkboy lay back on the bed. Her body covered his.

"Ain't you gonna write your letter? Letter to your mama an' daddy?" Ruby's cheek smothered Darkboy's.

"My mama and daddy," Darkboy said excitedly, "can wait."

And that was when Ruby's strong body became tangled in Darkboy's, like thick vines.

Darkboy and Ruby had two suitcases and two train tickets for Saint Louis. The train tickets were a wedding gift from the band. Ruby and Darkboy stood on the train's platform.

Darkboy was dressed nice; so was Ruby. The train was in the station, and all looked well.

"We've got our train tickets, Ruby!"

"Yes, Darkboy!"

"And we're all set to go to Saint Louis."

It sounded all so romantic to them.

"Darkboy, doesn' never have a ticket to ride a train 'fore."

"But you've been on a train before today, right?" Darkboy teased.

Both Ruby and Darkboy knew firsthand what the inside of a train car looked like, felt like—cold or warm, damp, huddled among strangers, frightened, hiding from the law, in and out of trouble.

"But this time ain't got to hide from nobody," Ruby said. "This time it gonna be real different riding the train along."

Darkboy held tighter to Ruby's hand.

The train roared.

Darkboy and Ruby laughed at the coincidence.

"Yes, ma'am! Real different, Ruby!"

Long Ray's head shook a mile a minute, along with the rest of the Windy Wind Five's, in tune.

"What took you honeymooners so long to get here?" Long Ray said.

Darkboy and Ruby couldn't believe what they saw: Long Ray and the band were in Union Station, and the train was on time.

"Mr. and Mrs. Slade!" Cool Hands said, grabbing Ruby's suitcase, still thinking he might be Ruby's official escort for the band's two-city tour.

"Don't they look like newlyweds? Bride and groom. Love birds. Look at them pusses!" Pinky said.

"Figured we'd surprise you two," Long Ray said, locking his arm with Darkboy's and glancing over to Ruby, who was still very much occupied by Cool Hands's fatherly attention. "Welcome you two, in style."

"Thanks, Long Ray. Guys."

"Couldn't very well let you and Ruby set foot in Saint Louis bare bones—without a parade—could we?"

"Well, thanks, Loose Lips, because Ruby and I didn't expect this kind of reception, uh, turnout, did we, Ruby?"

Ruby moved seamlessly from Cool Hands and to Darkboy. "Uh-uh, Darkboy. Doesn'."

"I guess when one talks, the others got to too," Pinky said. "Sounds like a marriage to me, all right. Like Darkboy's henpecked already!"

"Don't pay attention to Pinky, kids," Long Ray said.

"Do they ever, Long Ray?" Pinky said. "Does anyone ever pay attention to Pinky Irving? It's my problem, man. I was abandoned as a child. Left on a damned door step, man, to fend for myself. I need *attention*!"

They howled.

"Have you two been practicing?" Long Ray asked, leading the congregation out of the train station "Because all of Saint Louis is excited. Word came in from the Hey-Hey Club—"

"What, Long Ray, by Pony Express?" Pinky cut in.

"Yeah, Pinky, Pony Express," Long Ray said, sucking his teeth. "As I was saying, word came that Ruby Midnight and the Windy Wind Five knocked them dead in Kansas City in the Hey-Hey Club. So now, it's like we've got this reputation that's bigger than life, uh, for right now."

"Say, the Flim-Flam Club is gonna be packed tonight," Pinky said, "Sardines in a can. Can get them in, but can't get them out."

The bus was outside the train station, making everything else around it look cheerful.

"Back to the bus," Pinky said dejectedly.

"The newlyweds first," Loose Lips said.

Darkboy reached out for Ruby's hand, and Ruby stepped aboard the bus. They sat in the front seat. And out of nowhere, rice rained down on them.

"Ha!" Pinky laughed. "Had some rice left over from Kansas City. From the city hall gig, man."

Ruby and Darkboy laughed, and then Ruby wiped off Darkboy, and Darkboy wiped off Ruby.

"By the way," Pinky added, "did them colored porters on the train treat you like white folk?"

Long Ray gunned the bus.

Long silence.

"Thought not!" Pinky laughed in answering his own question.

Long Ray and Darkboy were at the Flim-Flam bar. Long Ray was drinking scotch, as was Darkboy.

"Ooo-wee, Darkboy, did I miss you two!"

"We missed you too, Long Ray," Darkboy responded.

"Bet you did." Long Ray winked. "Guess you and Ruby didn't have much time to do anything but—"

"Wrote Mama and Daddy. Found the time to."

"Hell, on your honeymoon?" Long Ray gulped down his scotch. "Uh … uh, good for you. Yeah, uh, good for you, Darkboy. What about Ruby?"

"No."

"No?"

"No, Ruby didn't write her parents."

"Did ... did Ruby talk about them—her parents—to you?"

"No, Long Ray."

"Not even with you?"

"No." Darkboy knew what he was doing with Long Ray. That part of Ruby's life didn't have to be exposed or discussed with him—her troubled past, how it was still with her, inside her gut, her soul. It didn't have to be revealed, examined, talked over, even if Long Ray could be trusted as someone who deeply loved Ruby, who would consider, delicately, Ruby's privacy. But he was Ruby's husband now, someone who would always want to be her protector if called upon—and now was the time to prove he could. It'd been thrust on him. The time had come for him to prove himself.

Long Ray wearily put his glass down on the bar. "Damn, Darkboy, what do we know about, Ruby? Really, I mean. What do we really know? It's like she came out of the midnight that night, like she told us how she got her name. Actually did."

"It bothers you, Long Ray?"

Long Ray shrugged his shoulders "A little, I've got to admit. Does it bother you, Darkboy? We've all got a past. You know, to live up to. A mirror to look back into. We just don't materialize out of thin air. We all have a past—some good, some bad—but it's what makes us who we are. What's in the mirror. Life's mirror, man." Long Ray grabbed the glass, then sipped from it slowly.

No, Darkboy thought, *the secret's mine and Ruby's for now. No one else's. Ruby's past will be protected—not discussed, picked over.*

"Did ... did she bleed?" Long Ray asked.

Darkboy was forced to shut his eyes but said nothing.

"Thought so. All along, Ruby was a virgin. Never had a man. Man have sex with her."

How could Long Ray think like that? Darkboy wondered. When Ruby sang, she sang so knowingly about life, as if she'd tasted its bitter fruit. But hadn't he known it too, despite that? Him—Jimmy Darkboy" Slade?

"I was right about Ruby," Long Ray said, putting his glass back down on the bar. "All along, all the time."

Had Ruby sung at the Flim-Flam Club or what!

During the band's five-night engagement, Ruby sang the blues like the "Father of the Blues," W. C. Handy, had returned to Saint Louis, Missouri. For those five nights, Ruby had rocked the blues until the Mississippi River turned good and black! Well, that was how they told it in Saint Louis now.

Out in the heartlands, Ruby and the Windy Wind Five had carved out quite a niche and name for itself. If they had landed on Saint Louis farmland in a spaceship, Ruby and the band might get requests for Fats Waller's "Honeysuckle Rose" from the local yokels.

It's really what Long Ray was after for Ruby, not necessarily the band. Yet the band had proven its worth, that it was as good as any jazz band currently working the jazz scene.

Ruby now had three show wigs, courtesy of the Windy Wind Five, to go along with her two nightgowns, courtesy of Ruby's new husband. The Windy Wind Five was on Sam Waters's rented bus, on its way back to Chicago. Long Ray had already told the congregation he was going to drive the bus back to Sam Waters's car lot and say, with his characteristic aplomb, "The Windy Five thanks you for the many memories, Sam!"

CHAPTER 20

"Don't worry, Ruby, we're almost home, baby."

Ruby took a look out the bus window for signs, for landmarks—physical things she knew were drawing the bus closer to Chicago.

"Chicago—it our home now, ain't it, Darkboy?"

"Yes, it is," Darkboy said, holding onto Ruby. "Home sweet home."

"We gonna make it a home," Ruby said shyly.

"Well, we're almost home," Long Ray announced from his driver's seat. "There, folks. We'll be saying hello to Chicago soon. Tipping our hats to the old gal and kissing the mayor. Well, sort of!"

"Gonna soak my butt in the tub. Promise you that. When I get home," Pinky said. "In a six-foot tub of ice and water and swear to never ride on one of Sam Waters's rented buses again—not for the life of me, man. Know Sam, the cat, overcharged you for this bucket of bolts, don't you, Long Ray? You gotta know that!" Pinky said.

"Stop complaining, Pinky," Long Ray said. "Sam's 'bucket of bolts,' as you call it, got us to Kansas City, Missouri, and back to Chicago in one piece, didn't it?"

Pinky checked his anatomy, feeling his bones like he was playing a xylophone, having had switched instruments from his sax.

"And here we are, lady and gentlemen," Long Ray called out, "at the mouth of the grand city of Chicago!"

"We home, Darkboy!" Ruby yelped. She kissed Darkboy, and both were aware it was the first time they'd kissed in Chicago.

"Ooo-wee, nothing like a Chicago kiss, huh, kids?" Long Ray said.

Ruby was still at the blushing stage but not Darkboy. "You said it, Long Ray!"

"Left Chicago poor, coming back to Chicago poor!" Pinky said.

"Listen to the cynic. Always the cynic."

"What that mean, Darkboy, cyn-cyncic?" Ruby whispered.

"Oh, it means—"

"Cyncic."

"Yes, *cynic*. Cynic, Ruby."

"Oh, cynic. Cyncic."

"It just means Pinky, uh, he's always looking on the dark, negative side of things. Anything. He'd see a dark cloud rather than a silver lining."

Ruby smiled. "Pinky don't mean it, Darkboy."

"Well, Ruby, sometimes, honestly, he does."

She nodded. "Well, maybe sometimes."

"Here we come, Sam, bringing it back to the lot!" Long Ray said.

"Yeah, you can have it back, Sam, so you can rent it to another sad, poor-ass band of jazz musicians on its way to Kansas City with a short supply of dough. Beat them out a buck. Another piggy bank pilfered," Pinky said.

Sam Waters had his bus back in his car lot, and it quickly emptied. The band got itself and the instruments off the bus.

Now it was just Long Ray, Darkboy, and Ruby. Long Ray was rolling his bass and carrying his suitcase, Darkboy his drum cases and suitcase, and Ruby hers, but they were walking about as light as spring with the anticipation of being minutes from the apartment building.

"Man, did we blow the lid off of Saint Louie," Long Ray said. "Saint Louis's hair's still standing on its end. Don't be surprised any if they want us back, kids, soon; I mean *real* soon."

"Would we go back out right away, Long Ray? So soon?" Darkboy queried.

"It's according to the money, Darkboy. Depends a lot on that. Money, now."

"Oh," Darkboy said.

Ruby eyed Darkboy.

"Begin thinking like businessmen now," Long Ray said. "Protect our interests. You do understand, don't you?"

"Uh, yes, sure, sure, Long Ray."

Long Ray stopped rolling the bass. "Ain't in this business to get rich; you know that, kids. Come from nothing, humble beginnings, same as every other jazz cat who's played this music. I know Jelly Roll, King Oliver, James P. Johnson—great musicians, great originators like them—when they died, they died basically poor. Nothing to show for their efforts. Anybody who has a pulse knows that."

Ruby thought of Miss Honey, buried in the back of Macguire's Baptist Church in Plattstown.

"The list goes on and on." Long Ray took a deep breath. "But Pinky, well, he was right: we went off to Kansas City poor and came back to Chicago poor. Pinky, sadly, *was* dead right." Long Ray extended his hand to Ruby. She took it. "But we're not going to let it happen to you, Ruby. Not to you, honey. What happened to those other great jazz musicians, singers—well, that won't happen to you. I swear to you, as God is my witness."

They continued walking, but Long Ray hadn't changed the sensitive subject. "Ruby could've made double, triple the money she made if we hadn't already cooked up the Kansas City/ Saint Louis deal in advance, Darkboy."

"She could've?"

"Easy. Damn, Ruby, those folk at the Flim-Flam would've paid a thousand bucks for a ringside seat. One thousand!"

"A ... a t-thousand dollars, Long Ray?" Ruby said as if her tongue didn't know how to pronounce *thousand*.

"Ruby, honey," Long Ray said patiently, "you're Ruby Midnight. Already the greatest jazz singer who ever lived, that the world has ever heard."

Darkboy had carried Ruby across a new threshold, and so that officially stamped the occasion they were home.

Of the two of them, Darkboy had the larger room, so Ruby moved out of her room and into Darkboy's.

"How's it in here?" Long Ray said. "Enough room?"

"Plenty, Long Ray," Darkboy said spreading his arms.

"Back to nine-to-five tomorrow, Darkboy," Long Ray said glumly. "Me, the elevator boy, taking white folk up to the penthouse. And you, the kitchen boy, scraping food off their plates down in the dungeon. None of them know about Kansas City, man. Saint Louis, do they? Nothing … none of that stuff. How special the band was out there."

"No … no, not at the Mayflower Hotel, they don't."

"Ain't supposed to. Hell, look, kids, it ain't about that anyway. It's about our music, not about them white cats. They don't have to know about it, as long as we do."

Darkboy knew just what Long Ray was getting at. So did Ruby.

"It's why we've got to take care of it like it's a newborn babe, Ruby," Long Ray said. "Have to."

"Y-yes, Long Ray," Ruby replied.

"The music, kids. And, uh, talking about the music, you feel like, uh …" Long Ray leaned his head like he leaned it into his bass, but this time it was in a northerly slant toward the front room, where the instruments were.

Only Ruby and Darkboy had something potentially upsetting to discuss with Long Ray. Something they'd had time to consider and discuss during their stay in Saint Louis, and they'd reached a strong conclusion.

"Got to tear up the Bluelight tomorrow night, kids. Set it on fire. Let Chicago's Southside know Ruby Midnight and the Windy Wind Five are back in town to reclaim its crown!"

Ruby and Darkboy walked into the front room with Long Ray. He pulled the bass off the wall and stood behind it, leaning his head into it. "Ain't you gonna sit down at your drum kit, Darkboy? It ain't gonna bite you, man. I promise."

Darkboy and Ruby were holding hands, presenting themselves as a united front.

"Marriage," Long Ray said with a sigh upon seeing the spectacle.

"Long Ray," Darkboy said firmly, "Ruby and I have given this a lot of thought. I just want you to know that—r-right, Ruby?"

"What, Darkboy?" Long Ray asked.

"A lot."

Ruby and Darkboy looked at Long Ray with grave concern. Darkboy cleared his throat and said, "Long Ray, Ruby and I can't stay in the apartment with you any longer, h-here."

Long Ray grabbed his head.

"L-Long—" Ruby started, but Long Ray cut her off.

"It's all right, right, Ruby. I-I'm all right." But Long Ray was reeling. "I just feel like I've been blindsided. But leaving here, Darkboy, you and Ruby? The apartment? F-four o'clock rehearsals? What we were about t-to do now? J-just now, man?"

No, Long Ray didn't seem to be all right.

"We married, Long Ray," Ruby said. "Darkboy an' me married. Got to be out on our own."

Long Ray put the bass back against the wall. "But, but I didn't think it would be this soon, Ruby, D-Darkboy. That's all. I, well, I just thought you'd settle in first. Yes, give it a little time, distance, you know. And then maybe look for your own place, say, in, in the future, not now. Not this soon. Sudden. Y-you caught me off guard. You really caught me com-completely off guard with this, kids."

"I ... I know," Darkboy replied, in tears.

"W-when, Darkboy? When are you and Ruby going to look for a new apartment?"

"Probably in another day or so—w-wouldn't you say, Ruby?"

"Yes, Darkboy."

"You kids, I ... I understand you kids have got to have your privacy. I do. I really, really do ... Darkboy ... Ruby." Long Ray's face looked anguished.

Long Ray had been tossing in his bed. Then he heard footsteps treading stealthily over the front room floor, the sound clear through his closed bedroom door.

First, it was Ruby's light footsteps he heard and then Darkboy's heavier steps. Each had gone into the bathroom to do what someone does after sex: wash up. *Darkboy and Ruby are no different*, Long Ray thought. But he could get used to this, the nights when Ruby and Darkboy made love.

Get used to it, not hear them in the bedroom. Even sleep through it before it began.

It was tonight that he was all messed up. Tonight, he was emotionally distraught. Tonight, he was being kept awake by the thought of losing them, of being without them—something that just hit him right between his eyeballs and stunned the living hell out of him.

He loved Ruby and Darkboy

They were family, a family he never had. They meant everything there was in life to him. Why hadn't he seen this in Kansas City, in Saint Louis—that it would have to be this, take on this kind of form, turn out this way?

"It seems you lose a piece of yourself every day," he said to himself. "Every damn day." Long Ray tossed, then turned. *Music—sometimes it can't take the place of life*, Long Ray thought. When someone meets a Ruby Midnight and a Jimmy Darkboy Slade, music takes a back seat, plays second fiddle.

"But, man, man, they're husband and ... and wife, man. Why should they have to sneak across a floor at night to get from their bedroom to the bathroom after sex so ... so not to be heard? Why? Why ... what for. Hell, man ... I know people, people in the real estate business in Chicago, don't I? Help, help Ruby and Darkboy move out the apartment myself, if I have to," Long Ray said in a much gentler mood. He rolled back onto his back and shut his eyes.

"Even though, for now, man, both are traveling light. Uh, very light, in fact."

Long Ray was thinking about the furniture, the Slades' furniture. *Now that's good for a good chuckle*, Long Ray thought. *The Slades' furniture.*

How many days had she been Mrs. Jimmy Darkboy Slade? Six, seven? Six—it just seemed like more. Ruby was up and about the apartment, making the bed, Darkboy's and hers, sweeping, mopping, keeping busy.

Wait until me an' Darkboy get our own apartment, Ruby thought. *Boy, am I gonna keep it spick-and-span!*

Darkboy and Long Ray were off to work at the Mayflower. They'd been gone a number of hours.

"He love me. Darkboy love me." Ruby was standing between the toilet bowl and the sink in the bathroom. "Darkboy love me."

Ruby still couldn't get over what had happened to her, the luck in her life, how things had changed so dramatically without there being any sense or sign or warning.

"Ugly." Ruby was looking at herself in the mirror. "Ugly black girl like me. Ugly black girl like me. Pick-pickaninny. Pickaninny girl. Mama call me. Nigger, nigger girl."

Ruby did not want to feel tears, feel or taste them, but she did. They rose to line her face.

"Darkboy love me. Darkboy love me. Darkboy love me. Darkboy love me."

But there was Miss Honey, before there was Darkboy, who loved her. Who thought her pretty, not ugly, not a pickaninny girl, a nigger girl, like her mother had.

Ruby's head turned from the wall mirror; she didn't know what face she saw, what person she was looking at and talking to.

Her voice—who would she be, what would she be, where would she be without her voice?

Ruby sat on the edge of the tub. She held her face in her hands. Her fingernails edged into her skin. She jumped back up and looked at her face in the mirror. And then, quickly, she took her face away from the mirror, as if she were playing a game of cat-and-mouse, hide-and-seek, with herself.

"Darkboy love my face. Darkboy love my face."

She wanted to feel pretty without wigs, without makeup, without the show dresses and high heels. When she and Darkboy made love, she wasn't in those things. Her body wasn't entrapped in them. When she and Darkboy made love, she was a "natural" woman. It was only her.

Ruby felt Darkboy's mouth on her skin. She sat back down on the edge of the tub, thinking of Darkboy, of how he held her in the night to make her feel pretty. Thinking that her mother had made a mistake, was drunk, too much in a drunken stupor to see her, to really see what she looked like—how pretty her little Ruby was.

But she still ached with the thought. Ruby's stomach was pained. She bent over. She moved over to the toilet. Her head was over the toilet.

"Mama. Mama."

She felt as if she were going to throw up. Puke. Her stomach felt every hurt of the past.

She could never be pretty.

She could never be pretty!

Darkboy, Miss Honey, the Bluelight Café, the Hey-Hey Club, the Flim-Flam Club, the miles of travel and applause and standing ovations and encores—the wigs, show dresses, makeup, spotlight could never, never make her pretty, make Ruby Midnight pretty.

"Mama, I is a pickaninny girl, Mama!"

Ruby held her stomach with everything in her, with her hands, trying not to feel the pain but feeling it; trying to block out the past but pressing it deeper inside herself; not wanting to think of Plattstown but thinking of it more and more; as if Chicago never existed, never was.

Not for one day of her natural-born life.

Long Ray and Darkboy were home from the Mayflower.

"Ooo-wee, fried chicken, man! Ruby's fried chicken tonight, Darkboy!" Long Ray and Darkboy were in the hallway. "Could open up a chicken shack, Darkboy, the way Ruby fries up fried chicken, man. Call it, I'm from Texas—"

"I'm from Louisiana—"

"Texas—"

"No, Louisiana."

"Fried—"

"Chicken."

"Hey, Darkboy, that sounds catchy: Texas Fried Chicken, man. Yes, Texas Fried Chicken! Sounds better than something like Louisiana, or ... or say, Kentucky Fried Chicken."

"I have to admit, Long Ray, it does sound like a winner, all right," Darkboy said, inserting the key into the door lock.

Ruby was waiting for Darkboy, wearing an apron, as he opened the door. "Darkboy." Ruby swooned.

"Ruby." Darkboy swooned back.

"I remember when I used to live here!" Long Ray teased.

"Oh, hi, hi, Long Ray," Ruby said.

"Oh, hi, hi, Long Ray," Long Ray parroted Ruby. "Ruby, honey, you and I are going to have to sit down and have a talk. A long, long talk, young lady."

Ruby giggled.

"Darkboy and I smelled supper out in, uh, the hall, Ruby—right, Darkboy? Crispy, juicy, and light, and perfectly seasoned to my delight."

Ruby had slipped into Darkboy's arms.

"Got a proposition for you, honey," Long Ray said.

Ruby was all ears.

"Listen to this, Ruby," Darkboy said, his voice sparking with skepticism.

"And good, Ruby. Listen good."

"Am, Long Ray." Ruby's forehead wrinkled.

"How … why, how about we, us, we open a chicken parlor, store, shop, shack—whatever you want to call it, right—open one right here in Chicago. We could go into the chicken business. The way you fry up chicken, all of us could live like millionaires!"

"Open up a jazz club," Darkboy said.

"Why not, Darkboy?" Long Ray said. "I've heard of worse Technicolor dreams and schemes, man."

They laughed.

"But all joking aside, Ruby. You do fry you up some mean fried chicken, young lady!"

"Thank you, Long Ray."

"Well, let me wash my hands. Of course, Darkboy doesn't have to wash his, since his hands have been in filthy, dirty dishwater all day."

For Long Ray, this had become a nightly, routine comment to Darkboy and Ruby, even before the two-city bus tour.

"S-so how was your day, Mrs. Slade?"

"Fine … it, it just fine, Mr. Slade," Ruby replied, playing along with this newlywed game.

Ruby and Darkboy kissed.

They were eating Ruby's fried chicken. Long Ray had had four pieces of chicken; Darkboy and Ruby were up to number two.

"Ruby," Long Ray said, reaching for his fifth piece of chicken on the platter. "Uh, being distracted by your fried chicken coming up the stairs, I forgot to tell you what happened today, honey. Guess who I got a call from at the Mayflower today, of all places?" Long Ray's grin was as wide as the China Wall.

"Who, Long Ray?" Ruby asked. "Know I ain't good at guessing."

"Zack. Zack Macketts called me at the Mayflower, of all people!"

Ruby was surprised. "What for, Long Ray?"

This was the part Darkboy didn't like—Long Ray had told him earlier about Zack Macketts's phone call, as if Ruby needed any added pressure.

"The Bluelight's sold out. Get this, Ruby—for the next six nights! There's not a seat to be sold nowhere, for no price. Couldn't seat a spider on the Bluelight's walls tonight, Ruby, Macketts said."

Long Ray was too busy eating the piece of chicken to see Ruby shaking. But Darkboy saw it, as if it were his own.

"What a night it's going to be for all of us, Ruby," Long Ray said. "Make...make it six nights, honey."

Darkboy and Ruby were in their bedroom getting dressed for the night's performance at the Bluelight. Darkboy was mostly dressed, almost there. Ruby wasn't. Uncharacteristically, she was lagging behind, slow tonight.

"Don't know what to wear?" Darkboy asked.

Ruby shook her head; it seemed hopelessly.

"Ruby, are, are you okay?"

"I … I doesn't know, Darkboy." Ruby stared blankly into the closet.

"Is the pressure—is it too much? Is it getting to be too much on you, b-baby?"

"I-I a jazz singer, Darkboy."

"I know that. But is the pressure getting to be too much for you? Is all of this happening to you too fast, t-too soon?"

"I got to sing." Ruby leaned back into Darkboy's arms. "Can't do not'ing, Darkboy. Can't do not'ing else but. Too ... too ugly to do not'ing else but—"

"Ugly! Ugly! Who said you were ugly? Where did that come from?"

"Pickaninny girl. Black girl. Nigger—"

"Don't say that, Ruby! Stop saying those things!"

"Mama say it, Darkboy! Mama right!"

"Your, your Mama was mean and cruel, a cruel woman. Hateful woman!" Darkboy said, his arms tensing around Ruby.

"Mama got eyes. Mama see, see me!"

"See what, Ruby? What she wanted to see? Your mother wasn't looking at you. Your mother was looking at her life—her life through her eyes, not through anyone else's."

Ruby turned to Darkboy with tears in her eyes. "I ... I doesn't know, Darkboy. I doesn't know what Mama see."

"Her eyes didn't see you. The beautiful you."

"I doesn' know what Mama see." Ruby continued to sob.

"She didn't see you," Darkboy said, shaking Ruby hard. "Do you hear me? Do you?"

"Mama never hear me sing."

Darkboy could feel the break in Ruby's heart and voice.

"I ... I doesn't sing to Mama, Darkboy. Mama doesn't let me sing to her."

Suddenly, Darkboy lifted Ruby off her feet, took her over to their bed, and laid her down.

"I got t-to get dressed, Darkboy. They waitin' at the Bluelight. I—"

Darkboy pressed his finger to Ruby's lips. "A minute."

"No, Dark—"

"You need a minute for yourself. With this. We won't be late. I promise."

"Long ... Long Ray, Darkboy."

"He'll understand."

Ruby nodded her head up and down.

Darkboy had dark thoughts. "I don't like your mother," Darkboy said in a sudden rage.

"I-I ain't trying to make Mama out bad, Darkboy, for you to hate Mama."

"I know that," Darkboy said, "but you can't change what she did—or what she did to you."

"No. No, doesn't try."

"But she—your mother—she buried it so far down inside of you, Ruby. Planted the seed."

"Can I stand up, Darkboy, n-now?"

"Why … of course. Of course. I'm your husband, not a prison guard." Darkboy chuckled.

"Do make it sound like that, doesn't I?" Ruby reached for Darkboy. She hugged his shoulders. "Sing good tonight. Like I standing in the middle of a green fields in Plattstown." It's what Ruby was imagining. "Free, Darkboy. Free!" Ruby was imagining.

"And I'm going to play my drums like I'm there with you, baby." Darkboy was imagining. "Out there in the green fields with you, baby. Okay?"

"Chicago feel good to me, Darkboy. Like I been on my way here all my life. This way. Com-coming to you, Darkboy. Running from home so I can come to you, fast as I can."

Darkboy thought of New Orleans, Cajun country, the drummers, the funeral marches, the specialness of everything those sights rendered him like gold coins, washing ashore at his feet, as lustrous as the sun darting out of clouds on a lazy afternoon, when the catfish jumped high up high in the blue waters.

He hadn't run from Louisiana, from home; it was on his own terms. But he had to leave home to become what he was.

"Darkboy, what are you and Ruby doing in there that you ain't out here!"

"In a second, Long Ray. In a second."

Ruby now realized what she was going to wear, which wig and show dress and shoes. She spied one of the wigs.

"The platinum one, Ruby?"

"Uh-huh," Ruby said coolly. "Bluelight Café ain't never seen me in the platinum one, Darkboy."

"Just the Flim-Flam Club in Saint Louis was so lucky. W-where you knocked them dead."

Ruby's eyes brightened.

"I'm serious now, kids," Long Ray called out. "Are you two coming out of there, out of that bedroom of yours, or not?"

Ruby put on a blue-platinum gown. "Okay, Darkboy?" And then Ruby put on blue high heels to match.

Darkboy heard Long Ray's breathing behind the door.

"Okay, Darkboy?" Ruby asked for Darkboy's approval.

"Okay, Ruby!"

Darkboy got up from the bed and walked over to Ruby, to collect her in his arms.

"And so, may I, Jimmy Darkboy Slade, escort you, Mrs. Ruby Darkboy Slade, to the Bluelight Café this evening, ma'am?"

Ruby pressed her lips together, her red lipstick softening her look. "Yes sir, you may."

The room door popped open.

"Ruby!"

"Ready, Long Ray."

"I-I should say, Ruby. I … I should say you are, honey."

"Was worth the wait, huh, Long Ray?"

"If Ruby could look any prettier, I'd marry her, Darkboy. And you know how square I am on marriage, kids." Long Ray offered his arm. Ruby took it.

But Long Ray knew he'd have to get his bass off the wall, and Darkboy knew he'd have to get his drum cases off the floor, but both knew it could wait until they at least escorted Ruby to the front door, as if they'd escorted her all the way to the Bluelight Café, just as they were.

"Ruby, you own this place. You own this town. Chicago's yours, honey!" Those were Long Ray's parting words to Ruby before she went out on the Bluelight bandstand.

The Bluelight crowd was thick, jarring, impulsive—reactive, a wild river in the night.

Darkboy had his drumstick in his hand, twirling it with great aplomb, showmanship; then he stopped. It was when Ruby kissed his cheek and melted into his arms, and he held her as if he were protecting her from the night, affording her shelter but only for so long, knowing she said she was going to sing tonight.

"Gonna sing like I standing in the middle of a green fields in Plattstown, Darkboy. Free, Darkboy. Free."

"We're on, Ruby!" Long Ray said.

Pinky, Cool Hands, and Loose Lips were up on the Bluelight's bandstand.

"Let's make music!"

And as soon as Long Ray, Darkboy, and Ruby got on the bandstand, they saw them—what Pinky, Cool Hands, and Loose Lips had already seen, sitting out in the Bluelight Café: cracker-white faces with fat black sunglasses wrapped around frosty, frigid faces.

Darkboy stumbled.

Long Ray already wanted to remake the night.

Ruby, innocent of anything and everything surrounding her, was at the microphone. And after the wave of applause, she waited for the spotlight that poured onto her platinum wig and then onto her blue-platinum gown and then her matching blue shoes, for Long Ray's definitive downbeat.

Ruby sang.

If a pretty butterfly were in a jar with red ants, what would be its fate?

Another person came into Zack Macketts's office as if he owned it. Ruby sat there like before, in front of the high desk, not behind it. This new person made his way behind the desk as the others preceding him had.

"Miss Midnight. Miss Midnight, my name's Fat Tony—Fat Tony Apollo, if youse wanna know alla it, as I'm sure youse do." He extended his right hand to Ruby, and Ruby's hand got swallowed in its massive mass of meat. "Pleasure is mine, Miss Midnight, is all mine."

Fat Tony Apollo sat down in Zack Macketts's chair. His head looked too small for a regular-sized hat, but his body was too big for the Bluelight office. Ruby didn't know what to make of him, so she looked at him as if he were not there.

"Youse, if I may say so, Miss Midnight, sing like a boid. Like a real divine, livin' boid!" Fat Tony Apollo, who breathed much heavier than he should, used his meaty hand to slap his thick thigh before continuing. "My family's from Naples. Speaks Neapolitan. Ever seen youse a Neapolitan sunset, Miss Midnight? Nothin' like it comes to mind. Enrico Caruso was born there. Enrico Caruso himself was born in Naples. Greatest singer the world's ever seen, Enrico Caruso, Miss Midnight—until you come along."

Fat Tony Apollo shut his eyes. "Hear Enrico Caruso records in my sleep since I was a little bit a nothin', Miss Midnight. His voice in my sleep. Could hum every note, every melody of *La Bohème, La Traviata, Pagliacci, La fanciulla del West, Rigoletto*—alla them operas, Miss Midnight. Puccini, Verdi, Leoncavallo, Rossini—alla them operas. "Still hum them in my sleep like a kid at night. Still. But tonight, Miss Midnight, tonight, I ain't hummin' Enrico Caruso in my sleep. No way. Guess how come I ain't, Miss Midnight?"

Courteously, Ruby nodded her head, not knowing "how come."

"Ruby! Ruby! I'll be hummin' Ruby Midnight tonight. Ruby Midnight an' only Ruby Midnight tonight!"

How many of these people have I seen tonight? How many have come and gone? Ruby asked herself. *The way he talks, the way he does his hands, the way he did.*

"How many do youse see tonight, Miss Midnight? How many o' them?" Fat Tony Apollo was gesticulating. "Fancy-smancy talk—*goombahs*!"

Ruby didn't know this talk, any of it—the sound of it was primitive, raw, by its own construction.

"Goombahs, Miss Midnight. Goombahs!"

He won't bother to explain, Ruby thought. *He too busy talkin'. Too busy.*

"Bright lights, Miss Midnight. Fame, Miss Midnight. You ever see your name in bright lights, Ruby? Stretched a block long? A city block long?" Fat Tony stretched out his short arms, all the way out. "'Round the corner, uh, the block."

Ruby didn't know what to think or how to react; she just kept watching Fat Tony Apollo stretch his arms until he stopped and then breathed heavy, far heavier than he should have.

"And ... and records, Ruby? Records. Records. The best!" Fat Tony's lips kissed his fingertips with a power, a passion, and a loud *smack*! And like the others had done before him, Fat Tony Apollo whipped a contract out of his suit pocket. "It's all yours, Ruby. Everything. The world's yours. Paris.

Germany. Italy. It's yours, Ruby! Your oyster pearl, Ruby. All yours. All youse gotta do is sign on the dotted line! It's all youse gotta do, Ruby, and it's yours!"

Fat Tony whipped a pen from his suit jacket. "The world's yours. Gift-wrapped. Pretty as the dress youse wearin'. Pretty, pretty as a Neapolitan sunset. The world's gonna love you, Ruby. Miss Ruby Midnight. Gonna love the earth youse walk on. The whole, wide, freakin' world!"

The band was in Long Ray's apartment. It was 2:36 a.m.

Four of them were drinking black coffee; two had declined.

"Smell like a barrel of dead fish!" Pinky pinched his nose.

"I ... I know, Pinky." Long Ray took three quick puffs off his cigarette.

"How many of them was there, anyway, Long Ray? Maybe ten, fifteen of them greasy-spoon cats?" Loose Lips asked.

"More like fifteen, Loose Lips."

"Yeah, yeah."

"Licking their chops like hyenas at the gate," Cool Hands said. "Always come in a pack, don't they? Tell me I'm wrong. Mistaken."

Ruby was sitting, and Darkboy sat to her right.

Long Ray had called for this get-together. What had happened tonight to Ruby had to be taken under careful, prudent counsel. All of the Windy Wind Five, its total accumulation of wisdom, knowledge, and experience, had been called into service to help Ruby, to guide her way through this morass. It was its sole mission, its sole purpose: to help Ruby.

"At least Ruby didn't sign anything!" Cool Hands said.

"No, no, I doesn't, Cool Hands," Ruby said, her eyes downcast. "Doesn't sign not'ing in the room."

"Shocked the living daylights out of you, though, I know, honey," Cool Hands said. "Didn't it?"

"Yes, it do, Cool Hands. Yes," Ruby said, bowing her head.

"Probably been planning alla this since Saint Louis," Loose Lips said. "The Flim-Flam Club."

"Word got to their ears quick," Cool Hands said.

"Cash registers jingling in hell, Cool Hands," Loose Lips said, "Can hear them damned cash registers!"

"New York," Long Ray said. "It's New York, isn't it, Ruby?"

"Yes, Long Ray."

"And every other place there is on the map. Paris. Germany. Probably threw in Italy too," Pinky said.

Silence.

"I ... I doesn't wanna go," Ruby said, turning to Darkboy. "I ain't going nowhere!"

Silence.

"But you have to, Ruby," Darkboy said weakly. "You have to."

"B-but I doesn't wanna, Darkboy. Go. Doesn't."

"Suppose you don't go." Long Ray took a few jerky puffs from his cigarette, then ground it hard down into the floor.

Pinky examined his shoes and then looked over at Ruby. "Missed opportunities—they kill you in this business."

"Someone always comes along," Cool Hands said. "There's always some girl they're trying to make a star. Make her out like she's gold. The hottest thing since—"

"Maybe not as good as you, Ruby," Pinky cut in.

"Yeah, ain't that the truth, Pinky. But those louses are still gonna sell them like she's gold," Long Ray said. "Like she's the best thing since Bessie Smith. Or, say, Ma Rainey. Doesn't matter to them, as long as they can make a fast buck in a fast town until word gets around. Cir-circulates." He turned to Ruby. "But you're the real thing. They don't have to do any fast maneuvering or flashy footwork to sell—"

"Ain't no Cracker Jack in a box," Pinky said, cutting off Long Ray again. "A dime a dozen, doll."

"You can get there, Ruby. You can get to all those places those people promised you. Ruby Midnight can get there," Long Ray said emphatically.

"So that's why you must consider it, Ruby," Darkboy said.

"Dark ... Darkboy, I—"

"The world owes you at least that much, baby."

The band knew they couldn't say any more than what Darkboy had already said with such youthful wisdom.

Darkboy let Ruby move from his side and out of the bed; then out the door without interrupting her.

After a few minutes, Ruby was back in bed. "Have to go, Darkboy." Ruby giggled.

Darkboy got up, went out of the room, came back, and climbed into the bed. "Me too, Ruby."

Both laughed.

He held Ruby's hand; there was heat in it.

"It gonna be okay, Darkboy. You gonna see."

Darkboy laid his hands across Ruby's hips. "I know it is, Ruby." He turned to face her. "I have all the agents' names and telephone numbers. So don't worry. But it's you, baby—it's you who's going to have to pick the one you want. The one who—"

"Make me feel comfor'ble. Can ... can you?"

"No, baby; it's your decision to make."

"Got to make a lotta them from now on, doesn't I, Darkboy? Them on my own."

Darkboy knew he played as pivotal a role as anyone, as Ruby's husband, in Ruby's decision, since it'd have an enormous influence on him. But he also knew he had to give Ruby as much space as possible so that she could work her way, develop through this process, the emotional and mental, all the requirements she'd have to meet in settling for success.

"Darkboy?"

"Yes?"

"Do you, can you, you ..." Ruby fumbled for words. "Call in sick to the Mayflower this morning?"

Darkboy laughed. "You know we just got in from our twelve-day road trip, Ruby."

"I ... I know."

"And I don't think the Mayflower would take too kindly to me—"

"Sorry, sorry, Darkboy."

Darkboy swallowed hard. He knew what Ruby was going through; the same thing he was, no matter his lofty thoughts before that he had tried to let anchor his taut, raw emotions. The game, the stakes, had been raised and had become omnipotent, all-consuming. Life was beginning to stretch out like a big, brawny river, and he and Ruby were being swept into its strong undertow.

No one had to tell him this. It was there, hairy as an ape, scary as hell.

Darkboy shut his eyes and tried to think of Chick Webb playing his drums at the Savoy Ballroom in New York City. He'd heard tales, stories from jazz musicians (Cool Hands and Pinky, to name two) about the notorious "cutting sessions." That's what Chick Webb was doing in his head now, at this very instant, thundering his drums so hard and ruthlessly and recklessly that he was hanging any drummer out to dry who dared challenge him.

Today is here, Darkboy thought. *And then the tomorrows. They are the ones no one—not even Ruby—can count on.* They were the stars Ruby knew nothing about. Lucky stars, unpredictable stars. Stars with little conscience or regard for Ruby toward the completion of her destiny.

What star had he and Ruby been standing under when, just yesterday, they were talking about how lucky they were to find each other in Chicago, in the heat and whirlwind of this dynamic city? Him from Louisiana. Her from Plattstown. And both were in Chicago in love, married, Mr. and Mrs. Darkboy Slade.

Mr. and Mrs. Darkboy Slade.

But hadn't he fallen in love with Ruby when he first heard her sing, like everyone else? Hadn't he wanted to take her away from something when he first heard her sing, like everyone else? How long would it be before she went to New York? And when would she come back to Chicago, back to him? But he was Ruby's husband. What did it mean in Chicago, "Hog Butcher for the World," as Carl Sandburg had described the city? Hogs slaughtered for a good price on the meat market. Who fixed the market's prices? Who? Him—Jimmy Darkboy Slade?

Chick Webb was drumming in Darkboy's head. He was cutting someone in a jam session at the Savoy Ballroom in Harlem. Killing his competition off, one by one. Drum master, mastering the world for as long as he could until some young cat, some hep, dynamo drummer walked through the Savoy Ballroom's open doors, carrying his drum kit, set it up, and then rolled his thunder, lightning quick, out the air until the master toppled, fell from grace, lost his crown, and was laid to rest—dead. A graveyard of dead bodies.

The stars said Ruby had to go to New York City.

Ruby had to prove she was the best jazz singer in the world. Even as she slept (she had dozed off in the bed), the light sound of her breath was the most compelling sound in the world. In perfect pitch, in perfect harmony with the universe, the forces that are—that be.

Even now, as Ruby slept lightly, she could drift Darkboy out on a cloud, for he could dock his dreams at paradise's door. Even now, as she slept, Ruby could hand Darkboy that piece of that, give it to him, and it was only New York, knocking for now, who wanted Ruby's hand, until life began beckoning her for more than what was there before.

CHAPTER 21

Darkboy stood in front of the window at Midway International Airport, staring wanly out at the Chicago sky, wearing clothes he'd worn for the second day—two days in a row.

"Well, she's gone. Ruby's gone, Darkboy," Long Ray said. "Ruby's never been on a plane. What about you? Twice been on a plane in my life. Twice. Don't ask me where to. I'm still shaking in my shoes."

Long silence.

"She couldn't take us, Long Ray."

"Uh, we discussed that, Darkboy. All, all of that before."

"Why should they want us when it was Ruby they came to the Bluelight for? Ruby can make any band sound great, can't she, Long Ray? Can't she?"

"I don't know if Ruby's gonna find another band quite like ours in New York City. The caliber of ours. But hope so. I know it doesn't feel fair. I know this is the first time you've had to face something like this head-on. Something as grave as this, man. Something that hurts the heart."

"But I have to be positive, don't I, Long Ray? Positive. At least do that much for myself—think positive."

"She's your wife, Darkboy. She'll come back."

"The apartment. I told Ruby I'd still look for the apartment. Our … our apartment."

"That's good. And I'll help you with that. How about that?"

"Thanks, Long Ray," Darkboy said, half smiling.

"You and Ruby'll have a place by the time she gets back. Make certain of it." Long Ray buttoned his outer coat. "Ready, Darkboy?" He saw

Darkboy hadn't buttoned his outer coat. "Better button up. It's beginning to get cold. Weather's changing. Cold in Chicago."

And it's what Darkboy began doing, buttoning his coat, as if he knew it was getting cold in Chicago.

The plane had landed. The plane had taxied. The plane was at LaGuardia Airport in New York City. Ruby was a bagful of nerves.

She ducked her head to avoid the overhead bin, then stepped out into the aisle, and then stood erect. She couldn't wait to get off the plane. All she had thought about, the entire trip, was Darkboy. He'd given her a book to read at O'Hare. She had told him last night, in bed, she was going to read a lot while away. That she wished to get better at reading. She told Darkboy it was something she had determined to do.

Ruby carried the book as she walked down the aisle—Langston Hughes's book of poetry. But it'd remained unread during the flight.

Where am I? Where have I brought myself? One minute here, the next minute there. The music wasn't inside her. The music had left her.

Ruby didn't want to cry.

Help me, Miss Honey. Help me. I doesn't want to cry, Miss Honey. Help me, Miss Honey!

Ruby was off the plane. She had her suitcase. He was supposed to be waiting.

"Ruby! Ruby!"

He was there! Fat Tony Apollo was at LaGuardia Airport. The one who painted Neapolitan sunsets and loved Enrico Caruso and could hum every note, every melody of *La Bohème, La fanciulla del West, Rigoletto,* "all of them operas" in his sleep was there at LaGuardia Airport, like he'd said. He was attired in a snazzy red sports coat, black pants, white shirt, black shoes, and a red bowtie that could light up Broadway.

"Here, here, let me take your suitcase!"

"Thank you, thank you, Mr. Apollo."

"Ruby." Fat Tony Apollo's fishbowl-of-a-face frowned. "Foist off, since, well, since I'm your agent an' I'm gonna be managin' you an' all, in this here enterprise of ours, why don't ya call me Fat Tony, or Tony, if youse like, if you ain't one stuck on nicknames."

Ruby smiled politely. "Tony ... or, or Mr. Tony. Ain't never called nobody Fat Tony before. Sound like you funning them, otherwise."

Fat Tony laughed. "I don't take no offense, Ruby. Eat too many meatballs to take offense to nobody calling me Fat Tony." He rapped on the taxi's window with his pudgy knuckles. "Back!" he said to the dozing cabbie.

"Oh ... sure, sure thing, Mr. Apollo!"

The driver rushed out the cab, took the suitcase from Fat Tony, and opened the car door for Ruby and Fat Tony to get in.

"You foist, Ruby."

Ruby got in the cab, then Fat Tony. The cabbie put the suitcase in the trunk, slamming it, but not enough for the cab to shake or jostle, since Fat Tony sat in the back seat.

"Back to Manhattan, where we started from—what you say?" Fat Tony said to the cabbie, while adjusting his red bowtie. "We gotta show this gorgeous gal, here, New York's bright lights!"

Ruby was in the ladies' room. It was clean and tidy. Fat Tony had told her this would be the club where she'd make her singing debut tomorrow night. The Downbeat Club.

What is Darkboy doing?

Ruby looked down at her wedding band. She was Jimmy Darkboy Slade's wife. What was she doing in New York City? What was she doing away from Darkboy in this strange place? New York City?

New York City was big and burly—she'd seen that. It was bigger than what her eyes could hold onto for such long periods of time. She looked at it star-struck, like anybody, like a stranger from the backseat of a New York taxicab.

But it would be tomorrow when she would have to sing for New York City. Tomorrow night, she would have to do it alone, without Darkboy, without the Windy Wind Five playing behind her.

"I doesn't know not'ing, Darkboy."

The book Ruby had carried into the ladies' room was the Langston Hughes book. When she got the chance between rehearsals and all, she would read it. *It's something from Chicago,* she thought. The ring on her finger, the book in her hand—her life shouldn't be sad.

The drums Darkboy sat behind could be anybody's drums. Any drummer's drums. They could make any sound they wanted. Darkboy didn't care. He didn't give a damn.

Darkboy was looking for a downbeat from Long Ray. Long Ray didn't seem to mind; he just wanted to get on to the music. The band was hired to play tonight in the Bluelight Café.

The first sound from the band in the Bluelight was flat. Nobody seemed to mind, neither the patrons nor the musicians.

"We stunk tonight, all of us. A skunk wouldn't want to be around us—we stunk so much. Stunk the fucking joint out," Pinky said.

"Hell, you think anybody noticed, Pinky?" Long Ray said.

"Shouldn't've played at all. The Supreme Court couldn't't've made a case for us not to," Cool Hands said.

"Legitimate case, you mean, Cool Hands," Loose Lips said.

"Might as well've been a funeral," Pinky said. "But who the fuck cancels a funeral? How fucking long can you keep a dead body, corpse on ice?"

"Darkboy, I—"

"Can I just put my drums away, Long Ray?" Darkboy said. "J-just let me do that much, o-okay?"

Tonight, they'd drunk too much liquor, Darkboy and Long Ray. Their walk up the street, the way their shadows moved, occupied space, silently, of course, but weaving in and out of each other like twisting trees all but gave them away.

"Darkboy is … is but the first night of this shit, man." Long Ray was rolling his bass as if he were standing behind a boulder, rolling it up a steep hill like Sisyphus.

"I love her."

"Nothing was the same tonight."

"It was worse than dying, Long Ray." Darkboy laughed cynically. "It had to feel worse than my own death."

"She's up there, Darkboy. Uh, when does she start at the Downbeat, again?"

"Tomorrow night."

"It had to come, Darkboy. Had—"

"They came without warning."

"Like locusts. Blackening the sky. Always do, Darkboy. Always."

"Are, are they that bad, Long Ray?"

"They've got their world—and, and we've got ours. And they intertwine."

"And now Ruby, Ruby's a part of it."

"Caught in it. Ruby's gonna know fame and fast."

"Let's stop for a second, can we? I've got to catch my breath, man." Darkboy bent over in order to breathe better. "My … my head—I don't feel good. So good."

"Ha, we're both drunk, Darkboy. Drunk as hell. Pinky, Cool Hands, Loose Lips—all of us got our heads bad. Tore up tonight."

The liquor had flowed at the Bluelight that night. Zack Macketts had made a sackful of money.

"All of us were as blue as the midnight without Ruby, Darkboy. Yeah, man, the Bluelight Café lived up to its billing."

"It's a nice club, Long Ray? The Downbeat Club?"

"Heard it was. Supposed to bring the best, showcase the finest talent. Say it's first class."

"So Mr. Apollo didn't stick Ruby in a hole? A-a dump, then?"

"No, just the opposite. Apollo put rouge on Ruby's cheeks. He shined the apple."

No longer was Darkboy bent over, but his stomach remained queasy.

"Man, we're going to have to set the alarm clock tonight, Darkboy, if we plan to get off to the Mayflower this morning. As bad as our heads are. F-feel."

Already, Darkboy was looking into a stack of dishes at the Mayflower and seeing Ruby in them, bright and clear.

Darkboy's room light was off.

A wig stared at him as if it were human, a real person. Darkboy could swear it was moving. At least his eyes were telling him as much. Not all of Ruby's clothes were out of the closet. Ruby hadn't taken all of her belongings to New York City.

"You are coming back, Ruby. Y-you have to come back."

Darkboy's mind flashed back to Ruby's last night at the Bluelight. The roses. The applause. But he was the one who was losing her, suffering loss, not them—those people sitting out in the Bluelight Café, applauding her. He was losing a wife, someone who was more to him than a jazz singer who made golden tones, beautiful sounds that God put in her throat.

He was losing Ruby, not them. He had to come home to this, this emptiness; not those people at the Bluelight, tossing roses at Ruby's feet, bouquets of flowers, applauding her to what seemed no end in sight—endlessly. His life was now what he was seeing, what stood before him, mountainous and unsure and vague.

How long would this go on, have to exist? That was the only question he could ask himself. How many more nights of this, not even hearing anything his drums spoke tonight? Just beating them, beating them mindlessly so they could hear themselves cry. Drumming. Drumming. Just beating them as if his drumsticks were making piles of anger deep inside the caverns of his ears.

"I wasn't making music. The Windy Wind Five wasn't—we weren't making music tonight. We were crying for Ruby. All of us, man. Crying out our instruments for her."

He was Ruby's husband. He was married to her. He knew her soul inside out, not just a song, a melody, but her song's soul, how it sang when it gave all it could give to a man.

Darkboy looked over at their bed. "It's lonely without you, Ruby. Lonely. Cold, cold as hell, baby."

But there wasn't much of the night left. He and Long Ray would be going off to the Mayflower soon. Hambone would smile his smile at him—someone, if anyone, who knew pain. Who knew cotton fields and a white man's whip lashing into his back like a black snake, whipping into the wind. Even if Hambone was never a slave, a part of that generation, his daddy was, who'd bled "their" blood on a white man's plantation.

But a drum, a drum and a woman?

What did Hambone know about a drum and a woman? A drum he beat on for love. A woman he touched for love. *What does any pain teach anyone about anything?* Darkboy thought. You hate a white man but love a drum, a woman—or do you hate them too?

Maybe he was too drunk to think, too much in pain to try. Or maybe ten or fifteen years from now, he'd understand this more. But now, he couldn't wait to get to the Mayflower to listen to Hambone's blues pour out from his radio; that had to be worse than his blues, five generations worse than his blues—at least a man's, a woman's, and a drum's blues.

Next night

The change dropped into the coin box, and all in the world felt good again to Ruby.

Ring.

Ring.

"Hello."

"Long Ray!"

"Ruby!"

"It me, Long Ray!"

"Ruby, I'll get Darkboy!" Long Ray said, letting the wall phone hang by its wire in the kitchen. He ran off to Darkboy's room. "Darkboy, it's Ruby. Ruby on the phone!"

"Ruby!" Darkboy dashed out the bedroom door and past Long Ray, who trailed him.

"Ruby!"

"Darkboy!"

"Tell her I love her!" Long Ray said.

"Ruby, Long Ray says he loves you."

"Tell him me too, Darkboy. Me too!"

"She loves you, Long Ray."

Long Ray smiled, then left the room.

"Darkboy."

"Baby. Ruby, the club. The Downbeat?"

"Ev'thing go great tonight, Darkboy."

"They loved you, Ruby!"

"Uh-huh."

"How did the band—"

"Band play good. Real good. We rehearse."

Darkboy smiled, about as pretty as the last penny in a poor man's pocket.

"I-I miss, I miss you, Darkboy."

"I miss you too, Ruby." Darkboy's feet shuffled. "The Downbeat Club, was it full, Ruby? Packed tonight?"

"Packed, Darkboy. It packed, all right."

"How many encores?"

"E-eight."

"You were counting?"

"Kind … kind a." Ruby giggled.

"There should've been more."

"Oh, Darkboy."

"Well, there should have, Ruby. For my wife."

Ruby felt goose pimples prick her skin.

"Uh, last night at the Bluelight, it was a disaster. The band, the music, the crowd."

"What 'bout tonight, Darkboy? How it go?"

Darkboy's body slumped. "Not much better."

Ruby felt all of him. "Mr. Apollo, he show me New York City, Darkboy. My eyes get tired—so much to see. Staying in Harlem, Darkboy. Up-uptown. Got a room. It nice. Real—"

"You—do you feel safe up there?"

"It fine. Ev'thing Mr. Apollo do for me, it turning out fine."

"Ruby, by the way, did you read the book I gave you, baby?"

"On the plane," Ruby said excitedly. "When I read it. Such pretty words Langston Hughes use. Write such pretty words in the book he write."

"They are, Ruby. Poetry. It's poetry, baby."

"Po'try?"

"But uh, you haven't read all of it?"

"Most a the book left to read. For me, Darkboy. Po'try."

"You'll—"

"Darkboy." Most of Darkboy's name lingered on Ruby's tongue. "Gonna call you soon."

"I … I know you will, baby," Darkboy said, shutting his eyes, reimagining just how Ruby looked at Midway International Airport. "Well, it's goodbye for now, Ruby, I-I guess."

"Darkboy … real soon I call you."

"I love you, baby."

"Darkboy, I love you, love you, love you too."

Long Ray was sitting in Darkboy's chair in front of his drums. He wasn't going to bother him; Darkboy had to ride this thing out; emotionally ride it out.

Darkboy had walked into the kitchen and walked out the kitchen, as if he were pacing, thrashing out his impatience.

"She's a hit, Long Ray. She's taken New York by storm. H-how many times haven't we said that before a-about Ruby? Tell me, man? Some place by storm."

Darkboy's dark skin was burning so brightly that Long Ray felt as if he could see his reflection in it.

Long Ray got up from Darkboy's drum set. He pulled his bass off the wall and started strumming it and then plucked it. "Man, oh man … the band's been sounding bad the past two nights. Shit. Off key," Long Ray said with seriousness.

Darkboy looked up at Long Ray, as if he'd shouted into his dream and had turned it back into a nightmare.

"This, I don't like. None of it. We're jazz musicians, not some down-and-out bargain basement jazz cats."

Darkboy looked at his drums, then realized he was doing just that—looking at them.

"We've been neglecting ourselves, the music, for the past few days. All of us. The whole damned band, man. The lot of us."

Darkboy's hand touched the snare drum's skin—it felt good.

"Life goes on, Darkboy; it has to, man. Ain't nothing us mere mortals can do to stop it. And we've been trying, and it's killing us. Downright killing us. Putting us down."

Darkboy straddled the chair, reached down, and grabbed his practice pads.

"It's a bad situation all the way around. But I don't know if time makes it better or worse. See, when I play this note"—Long Ray plucked another string on the bass fiddle—"it just keeps vibrating until it stops. That's life—hear it? There's a life in that note."

"I have to get a hold of myself, don't I?"

Long Ray was sympathetic. "I'm just talking to you, man to man, that's all. Ruby's inside all of us. None of us was given a pass, free pass, man. But Ruby's not gone forever."

"No, no, she's not."

"She's in New York temporarily. Y-you didn't think—"

"It's the first time for me, Long Ray."

"Separation, no, Darkboy. I haven't forgotten."

"So what are you going to say to the guys, Long Ray?"

"Say, why, ha, why, to get off their asses and back in gear, that's what. Un-unless Zack Macketts is gonna throw all of us the hell out of the Bluelight!" Playfully, Long Ray strummed a series of consecutive notes on his bass. "Been noticing how the cat's been looking at us. One more night of our shenanigans, uh, shit, how we've been conducting our business on the bandstand, and I think that white cat's gonna pop a vein in his neck."

"We have been sounding bad, awful bad, Long Ray."

"Like five-day-old milk. Atrocious, Darkboy. Just—but the Bluelight's audiences have been the same as us, no different: off key, man. On the skids." Long Ray laughed.

"But not tonight, not if I can help it," Darkboy said, rubbing his itchy leg.

"Shucks, man, hit the cats with some rim shots, Darkboy. Drop some rim shots on them they'll never forget, huh?"

"Rim shots, cymbals."

"The whole nine yards. It's our job to bring life back into the club. Resuscitate the old girl."

Darkboy's face crackled. "We're jazz players but, but entertainers too, Long Ray. People pay to hear us play, s-so we can't disappoint them, no matter the situation. No matter how bad it gets."

"Darkboy, before we commence, my bladder got so excited, it's about to burst, man. Pinky ain't the only one who's been peeing a lot, whose bladder needs work on!"

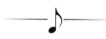

Ruby didn't want to let go of the phone; she pretended Darkboy still was on the other end. She entertained the next time they would speak— how it would feel—because her heart felt so rich and full, still so much in love with Darkboy, it continued to hurt in new ways. But Darkboy's voice made her so happy—it brought her back to life—that her life wouldn't spiral out of control.

Ruby yawned, covered her mouth, and stretched her arms. "I can stretch myself to the moon," Ruby said. She felt about as awake as a night owl perched on a branch. Ruby laughed at herself as she made her way up the short hallway, and away from the hall phone. But hearing the door behind her crack open, temporarily halted her.

Ruby turned. "Oh, hi ... hi, Happy. Hope I doesn't 'sturb you none."

"Not at all, Ruby. Just heard you up, that's all."

Happy Gillingham was big. When Ruby first saw him, she thought he could push one of Sam Waters's buses out a ditch by himself, even if he walked with a crutch.

"Glad you smiling, Ruby. It's what I try to do, through it all. Rain or shine."

William "Happy" Billingham told Ruby he'd been a professional fighter but was in a barroom brawl five years earlier, and half his kneecap had been blown off by a shotgun blast. It had ended his boxing career. Happy's right leg had been amputated from the kneecap down. Happy had told Ruby that he missed boxing a lot, but now he was working for Fat Tony Apollo, who told him to keep an eye on his property, the building that Fat Tony owned, and "otherwise" (meaning Ruby).

"The way you sing, Ruby, don't need to be sad."

"Thank you, Happy, but—"

"I ... I know," Happy said, tightening his robe around his burly-bruiser of a body and leaning lightly on his crutch. "You away from home."

"Where you from, Happy?"

"Travel, uh, up from Memphis, Tennessee. Ain't got nothin' but fightin' on my mind at the time. Fightin' an' fame. Not the blues, mind you."

"I ain't never been to a boxin' match."

"You like it, Ruby." Happy laughed. "Till somebody gets hit, that is. Women don't like it much when they see them get hit. Squashed. Squeamish. What it comes down to mostly with women."

"Faint ... faint way?"

"Sometimes."

"Well ..."

"Gets lonely, this time of night, don't it?"

Ruby nodded.

"I wake easy. It's how come I heard you up. I wanted it so bad, Ruby," Happy said, "to be heavyweight champion of the world like, like Joe Louis."

Ruby looked down at Happy's amputated leg.

"At night, sometimes I wish the doc don't cut it off—the durn, damn, damned thing off. Make me a new one. Start all over again. But I can't, Ruby. Ain't no way that I can." Happy seemed embarrassed, but Ruby's eyes softened, as if protecting him. "So ... I ..."

"Doesn't know what I do wit'out my voice. My, my singing."

"G-guess not. You come up from ..."

"Plattstown."

"We're all runnin' up here to New York from something to find something, ain't we, Ruby? Me a boxer. Pug. P-prizefighter. You a jazz singer. Me from Memphis. You from Plattstown."

"An' New York got us, Happy."

"Yeah, Ruby, got us, got us all right. Do you dream about it, what you after at night? Do it wake you up? Trouble your sleep, Ruby? Keep it stirring?"

"No. Uh-uh."

"I wake easy. Don't know if it's the pain in my leg or ... Don't lose your dreams, Ruby. Don't let nobody take them from you. Take it from a boxer. Nobody pull no rug from under you. Night, Ruby."

"Night, Happy."

"Keep smiling."

The lights were on in the one-bedroom apartment. "The book, Darkboy's po'try book." It was on the bed. "Got to read it. Got to lie to Darkboy I do. I already do it, so ..." Her hand glided over the book. "So I can't take it back. Not like a fib. But I know the words be pretty. Lang'on Hughes's words be pretty an' nice in the book. What Darkboy want me to learn. Po'try book. Po'try book."

Ruby's eyes shut. "Sing for all them white folk. They like me, but, but I can't stay in they hotels. Ain't right to do. Mixing wit' coloreds. Wit' us that way." Ruby looked at her room. "Mr. Tony give me a nice room in his place. Way it s'pose to be: colored wit' colored."

Ruby was about to open the Langston Hughes book when she thought of William Happy Billingham and what he'd said. "I does have dreams waking me in the night, Happy."

There was something driving her. Something. It had been there ever since she'd met Miss Honey, put on that white dress, gone off to Macguire's Baptist Church, sat in that front pew, and sung. The whole church had fallen silent, as if it were listening to some kind of miracle child with a golden voice, singing in their midst. She'd run from Plattstown for something that had to see the light of day.

"Mama ... an' Daddy ..." Ruby said, as if both were in her one-bedroom apartment in Harlem with her.

She'd run away from Plattstown. Was it because of them, her mother and father, or because she wanted to be a jazz singer, *had* to be a jazz singer? She'd dreamed of it in her urine-soaked bed—oh, how she'd dreamed of it at night. Miss Honey had put a dream in her that her mother couldn't take from her or destroy.

She wouldn't let her do that, not to her dream. She'd run away from home, traveled with a suitcase, run off with her dream. There couldn't be anything bigger than her wanting to be a jazz singer, Ruby thought; otherwise, she'd still be in Plattstown. She'd still be with Millicent and Man Martinson (if he was still there). But she was in New York City, Harlem—a jazz singer. The past couldn't take away her future, snatch it from her.

And she had a future. Mr. Tony said she had a "fantastic, spectacular" future. He kept telling her of those places she'd never heard of, never dreamed of, but now could. She could dream of those places a thousand times at night, over and over in her bed. It's how close they were to her: rainbow days and sun-kissed skies.

Ruby looked at her wedding band and cried. She'd have to get used to this, being away from Darkboy. Split apart from him like this. To become what she'd dreamed of becoming meant this. She wasn't dumb or stupid.

She put down the book. She stood over her suitcase and then knelt down on the floor. When she held the album cover, Ruby's heart thumped.

Ruby giggled.

And she felt different kinds of tears in her eyes. Tears of joy, not sadness. Holding onto a record of Miss Honey's that she'd buried under her house's front porch in the dirt, a record that she'd never played—never heard.

Miss Honey's record. Miss Honey's record.

She carried it, always, in her suitcase; always there.

"New York, Miss Honey. You, you back in New York, ma'am."

It's something Ruby had said repeatedly to Miss Honey since the two had landed together in New York City from Chicago two days ago.

Months later

Many things in the lives of Ruby Midnight, Darkboy Slade, and the Windy Wind Five had transpired.

For starters, Ruby was still in New York City, knockin' 'em dead. And the Windy Wind Five had arranged a return trip to the wild, wild west— Kansas City, Saint Louis, plus a few other cities and towns, stops along the way. The tour had been arranged by the band, with the club owners' full knowledge that one Miss Ruby Midnight no longer sang with the band.

The tour was a great success. More tours were to come. The Windy Wind Five had built itself a solid, much-respected reputation.

It'd been five months since Ruby had left Chicago for New York City—Darkboy could tell you that much. He could also tell you how lonely a day feels and how his drums drummed him further and further into the night, bitter and sweet and then back to bitter again.

$$\text{\textnumero}$$

It'd been arranged by phone: Ruby was coming back to Chicago, back home.

Darkboy had spoken to her on the phone the past evening. It'd been that simple, that fast. Darkboy was on cloud nine, as high flying as a kite—any cliché that fit, Darkboy used.

The moment when it occurred, Darkboy had no idea how he'd handle it. Would Ruby look the same? Her voice sounded the same over the phone, but physically—physically, how did she look? What had she grown in to after five months? Just what had New York City done to her, for her?

Darkboy was talking to his drums, to Chick Webb, but tomorrow, at Midway International Airport, would he have his answer when he saw Ruby and her suitcase and that she was back—back home in Chicago with him, her husband, Darkboy Slade.

CHAPTER 22

Darkboy was jumpy. But he'd see and feel her in a closet with a thousand coats piled on him. No time or distance would change that.

"Ruby!"

"Darkboy!"

And the world seemed to be filled with sharps and no flats—so much worth living in.

How could Darkboy not see anything in the airport but Ruby, this woman, his wife, the person he loved? How could he not see the five months without her but this second, this moment with her. Holding her as if the mean-tasting Chicago wind was whistling in her eyes, trying to steal her from him for another five months, bitter with tears, melancholy, Chick Webb, talking into drums, Mama, Daddy—*help me, please help me*!

Within minutes, it seemed, they were in the taxicab, being whisked away. There seemed to be almost too much happiness in them, of both feeling reborn.

"Long Ray's at the apartment, isn't he, Darkboy?"

"Yes, Ruby."

"He … he wouldn't. He wouldn't be in the way, Darkboy," Ruby said jubilantly.

"I know, Ruby. But you know Long Ray; he's always kind of laid-back in the shadows."

"Or ten feet in front of us." Ruby laughed.

"When it came to you and me, Ruby."

He was in love with her; nothing at all had changed in the past five months of separation.

"I want to see him s-so bad, Darkboy."

"Don't worry, Ruby; the feeling's 100 percent mutual. The guys at the Mayflower said Long Ray was so nervous yesterday, about today, that he was actually stopping the elevator between floors. Of course, I didn't see it firsthand, with me being down in the kitchen with Hambone."

"But Long Ray, he … he didn't deny it, did he, Darkboy?"

"Uh-uh. Ha. He was embarrassed, but no."

"I was nervous like that yesterday too."

"Were, you were?"

"Yes … I … except I didn't stop elevators between floors. No way. But, Darkboy, I was nervous right down to my shoes—as Long Ray would say."

"Ruby, don't make me laugh any more than what I am. Ha ha ha."

"It's true."

Then Darkboy—suddenly, unexpectedly—wanted to make love to Ruby in the taxicab's back seat. It'd been five months without her. It'd been so long since they'd made love. He felt like an animal. Wild enough to be tamed. Dangerous enough to be caged.

Ruby felt the fire burning in him. His desire of her. It was what she felt inside her too. It was bubbling chaotically in her. She remembered their nights, those nights, their lovemaking.

The sweet love.

The warm sheets.

Darkboy had to cool his temperature, scale it down. He smiled responsibly, amusingly, patting his head while doing so. The sudden rush of primal passion seemed to have subsided, been enough to give vent to it for now, just what five months without each other had sexually manifested.

Ruby looked out the cab's side window.

"It's not New York City," Darkboy said.

"Oh, Darkboy, it's Chicago. It doesn't have to be New York City."

"I … I know, but—"

"There's just more of New York. Bigger—"

"Better."

"I don't know."

Darkboy wanted to believe her; he really did.

The cab had reached the apartment. The suitcase, when Darkboy picked it up, felt light. It had bothered him from the time he'd picked it up at the airport until now.

Why is it packed so lightly?

The Chicago wind ripped into their clothing, as if it were trying to whipsaw them.

"Darkboy, I-I've never felt a wind like this!"

"Get used to it, Ruby. Get used to it," Darkboy said, holding his hand on his head like he was holding a hat about to blow off in the wind. "Chicago. Long Ray says this is the real Chicago!"

The two of them scampered up the front-porch steps as if the hound of the Baskervilles nipped at their heels.

The key slid into the lock—and that's when all hell broke loose.

"Ruby!"

The Windy Wind Five, excluding Darkboy, grabbed Ruby so fast that it was as if an octopus had escaped the aquarium.

"Darkboy didn't tell me!"

"He wasn't supposed to," Long Ray said.

"Otherwise, we'd shoot him like an ostrich if he did!" Pinky said.

Cool Hands took Ruby's hands. He blew on them. "New York's Mr. Hawk is nothing, a thing compared to Chicago's Mr. Hawk, wouldn't you say, Ruby?"

"You look pretty, Ruby," Loose Lips said.

"Real pretty, Ruby," Cool Hands said.

"Thank you, Cool Hands. How else am ... am I supposed to look when there are five handsome men surrounding me?"

"But we ain't staying long, though, Ruby," Pinky said, looking at Darkboy. "So don't think—"

"We're not chasing you away, Pinky," Darkboy said with a laugh. "Are we, Ruby?"

"No, Darkboy, no, not at all."

Long Ray sat Ruby in a chair as if she were a queen. Ruby looked around the apartment.

"Nothing's changed, Ruby."

"But the picture, Long Ray," Ruby said, pointing her finger at the wall.

"Oh, that. Uh, there was a crack there, uh, so Darkboy and I stuck a picture over it—that's about all. Uh, it. Yeah."

"Oh," Ruby said bashfully.

"Must've been a hell of a crack!" Pinky cracked.

"Was!"

"And so who have you met in New York, Ruby?" Cool Hands asked. "What particular jazz musicians of note?"

"Oh, just about everybody, Cool Hands. Every—"

"What about Teddy Wilson?"

"Yes."

"Uh … Coleman Hawkins?"

"Yes."

"Dizzy Gillespie?"

"Hey, Ruby, what about Daffy Duck!" Pinky asked.

Long Ray's fist rapped the table like a gavel. "Okay, it's time to go. Get the hell out of here!"

It was another moment Ruby was sure to remember—the band hugging her, kissing her, sharing her. This wonderful wreath of reward.

This was Ruby and Darkboy's time to be alone.

"Ruby, if you don't mind," Darkboy said, in some obvious form of apology. "I have something to show you. And the only way"—Darkboy stood by Ruby's coat—"is for you to put your coat back on, and for us to head back out into the cold, I'm afraid. Are you game?"

Darkboy held Ruby's coat out in front of her as if he were a matador, angling it just enough off from the bull.

"Uh, yes, Darkboy. I'm game."

Darkboy slipped the coat over her shoulders. He put his coat back on. "Bundled tight?"

"Real tight, Darkboy!"

The key slipped into the lock.

"The apartment's ours, Ruby! The rent's paid for the month of November!"

"Darkboy!"

"The apartment's not much to speak of."

"But, but it is, Darkboy!"

"See—you want to see our bedroom?"

"Yes, yes, our bedroom!"

A bed was in the bedroom, along with a bureau with a tall mirror. It was old wooden furniture.

"When, Darkboy, did you find the apartment?"

"Actually, Long Ray and I found it three weeks ago."

"You've had to pay rent for three—"

"Why? It's okay."

"And, and the furniture, Darkboy. The bed and the—"

"Don't worry. It's just the windows that need curtains."

"A woman's—"

"Yes," Darkboy interrupted, nodding his head, "a woman's touch."

Ruby and Darkboy's apartment was two blocks from Long Ray's, around the corner.

"Ruby, I mean, as long as you like it." Darkboy felt that animal urge in him return. He battled it for a second time.

But then he kissed Ruby in the middle of the room. She wasn't surprised. But it was done with affection, not at all sexual; Darkboy's body didn't press against hers.

"Ruby, when was the last—"

Ruby pressed her finger to Darkboy's lips.

He started again. "How have you ..."

"I don't know, Darkboy."

He let go her of her. "I pour all my sex, all of it, into the drums," Darkboy said, turning to Ruby, shamefully.

Ruby wondered, *Do I do the same with my voice, nightly, from the bandstand when I sing?*

"Beat them sometimes. I do, Ruby. Beat them."

Ruby walked up behind Darkboy and held him.

"Oh, Ruby, oh … baby," Darkboy said, sliding his head down onto Ruby's shoulder. "It's been so hard."

"I … I know."

"Five months—and I felt every day of it like thorns. And now you're back."

Ruby tensed.

"Back home."

"Yes, Darkboy, back home."

"With me."

Ruby and Darkboy were back at Long Ray's apartment.

They'd eaten out at a neighborhood restaurant. They'd toasted themselves with wine. They'd laughed at the wind, holding each other's hands as if it were spring eternal—an extravagant pause for enthusiastic young lovers.

When they got to Long Ray's, they laughed as if there were no tomorrows and teased each other as if they were children or a puppy chasing its tail, awash in the absolute pleasure of it.

Ruby and Darkboy had spent the afternoon like this, totally engrossed, immersed in catching up with what had been, for them, their yesterdays; what they had given up for what they now were—singer, drummer—this curse of talent that was theirs. In each other's arms, they were young, untouched, pure, free, unburdened. It was as if they could be these two entities, their feet not touching ground but lifted from it instead. It was an afternoon unplanned, not organized, but as spontaneous as music, when riding cleanly on a jet stream, becomes so carefree and unambitious and delirious. Dreams don't die, nor do they leave the world empty.

This was like old times. The Bluelight Café overflowed with Chicago folk. Long Ray had announced the previous night, from the Bluelight bandstand, the triumphal return of Ruby Midnight.

"Oh, there you are," Long Ray said anxiously, finding his pack of cigarettes. "Man, do I need you now. Right now. This instant." He struck a match. His hand wobbled. He grabbed it with his other hand. "Steady now."

He was on the bandstand by himself. It was about an hour before showtime. Long Ray needed this time to himself. His stomach was in knots. He'd downed a scotch, but it did him little good.

"Pinky."

"Long Ray."

"Yeah, that is you, isn't it?"

Neither had expected to see the other. Pinky had come in from the club's side entrance.

"Man …" Long Ray said.

"Yeah, I know what you mean," Pinky said. "Did you see what Ruby came in the apartment with?"

"Yeah. Damn!" Long Ray said roughly.

"Man, who's kidding, fooling who? This is when I hate this bullshit. Hate this shit straight up and down my fucking spine!"

"Making our money on the road. Making our fame there," Long Ray said.

"There ain't no other way, Long Ray. It's always been this way—got to get the whole world in on it. The whole fucking world's got to hear what you got. Your music's got to say."

Long Ray choked on his cigarette. "You know, Pinky, I hate these damned things. Really, I do. Hate the hell out of them. These fucking things!"

Pinky put his sax case down on the floor. He took the sax out the case, gazing at it lovingly, then put it back inside the case. "I could write me a book about love, man."

Long Ray puffed on a freshly lit cigarette. "We all could, but they'd just be words on the page. Can say we're lucky that way."

"Lucky?" Pinky said. "How you figure?"

"Great writers in the world come close to it when they write about love. But music … damn, Pinky, music." Long Ray looked out into the Bluelight Café. "They're all here to see Ruby tonight, Pinky. It's the only reason they're here. To hear Ruby's voice. Hear her sing."

Pinky looked out to where Long Ray squinted his eyes. "Yeah, they're all here, every single one of them. B-back tables and all," he said, looking away from this crazy, developing scene.

"How many writers can make sense out of love, Pinky? You know of?"

The applause was edgy but then stopped. Long Ray could feel the spotlight bake him, making it feel like it'd changed color.

"Ladies and gentlemen. Ladies and gentlemen!" Long Ray sounded like a record stuck in the same cool grove. "Ooo-wee, do I sound nervous. Well, guess what? I am!"

"So are we, Long Ray. We all sittin' in the same boat out here. Oars stuck in the water—no different!" Joe Flowers shouted from his front row table, from out of the Bluelight crowd, with his usual assertiveness.

"Why, hell, this isn't easy, Joe. Our little girl is back. Back in the Bluelight. Our queen. Our grand lady of jazz, is back in the Bluelight."

A delicateness lit Long Ray's face. "We all knew from the instant we heard Ruby Midnight sing in here that the Bluelight was meant to be her back door, her passport, if you will, to open out to the world." Long Ray's smile was as snappy as Duke Ellington's tux and tails. "So without further ado or delay from me, and … and with a father's pride inside, I announce the triumphal return of none other than Miss Ruby Midnight to the Bluelight Café audience!"

Ruby took the stage and stood in the spotlight, and the Bluelight's audience rose to its collective feet and applauded Ruby and the band and kept it going. Finally, quiet descended on the Bluelight, and Ruby waited for Long Ray to execute the band's downbeat, getting his attention with her eyes, softly. His body leaned into his bass at half-tilt, and when it happened, Ruby turned gracefully to the Bluelight's microphone to sing. Indeed, it was like old times again for Ruby Midnight, the Windy Wind Five, and Joe Flowers, and the Bluelight Café's audience, as if New York City had never happened, had never come between them.

The walk from the Bluelight to Long Ray's apartment was like old times too, as if they'd returned for Ruby, Darkboy, and Long Ray in Chicago. Long Ray rolled his bass about ten feet in front of Ruby and Darkboy. As usual, Long Ray gave Ruby and Darkboy their space. But Darkboy called out to Long Ray, and Long Ray waited for Darkboy and Ruby to catch up with him.

"Tell me how you felt again, Long Ray, before you introduced Ruby tonight."

Long Ray's body did a shimmy shake.

Ruby and Darkboy laughed.

"He looked calm, once he began, though, didn't he, Ruby?" Darkboy asked.

"The world seems calm at daybreak, Darkboy," Long Ray answered. "But don't you think the worm is turning in his hole? A robin's lurking somewhere near?"

Darkboy patted Long Ray's back.

"I was scared to death. I-I was speaking for everyone—y-you know."

The three stood outside the apartment on Donna Street. Long Ray stepped onto the first step. "Guess I'll be seeing you two later," he said, turning to them in the dark.

"Yes, Long Ray, Ruby and I are going around the block."

"Good ... good night."

"Good night, Long Ray," Darkboy and Ruby said in unison.

Ruby and Darkboy watched as Long Ray carried his bass up to the front porch and vanished behind the doors.

Darkboy held Ruby around her waist, even with his drum kit and the cold numbing his hands. He could feel a small sadness in Ruby's body.

"Ruby," Darkboy said as they both walked.

"Long Ray knew we were going back to our apartment tonight. No four a.m. practicing, Darkboy."

This was to be their night, and each recognized it. They'd had a honeymoon, two nights alone, to themselves since they were married but not since then, not since Kansas City, Missouri.

"It was great tonight," Darkboy said, speaking into the stiff wail of a wind.

"Sure was."

"You dream of nights like tonight."

Ruby sighed. "In New York, I dreamed of it."

"Me too, in Chicago, Ruby."

"Dreamed of how it was going to be for me when I came back to Chicago, Darkboy."

"It's funny how …"

"What, Darkboy?"

"We were separated but not really."

"And just think: we didn't even rehearse."

"Rehearse. You thought about that too, Ruby? But as soon as you opened your mouth, uh, I mean—"

"Darkboy, I did open my mouth," Ruby said, then playfully covered it.

"I … I know you did, baby. But when you open your—when you do it, should be described more, well, more special, elegantly than that—that's all," Darkboy said softly.

"Thank you, Darkboy."

"Don't mention it. Everybody shortened their solos tonight. Four, five bars, and out. They didn't want to get in trouble with the Bluelight crowd, not on their life, including me!"

Ruby blushed.

"Those people came to hear you sing, Ruby. Not the band play. To make fools out of ourselves."

"Oh, don't say that, Darkboy."

"What, not the obvious?"

"I could get a big head."

"Ruby, you know what? Sometimes I wish you would. Because sometimes I think you don't realize just how great, how astonishing, you really are."

"I-I don't want to, Darkboy."

Darkboy knew he'd hit a nerve in her, something solid, even though Ruby's voice had no agitation in it. *It's her past, her damned past!* Darkboy thought. That dark drape dropped over her life. Her mother and father—those two. Even if they had heard her sing, nothing in Ruby's life would be different for her.

They were a little way from the apartment on Dixon Street, and already their bodies were beginning to heat up in the cold. Darkboy could feel himself inside Ruby, between her strong thighs, inside the warmth of her—her vagina.

And Ruby could feel the beauty of Darkboy, the strength in him, the power and gracefulness of his movements, the rhythm in his responses to her—his penis.

"Ruby, we'll ... we'll be out of the cold soon, baby."

But Ruby hadn't been cold since Darkboy had put his arm around her waist, and that was two blocks back.

They were in the new apartment. The lights were on. There were shadows on the walls.

"Darkboy, can, uh, may I ..."

"Go right ahead, Ruby; it's what it's there for." Darkboy laughed, looking at the bathroom.

Ruby entered the bathroom, and then her skin turned an ashen white, for the night was about to slip out of her hands. Ruby had been carrying this torture inside her since New York City, since she had boarded the plane at LaGuardia Airport. It'd been torture, this secret in her, hiding, ensconced. She'd never done this before—yes, maybe with Miss Honey, keeping her mother from knowing she was going to Harding's Boarding House when her mother was drunk.

Yes, she'd harbored secrets inside her before, but they had to be that way. But this secret had a heart and a soul, blood in it. It could bleed. It could cry. It could blow the world apart into pieces.

Ruby saw herself in the mirror. Life was asking her to be a woman (no longer a girl), to be Miss Ruby Midnight, and she did not know how. She could sneak off to Miss Honey's boarding house while her mother was drunk. She could run away from home for good in the dark of night, but this ...

"Darkboy, how ..."

"Did you say something, Ruby?" Darkboy asked from in front of the lightweight door.

"No, Darkboy," Ruby replied. "I-I didn't."

"Oh, I thought I heard ... that you had."

"No, Darkboy."

Then Ruby, for a split second, heard the applause—the ringing, thrilling applause—from the Bluelight Café that night. Its approval of her. Adulation. Its acceptance of her, Miss Ruby Midnight.

Now it was weighing in her ear, maybe bigger than what it'd ever been. *I must get back out to Darkboy.*

Ruby tried to pretend, to think of this as just another performance at the Bluelight, in a club where everyone applauded her, approved of her, accepted her.

"Ruby, I thought ..."

Darkboy saw the look on Ruby's face when she came out of the bathroom, and it totally unnerved him, for some reason.

"Darkboy, I want a divorce!" She had said the words coldly, heartlessly, not anything like the Ruby Midnight Darkboy knew.

"D-divorce? Divorce me?"

Ruby fell to the floor.

Darkboy ran to her. "Ruby! Ruby!" He cradled her in his arms. "Ruby ..." Darkboy was afraid to leave her, to go to the bathroom for water. Instead, he picked her up and carried her into the bedroom, laying her down on top the bed. "Ruby ..."

Ruby's name spun through the dark room as if Darkboy's black skin had been stripped of its beauty. He was holding her, protecting her, trying to keep her safe.

"Darkboy ..." Ruby seemed barely conscious. Her eyes fluttered. "What ... where ..." And then her mind traveled back "What did I say, Darkboy? Tell me. Tell me!"

"Oh, Ruby, baby!"

"What, what, Darkboy?" Her eyes remained unstable.

"That you want a divorce, Ruby. Y-you asked me for a divorce."

"D ... did ..." Ruby shut her eyes, for her mind was back in the bathroom, behind the door, struggling with herself, not believing her heart, how it could burst, but there was a deceit in her like a poison, and she mustn't let it kill her—not for Darkboy's sake, not for love's sake, not for anything.

"Ruby."

Her head was pressed against the front of Darkboy's black tuxedo, the one he'd worn when he and Ruby had gotten married in at city hall in Kansas City, the one he'd played in that night behind his drums for Ruby's triumphal return home to Chicago.

"I'll get you a glass of water." He felt it was safe to leave her.

The room was spinning for Ruby. Ruby's head was spinning and the bed was spinning inside the room with her. But she did not want to open her eyes.

Darkboy was back. "Here, here, Ruby." Darkboy lifted Ruby's head. "Here."

Her lips touched the edge of the glass, and Ruby began sipping the water.

"Good ... good, Ruby. That's good. Do you feel better, better now?"

Ruby nodded.

"Do you want more water?"

"Uh-uh, no, Darkboy."

Darkboy put the glass of water on the bedroom floor.

"Darkboy! Divorce! I'm scared!"

"So ... so am I, Ruby. I am too!"

"Mr., Mr. Apollo wants me to go to Paris, It-Italy, Germany, Darkboy. He"—Ruby grabbed Darkboy—"said it wasn't going to work, Darkboy. That being, that being married to you wasn't going to—"

"He can't say that, Ruby. That white man can't say that!"

"But, but w-would you go with me, Darkboy? Go, t-travel with me?"

"But I'm here, Ruby. Here. Here in Chicago with the Windy Wind Five. I-I don't want to be—"

"Mr. Ruby Darkboy Slade Midnight."

"No, Ruby. Not that—Mr. Ruby Darkboy Slade Midnight; it, it would kill me. Yes, kill—it would, it would."

"Mr. Tony, Mr. Tony said it would. Mr., Mr. Tony said it would."

Darkboy's heart sank: Fat Tony was right. On that score, the white man was right.

Their breathing became erratic in their exasperation; nothing inside them was working right.

"You carried this with you from New York."

"I ..." Her voice died.

"Y-you thought it through," Darkboy said softly, nonjudgmentally. "You thought it through, didn't you? Five months, Ruby. F ... five months."

Ruby wanted to forget those five months spent away from Darkboy in New York City, but her mind wouldn't allow her: five months of singing in top-notch jazz clubs, a rising star brushing up against fame and glamor.

Darkboy stood. He felt flat. "You can have the divorce."

Ruby opened her eyes.

Darkboy turned to her. "It's not your fault, Ruby. Not anyone's fault. W-we didn't know what to expect. What we were d-doing. G-getting ourselves into."

Ruby's foot inadvertently knocked over the glass of water on the floor. "Oh … I'm sorry, Darkboy. I'm sorry!" Ruby flew off the bed and was on her hands and knees on the floor, patting the spilled water with panic in her hands.

"Ruby, Ruby, stop!" Darkboy grabbed hold of her arms, holding them, looking at the tears glistening on her face.

Both were on the floor on their knees, in this small puddle of liquid, drowning in some awful, awful way, when Darkboy felt Ruby's wet hands, hot as blood, touch his skin, giving him, it seemed, life.

Darkboy panicked. Warm juices flowed in him. The thought of Ruby. The days and nights. Five months of longing in his loins.

Ruby drew nearer to him, her body becoming a part of his—something like before in Chicago. And then it was as before, this connection they made, this thing they realized possessed them.

Darkboy lifted Ruby off the floor and put her back on the bed. Ruby's mouth made love to Darkboy. Ruby remembered how it was, how it always was, whenever she and Darkboy made love.

"Ruby are … are we doing this? Really doing this?"

She crawled atop Darkboy. Ruby's black flesh burned. Her black thighs twisted around Darkboy's body. Ruby and Darkboy had to make love, at least for now, this moment, to cancel out the future tonight. To forget there was to be a tomorrow.

"I love you, Darkboy."

"Yes, yes, Ruby."

Now their bodies were naked and engaged, Darkboy penetrating Ruby gently with his penis.

Ruby was asleep on her left side. She rolled over to her right side, into the middle of the bed, and opened her eyes. "Darkboy!"

Darkboy no longer was in bed with her. *When did he leave—when?*

Ruby rushed out of the bed and into the front room, where the sun poured through the window. And then she realized she was naked in this shadeless room. She ran back into the bedroom and saw her midnight-blue dress was off the floor (where it'd been last night) and hanging on a hanger on the back of a closet door. She didn't know what to think.

Ruby put the dress back on, but then realized she had to take it off again to take a shower.

"Darkboy didn't run." Ruby recalled seeing his drum cases; they were still in the front room. She opened the door and looked at them again, then relaxed. "What have I done? Divorce, t-then lovemaking?"

Darkboy hadn't run away, but he wasn't in the apartment.

As Ruby stepped out the shower, she heard the front door open and then close.

Darkboy!

Ruby was rushing to dry herself. She was rushing to find out why Darkboy had left their bed. But he'd probably come into the bathroom. They'd showered together before in Kansas City, Saint Louis, and Chicago.

Ruby slowed down.

Minutes later, Ruby opened the bathroom door.

Darkboy's head turned.

Ruby regarded him, shyly.

Darkboy was standing by his drums. "Good morning," he finally said.

"Good morning."

Suddenly, Ruby felt she and Darkboy were complete strangers. *No wonder he never came into the bathroom*, Ruby thought.

Darkboy unzipped one of his drum covers and pulled out his drumsticks. He looked down at them and played with them in his hands, as if they were toys, not instruments.

"Where'd you go this morning, Darkboy?"

He hesitated for a moment. "You were sleeping, Ruby. And hard. I didn't want to disturb you," Darkboy replied, without answering her question.

"You hanged, uh, hung, yes—you, you hung my up my dress, Darkboy."

"It was on the floor. Sure," Darkboy replied, stating the obvious. "So I hung it up."

"Thank you."

Darkboy bounced one of the drumsticks up and down in his palm.

Rudy headed for the bedroom.

"I showered too. Before I left this morning."

Where'd you go, Darkboy?

Darkboy did not follow Ruby into the bedroom, but he heard a slight commotion, some sort of confusion, in Ruby's feet. "I, uh, put your high heels on my side of the bed. Uh, under the bed, in fact. Sorry." Darkboy stood in the door frame; neither hid their broad grins. "Let me get them for you."

"That's all—"

"No, let me."

Darkboy tossed his drumsticks on the bed and then, with a quick knee bend, placed his hand beneath the bed and pulled out Ruby's blue shoes, which matched her dress. "Here they are." Darkboy handed them to her.

"We got divorced last night, d-didn't we, D-Darkboy?"

"Yes, we did, Ruby."

"I feel sick to my stomach."

"So do I." Darkboy's face looked his age.

Ruby sat on the edge of the bed, holding her shoes. She put them on the floor and leaned back and picked up Darkboy's drumsticks. "Here, Darkboy."

Darkboy took the drumsticks from her hand.

She leaned her head down on his shoulder.

The apartment door closed behind them. Ruby looked back at it; so did Darkboy. They reached the top of the landing.

"I'm not going to keep the apartment." Darkboy said, seeming to read Ruby's mind. "The month's rent is paid for, but I'm not going to keep it after the month's up. It was for us anyway."

Ruby thought of the bed, of the dresser, but not about the towels and washcloths, not about them, of course.

"The bed," Darkboy said—and Ruby wished Darkboy had said *our* bed. "I'm going to sell it, if you're wondering."

Ruby walked in front of Darkboy, her heels making tiny clicking noises each time they struck the wooden steps.

"The, the dresser too," he added.

"The washcloths and towels, Darkboy. What about them?"

Darkboy opened the building's front door for Ruby. She was the first one off the porch and onto the sidewalk.

Ruby felt the cold day. "Your drums, Darkboy."

"They'll be all right. Okay in the apartment."

Ruby waited for him. She watched Darkboy as he came down the steps, her eyes sitting squarely on him.

Darkboy twisted, a tricky grin on his face, breaking the gloom and tension. "Ruby, I have something to show you." He took about ten steps and then was there. "Here's where I was this morning, to answer your question." Darkboy's hand patted a brown car. "I rented it to drive you back to Midway International Airport this morning."

"I don't deserve it," Ruby said, stepping away from the car.

"You don't deserve it? Then who does?"

Ruby was in shock. "Darkboy, I were ... uh, honest, I wasn't honest w-with you, Darkboy. I c-came back to Chicago and stayed at Long Ray's apartment, and, and sang at the Bluelight and, and I wasn't honest with you. I ... Mr. Tony, an-and I—"

"I don't want to talk about him now—right now, okay. I don't want to talk about Fat Tony Apollo. It's you I'm driving to the airport in this car this morning, Ruby, not Fat Tony Apollo."

Ruby remained bewildered.

"Now, you can stand there if you want, or you can get in. Because this car's going to Midway Airport this morning, once we leave Long Ray's. It's why I rented it. Not for any other reason, baby, than to take you to the airport."

Darkboy carried Ruby's suitcase.

The brown car had gotten Ruby and Darkboy to Midway safely. There was time to kill. The flight was for 1:05; it was 12:16. They'd found a corner in the airport, this tiny space that no one else occupied. Ruby had changed out of her show dress and Darkboy out of his tuxedo before they left the apartment.

"How much will we remember about last night?" Darkboy had to ask, felt compelled to ask the question. "Ten, fifteen years from today, Ruby?"

"Ev-everything, Darkboy."

"May-maybe we will; maybe we won't," Darkboy stared at the concrete wall.

"Y-you don't want to look at me, Darkboy?"

"Baby, it's not that," he said, still not looking at Ruby, "it's just that I don't want to make this, this thing worse, any worse than it is."

"Did we say enough last night, Darkboy?"

"I don't know. I ... I can't speak for you." Darkboy stared at the concrete wall again, his voice hardening. "Hell, I ... I can't even speak for myself." He began twisting the wedding band on his finger.

"You're not—are you going to remove, take it off, Darkboy? Please, please don't take it off. Please don't do that!"

Darkboy was now conscious of what he'd been doing. "No, no, we're ... we're still married, Ruby. In, in the eyes of God, we are."

"How do we do this Darkboy—g-get d-divorced?"

"Didn't Fat Tony Apollo tell you?" Darkboy asked bitterly. His voice softened. "He's going to show you how. Long Ray t-told me. Long Ray said Fat Tony Apollo, h-he knows people, Ruby. All, all the tricks of the trade." Darkboy heard Ruby turn from him. "I'm sorry!"

"I-I could beat the world, Darkboy. B-beat it with my fists!"

"Here, here, sit down."

"Yes, I'll feel better if I sit down. I-I just—I just need to sit down, Darkboy. S-sit down. Yes, yes, I ..."

Both stood. It was 12:55.

Darkboy was walking with the suitcase. He stopped, putting it down. "Goodbye, Ruby."

"Good ... goodbye, Darkboy."

Darkboy let go of her.

231

Darkboy had parked the brown automobile in front of a red fire hydrant, across from Long Ray's apartment building. He yearned to be alone. He should have gone elsewhere. He should have parked the damned car elsewhere. Why had he thought to come home? *I don't need Long Ray right now. I just need to be left alone. To myself.*

Long Ray tried to open the car's passenger-side door, but it was locked. Darkboy's and Long Ray's eyes made direct contact.

Long Ray blew on his hands.

Darkboy didn't need a hint. He leaned over and unlocked the door.

"Thanks."

Darkboy looked straight ahead.

Long Ray looked straight ahead, as if the car was going to take him and Darkboy off someplace.

Before renting the car, Darkboy had dropped by the apartment and told Long Ray of the divorce. Obviously, Long Ray was shocked.

"Darkboy, lookit, you're gonna get yourself a ticket, man, if you park here. Ha. You know good and well how these Chicago cops are about these things."

"They can give me all the tickets in the world. Man, who gives a damn?"

Long Ray blew on his hands again. "Sun or no sun, it's cold as hell out here. Just wonder how much cash the devil paid God to make this wind blow how it's blowing. Really, really wonder."

Darkboy's head swung away from Long Ray, and then back, and then his eyes looked Long Ray up and down, as if he were somebody's paid fool. "Whoever said there's a God, Long Ray, is a liar!"

"Let's talk, Darkboy," Long Ray said sternly. "You and me; let's talk about it." No longer was he going to coddle Darkboy, no matter how fresh the pain of losing Ruby was. "Talk, you and me, man to man."

"Talk about 'it'!" Darkboy said, practically in tears. "What the hell's there to talk about when Ruby just left me, man? Went back to New York. My wife is divorcing me, Long Ray!"

"Darkboy, I-I don't have pretty words to—"

"Who's asking you for pretty words, Long Ray? I'm not asking you for pretty words. I don't need pretty words. I just need Ruby. I'm not afraid to say it, Long Ray. I cried. I cried last night. Cried! Is … is that a man? Is … is that being a man?" Darkboy was shaking.

"I know you did. You had to."

"As a man, as … I'm ashamed to say it, admit it. As a man."

"But we all have. Where'd you come off we haven't? We've all been in love. All been where you are. Damn. Damn. We cry. We all cry. A man cries. Any man."

"What was I thinking, Long Ray? Five months she was in New York City."

"No one has the answers. The key to that. No fucking one."

Darkboy began laughing. The car keys dangled from the ignition. "I had to take Ruby to Midway. I-I had to, Long Ray. Just Ruby and me—I didn't want anyone else to drive her. No one else but me. You see that, don't you, Long Ray?"

"You know, it was the suitcase, Darkboy. For me. It was the damned suitcase, man—all along, that did it for me."

"Light, light as a feather."

"Expected two suitcases if she was coming back to Chicago, to Chicago to, to stay. To make this headquarters."

"Yes, at least that, Long Ray. Two."

"Considering she was gone for so long. Ruby had time to buy more clothes up there, you see, more than what it was she was bringing back to Chicago. Pinky and I took notice. T-talked about it in the club last night. He saw it too. Same as me." He hesitated for a moment, unsure of how to go on. "Uh, a-about tonight, Darkboy. Uh, want me to call Cole Young? See if the young cat's available tonight for the gig?"

Darkboy looked relieved. "Yes, yes—would you, Long Ray? Do that? I … I can't drum tonight. Not at the Bluelight. I …" Darkboy was crying.

"Cry, Darkboy. Cry, man." Long Ray said. "Cry your eyes out. Don't hold back nothing, man. A fucking thing. Not a fucking thing."

Minutes later, Long Ray exited the car.

"R-Ruby's not coming back to me, is … is she, Long Ray?"

"No. Ruby's voice won't let her." Long Ray stood by the open car door. "Darkboy, move the car from out here, okay? I don't want you to get a parking ticket. Okay. City violation, okay?"

"I'm taking the car back anyway. I have no more use for it. I'm taking it back to the rental company."

"D-drive carefully. Okay, I'm gonna make that call to Cole, see if he's available for tonight's gig. Gonna do that as soon as I get upstairs. Call the young cat at his place."

The car door closed. Darkboy tensed. His hands gripped the steering wheel. He dropped his head down on top it. "Chick Webb. Chick Webb." But Darkboy knew Chick Webb couldn't help him now. He knew that what Chick Webb had learned in his drums, he was now beginning to learn: about life. It'd been passed down.

Long Ray was on the building's stoop, looking back at the brown car. He knew Darkboy was sitting in the car, so he wouldn't be issued a parking ticket for parking in front of the fire hydrant. The cop would, more than likely, simply ask him, politely, to move the car.

Long Ray blew on his hands. "Damn if the devil ain't paying cash to some damned body today!"

CHAPTER 23

Harlem is right over the bridge, Ruby thought. Right over the bridge, and she'd be back in Harlem, she and Miss Honey. Right now, she was in the back of a taxi that had just left LaGuardia Airport in Queens.

Ruby began twisting her wedding band, as Darkboy had done with his. When would he take his wedding band off his finger?

How was Darkboy going to live without her?

How was she going to live without Darkboy?

She was supposed to sing tonight; she wouldn't.

Was Darkboy going to play his drums at the Bluelight tonight?

She'd never missed a show, a singing engagement. She's sung when she was sick, when she couldn't make her voice do what she wanted it to do. But tonight, she would not sing gay songs, sad songs, or love songs. Tonight was her night to be alone, to herself, her and Miss Honey.

Miss Honey had to know. It was in her voice that she had known heartbreak—the love of a man.

Ruby paid the cabbie, and when she turned, a mountain-sized shadow covered her.

"Ruby, let me take it for you."

"Thanks, Happy."

"Heavier than before, when you left for Chicago. Much. Not that it's so heavy now for someone strong as me."

Ruby smiled.

Happy Billingham was in tan slacks and a white T-shirt. "Know it's cold in Chicago." They'd reached the building's entranceway. "Fought there a coupla times in the winter. Won, too. And you can believe me, Ruby. Ain't lying to you on that."

Ruby laughed.

"So know that wind don't mess around with folk much. Keeps you moving, don't it?"

Ruby and Happy were inside her one-bedroom apartment.

"Put it over there? In the corner there?"

"Yes, thank you, Happy."

Ruby began twisting her wedding band.

"Uh, Ruby, ain't you gonna take off your coat?"

"Why, why yes, Happy. Of course. Why … my coat."

Happy helped Ruby with the coat. "You and your husband, uh, Dark …"

"Darkboy, Happy. I asked him for a divorce in Chicago."

"Oh … I'll, then I'll hang this up for you," Happy said, removing the coat from Ruby's arm. "D-don't hold it against yourself, Ruby."

Ruby seemed confused.

"Had me a girl and left her. Come here to New York to fight. Wasn't for her. Had to fight. Had to. All I want to do was fight." Happy struck what seemed to be a boxer's pose without knowing it, balancing himself on one leg. "It was in me. Young as I was. Always was. Gotta be a fighter. Come up here to New York. Wasn't nothing else for me."

Ruby sat. She stared intensely at Happy.

"Don't hold it against myself. Not to this day. Can't go back, though; she ain't gonna want me. I took off on her. Run off on her when we was at our best. All I'm saying. Young and wet behind the ears. Just learning about love." Happy relaxed. "Can't go back—don't near way wanna. My girl's married. Got herself a family, so, so Mama tells me. An' I got this, Ruby, this now. This bum leg of mine to carry around with me."

Ruby looked at her suitcase, not at Happy's leg.

Happy grabbed his crutch off the wall. "Gotta go. Some things I … oh, but, by the way, Mr. Apollo wants you to call him. Said the first thing you get in I was to tell you. But I figured I'd—"

"I'll call him, Happy. And thanks."

"Look, Ruby, it ain't easy." Happy frowned. "T-that I know. Still think of … of Veronica—what's her name? Veronica Victoria Beauchamp. It been twelve years and still think of her. Nobody else come to mind. Can't replace her. Nobody can. Don't care what nobody say, Ruby, how they put it to me." Happy took Ruby's hand, then released it. "But when this thing happen, the bullet, it shattered my kneecap an' ... well, all my dreams go down with it. End of the game. T-them for good. The trail for me."

Ruby didn't know what to say.

"And if I got to choose between getting Veronica back and my boxing, durn, I-I know which I'd choose, Ruby. Always have."

Ruby had made the call to Fat Tony Apollo. What could she have said?

Fat Tony only asked if she thought she could perform tomorrow night at Eddie Condon's club. She'd said yes. But who knew now? Who knew? She felt alone, lonely. Plattstown rushed back to her mind in all its venality. There were those green, green fields, but now, even those she hated.

Ruby shut the bedroom door. "How am I going to live the rest of my life without Darkboy?" She could say Darkboy's name a million times and not tire of it.

Darkboy. Darkboy. Darkboy. Darkboy.

Until she went crazy.

Happy, the bullet, his knee—it all came to mind. How could she forget how he looked? How could she? She didn't want to forget. "Happy said all his dreams were taken from him. Miss Honey, it's, it's what Happy said, ma'am. It's what he said, Miss Honey. If I couldn't sing, never sing again, but ... but could have Darkboy back ..."

There was the book; Ruby was looking at it. It was on top of the other books, the books that helped her become smarter, brighter, reading them, borrowing the words, and listening to white folk, rich and dignified white folk, talk in the nightclubs, tables away from her table, when she was in between sets. Mimicking them.

Her English—she had worked hard, slavishly, on her English. Day and night. Darkboy noticed right off. From telephone call to telephone call, he consistently commented on it. She felt good about that—Darkboy's acknowledgment of what she diligently was trying to do in improving herself.

She told him his book had started it. She told him his book had started her on the path of self-improvement. The Langston Hughes book. The book with all the pretty words in it. Poetry. And the five months. For five months, all she did was work on her English, trying to master it. She no longer wanted to be a country girl up North from the South, someone who could hardly talk and walk right, hindered, handicapped. No one had to know cotton was in her hair, in her hands; that she was afraid of bugs, the insects that crawled on the cotton plants when, as a little girl, she picked them. Nobody had to know Ruby Martinson was a child laborer on poor, small farms—somebody who wasn't anybody in Plattstown.

But now she was Ruby Midnight. Her mama didn't know. Her daddy didn't know. Nobody from Plattstown knew. Nobody knew what she'd grown into—Ruby Midnight, jazz singer, star. Nobody from Plattstown knew Ruby Martinson was now Ruby Midnight.

Nobody.

It was the way she wanted it. It was the way she would always want it. Ruby Midnight was not Ruby Martinson. Ruby Martinson was not Ruby Midnight. Ruby Martinson was dead, buried in Plattstown. There was no trace of her; nobody could find her. Her grave was unmarked. There was not even a smell, nobody's bones—nothing.

"Ha …" Ruby laughed girlishly. "It's, it's funny. Funny."

She and Miss Honey were in New York. They'd been to Chicago and all those other places in between, but now, now they were in New York.

Ruby looked to her left to the light switch. "I … I ought to keep the lights on."

How long would she remember their last kiss at Midway International Airport that day?

As long as Happy had remembered Veronica and wanted to go back to her but couldn't. Veronica Victoria Beecham was married. She had family. Happy had lost his dearest friend.

The one person who meant the most.

Darkboy had asked about the crowd at the Bluelight that night, and Long Ray had said it was half-empty. That was about as much as Darkboy and Long Ray had talked when Long Ray got in from the Bluelight. Darkboy had not asked Long Ray about Cole Young or how he'd played the drums—if Cole Young had done a good job drumming. He'd only asked about the Bluelight crowd, and Long Ray said it was half-empty.

What, if anything, did I expect? Darkboy thought. *What else, in God's name?*

Ruby was gone forever—for good.

Darkboy was in bed.

One minute he was hot; the next minute, cold. His body was in a state of horror, in a bad, bad fix. And this was only the beginning without Ruby. This was his first night of this, knowing Ruby was never to come back to him, to Chicago.

This was the first night.

Before—five months ago—he could think ahead, down the road. Think of what lay ahead for him and Ruby—imagine it. But what did he see, had he really seen for them?

Darkboy's body felt cold. There was that cold back in it. That Chicago winter back in his body. Mean. Nasty. A cold that could chop off bones at their joints. A cold that could kill him.

And it could happen at any time.

"Darkboy." It was as if Long Ray's voice had sliced through the air.

"You're up." The cold in Darkboy's body dissipated, and now it was hot.

"Can't sleep, Darkboy. Not a wink. Not for the life of me," Long Ray said, sounding depressed. Long Ray knew his way around Darkboy's room in the dark. "Floor's cold as hell." Long Ray stood in front of the window. The light in the room made Long Ray's silhouette seem even starker. "I was thinking of Ruby too."

Darkboy decided to come right out and say it; there was to be no beating around the bush. "What was I doing, Long Ray? Wearing blinders? She wasn't coming back to Chicago to stay, n-no matter how hard I wished it."

Long Ray's eyes saw a star but wouldn't comment on it.

"I-I wonder if Ruby's looking out the window and seeing the same sky you're seeing, Long Ray."

The beauty and purity of that line, the simplicity of it, that thought, stunned Long Ray.

"Tonight's hard on her too, Long Ray."

"Hell, hard on everybody."

"How did Cole Young play tonight?"

"You know, I didn't hear him. To be honest with you, plain and simple, I didn't hear the cat. Is-isn't that something for me t-to admit? Isn't that the craziest thing you ever heard anybody say in your life?" Long Ray turned back to the window, hoping his eyes would see that star again.

"I don't think I'll love again."

"Uh-uh." Long Ray shook his head. "Not like that."

"Will she? Ruby?"

"No."

"It's not, it's not good to love like that, is … is it, Long Ray?"

"Darkboy, I don't know, man. I don't know. Who's to say?"

"Look … look at me. Look at me, man!" Darkboy insisted.

Long Ray couldn't. "It's gonna snow today. It's what's gonna happen. Hope it's the last of it. Hope like hell it's the last snow that drops out of the Chicago sky this winter."

"W-what are we afraid of, Long Ray? Tell me."

Long Ray's eyes moved back to Darkboy, this figure buried in the dark, away from the window's slit of light but where there was something to look out on, eyes to hang on to something. "A-afraid of, Darkboy?"

"You, you're not afraid of the snow, are … are you?"

"No, I didn't—no, it's just that—"

"I'm going to die. I feel it."

Long Ray's tongue tasted the sweat in his mouth, what he'd tasted in his bed that had made him rise out of it and walk across the cold floorboards, barefoot, and into Darkboy's room.

"Are you afraid of dying, Long Ray? Are you? I've got to know." But before Long Ray could answer, or whatever it was he was thinking to do, Darkboy said, "I'm not."

Is that youth talking? Bravado? Long Ray thought. *Or is life already squeezing the blood out of Darkboy?*

"Every-everybody's afraid of dying, Darkboy. Any man walking the face of the—"

"No. No. Not me, Long Ray. Not me. Love … love's taught me that."

Darkboy shivered. "All I have now are memories, memories. For the rest of my life. Every day of it now."

Long Ray looked back out the window and then turned to leave Darkboy's room.

"Leave-leaving, Long Ray?"

"Yeah."

"Her English. It's better, so much, much better, isn't it? Much, much better now."

"Yes, it … it is. Much, much better. Ruby's English is … better, better like you told us it was."

"The … the Mayflower Hotel, h-how many floors does the elevator climb to again?"

"Twenty-three, Darkboy. Twenty-three floors up."

"Must feel like you're … you're at the top of the sky, man. When you're up in it."

"I don't know, Darkboy. I'm inside, like I told you before—you never feel how high up you are from the inside of something; there's nothing to look down on to make it seem high."

Darkboy's voice quavered. "But you're off the ground, in … in the air."

"Right, right. Off the ground, in the air."

"High, high up where … where no one can touch you, Long Ray. Way up there on the twenty-third floor, where no one can touch you, man."

It sounded silly, Long Ray thought, while crossing the bedroom's cold floorboards. What Darkboy had said sounded silly, but it's what love could do to you, and Darkboy and Ruby were so young. And it was the memories that both would have to carry with them for the rest of their lives, like Ruby would carry her voice and Darkboy, his drums.

"You're not going to die, Darkboy," Long Ray said, facing the door.

The cold stung Darkboy's body, running through his legs, down to his toes. And he shut his eyes with a deep conviction, after hearing what Long Ray had said and the door had shut.

No, Chick Webb can't save me now.

CHAPTER 24

Four years later

Time had been good to Miss Ruby Midnight. If there ever was this thing called success, where Ruby could mark her days by her accomplishments, then Ruby Midnight had been lucky; she could do that.

Ruby had been to all the great showcase venues. The great countries. The great cities and capitals of the world. She had lived a jazz singer's life. Her home base was still New York City, Harlem, but in a different section of Harlem, a more upscale, swankier section of Harlem: Sugar Hill. She lived in a brownstone big enough for big parties (if it was her thing, which it wasn't). Ruby was living a good life. She could afford it. She was making excellent money, the kind where she had to pinch herself every morning when she woke and every night when she fell asleep.

"Ronny and the guys said hello, Ruby."

"That was sweet of them, Happy." Ruby smiled.

Happy Billingham was pushing a shopping cart full of groceries into the kitchen. He'd done Ruby's grocery shopping. "Eggs—durn, you forgot eggs on the list," Happy said, opening the refrigerator door and noting Ruby was down to two eggs by pointing his finger to each egg individually.

Ruby was at the kitchen table. She was in black slacks and a black-and-gray top.

"Hit me when I looked at the egg section. 'Ruby, she's outta eggs,'"

Happy said. "Ronny caught me talking to myself, as usual. Can't duck the guy."

Ruby laughed. "Thanks, Happy. One day I'll learn how to fill out a grocery list properly. Last time it was—"

"Bacon. You must have something against pigs and chickens," Happy squealed. "Ever kill you any? Back home in Plattstown?" Happy leaned back on his crutch.

"A chicken but not a pig. We weren't rich enough to own pigs. My … my parents, t-that is, on, on our farm, that is."

"Man, Ruby. Ha. Don't wanna kill you a pig. Messy business. Ain't pretty—not that nobody ever brag it was."

Ruby got off the chair to help Happy put the groceries in the kitchen pantry and cabinets.

Happy winked. "Guess you can buy you a fancy farm full o' pigs in Plattstown now, huh?"

"Uh, guess so." Ruby laughed. "But not if I had to turn them all into bacon."

"Come on, now, Ruby; durn, a pig's a pig. Don't have to have you no love affair with them. Get cuddly, all affectionate. A pig!"

"I think I would, though. Probably."

Happy looked at Ruby as she turned to go into the pantry with a few groceries. "Yeah, you probably would, Ruby, knowing you. How you get. Yeah, sure would." Happy chuckled.

Ruby came out of the pantry.

"How many days before you know, before Mr. Apollo tells you something?" Happy asked.

"Who? Tony?"

"'Who, Tony?' D-don't get all cute with me. You know my durn head's beating like a drum since Wednesday evening, an' it's Friday—an' I'm about to die from the stress it's putting on me. Beating the living daylights outta me, Ruby."

Ruby sighed. "This evening I should know. Have an answer —h-hopefully."

"*Hopefully* is right. Because, Ruby, look at you, standing all cool like your skin ain't got a wrinkle in it, when you know durn well you excited as me. Ain't you?"

"That I am, Happy. Yes."

"I know the deal gonna get sealed. Mr. Apollo got that thing about him. Man, if he was my fight manager back when—have me a million bucks by now. Rolling in dough. Sitting pretty as sunshine."

"I'm trying my best not to—"

"Billie Holiday done it, sung at Town Hall. Why not you, Carnegie Hall? Next. Man, love that white gardenia in Billie's hair. Love it to death."

"I love Billie, period."

Happy slowed down. "Them drugs gonna kill her. Uh-huh. Durn drugs. Worse damned thing for you." Happy pulled a chair out from the kitchen table and sat. "Fool around with them. Get hooked on them." Happy's eyes seemed to have a moment of contemplation before he spoke again. "Almost get mixed up with them when this here thing happen to me," Happy said, looking down at his leg. "Sometimes forget what's right from wrong. Have to fight it off. Was the biggest fight of my life up till then. Was. Staying away from drugs … From, from temptation. Bigger than any fight I fight in the ring—for sure for me."

"When you're depressed …"

"Can sink fast as a tub. Go straight down to the bottom of the ocean fast, real fast." He shut his eyes. "This entertainment business you in is tough, the road—but she probably growed up missing out on something, Ruby. Betcha that. Billie Holiday got ghosts in her closet from somewhere far."

"I know."

Happy was back up on his crutch. "Now, we got plenty of eggs."

"Plenty, thanks to you."

"Uh, listen, Ruby, things gonna work out like I … it oughta. I'm buying the champagne, okay? For everything, okay, on that day?"

"Not too much for me," Ruby said coyly.

"Watching your cups, huh?"

Ruby laughed. "You know champagne tickles my tonsils."

♪

The news Ruby received from Fat Tony Apollo was the best news she possibly could have received. In two months, she'd be presented in concert

244

at Carnegie Hall. Billie Holiday had performed in concert at Town Hall, just months earlier, and now Fat Tony Apollo had booked Miss Ruby Midnight for what was probably the most prestigious concert hall in the world.

Fat Tony had guaranteed a sell-out, the likes of which Carnegie Hall had not seen.

"Happy!" Ruby hoped Happy could hear her through the thick upstairs rugs in his apartment below hers. Happy had become kind of her bodyguard, chauffeur, companion, and friend. Fat Tony had arranged the financial end of the brownstone purchase for Ruby. Happy's apartment had two bedrooms, a living room, bath, and kitchen, although Ruby did all the cooking for them: breakfast, lunch, and dinner.

"Man, you got some pipes, Ruby! An' not just for singing!"

"I see you've got it!"

Happy hoisted the champagne bottle in his right hand. "Just need the champagne glasses."

Ruby ran into the dining room and came back with two champagne glasses.

"Well ... here's to Carnegie Hall! First colored woman in ... in the history of the Negro race to, well, what the hell, never was any good with toasts." Happy popped the cork in the champagne bottle. After pouring champagne in the two glasses, he said, "To Carnegie Hall, Ruby!"

"To Carnegie Hall, Happy!" Ruby began giggling.

"Tick ... tickles your tonsils, huh? Man, I did pour you a little, like you said." Happy took his sip of champagne. "You know, I bought the bottle Wednesday night, don't you, Ruby? Three days ago. Guess you was wondering how I got hold of a bottle so fast."

"Come to think of it, yes, but no, I—"

"Ha. Come on, Ruby, Miss Ruby Midnight at Carnegie Hall. Gotta be a sure bet anytime. And with Mr. Apollo behind it, backing you, putting the deal together ..."

As soon as Ruby and her small entourage entered Carnegie Hall, Ruby felt an architectural greatness within the concert hall's historic walls. As a singer, not only did Ruby want to rise up to the hall's greatness and expectation but top it in a setting ruled by classical music and world-renowned opera singers and their musical mastery and unmatchable public popularity.

Ruby's jewelry was exquisite. She and Fat Tony had had a private sitting at Cartier's. Many satin-lined trays of sparkling diamonds had been displayed for them, then examined, and then purchased, with the forethought that they had to match Ruby's Carnegie Hall debut—the night when Ruby Midnight undoubtedly would be crowned by her fans and music critics alike as jazz's new reigning queen.

After substantial vocalizing in her private dressing room, Ruby knew she was in marvelous voice. It was that something in her voice that felt like a drop of warm, melted honey. It's how she hoped her voice would feel, and tonight was no exception. She and the band had laid out the songs, of course, from A to Z. Fast, fast, fast numbers, and then slow down the tempo a bit, and then absolutely slow the tempo down with a bluesy number, and then back to fast, fast, fast numbers.

Ruby's dressing room was ringed with assorted flowers. Fat Tony had made sure of it. She was spending this time alone in her dressing room in order to embrace the significance of silence, of meditation, of winding through herself to gain the spiritual balance. She needed that to express every aspect of her being as an artist and person for an audience that would know much about her life, as the Bluelight audience in Chicago had—and audience who had helped shape her as a jazz singer and a person. Who had helped put her on the world's great stages. And who, tonight, had helped put her before Carnegie Hall's bright stage lights for final acceptance, significance, and elevation.

"Ruby, need I say more?" Happy asked.

"No, Happy," Ruby said, turning toward Happy—she'd been expecting him for the past few minutes. "It's time."

"Ruby, you look real, real pretty tonight. S-sure do."

Ruby stood. Her wardrobe looked as rich as Carnegie Hall. Her dress was as shiny as a silver dollar. Her hair was chestnut red and gleamed. Her perfume was silky, subtle, and sensuous.

"Mr. Apollo, he's out in the wings, waiting on you," Happy said emphatically, taking her by the hand. "The band's behind the curtain, warming up."

She could hear the band in the distance.

"Great night, ain't it, Ruby? To be alive, ain't it?"

Ruby was ready for this night at Carnegie Hall.

Fat Tony saw her and called out, "Break a leg, Ruby. Break a leg!"

There was a long slit running up the side of Ruby's shiny silver dress, revealing a sexy leg, one Carnegie Hall had never seen walk across its stage before—at least not a colored woman's.

"Happy, pinch me, would you?" Ruby said, shutting her eyes.

But before Happy could, Carnegie Hall's maroon curtain opened to the one-month sold-out Carnegie Hall audience.

Fat Tony and Happy hugged, and then the band hit its first sizzling note, and Ruby sang, and it was history-making in a city recognized for its sophistication, and opportunity, and as one of the great cities of the Western world.

Ruby was floating on cloud nine—she owned it. Carnegie Hall's applause had rung up to the rafters for her.

"Seven encores, Ruby, an' still counting," Happy said. "And there would've been ten more, if Mr. Apollo didn't tell the band to leave the stage when he done. Pack it in."

Ruby leaned back her head in the stretch limousine. She was in the back seat, still in her Carnegie Hall wardrobe. She and Happy had just left the after-party thrown by Fat Tony.

"You had them, all of them, eating out of the palm of your hand, Ruby," Happy said, looking at her from the rearview mirror. "How's that feel?"

"Sometimes you know, Happy," Ruby said with a sigh. "And sometimes you don't. You're, you're so wrapped up in the song, the moment—that's when you don't know what's happening around you."

"Honest?"

"Honest."

"But you know when everything's right, don't you? When it's clicking for you."

"Absolutely, Happy. Absolutely."

"Gotta feel like"—Happy shifted his big butt in the car seat—"when I used to throw the perfect jab in the ring. Durn, Ruby, knew it right at the second I uncork it, can knock out a gorilla."

"A gorilla, Happy? Ha ha."

"Well ... maybe a baby chimpanzee. One with a big head. How's that!"

They laughed.

"Uh, Mr. Apollo said he wants to do it again. Overhear him at the party. Was talking to some big shot with big money."

"Yes, uh, he did mention it, actually, Happy, before we left the party."

"Ruby, man, you could sing at Carnegie Hall for a year, 365 days, an' still sell out the joint every night."

"You know, it's good having a friend like you, Happy."

"Hey, Ruby, don't you ever, you know—just sit down an', well, look at yourself an' know just how great you is?" Happy looked in the mirror again at Ruby, driving one-handed; the other hand grasped the top of his crutch.

"I think, just think it's God's work, not mine. God who's great. You know, it didn't have to be me."

"Yeah, it don't. None of us knows how any of it works, no way. Guess it's better you don't think of it."

"I've just accepted it," Ruby said.

"How great you make everybody feel tonight in Carnegie Hall. Out of this world. Just because of that voice of yours. And the love you got in it," Happy said. "White and black feel it alike."

The makeup was off her face, the wig off her head, the gown off her body. It was as if Ruby had been stripped naked.

She was in her bed and had been sleeping for well over an hour. When she and Happy got in from the concert, they were exhausted. Any church in Harlem open for business the next day, Sunday, wouldn't see William Happy Billingham or Miss Ruby Midnight sitting in its pew—that was certain. Both had yawned simultaneously when they got inside the brownstone.

"Good night, Ruby," Happy had said, as weary as if he were carrying a Tennessee mule on his back.

"Good night, Happy," Ruby had said, as if she were carrying Plattstown on hers.

Ruby had made a beeline for her bedroom and all she was garbed in at Carnegie Hall came off. The wig, the makeup, the dress—it's when she looked in the mirror and cried at her success and, at the same time, her failure. The integration of both felt too emotionally impactful.

She had reached her bed and had said her prayers, and all was quiet in the room, the neighborhood—as if the block was sleeping inside a cradle too delicate, even for a Harlem night, to rock.

When Ruby's head first touched the pillow, she'd fallen immediately to sleep. It was sleep she more than deserved after Carnegie Hall.

"Mama! Daddy!" Ruby looked around the room, and right away, it was Darkboy who'd awakened her, not her mama and daddy.

Did he know? Did Darkboy know about Carnegie Hall? Did he?

And if he did, how? How did he find out? And what did he do? What did he do when he found out?

Ruby's eyes burned. Her greatest triumphs were now her greatest failures.

It's how Ruby perceived it. In her heart of hearts, that's how she perceived it. She still loved Darkboy. After four years of separation, she still loved him. Her shame still burned as brightly, if not brighter than before.

They'd not been in touch for so long. For so damned long. It was nobody's fault. What they'd done had changed them, literally had swallowed them whole.

She had sung to him that night.

From the Carnegie Hall stage, she had sung to Darkboy. Every night, whenever she sang, wherever she sang, she sang at least one song to Darkboy. But tonight, at Carnegie Hall, on that historical stage, in front of those glamorously dressed folk (mostly white), she sang all the songs to Darkboy, the encores—all of them.

The band was a world-class band.

The band had played like the Windy Wind Five.

Ray Brown had played like Long Ray on bass; and Tommy Flanagan had played like Cool Hands at his piano; and Dizzy Gillespie had played like Loose Lips on trumpet; and Ben Webster had played like Pinky on tenor sax; but the drummer--no drummer in the world could drum like Darkboy.

None.

Where would they be today if she hadn't left Darkboy, left Chicago? Where would she and Darkboy be today without the divorce?

She thought about children—a houseful. *I'm a woman, a woman first*, Ruby thought. A boy, a girl, children—many. She thought about it, a family, something she never had; something she'd always want.

"It ... it wasn't to be, Ruby," she told herself.

Ruby was tired of hearing herself repeat the same old song. She was young. In many ways, she was still a child, yet grown in many other ways. Her mama and daddy—she thought about them, if they were still drunk every day of their lives. She still didn't want to see them. They hadn't come for her. She wasn't going to go back to them. It was finished, final. She had nothing to prove to them; dying would probably be the best thing for them.

She looked around the bedroom. "Darkboy, it's you; it's you I love."

What would she say to Darkboy if he walked through her bedroom door? Would they make love?

Darkboy had made her a woman.

"Darkboy, it's you; it's you, you I love."

Time could not clear from memory Darkboy's strong back or his strong arms or his strong hands, yet how gently his hands held her whenever they made love. Darkboy did not know his own beauty, only she did. It wasn't Kansas City, or Saint Louis, or Chicago, but now, in Harlem, thinking of Darkboy, she felt those nights with him in her more and more. It made time stand still in some childish but adult way that she had no control over or felt she ever would be able to wipe from her memory.

But what would she do if she saw Darkboy? What would she say? Had they become strangers? Was what they were one of the songs she'd sung from the concert stage tonight—the lonely song, the hurting song, the blue song?

Or would Darkboy play his drums behind her, and it would happen like magic all over again for them? Would it be like before, sparkle and shine—this thing that could only be considered because of its strangeness and oddity and then disposed of, as if it was never so strange or odd but awake in their hearts from the first days of conception?

Can an audience's applause ever be a substitute for love? Can it? Can it ever replace love? Did she think that it could, four years ago, when she'd left Darkboy in Chicago?

The applause no longer rang in her ears. But Darkboy's drums—they still rolled through her mind, making gorgeous sounds. The bass drums, the snare drum, the trap drum, and cymbals, making different sounds, new bridges for colors.

She had a jazz career, was a jazz singer. She and Miss Honey were in New York City and had traveled the world, only just how far had they traveled?

Happy had thrown that jab he'd thrown so many times that he knew when it was the real thing. Plattstown had taught her so much—her mama and daddy, the folks in Plattstown. She knew love when it came along. She knew the moment it touched her. Miss Honey, her voice—her. Darkboy, his drums—him.

That was love.

But now she had sung at Carnegie Hall. She could say that. Fat Tony Apollo could say that. It would go on her résumé, her press releases: Miss Ruby Midnight, concert at Carnegie Hall.

But did Darkboy know about it? She knew she would not hear from him, not ever, so why now?

Ruby closed her eyes, hoping, knowing if Darkboy stood outside the bedroom door, her eyes would open before the door did, before Darkboy even uttered a word or reached her.

"This is the last cigarette until tonight, Darkboy. I swear on a stack of Bibles. The last one. I'm not going to let these damned things be the death of me or my bass, man." Long Ray glanced over at the bass, parked against the front room's wall.

Darkboy and Long Ray's 4:00 a.m. practice session was over. It was

5:22. They were in the same apartment in Chicago, the same street (Donna Street) in Chicago, overlooking the same view from the third floor in Chicago.

"Gotta quit these cancers sticks. Get serious about it. Before they retire me. I do have much bigger shoulders than them."

"Long Ray—"

"Don't say it, Darkboy, because I know I'm beginning to sound like an old windbag. Shit, b-but it's not that simple, man. There's something in these damn things those tobacco companies ain't telling us. 'Cause I've got my suspicions."

Darkboy eased himself from behind his drums. He was still Jimmy Darkboy Slade, elusive, painted a pretty black. "I'm glad I don't smoke."

"Started this thing when I was nine. Would sneak some puffs off my granddaddy Henry's corn pipe. Then, when I was ten, started smoking for real behind Ronald's, my best friend's, barn."

Long Ray, after four years, still looked the same, with little wear and tear. "Smoked a half pack a day. Daily. It must've looked like a smokestack in back of Ronald's barn. Or Indians sending off smoke signals from a wigwam. How's that?"

Darkboy stood at his bedroom door. His eyes were red but not because of the hour; it was because of the booze in the Bluelight bar that Bartender Bob had poured. "I'm going to turn in, Long Ray." Darkboy yawned. "I don't know about you."

Long Ray couldn't avoid noticing Darkboy's eyes; anyone who loved Darkboy the way he did couldn't avoid it. "You … you've got to stop it, Darkboy."

Darkboy didn't flinch; for him, it wasn't anything to flinch at.

"Fucking stop it, man," Long Ray said more passionately.

Darkboy shrugged his shoulders; he'd heard it all before from Pinky, Cool Hands, and Loose Lips. He could beat his bass drum to their tired tune a thousand times over by now.

"Ruby's not coming back!"

"You can go to hell!"

Long Ray didn't say anything more. He'd made peace with himself.

"You, you just worry about your cigarettes, man. Beating your own damned habit, and don't worry about mine!"

Long Ray felt the cigarette heating his fingertips. His fingertips smelled no better than tobacco.

If only the Windy Wind Five had been at Carnegie Hall that night with Ruby, been the band to back Ruby on the Carnegie Hall stage—Long Ray had entertained the thought countless times. But such a possibility had long been chased away by reality. There could be no reunions between the band and Ruby. Their farewells, goodbyes, had taken place four years ago at the Bluelight. It was in front of everybody.

Because of Darkboy, in deference to him, Long Ray had kept his distance regarding Ruby. There'd been no mention of her, no communication with her since Chicago. It hurt him. It was not his choice to do this, but Darkboy had to be protected. Time had not become the great cure or healer for Darkboy; instead, it'd become the great burden. Darkboy was under a big rock. It'd fallen on him. Every night, they heard her. Every night, when the band played, they heard Ruby Midnight—even Long Ray. She was always on the bandstand with them. Ruby was in his bass, in Pinky's sax, in Loose Lips's trumpet, in Cool Hands's piano—not just in Darkboy's drums. They heard and breathed with her every night they played.

What man wouldn't go crazy, drink too much, hit the liquor bottle and hard?

Ruby Midnight was on the bandstand. She ruled their hearts and souls. She lived in them. They carried her onto the bandstand with them. He and the band were in love with Ruby in a different way, with a different kind of passion, with more sobriety. But Darkboy unfurled mad rhythms, mad frenzies, mad spins and turns, mad episodes, mad beginnings and endings—mad pictures of pain and dark matter descending far down into dread.

And they'd all stand there on the bandstand, transfixed, not knowing what part of him he'd just rent, torn, found no more use for—driven as he was.

How much longer could it go on? He loved Darkboy; all of them loved Darkboy. Ruby was winning; love was winning. The rock was on top of him, and he couldn't push it off. Nobody could.

Nobody.

"Ouch, man!" The cigarette's ember had touched Long Ray's fingertips. "Damn, who needs these goddamned things?" Long Ray dashed the cigarette in the ashtray. He'd wanted to stomp on it but also wanted to keep himself under control. He could do that for Darkboy. He'd tried to be the voice of reason. Four years ago, he's taken on the role. Four years, but tonight it felt as if seven days had passed—days he could count as simply as the last days of summer but which were as brutal as winter.

Long Ray walked over to his bed and lay down. He stretched his body. "Why God? Why'd you put them together so you could break them apart? It makes no sense, man—none." Tears ringed Long Ray's eyes. "Darkboy, it's all gone. The beautiful glitter, man, shine. He tried. Shit … Lord knows Darkboy tried. He wanted to understand too. H-he wanted to say he, he could do it, God, make the sacrifice for Ruby. But Ruby Midnight was born to sing. Born. Born. He had to fall in love with her."

Long Ray shut his eyes. "It was in his drums, Chick, Chick Webb's drums. Dark … Darkboy's world. Darkboy thought he could live with that—that that's all there was to life, to living, defined life: Chick Webb and his drums."

But then Ruby Midnight had come along.

"Ruby, man." Long Ray saw that night again—a young girl, pretty but scrawny, and with eyes that made the world see, that forced him to look into them by their absolute, astonishing power. A young girl lost but now found, with a cardboard suitcase hugging her leg like a friendly cat.

"She came for you, Darkboy. Ruby. T-to take you away to places you-you'd never been. To open up a new world for you where … where you and your drums and Chick Webb couldn't go. Ruby took you into that world. And now, now you can't get out. You can't escape it—you're lost. Literally lost. You don't know how."

Long Ray wanted to play his bass in the worst kind of way. Dammit if he didn't want to pluck its strings. His bass had been his heart; it'd never broken his heart, not like a woman. His bass wouldn't go off to New York City without him. It wouldn't want to go to Carnegie Hall and sing before thousands of people. His bass wouldn't.

And then Long Ray heard how foolish he sounded. "Darkboy, you're not a fool for loving Ruby too much. But I can't tell you that. How in the hell can I tell you that … that loving a woman is loving too much?"

This was the worst he had cried.

Darkboy was in his room. He'd drunk too much. He and Long Ray were lucky that they didn't have to worry about the Mayflower Hotel day jobs anymore—the band was in great demand, practically everywhere. Now they were full-time musicians. Darkboy could sleep off his drunk without worrying about work. He could sleep until his hangover stopped.

Was he going to die?

He was beginning to see things too clearly now, too vividly. It's what people say happens before they die—seeing their lives roll back to them with clarity. And it was happening to him. Why was tonight so bad?

Long Ray had to mention her name. Yes, he had to. He had to get rough with himself; the bottle—had it become his only salvation? And he hated liquor. The taste—he hated its taste. But he was drinking like he didn't hate it. He was drinking like he didn't, but he did. Never mind what it was doing to him.

But what did it do *for* him? What healing power did it possess? What healing did it do for his soul? He and Long Ray never talked about it. He'd never talked to anyone about his feelings. For five years, it'd been this way. He wrote his mama and daddy, but that was two years later, after the fact. He told them that he and Ruby had divorced, making it sound as if they'd been married for two years, that it hadn't gone all wrong for them—soured, fallen apart, on hard times so fast, overnight—after only five months of marriage.

But how could he explain what had happened? That it had nothing to do with not loving Ruby or her not loving him. It had nothing to do with that. How could he explain what was in the soul, what was mightier than what it should have been or could have been?

They knew the love he had for his drums. His mama and daddy knew that; it's why they let him leave home at sixteen to find his way in the world. But they could never understand the responsibility some people owe the world, the gifts God had given them, or what a musician's life was.

"Long Ray. I-I owe him an apology, don't I? D-don't I? I do," Darkboy asked himself. He didn't need the light to find his way to Long Ray's room.

He saw his drums in the dark and the powerful shape of Long Ray's curved bass, standing upright against the front room's wall.

They were musicians all right; it was their sacred calling.

"Sorry ... sorry, Long Ray. Sorry." Darkboy knew Long Ray was awake.

The sheets rustled. "For what, Darkboy?"

"Four years—and I haven't talked, dis-discussed it with anyone: Ruby."

"Bottled it up. Wouldn't let it out."

"So ... so everyone else had to do the same. Suffer too."

"Yes, I guess so."

"Couldn't even admit it to my mama and daddy. We just got married too young. Ruby and I. We just didn't know what life had in store for us."

"How could you?"

"Maybe if we had turned—"

"To someone?"

"Yes, Long Ray."

"It wouldn't've made a difference. You don't want life, old cats like us, to take that kind of joy from you. Y-you have to feel love to know it. To know what it is, Darkboy. No one can do that for you but you."

Darkboy felt it now—love—running deep in him. "Ruby is gone, isn't she, Long Ray?"

"I had to tell you that. Had to lay it on the line for you." Long Ray didn't speak for a moment but then said, "But now you've got to—you've got to start taking care of yourself ... yourself, Darkboy." He could hear Darkboy's body droop. "Make yourself the number-one, top priority. I know I'm making it sound simple when it's not. But day by day, Darkboy. Day by day, you've got to make it work."

"Long Ray, the Carnegie Hall concert—I was proud, man. So proud of her. It's like we, the Windy Wind Five, helped put Ruby on that stage. Helped her get up there."

"Man, Darkboy, it's how it felt all right. At the time."

"In your heart. In your heart—"

"Yeah, Darkboy, yeah. I know what you were gonna ask me. In my heart, I wished we could've backed Ruby that night. Been her back-up band at Carnegie Hall."

"But not with me as the band's drummer."

"No, not with you."

"See? See? I took that away from you. I hate it, man! I hate love! Hate it. Hate it! Hate it!"

In a shot, Long Ray was out the bed and holding Darkboy, holding a young man who'd already lived too many years with a bliss that could kill.

"I-I see her, Long Ray. I see Ruby. I … I saw her on TV. I … I turned it off. I … I listen to her records."

"I know, know that."

"But, but not for long. Very long."

"Yes, uh-huh," Long Ray said, holding Darkboy's head to his chest, patting it as if Darkboy were a young boy in his arms.

"I can't stand to listen to her but for so long. Ru … Ruby's voice. My drums … I hear my drums in … in Ruby's voice, man. Hear me, Long Ray. I-I hear my drums in … in Ruby's voice."

Long Ray rubbed the back of Darkboy's head.

"She's singing to me. Ruby's always singing to me."

"Right, right. All the time."

"And her, and Ruby's voice is in my drums, speaking to me. Am … am I going crazy? Mad, mad, Long Ray? Am I?"

"No, Darkboy. No!"

"Does she know it? Does she? I see … see her, though. I-I see Ruby!" Darkboy broke free of Long Ray. "See, see … I …" He stood in the middle of the room. "She … she's pretty as ever, Ruby. Ruby is … man." Darkboy stood in the dark, burning with a fever. "She … she comes to me. Comes to me at night, at night. Ruby. Am I going crazy? Am I going mad? Ruby comes to me at night in … in my bed. Am I going crazy? Am, am I? Am I? In … in my bed, Long Ray!"

It was minutes later when things calmed.

"I, I'm going back to my bed," Darkboy said. "I just wanted you to know that I was sorry, sorry about everything, that's all. I'm glad we talked. Glad about that. T-to empty things out. Yes, t-to talk. Good night, Long Ray."

"Good night, Darkboy."

Darkboy didn't need the light to find his way back to his room. He saw his drums in the dark space, and Long Ray's powerfully shaped bass standing upright against the wall.

Darkboy stopped in his tracks: *Man*, he thought, *can I play the drums. Can I, man.*

Darkboy couldn't wait to get to his bed. If he could just get to his bed, all of his problems would be solved, would go away, would be completely eliminated from his consciousness.

He lay on top of the bed, his body still, his red eyes open, still not knowing where to look, where to turn in the dark. His arms fell off to the side of the bed. His hand extended down under the bed, feeling, searching for it, until it was in his hand. Round, full, warm. Darkboy sat erect now and twisted the cap with his free hand. And he brought the liquor bottle to his lips. Darkboy was ready, anxious. His head tilted backward, and the bottle tilted back with his head. The liquor ran through Darkboy, into him, generously, as he wiped his mouth with his hand and then drank more of the quarter-filled bottle.

And she appeared, came to him. His eyes were shocked by her. But she came to him every night. Every night in this way ... slowly ... silently ... deliberately.

"Ruby." His voice was as free as light.

Darkboy put the bottle back down on the floor, capping it, standing it upright, having no more use for it for now.

"Ruby."

CHAPTER 25

Three nights later

Right off, Darkboy had noticed her: tall, shapely, bosomy, and sexy, in a shiny red dress; a black woman who'd sat in the club's front row to, what seemed, her overt delight. But what he noticed most about her, during the band's first set, was how this sexy black woman shut her eyes when he spun drum solos from the stage. The raw pleasure on her face and the trail of her breathing, how it relaxed and seemed in rhythm with him and the drums, no matter what music or rhythm he played.

In a way, it had rocked Darkboy's system to feel what this woman had done to him; something so powerful, connecting him to a yearning pulsating in him, with no prospect of future relief.

Darkboy tried not to look at her whenever she shut her eyes, pretending she wasn't there, but failed badly. She was dragging him down into where she was, into her breath; this feeling of penetrating, then breaking his resistance from no longer wanting a woman, from no longer needing a woman.

It was a feeling that she was the woman who felt the passion still dominating him, the drum, which was still real, whole, had not deserted him. And that she was in the Bluelight Café at that very table, at this very moment in time, to reawaken his sexual yearning for the sake of his sexual healing.

The drumsticks skimmed across the drum's surface at top speed. Then there was the heavy emotional pounding, beating of them. Darkboy tried his best to make the intense moments submit to his cries, the desperation in him that was driving him into a place of his most profound darkest pain and fear.

Sex. Sex. Sex.

Darkboy's drums sat on the Bluelight's stage.

It was a first.

"Well, it's done, gentlemen. Over with," Loose Lip said.

Darkboy had left the Bluelight with the woman.

Long Ray, Pinky, Cool Hands, and Loose Lips had witnessed the event.

Each had a drink. They stood, united, at the front of the bandstand.

"Don't know how the boy did it. Held out for as long as he did," Cool Hands said.

"Shit, ain't got nothing to do with Ruby. Sex, man. Not the love Darkboy still has for her," Pinky said.

"I've watched him over the years. Saw how hard he tried," Long Ray said. "His bond he kept with her."

They all agreed, shaking their heads.

"Dames. Street prostitutes. Darkboy never had any fucking use for them," Pinky said. "Not like some of us, when times got rough."

"The girl he's with tonight—she's no whore. Just willing," Long Ray said. "Loose with sex."

Long Ray got his bass, and soon followed Pinky, Cool Hands, and Loose Lips out of the Bluelight Café.

The Ambassador Hotel was a few blocks away from the Bluelight Café. There were twenty rooms on the second floor.

Marlena Grace and Darkboy stood in front of room 16B.

Earlier, Darkboy had asked her name; he didn't want her to be a stranger to him.

Room 16B's door opened.

The light switch cleared the darkness. The room was clean; the bed, immediately available to Darkboy and Marlena Grace, was a few feet away.

It was June. A warm night, not hot or sultry.

It was sudden. Marlena Grace turned her head to Darkboy and breathed into Darkboy's ear and eased her hand up under his shirt and touched his sweaty back.

"All night I've wanted you, Darkboy. Umm … baby. But I've told you that shit at least ten times by now. On the way over—haven't I?"

Darkboy felt nothing, but then, everything, as if he were trapped inside her thighs, no longer seeing her eyes shutting sensually in the Bluelight, the drums, their music, their common ground, their lustful connection. Now her eyes were wide open and passionate; her sweet body in the room to please him.

Marlena Grace's fingers had located the zipper to her shiny red dress when Darkboy's hand abruptly stopped her. "What are you doing, baby?"

"I can't! I can't do this with you!"

"Have sex? Sex? You don't want my shit?"

"I'm sorry. I'm sorry. I'm in love—"

"Love, love—this has nothing to do with love, just us, baby. Us. You are a man, ain't you?"

"Here, here, take this!" Darkboy yanked his wallet out of his back pocket and handed her the bills.

"I don't want this! I'm no fucking whore!"

"It's all I can do. Can do for you!"

"Then get out. The hell out!"

"No, take it, take it. Take the money, Marlena!"

Marlena Grace slapped Darkboy's face and then fell across the bed, covered her eyes with her hands, and cried hysterically.

When Darkboy shut the door, all he could see was a vision of Ruby.

Ruby's fragrance.

Ruby's touch.

Everything Ruby had left behind in Chicago.

Awake in his bed, Long Ray heard the apartment door open and close.

Darkboy couldn't do it. He pressed his hand to his forehead. *I knew it wouldn't work with that woman.*

Long Ray took the cigarette out of his mouth and simply watched the smoke ascend to the ceiling before crushing the cigarette in the ashtray; then he puffed his pillow and stretched out more. "There has to be a time, yeah, of course, when it will work for him. Man, I know that."

Now, Long Ray heard Darkboy's door close for the night. "Ruby. My darling girl, Ruby. Darkboy's safe," Long Ray said.

CHAPTER 26

Two years later

"Ruby, don't know about you, but I'm gonna sleep all day. Need to catch a break now an' then."

"You don't ask for much."

"Nah—can't say I do. Honestly can't."

Ruby was in the back seat of the car, as usual, as Happy chauffeured the gray Cadillac. They'd just come from the Five Spot and had seen Billie Holiday sing there. Billie had invited Ruby to the bandstand to sing, but she'd begged off, much to Billie's disappointment.

"She's dying, Ruby," Happy said, after there'd been a short silence. "Billie's dying right before our eyes. I know it's what you thinking. Was on your mind."

"Yes," Ruby said softly.

"Was drinking her liquor down like water. Was in her eyes, in her voice. Can't hide it for nothing. Heard it sitting there all night."

"But she sounded wonderful. She just lost Lester Young. May-maybe she's—"

"No way. Not about to let you off the hook with that one. Durn, Ruby, Billie Holiday been boozing an' ... an' shooting up dope for near as long as I can remember. Lester Young ain't added to Billie's woes, her habit—him dying."

"And her voice? This is a rough business, Happy," Ruby said sadly.

"Was thinking of Joe Louis before. Was. Yeah, too many durn fights in his skin. Too many nights when he should hang up his gloves an' call it quits—say he wasn't gonna do it no more. Knowing his career was over but still him trying to be what he was, as if time stand still when it don't. Not for nothing. Not for nobody. Just don't want him to go out like that. Be remembered like that. Fight until he can't. As great a fighter he was. But it's the money, money. Ain't no different. And them back taxes the government say he owes."

"No, it isn't, Happy. Our bodies taking a beating too. Our voices. A singer's voice."

"Singing every night like y'all do," Happy said sympathetically.

"To please people, and, I must admit, ourselves."

"Billie have to live. Make a living."

"She lives through her songs. Everything else around her, maybe, at times, may be rotten," Ruby said, "but it's all right when she sings, no matter how sad or depressing they are."

Happy's voice scaled down. "They gonna call her a junkie. An alcoholic, Ruby, when she's done. When she dies. Gonna drag Billie Holiday's life through the mud."

"Well, let them try, but there'll always be her records—something people can hear for themselves. They'll be there for the next generation of jazz singers to appreciate and love. Lend some sense of who she was, Ruby said; trying to feel how the future can reveal the past's significant value.

"Man, just glad you ain't got no vices." Happy chuckled.

"Except one—singing!" Ruby exploded with laughter.

"Man, I can live with that!"

One year later

He loved her. Sure, he loved her after all these years. He loved Miss Ruby Midnight. But she was the exclusive, sole domain of Jimmy Darkboy Slade. He knew this was hurting him more and more. He wasn't getting any younger. The pain was beginning to come more often now, especially at night, and sharpen with time.

At times, he wanted to quit this job that Fat Tony Apollo had given him almost seven years ago. At times, he wanted to leave Ruby's side. It was becoming too tough for him. He'd fallen in love with her. The last six years of pining for her, of hoping, was a long, long time—hoping to turn that corner, of making some kind of gain. It was taking its toll; his heart was hurting big time. Big time.

She'd never recovered from Jimmy Darkboy Slade.

It just wasn't in the cards for Happy—for him and Ruby. It wasn't to be. Jimmy Darkboy Slade was as alive in her as if she'd just gotten off the plane that day from Chicago, after she'd gone there to ask Darkboy for a divorce.

One day, he'd have to leave Ruby. Come up with some excuse; stop doing what he did for her before he ruined it between them—what they had. He was listening a lot to Billie Holiday's recordings, the sad songs she sang that were her life, but he was feeling the feeling that Billie Holiday felt, of unrequited love.

She was still Mrs. Jimmy Darkboy Slade. He remembered the wedding band, the ring, when finally it was off her finger. Three years back? Jimmy Darkboy Slade had not left her side, not once. But one day, Happy knew, he would. Veronica was a flicker in his heart; Ruby was a flame.

Billie Holiday said a lot to him in her songs. Maybe she was going to die, but she'd saved him.

Three months later

Ruby opened the door for Happy, and he entered the room. Ruby looked up at him. It was midafternoon, July, and a big fan blew air over by the gold sofa.

"Why so gloomy, Happy, on such a beautiful—"

"Ruby, I got to confess something to you. I gotta do it now, 'cause by the end of the week, I'm gonna be leaving New York. Heading back to Tennessee."

"Ten-Tennessee! What are you saying, Happy?" Ruby grabbed Happy's hand and led him over to the sofa. "But why?"

"I love you, Ruby."

"Love me!"

"Yes, yes," Happy said, gripping his crutch harder. "I'm sorry; it wasn't supposed to come to this, b-but it does. Can't help it. I tried, I tried, oh, how I tried, Ruby. But … but …"

Ruby saw the pain she'd put in Happy's eyes. This was information she'd never seen coming.

"I'm sorry, Happy."

"Sorry," Happy said, lifting his head, "but I wasn't to fall in love with you, Ruby. Mr. Apollo don't hire me for … for that. Any of that." Happy, this huge man, stood and leaned on the crutch. "But I do. All I can say. And you ain't to feel bad or nothing. I'm the one who was dreaming, not you. Romancing. Durn, Ruby, ain't nothing you got to feel bad about."

"I don't know what to say. This still hasn't sunk in," Ruby said, shaking her head.

"I'm heading back to Tennessee. Already put a call in to relatives down there. They gonna take care of me. Find something for me to do down there." Happy laughed, even if tears filled his eyes. "You the best friend I ever got, Ruby. But I was mixing it with love on my part. But you love somebody else, something I ain't gotta tell you, do I?" Happy looked into Ruby's eyes, which were as hard as diamonds. "Something you already know. Darkboy Slade been with you for a long, long time now. You falling in love with him in Chicago an' all. Y-you know."

Ruby was to see Happy later. He was to drive her to the Tattle Tale Club. She still hadn't recovered from this afternoon, with Happy's confession of his love for her—the shock of all shocks.

She was drinking tea with honey and lemon. How much in the dark was she? How dark was her tunnel? How much in love was she with Darkboy that she could only see one man and the thought of anyone else frightened her?

She was twenty-six years old, and still, no man other than Darkboy had touched her. No man other than Darkboy had made love to her during all of her traveling, and all of her fame—this fabulous life she lived. She had educated herself, but she was still a young girl from Plattstown who was simple in her ways and heart. That part of her had not abandoned her.

She had learned to talk to kings and queens, as Miss Honey had said one day she would, but she was still a simple girl from Plattstown, as she was sure Miss Honey was before dying.

Miss Honey felt it was fate that had sent her home, God's guiding hand at work. But it still had something to do with who Miss Honey was far down inside, the splendor of her journey, of Macguire's Baptist Church and Mr. Jasper P. Bean, the organist; of the back roads and the beautiful green fields, sending her home to Plattstown to die. For it to be her final resting place.

She must never forget that. Just like she could never forget Darkboy. Darkboy hadn't left Chicago—playing drums, playing his drums. *Memories make a life drift back to another time, another day or night in a person's life*, Ruby thought.

"The night I was with Billie, I saw the spotlight shine on her face at the Five Spot, with the white gardenia in her hair."

She and Billie had talked about Lester Young that night. His death. He was the one who had nicknamed her "Lady Day"—and she was the one who had nicknamed him "Prez." And Billie had sung every song she'd lived that night. Only Darkboy had stayed on Ruby's mind, like now— just Darkboy and no one else—as Billie had sung with the spotlight on her face, counting years, marking time and years—things that don't die but live into the night and into the next day; there, to radiate in sunlight. Darkboy was forever worthy of her memories, as Billie's voice had told her at the Five Spot.

Was Darkboy any better off than she was?

It'd happened at the Bluelight Café that night. Darkboy had collapsed on the bandstand while drumming. He was rushed to Providence Hospital. It was Darkboy's liver—Darkboy's hard drinking.

This was an emergency. Things had gone badly for him.

"Where's the damned number?" Long Ray had screamed at the top of his lungs, dumping the table drawer onto the floor.

It'd come in an envelope so many years ago, mailed to him.

There, I got it!

She'd written only:

Long Ray,
212-555-5641
Ruby

What the hell else was there for Ruby to say? It was for an emergency, for now.

Long Ray collected himself.

Darkboy's dying. He's fucking dying, man! How will I say it to Ruby?

The operator got him through to the New York number.

"Darkboy?"

"Ruby, it's—"

"Long Ray!"

"Ruby, it's good hearing—"

"Oh, Long Ray, Long Ray, it's been—"

"I know, Ruby, I know."

Now fear struck her. "Darkboy, Dark—"

"How do I say it, Ruby? In God's name ... how do I?"

"He's—"

"Dying, dying? No, not yet, Ruby. But it's his liver. It's his liver. His drinking. It's serious. He collapsed tonight at the—"

"Darkboy collapsed!"

"So you've got to come out to Chicago. Get here. Fly back home."

"Darkboy needs me, Long Ray!"

"Yes. It's the only reason I called. This is an emergency, honey."

Long Ray went back to Providence Hospital and was at Darkboy's bedside. Darkboy was conscious, coherent, still able to communicate. He was in a long white hospital gown.

"Long Ray, I'm dying. I-I feel it."

"Darkboy, listen, you're not going to die. I won't let you."

"B-but I am."

Long Ray's big hand squeezed Darkboy's hand, hard. "Feel that, Darkboy—that's life, man. Feel it."

"My, my drums."

"Your drums? Are you kidding? They're okay. They're back at the apartment. Pinky took them back to the apartment for you."

Darkboy's voice softened. "I meant after, after I die, Long Ray. It's what I meant."

Long Ray chose not to reply.

"My drinking. My drinking—it took all the joy out of my drumming. B-but I still loved it, Long Ray. Still thought of it, just lost the joy because of my drinking."

Long Ray hated this past-tense talk Darkboy was doing, making his words smell like death.

"Mama and Daddy—I would love to see them. S-see them before I die. Die, I die."

There was spittle on Darkboy's chin, so Long Ray wiped it with a towel. "There, Darkboy."

"Look a mess, I know."

"Right. You don't look exactly like a beauty queen from New Orleans."

"I-I want to look like New Orleans, Long Ray. A ... a funeral march. Chick Webb, man. In my black suit, my black tie when I die. It's what I want to look like, Long Ray. Man, Long Ray ... What I've always wanted to look like my, my whole life: New Orleans, a funeral march, Chick Webb rolling thunder. H-his drums banging out l-life."

Long Ray wouldn't tell Darkboy why he'd gone back to the apartment. He wouldn't tell him that Ruby was coming to Chicago. That she was on her way in from New York; that she was taking the first flight out of LaGuardia Airport.

"Ruby!" Darkboy called out.

Long Ray had expected this, but now that he heard Ruby's name, it rattled him.

"I love her, Long Ray. But it's best that she's not—"

"Here? That Ruby's not here at the hospital with us?"

Darkboy's skin reddened. "Not here to see me like this. My skin dying. Seeing me at my worst, Long Ray. Not my best. W-when I was at, at my best, Long Ray. Pretty ... when Ruby thought I was pretty l-like a girl."

He swallowed hard and took a deep breath. "That I would never die. Our love never die either. Our love either. But everybody dies. Everybody and everything. Everything must die. Me, you, Ruby, the—"

"Darkboy, there you are, man!" Pinky said, charging into the hospital room.

"Pinky, Darkboy hasn't gone anywhere," Long Ray told him.

"Better not! That bed looks awfully comfortable from here!"

"Hi, hi, Pinky."

Pinky stood at the side of the bed, bent over, and gave Darkboy a big bear hug.

And Long Ray thought of Ruby again. That she was probably on the plane by now, flying out of LaGuardia Airport, and into Midway International Airport. And a lovely sense of balance fell over him, how Pinky was hugging Darkboy, as if he would be around to celebrate his birthday in October, just two months away.

CHAPTER 27

The next morning, Darkboy's hospital room was empty and calm. Long Ray had left Providence Hospital but told Darkboy he'd be back by late morning. Darkboy hadn't panicked. Long Ray had done enough, he'd thought when he'd left. He wanted this time to himself anyway, to think. To make sense out of his life, since, truly, in his heart, he felt he was going to die at the age of twenty-nine, and that he would never see the people he loved most in his life: his mother, father, and Ruby.

A nurse had been in and out of the room, performing the duty of keeping him comfortable and stress-free.

Darkboy was asleep when Ruby arrived at Providence Hospital and went up to Darkboy's floor. She had checked in at the front desk and was told Darkboy's room number. She had been fretful on the flight from New York. It was nine fifty-five. She never imagined something like this, where the world seemed to be coming to an end for her and Darkboy. She saw Darkboy's life as not that of someone who had succumbed to liquor but of someone who had fought the same mental battles that she had when she felt desperate and continually connected to her heartbreak, but she'd found other ways to suppress it, not end it, for the past eight years of her life.

She stood amid the second floor's activity at Providence and felt anxious, knowing the seriousness of each step she took down the corridor. Long Ray's voice couldn't hide his fear of the unknown, of what Darkboy was up against, what his life had suddenly, sadly, turned into, and she must be prepared for what she saw.

Darkboy's still beautiful. Darkboy's still beautiful.

Ruby's lips touched Darkboy's forehead and then her hand held his, and Darkboy felt something but thought he was dreaming—a connection to something else, another time and place, but the place was still unfamiliar to him, as if he were playing in a field of luminous green grass and delicate-shaped fragrances, not New Orleans, but some other place, but it was brightening him, his spirit, making his body breathe better, stronger. And his eyes—he wanted to open his eyes.

"Ruby ..."

"It's me, Darkboy."

"Y-you're here, Ruby. In Chi-Chicago, Ruby. With me."

"Don't move. Don't you dare try. Stay still, okay? Right where you are."

"B-but—"

"I won't leave your side. Don't you worry. Not ever again."

Darkboy kept his head on the pillow and looked up into Ruby's dark eyes. "I thought I was dreaming."

"You weren't."

"I thought I had died and—"

"I won't let you die, Darkboy."

Darkboy's eyelids stopped fluttering. "You won't let me die? You won't? No, no, you won't, Ruby. You have come to save me."

CHAPTER 28

Three months later

So many remarkable things had developed for Ruby and Darkboy over the past three months. Darkboy was not only back in good health—he'd sworn off liquor—but had moved to New York; Harlem, to be more specific. He'd moved into the brownstone with Ruby, and he and Ruby were to remarry. It would be a December wedding, but not at city hall in front of a justice of the peace. They were going to do their second wedding up big.

Finally, Ruby had sat down with Darkboy and told him about Miss Honey Gillette, how it all began for them down in Plattstown—the religious experience she'd had of Miss Honey taking her under her wing; the mentorship; the record of Miss Honey's that she'd carried everywhere she'd traveled in the world; and that she'd never played the record, something she felt so personal and deep in her heart that Miss Honey had not wanted her to do.

Darkboy had left Chicago and the Windy Wind Five. It wasn't easy, but he and Long Ray, Pinky, Cool Hands, and Loose Lips understood it was the only thing he could do to regain control of his life and to be happy. He would play his drums in a band behind Ruby whenever possible and had been in demand on the New York jazz scene, having attracted fast attention.

Over the course of the three months, Ruby had canceled any number of singing engagements, with the support and encouragement from Fat Tony Apollo, while she helped Darkboy heal. When she performed her overseas gigs, Fat Tony made certain Darkboy traveled with her band. Their careers and personal lives were not to be put at risk. This had become top priority.

Ruby wasn't going to let Darkboy die, not until both of them were at least ninety-two.

Ruby, in a midnight-blue dress, high heels, and a silver necklace with diamonds, rushed out the brownstone's front door and looked down from the stoop.

"Good, it's here," Ruby said, clapping her hands. "Darkboy, hurry up," she fussed.

"Ruby, I'm trying my best," Darkboy said, stepping away from the hallway's tall wall mirror, and looking down at his shiny black shoes, and making sure the tuxedo Ruby told him to wear for the afternoon's special festivities looked just right.

"Wait until Darkboy sees his surprise!" Ruby said, rubbing her hands.

Darkboy stepped out of the brownstone and on to the porch; then he shot down the steps.

"Hey, Ruby, what's that?"

A lovely yellow roadster was parked in front of Ruby and Darkboy's brownstone.

"I rented it," she said without cracking a smile. "It was dropped off while we slept."

"Oh, I … I wondered how—"

"Come on; let's get going, so I can show you the other surprise!"

"You know I can't wait, baby, f-for that one!" Darkboy's body was running on a ton of nervous, jittery energy.

They hopped in the car, and Ruby handed him the keys. Darkboy leaned over and kissed her.

"Mmm," she said.

"And by the way, when are you going to learn how to drive, Miss Midnight?" Darkboy teased.

"To 136th Street and Lennox Avenue, please. We mustn't be late."

"So, I see you're avoiding my question."

"Kansas City's a long time ago, Darkboy, when you tried to teach me how to drive a car." Ruby winked alluringly.

Darkboy's beautiful black skin gleamed. "Man, Ruby, don't remind me. Okay. We had a ball. Didn't we? You driving the car. Practically hitting that cow, ha ha, in the road."

"Poor little thing." Ruby giggled. "He didn't stand a chance."

"With you behind the wheel, no. None," Darkboy said, rolling his eyes.

Ruby had made it her business to rent the yellow roadster off the car lot, just so she and Darkboy could be reminded of Kansas City and the "ball" both had had on that grand, sunshiny day in Kansas City, Missouri.

"By the way, Darkboy, do you know how to get over to 136th Street and Lennox Avenue?"

"Of course."

"You're sure?"

"I'm a Harlemite; of course I'm sure. New Orleans, Chicago, and now Harlem."

"Harlem, Darkboy," Ruby said with a sigh.

The yellow roadster threaded its way through the busy, boisterous Harlem streets, stopping at a long stretch of one stoplight followed by another on their way to 136th Street, the north side of it. Darkboy did know his way around Harlem, especially its jazz clubs: Minton's, the Cotton Club, and many more of the distinguished clubs where Harlem's jazz clubbers brought their love and dedication and hunger and pride—just like all of Harlem and its rich diversity and bustling, forward-looking spirit.

But Darkboy's romance was with his renewed romance with Ruby and the beginning of his romance with Harlem. Darkboy was not a professor or academic to examine the vast, impoverished status of poor people of Harlem; instead, he was a jazz musician who knew that music blessed this place, granting it a sense of the talents that it could present on a world stage and be consumed and respected because of them.

This was Darkboy's new home—his new shiny apple.

"The Apollo, Ruby!"

"My eyes never tire from looking at it, Darkboy," Ruby swooned. "The Apollo—a home for so many of our talented Negro artists to perform and gain a sense of recognition for their work. It definitely inspires me."

"When we played there last month—"

"I had so much fun showing it off to you." Ruby smiled, while enjoying Darkboy's pretty smile. "Guiding you through every part of the place."

Darkboy turned on 136th Street, and his breath caught in his chest. His eyes practically leaped out of his head when he saw what stood tall before him.

"Your eyes, they're not playing tricks on you, Darkboy. No, they're not!"

The building's fabulous red marquee over the nightclub's beautifully designed entrance read in bold, red lettering: Miss Ruby Midnight and Darkboy.

"It's ours—yours and mine," Ruby told him. "We'll be partners with Tony, the two of us partners in the nightclub with Tony. Co-owners, Darkboy. Co-owners. It'll be our home base. We'll run the club. Do all the booking and hiring of bands and staff. Ev-everything ourselves, honey, that's necessary to make it work."

Darkboy could barely park the yellow roadster at the curb; he was so amped.

Out of the car, Ruby and Darkboy rushed toward the club.

"The inside's not finished; it's still raw. It needs a lot of work, but Tony and I wanted to get the marquee up so you could see for yourself what we've done up to this point," Ruby said in one breath.

From Plattstown to this, Ruby thought. *How lucky can a person be? Thank you, Miss Honey. Thank you. Thank you, ma'am.*

About thirty yards from the club, they saw Fat Tony Apollo's white limo gliding coolly down the street. It stopped about forty feet from them, with the back window open. Fat Tony's head popped out the limo's window.

"Hey, how's youse like it, Darkboy? Huh!" Fat Tony yelled.

"Fine, Tony. Great, man. Great!"

"Yeah, great, Darkboy. Great!" Fat Tony said.

Ruby whistled loudly.

"Ruby, what—what's that?" Darkboy said, flabbergasted. "And hey, I've never heard you whistle."

Silky-sounding music drifted from the club's front door.

Darkboy's shock doubled.

"Why, that's Pinky on sax," Ruby said, "and Loose Lips on trumpet, and—"

"Cool Hands on—"

Long Ray leaped from the front of the club. "Hurry up, kids. The Windy Wind Five can't wait all day!"

"Long Ray!" Darkboy said.

Ruby laughed. "Yes, Long Ray!"

"That's why you whistled!"

"He's been waiting for us, Darkboy. It's how Long Ray and I planned it, honey."

Fat Tony was halfway out of his limo, a little way up the block.

"Let's get going, baby" Darkboy said, grabbing Ruby's hand. "Like Long Ray said, the Windy Wind Five can't wait all day!"

They ran, then stopped, then kissed sweetly under the Miss Ruby and Darkboy nightclub's red marquee.

"Love you, Ruby."

"Love you, Darkboy."

Darkboy held Ruby's hand again and then disappeared into the club.

Fat Tony, dashing down the block, was trying his darndest to catch up to them.

His legs spun like crazy.

Man, oh man ... did they.

Man.

ABOUT THE AUTHOR

Denis Gray is the author of fourteen published novels. He lives in New York with his wife, Barbara.

Printed in the United States
By Bookmasters